Two and a half thousand years before the Cataclysm that tore Krynn asunder, it held sway over half a continent. Carved out of plain and forest by the savage hords of a warlord, it is now wracked by internal strife. Meanwhile, the empire's foreign rivals wait and watch with keen anticipation.

Into this tumultuous time is born Tol, a farmer's son. With clear mind and strong arm, he ascends from lowly foot soldier to the glittering halls of the imperial palace.

His journey begins here.

The Dragonlance® Saga

By Paul B. Thompson & Tonya C. Cook

A WARRIOR'S Journey

The Ergoth Trilogy
volume one

Paul B. Thompson
Tonya C. Cook

A WARRIOR'S JOURNEY
©2003 Wizards of the Coast, Inc.

All characters in this book are fictitious. Any resemblance to actual persons, living or dead, is purely coincidental.

This book is protected under the copyright laws of the United States of America. Any reproduction or unauthorized use of the material or artwork contained herein is prohibited without the express written permission of Wizards of the Coast, Inc.

Distributed in the United States by Holtzbrinck Publishing. Distributed in Canada by Fenn Ltd.

Distributed to the hobby, toy, and comic trade in the United States and Canada by regional distributors.

Distributed worldwide by Wizards of the Coast, Inc. and regional distributors.

DRAGONLANCE and the Wizards of the Coast logo are registered trademarks of Wizards of the Coast, Inc., a subsidiary of Hasbro, Inc.

All Wizards of the Coast characters, character names, and the distinctive likenesses thereof are trademarks of Wizards of the Coast, Inc.

Printed in the U.S.A.

Cover art by Brom
First Printing: May 2003
Library of Congress Catalog Card Number: 2002114087

9 8 7 6 5 4 3 2 1

US ISBN: 0-7869-2965-0
UK ISBN: 0-7869-2966-9
620-17969-001-EN

U.S., CANADA,
ASIA, PACIFIC, & LATIN AMERICA
Wizards of the Coast, Inc.
P.O. Box 707
Renton, WA 98057-0707
+1-800-324-6496

EUROPEAN HEADQUARTERS
Wizards of the Coast, Belgium
T Hosfveld 6d
1702 Groot-Bijgaarden
Belgium
+322 467 3360

Visit our web site at **www.wizards.com**

For Sara

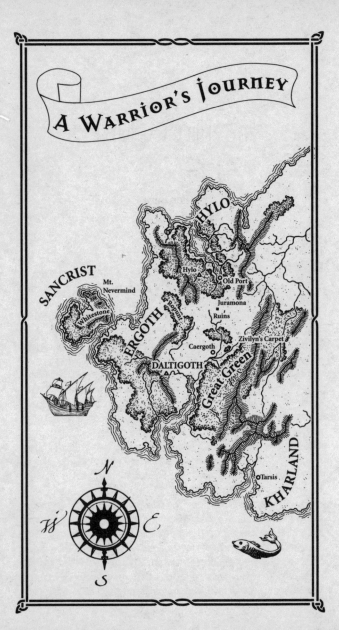

A WARRIOR'S JOURNEY

SANCRIST

Mt. Nevermind

Whitestone

HYLO

Hylo

Old Port

Juramona

Ruins

ERGOTH

Zivilyn's Carpet

Caergoth

DALTIGOTH

Great Green

Tarsis

KHARLAND

N

W E

S

Prologue:
The Prince's Charge

Tarsis, Year of the City 224

From Valgold, Prince of Vergerone, to Hanira of the Golden House, chosen voice of the guild of jewelsmiths.

Secret! This document is not to be shared outside the Golden House!

Greetings, Lady Hanira. Let me be the first to congratulate you on your accession to the ambassadorship to Ergoth. As a former emissary to the imperial court myself, I feel obligated to give you a foretaste of what awaits you in Daltigoth.

Since the founding of the Ergoth Empire by the savage warlord Ackal Ergot just two years after the founding of our own sovereign city, there has been continual conflict and competition between us. The Bay War, the Mountain War, the War of the Silver Skulls checked the southward expansion of Ergoth's mounted hordes, but each time at enormous cost to the city's treasury. The great drain on our coffers continues so long as we are forced to maintain a mercenary army in the field to deter Ergothian aggression.

Lately the crisis has been focused on Hylo. Large numbers of itinerant Ergothian merchants have infiltrated the kender kingdom, infringing on the natural monopoly of trade Tarsis enjoys there. The kender, lacking patriotic feeling, have done little to resist this peddler invasion. Ergothian traders supply considerable quantities of food, cattle, leather, textiles, and wine from the large farming estates of their western provinces.

Paul B. Thompson and Tonya C. Cook

Our merchants provide similar commodities. But as these must come by sea and from further away, our prices tend to be higher than the Ergothians'. Witless kender, not realizing they are selling their independence for the sake of cheaper cloth, increasingly choose Ergothian goods over ours. There is evidence the emperor's agents have bribed Kharolian pirates to harass our ships as they round the continent on their way to Hylo. It is for this reason that every convoy from Tarsis must be escorted by armed galleys of the City Navy, an expense that only serves to increase further the cost of our trade goods.

Trading rights in Hylo will therefore be one of the foremost topics of your discussions in Daltigoth. As chosen chief of the guild of gold, silver, and jewel makers of Tarsis, you are accustomed to dealing with wealthy and powerful clients. This will serve you in good stead in dealing with the proud but violent Ergothian nobility.

Shortly after I returned from Daltigoth, it was announced that the king of Hylo, Lucklyn I, had openly declared his vassalage to the emperor. If true, this is a setback for us, but not a fatal one. Money and trade are more important than feudal loyalties, so if you can wrest concessions in Hylo from Ergoth, then the kender king can bend his knee to the emperor as deeply as he likes.

Great things are astir, Lady Hanira. The dormant war between the Ackal and Pakin dynasts has flared anew since the assassination of Emperor Pakin II, an Ackal in spite of his name. The Pakin Pretender has raised an army of unknown size in the north and threatens several minor provincial strongholds. Forces loyal to the Ackal heir are moving to destroy him. Do not become entangled in this brutal, confusing struggle! The intricacies of the Ackal-Pakin feud would confound the wisest sages in Tarsis.

For example, the murdered emperor, Pakin II, chose his regnal name in an attempt to reconcile both sides to his rule. Far from being reconciled, the Pakins' response was to slay him with knives in his own council chamber. His brother (likewise an Ackal) took the throne as Pakin III, in honor of his slain sibling. Pakin III is no gentle conciliator. He will send his hordes to the ends of the world to track down the Pakin Pretender, and will not rest until the Pretender's head decorates the palace roof in Daltigoth.

For all his ferocity, the current emperor is a just and honorable ruler. But his opponent is neither. The Pakin Pretender is by all accounts a vicious, treacherous man, and potentially a worse enemy than his Ackal rival. His troops are little more than bandits. They have sacked peaceful villages near the Hylo border, robbed caravans, and tortured Tarsan merchants to death.

Master Vyka, of the White Robe Council, tells me the Pretender does not blanch from practicing black magic. Among his closest advisers are known Black Robes, including one Spannuth Grane, believed to have been involved in the murder of Pakin II and under sentence of death in Ergoth for his various sorcerous crimes.

Assure the emperor of our best wishes in his struggle against the Pretender. At the same time, we are sending a fleet of fifty galleys to Hylo to impress the kender with the power of Tarsis. They are feeling pressed these days, not only by imperial power, but by the Pakin Pretender's forces. Our High Admiral, Anovenax, has instructions to land the army of General Tylocost if need be, to convince the kender of the wisdom of retaining their ancient trading relationship with Tarsis. That relationship is worth thirty million gold crowns a year to us, or a quarter part of all revenues of the city. Our hegemony over Hylo must be preserved—without war, if possible, but preserved nonetheless!

May Shinare guide and protect you, lady. Remember you are going to a splendid but savage place, where men kill for honor and massacre for glory. As a woman, you may find the Ergothians' notions of honor peculiar, but you are well-equipped to take advantage of their weakness for feminine glamour. I trust a woman of your experience, wit, and talent will accomplish far more in Daltigoth than I ever could. And

3

if not—well, Lord Tylocost has fifty thousand mercenaries ready to take ship to Hylo.

All success to you, Lady Hanira! The hopes of your city go with you!

(sealed)
VALGOLD, PRINCE OF VERGERONE
from the Griffin Palace

A Strange Harvest

Again and again the blade rose, lingered for a moment in the clear spring air, then fell to earth with a thud. Each blow cleaved in two a clod of red-brown clay. Inside each broken clump dark soil gleamed, heavy with moisture from the snows of winter. Night still held enough chill to preserve crusts of ice in the deep shade of the woods, but here in the onion patch the newly turned ground had thawed and was soft.

Tol labored tirelessly, pulverizing the weed-woven dirt. His father had plowed the field at dawn. While his father returned the borrowed bullock to their neighbor Farak, Tol finished preparing the soil. He had to be done by midday, when his mother and sisters would come with dried onion bulbs, carefully stored through the winter in the root cellar beneath their hut. By sundown the field would be lined with little hillocks, each tiny mound holding a single bulb. If the hard yellow seedlings survived until summer (and fewer than half would), each onion would mother three or four others. With good rains and fair taxes, Tol's family would harvest enough to feed themselves and have some left over to barter for things they did not grow—like apples, Tol's favorite fruit.

Halfway through one swing, Tol heard a strange sound. For the first time he broke his rhythm, hoe held high over his head. The sound was a distant rumble that rose in volume, then fell, seeming to fade into the hills behind him.

Tol lowered the hoe. He turned his head slowly, trying to gauge the source of the strange noise. It seemed to begin beyond the two tall hills northeast of the onion patch. They often masked thunder, making it hard to judge the distance of an oncoming storm. A breeze lifted his long, loose hair and tossed it in his face. He combed the thick brown strands aside and squinted against the morning sun.

Another sound reached his ears. He recognized this one—though he heard it seldom—and knew it for an ominous portent. Bright and hard, it was the clash of metal on metal. He realized then the strange ebbing and flowing noise must mean a battle was raging nearby.

Tol took a step backward, uncertain. Should he run home and warn his family? He glanced over his shoulder in the direction of their homestead. It was five minutes' walk away, but if his father returned and found him gone, his work not yet finished—Tol shook his head at the thought of Bakal's certain wrath.

Last autumn there had been other battles. Swarms of mounted men, clad in bronze and iron, had fought to possess the Great Road that ran through the southern end of the province. Once, Tol had seen a small mob of warriors bearing green streamers. They rode helter-skelter north, pursued by a larger band of fighters under a scarlet banner. The green riders had burned six farms and killed the local healer, Old Kinzen, when he couldn't save their leader from his wound. Tol's father and his cronies sat around the fire all winter, drinking plum dew from a stone jug and talking in anxious voices about war. The emperor's Great Horde was fighting itself, they muttered. Men of Ergoth were making war on each other.

Tol understood little of what was said. The affairs of men were not for women and children, and the ways of warriors were even more remote. All he knew was, where men went with horse and sword, blood and fire followed.

Suddenly a truly mighty shout went up, echoing off the intervening hills and penetrating Tol's worried ruminations.

He heard a terrific crash, as if all the trees in the forest had fallen down at once. The plowed earth beneath his feet shivered. His fingers tightened nervously around the hoe handle.

The strange ground tremor did not subside, but grew stronger. An indeterminate rumble of combat gave way to the sounds of individual hoofbeats and shouting voices. It rose steadily in volume. The fight was coming his way!

He cast about for a hiding place. The onion field was a shallow, bowl-shaped depression between three hills, about thirty paces long and half that wide. Other than Tol himself, the only thing in it that morning was a chest-high pile of compost his father had dumped the day before. Formed from the family's refuse collected all winter, mixed with the scrapings of the chicken coop, it was a malodorous heap.

Tol didn't hesitate. He sprinted for the compost pile, leaping nimbly over the newly turned sod. Better to lie in filth than be trampled by a warrior's charger, or hacked to death by an iron sword!

Before he reached cover, a lone horse appeared in the cleft below the north hill. Tol's panicked dash halted abruptly when he spied the coal-black beast. It was an enormous animal, and it was riderless.

When the horse galloped by, eyes bulging, teeth bared, foamy sweat streaking its ebony neck, Tol saw why it was so terrified. Gripping the animal's mane was a man's hand, fingers tightly knotted into the long strands. Severed below the elbow, the limb thudded rhythmically against the horse's neck. Blood stained the blaze on the horse's chest.

Hardly had the first runaway steed gone by when two more rounded the base of the hill. Neighing frantically, they weaved this way and that, almost colliding. They shied from Tol and cantered off. One animal had a wound on its rump, but neither bore a rider, or even part of one.

Someone blew a ram's horn close by. The sudden blast sent Tol scrambling again for the compost pile. With the wooden blade of his hoe, he began hacking out a niche large enough to hide in.

He'd made only a shallow hole when a fourth horse appeared. Unlike the others, this animal had a rider, slumped forward over its neck. The horse came on at a steady trot. He was a magnificent stallion, broad and strong, the color of morning mist. Heavy mail trapping coated him from head to tail, the small iron rings sewn to rich crimson cloth. He came directly to the amazed Tol, and stopped. The reins fell from the unmoving rider's hands.

At first Tol could only stare dumbfounded at the apparition looming over him. When the horse dropped its head to nuzzle his chest, he started violently, but regained his wits enough to speak.

"Sir? Master?" he said tentatively. The slumped rider did not reply, so Tol edged closer. The huge, dappled-gray horse watched him closely but did not shy, so he circled to the side to see the man's face.

The rider was a burly, yellow-bearded fellow. He'd lost his helm, but his fair hair was still matted from its weight. Fresh blood dripped from his slack fingers, and a nasty gash scored his left temple.

"Sir?" said Tol again, daring to touch the rider's dangling hand. The limp fingers suddenly seized his arm. Tol tried to pull free, but the man's grip was surprisingly strong.

"Boy," he rasped, "don't make a sound if you want to live!"

Tol hadn't yelled when he was grabbed, and he wasn't about to do so now. He simply nodded.

"All is lost. The Pakins have won the battle. They will come for me," the man murmured. He coughed, and his hand relaxed, releasing Tol.

The ram's horn bleated again, very near, and Tol understood its significance. Hunters used horns to signal each other when tracking prey. This man's enemies were hunting him like a wild animal.

Tol slapped the horse sharply on the flank. The powerful beast gazed at him contemptuously. Surprised, Tol picked up the reins and tried to lead the horse away. The broad hooves never budged. It was like trying to shift an oak tree.

There was a rumble of many hoofbeats, growing louder, and Tol was torn. If he ran away, the unconscious warrior would certainly be caught and killed. If he stayed, the man's enemies might slay him too!

His gaze fell upon the hoe, lying at his feet where he'd dropped it. The sight of it gave him an idea.

He planted his hands against the horse's side and shoved. To his relief, the startled animal shuffled sideways a few steps. Tol cupped his hands under the injured man's left heel and heaved. The warrior was big, and weighted down with much metal, but the gods were with Tol. The man rolled off his saddle and fell heavily to the ground.

Tol tore the scarlet band from the warrior's sleeve and laid it over his face. That done, he attacked the compost pile once more with his hoe, flinging rotting leaves and manure over the unconscious man. Not satisfied with the amount he was shifting, he dropped to his knees and plunged his hands into the stinking heap. In short order the fallen warrior was completely buried.

Filthy up to his elbows, Tol confronted the horse, shouting and waving his arms. The stolid animal merely snorted, short plumes of mist furling around its wide nostrils.

"Stupid beast! Get away! How can I hide your master with you here?"

The war-horse only shook its big head and refused to move. In desperation, Tol did something his father had told him never to do: he swatted the animal hard on the nose, a blow no horse will bear.

The gray stallion finally woke to anger, rearing high and lashing out with its metal-shod hooves. Tol dodged briskly. A single blow from those heavy hooves could crack his skull open like a walnut.

The outraged horse trotted away. It followed the natural draw of the field, disappearing in the direction of the south woods. Hardly had the stallion merged into the morning haze than several riders burst from the defile. The lead warrior spotted Tol immediately and shouted. Whipping his long sword in a circle around his head, he led three companions toward the boy.

Tol's heart hammered against his ribs, but he concentrated on working the soil with his hoe and on keeping his eyes from straying to the compost pile. In moments he was surrounded by mounted men, each wearing a strip of green cloth tied around his right upper arm.

"It's just a peasant," said one, reining in his prancing charger. "And a smelly one at that."

"They're all smelly," said another, bearded face twisted in disgust.

"Look here, boy," said a third, whose helm bore a green feather plume. "How long have you been here?"

"All morning, master," Tol replied. He was surprised by his own coolness. Though his heart was racing, his tongue was calm. No quaver spoiled his voice.

"Seen any riders come by? Riders with red trappings?"

"Yes, my lord." Tol ceased his labors with the hoe, but kept his eyes downcast.

"How many?" asked the man in the green-plumed helmet. Tol shrugged, and the tip of a nicked iron saber pressed into his ear. "Loosen your tongue, boy, or I'll have it out for good."

"Three horses, good master, with no men on them! And one with a rider."

All the warriors but one had spoken. Unlike the rest, this fellow wore a closed helm. Its fiercely grinning, hammered bronze visor covered his face completely. As tall as his companions, he was of slighter build, and even to Tol's unschooled eyes his arms seemed finer and more costly.

"What did the rider look like?" the visored man asked, voice low but carrying.

Tol looked up at him, then quickly back down at the ground. The evil, grinning metal visage filled him with dread. Even though he was farthest away and his sword was sheathed, the visored warrior somehow seemed the most dangerous of them all.

"He was a big man, lord," Tol said truthfully, "with hair

and beard the color of straw."

His answer obviously pleased them. "Odovar!" said the horn bearer, glancing at the masked man. "Which way did he go, boy?"

Tol indicated the tracks of the big man's horse. "Yonder, lords."

Standing in his stirrups, the rider with the ram's horn put it to his lips. He blew a loud, wavering note. Iron blades flashed as each warrior lifted his weapon high.

The visored warrior said, "Remember, men: the weight of Odovar's head in gold to him who brings it to me."

With whoops and yells, the riders spurred their massive horses and galloped away.

The visored man lingered and Tol felt his gaze on him. Curiosity overcoming his natural caution, Tol ventured to ask, "My lord, who are you? Why do you fight?"

To the boy's surprise, the man deigned to answer.

"I am Grane, commander of the northern host of the Pakin Successor. I am sworn to return the house of Pakin to its rightful place on the imperial throne," he said. His voice betrayed amusement. "Does that satisfy you, boy?"

Tol nodded dumbly, though in fact the words meant nothing to him.

Grane reached back to a leather saddlebag. He lifted the flap and thrust his hand inside. When he withdrew it, something brown and furry squirmed in his gauntleted fist. He tossed the creature to the ground and muttered words Tol could not understand. A strange breeze began to blow, rushing inward, toward the fist-sized brown creature.

The furry form swelled and as it expanded its fur darkened from brown to black. Terrible yowls sounded from its mouth, as though the growing was painful in the extreme. Horrified, Tol stepped back quickly, almost stumbling over the pile of compost. When it stopped growing and raised its head, Tol gasped. The night-black creature had long fangs and green eyes, vertically slit like a cat's, but was half again as big as any panther Tol had ever seen.

11

Paul B. Thompson and Tonya C. Cook

"Vult, seek. Find Odovar," commanded Grane. The leonine beast uncoiled muscular limbs, revealing fur-covered, manlike fingers and toes. It lowered its nose to the ground. Catching a scent, it opened its jaws and let out a low, wavering yowl that made the hair on Tol's neck rise. Its fanged maw was large enough to swallow Tol's head.

"Find him, Vult. Find Odovar!"

The hulking cat creature stalked forward, and Tol was suddenly very afraid. Could this unnatural beast scent its prey through the moldering compost?

Eyeing him up and down, the panther sniffed Tol. A snarl gurgled in its throat. Tol forced himself to remain still.

The great panther's head swiveled toward the rotting manure pile. It drew in a deep breath. Plainly disgusted, the beast padded away, along the track left by the hidden man's horse.

"You have lived through a great day, boy," Grane said, snapping his reins. "Tell your children you saw the victor of the Succession War this day!"

He urged his mount to rear, then rode off behind the creature Vult, sunlight shining on the gilded peak of his garish helm.

Tol watched man and panther vanish into the woods. He waited several interminable minutes, just to be certain they wouldn't return, then hurried to the pile of compost. He clawed away the manure until he found the scrap of red cloth over the hidden man's face. He whisked it off and saw the man's eyes were open.

"Are they gone?" the warrior muttered. Tol nodded, and the fellow sat up, scattering clumps of compost. "Grane, the blood drinker! Someday, I'll—" He made a fist, but winced from the effort.

"Help me up, boy," he said. Tol gave him his shoulder, and the hulking blond warrior rose unsteadily to his feet.

Looking around, he asked, "My horse—how did you get Ironheart to leave me?" Tol explained what he'd done. The warrior barked a short, harsh laugh. "You're lucky he didn't

12

stamp you into your own manure pile, boy!"

Tol staggered a bit under the weight of the big man. "My lord, you are called Odovar?" he asked.

"Aye, I am Odovar, marshal of the Eastern Hundred. Grane and his damned Pakins have ambushed my troops, but I'm not done yet." Odovar squinted at the sun to orient himself. "It's a long walk back to Juramona. Have you a horse, boy?"

Tol confessed he did not, then asked, "What is Juramona, lord?"

"The imperial seat of this province, and my stronghold. It lies two days' ride due east of here." Odovar coughed, grimacing. "Two days' ride is eight days' walking, and my head is still thundering from Grane's blow. Fair broke my helmet, it did."

Pushing Tol away, Odovar tried to walk unaided, but his knees buckled immediately. He sank on his haunches.

"I'll not make it with the land heaving under my feet like this!" he declared. "Help me, boy."

Again Tol braced him, and Lord Odovar managed to stand once more. "Lend me that stick," he commanded, and Tol gave him the hoe. The warrior braced the wooden blade into his armpit and essayed a step. The hoe handle was short but stout, and bore the big man without cracking.

"This is good seasoned ash," Odovar said. "I'll take it with me."

Tol winced. His father had made that hoe. It was the only one they had. Without it, planting the onion crop would be much harder. Even so, he dared not deny so powerful a lord.

"Don't look so downcast," Odovar said. "I'll pay for it. One gold piece will buy an armload of hoes."

The warrior limped a few more steps, then halted, swaying drunkenly. "Damn Grane and all the Pakins!" he thundered. "My head feels like a poached egg! Come with me, boy. I need you."

"But my father—my family—"

"Do as I say!"

Worried but obedient, Tol put himself under Odovar's other arm. Between the strong boy and the sturdy hoe, the injured warrior made better progress. He asked Tol his name and age. To this last, the boy could only shrug and say he didn't know.

"You don't know?" Odovar repeated, and Tol looked away, ashamed of his ignorance. "Well, you're a strongly built lad, whatever your age."

The tumult of battle had faded, and once the marshal and the boy passed through the cleft in the hills Tol beheld the scene of the fight for the first time. Spread below in a narrow gap in the trees were dead men and horses, heaps of them. Tol had seen dead men before, but never so many at once. The air was heavy with the smell of blood, like the farmyard when his father slaughtered a pig.

"They took us by surprise," Odovar said, grunting. "Ambushed in column we were, blades sheathed and spears ported. We had not a dog's chance."

Most of the corpses bore red armbands. A few wore green, like the mysterious Grane. Tol asked about the significance of the colors.

"Red is the clan color of the Ackals, rightful rulers of this land," Odovar said, touching the scarlet cloth tied around his own arm. "Green is for the house of Pakin, who claims the throne of Ergoth for their lord, the Pakin Successor."

"Ergoth? What is Ergoth?" Tol asked. Out of the many confusing words, he seized on the one he'd heard his father use.

Odovar stopped hobbling and regarded him with surprise. "All of this!" he said, waving a hand to the horizon. "This land is Ergoth. I am Ergoth, and you. We are all subjects of his glorious majesty, Pakin the Third, rightful emperor of Ergoth since the assassination of his brother."

Now Tol was truly confused. The concept of "Ergoth" eluded him, but no more so than the notion that Lord Odovar could be the subject of someone named Pakin, when Pakins were the very enemies he was fighting. Questions formed on his lips, but he held them back for fear of seeming stupid before the great lord.

In the midst of the narrow battlefield there was movement.

A chestnut horse floundered, tangled by its own reins. Odovar sent Tol to free it. The boy unwound the leather traces from its legs and the animal bounded to its feet. He brought the horse to Odovar. With much heaving and grunting, the warrior managed to mount the tall horse. Odovar's face was ash-gray now, and beads of sweat stood out on his brow.

Hoe on his shoulder, Tol prepared to return to the onion field now that Odovar had found a mount. However, the warrior chief tossed the reins to him, saying, "Lead him, boy. If I try to ride, I'll fall off for sure."

The sun was nearly at its apex. By now, his mother and sisters, laden with spring bulbs, would have set out for the onion field. He had to get back. His father would be angry when he saw he hadn't finished his work.

He tried to explain this to Lord Odovar, but the warrior interrupted him—or perhaps hadn't even heard him, so pale and sickly did he look.

"Go east," Odovar said, his breathing labored and loud. "Whatever happens . . . go east. Get me . . . to Juramona. My people will . . . reward you well." He then slumped forward, unconscious, arms hanging limply on either side of the horse's neck.

Tol twisted the reins in his hands, mind working furiously. He could leave the wounded marshal here and return to work, but the man would likely die if he did. On the other hand, Odovar's request was daunting. Tol had never been more than a day's walk from home, and then only with his father. He had no idea what lay beyond the green hills east of the farm.

Juramona. The very word seemed mysterious and remote, like a mountain on Solin, the white moon. Could Tol actually go to Juramona? Could he leave his family and make such a fantastic journey?

It was Odovar's mention of a reward that finally settled the question. If Tol returned home with gold, his father wouldn't beat him for abandoning his chores half done.

Laying the reins over one shoulder and his hoe on the other, Tol began the trek east.

❦ ❦ ❦ ❦ ❦

The land beyond the hills was flat and dotted with trees. From time to time Tol spotted riders in the distance. Since he couldn't identify them as friend or foe, he hid himself and Lord Odovar until they had gone by.

Mid-afternoon found Tol's stomach knotted with hunger. He should've been home eating his mother's beans and cabbage. Instead of enjoying that hearty fare he was wandering this endless expanse of grassland, leading a horse with a dying man on it. This was not how he imagined the day would go when he awoke that morning.

He entered a grove of pines. The horse, until now placidly following Tol's lead, began to pull away toward the left. Tol smelled water too, so he let the horse choose the path. They soon came to a small brook.

Tol tied the reins to a sapling and fell on his belly to lap the cold water alongside the animal. Looking up from his drinking, he saw that although Odovar's eyes were still closed, his color had improved. His butter-colored mustache puffed in and out with each breath.

Tol wandered out of the pines, kicking through the tall brown grass in search of anything edible—nuts, seeds, windfall fruit. There was nothing. The land hereabouts was as clean as his family's root cellar come spring.

As he stood bemoaning his hunger, he suddenly heard voices. A line of spearpoints advanced through the trees. Tol dropped to his knees. He couldn't get back to Odovar without being seen, so he waited nervously to learn who the strangers might be.

They were warriors, though not so richly armed as Grane or Lord Odovar. Their helmets were simple pots, and their breastplates boiled leather studded with bronze scales. Most were bearded. Each carried a spear with a short strip of cloth tied behind its head, and each wore a similar strip of cloth tied around his left arm. The cloths were red.

Tol popped up so suddenly the lead horses reared. Spearpoints swung down, aiming for his chest.

"Who goes there?" demanded the rider in the center of the group of ten. His helmet bore a brass crest and his auburn whiskers were sprinkled with gray.

"Friend! Friend!" Tol cried, holding his hands high.

"It's only a peasant boy," said a nearer warrior. He lifted his spear away from Tol's face. "Too bad he's not a rabbit. I could eat a rabbit just now."

"I could eat a peasant brat, myself," said another, and the company laughed.

"My lords, who is your master?" Tol asked quickly, wondering if men of war did indeed eat children when they could not get rabbits.

"We serve the marshal of the Eastern Hundred," said the one with the gray-flecked beard and brass-crested helm. "Odovar of Juramona—or was, till he perished this day in battle."

Relief coursed through Tol and he cried, "No! He lives yet!"

Brass Helm guided his mount closer. "What say you, boy? Have you news of Lord Odovar?"

"He lives! He is yonder, in those pines!"

Plainly unimpressed, the elder warrior called out, "My lord Odovar! Are you there? It is Egrin, of the Household Guards!"

Wind sighing through the grass was the only answer.

"He is there," Tol insisted, "but hurt. A man named Grane hit him on the head."

The name echoed through the mounted men like a thunderbolt.

"Grane!" Egrin exclaimed. He gestured, and one of the men thrust his spear through the collar of Tol's jerkin. Using the pommel of his saddle as a fulcrum, he hoisted the boy up onto his toes.

Ignoring Tol's protests, Egrin snapped, "Watch him. The rest of you, spread out. This smells like treachery to me. If it's a trap, spit that boy like a partridge and get out of here. Report back to Juramona. Understand?" The warrior holding Tol nodded.

The riders made a half-circle and approached the pine copse quietly. Egrin went in, and let out a shout.

"By the gods! Lord Odovar is here!"

Tol found himself dropped unceremoniously to the ground. His erstwhile captor spurred forward, joining his comrades by the brook. Fingering the hole in his good leather shirt, Tol followed.

Egrin had Odovar sitting upright on the chestnut horse and was holding a waterskin to his lips. The burly chieftain gulped the contents. His face reddened, and he pushed the neck of the skin away.

"Mishas preserve me!" he spluttered. "You give a dying man *water*? Have you nothing better?"

Egrin smiled and pulled a hide-wrapped bottle from his saddlebag. "Applejack, my lord?" he said, offering it to his commander. Odovar drew the stopper and took a long swig.

"I rejoice at your survival, my lord," said Egrin. "We thought you dead in the ambush."

"So I would have been, if not for this boy." Odovar wiped droplets of hard cider from his mustache with the back of a dirty hand. He told the company Tol's name, then drained the bottle and demanded an account of the battle from Egrin.

The veteran soldier reported that he and his men, sent by Odovar to scout the woods ahead of the main band, had been cut off by a superior force of Pakin warriors. When it looked like they would cut their way through anyway, a wall of fire leaped up between them and the Pakins, driving Egrin back. By the time he rallied his men and returned, the Pakins had vanished, and there was no sign of Lord Odovar, alive or dead.

"Strange to say, my lord, after the fire had gone, there were no ashes or coals, no sign of burning at all," Egrin finished.

They exchanged a meaningful look and Odovar said, "So, Grane is using his magic against us. We will return to Juramona at once. The Pakins may move to strike there."

Egrin formed up the men and took the reins of Odovar's horse himself.

Through all this Tol had been squatting to one side, watching and listening. So the great lord Grane, whoever he was, had magic on his side. That explained the strange creature he'd drawn from the small pouch on his saddle. Tol knew little of magic. His parents spoke of it only to curse it, but the rare passing mage or itinerant cleric who stopped at the farm for water or food seemed kindly enough to Tol. One had even done tricks to amuse him and his sisters, levitating stones and making doves appear from his floppy hat.

As the warriors set out, Tol stood. It was nearly dusk, and a bite in the air announced the cold night to come. He would have a long, chilly walk back to the farm.

A big roan horse blocked his path. Tol looked up and saw Egrin studying him.

"What about the boy, my lord?" the elder warrior asked. "What shall we do with him?"

"Eh? Do with him?" repeated Odovar, his words slurred by cider and fatigue. He shook his head as if to clear it and said forcefully, "Bring him!"

"As you wish, my lord."

Tol was surprised, but before he could speak, Egrin leaned down and took hold of his collar. With no obvious strain, the warrior hauled the boy off his feet and set him on the saddle behind him.

Torn between curiosity to see this Juramona and fear of leaving his family, Tol cleared his throat and said, "My folks will wonder what's happened to me."

"We'll send word," Lord Odovar muttered, eyelids closing. His head drooped.

Egrin gave the boy a shrug, implying they would get little else from the exhausted marshal.

They rode out as the sun set at their backs, stretching long shadows from the sparse trees and washing the plain in strong colors. The clouds above seemed afire, blazing with the bold red color of Lord Odovar's Ackal clan.

If it was an omen, it was not one Tol found any comfort in.

Chapter 2
Day Begins at Midnight

Odovar's men rode all night without pause. They kept their animals at a steady walk, and ate and drank in the saddle. Conversation was sparse. When at last they halted, it was only because Lord Odovar had toppled from his horse. Egrin dismounted, hurrying to his commander's side.

Tol was grateful for the respite, and got down as well. He'd never ridden a horse before and was quite sore from the experience.

"My lord, your head wound is graver than I thought. Do you know me? Do you know where you are?" asked Egrin.

"You're Egrin, Raemel's son, the warden of the Household Guard. I am Odovar, marshal of the Eastern Hundred. I'm sitting on my arse in the grass, and I smell like I've rolled in manure."

Egrin grinned. "Yes, sir. Can you rise?"

"If the sun can do it, so can I."

Without help, the bleary nobleman got his feet under him. Egrin snapped his fingers at Tol and pointed at Odovar's mount. Tol fetched the chestnut horse. After a few steps the horse snorted and stopped, head bobbing, eyes rolling.

"Come on boy, stop dawdling," Egrin said gruffly. "I thought farmers' sons knew how to handle beasts."

The other horses began to stir, and one of the warriors said, "It's not the boy, sir. They've gotten wind of something."

Egrin drew his curving saber in a single swift motion. Though shaky, Lord Odovar bared his weapon too. The mounted men formed a circle around them, facing outward with their spears presented.

The night around them was still. The red moon, Luin, was low on the southern horizon, pouring sanguinary light under a shelf of high clouds. Wind rustled the tall grass briefly, then died.

A low, gurgling snarl reached them.

"Panther!"

Egrin dismissed Tol's fears, saying a wild cat would never stalk ten armed and mounted men, but he ordered one of the men to make a fire, so they could better see their surroundings. Wielding iron and flint, the Ackal warrior soon had a modest blaze going.

Tol heard a sharp intake of breath behind him. He turned and saw two wide red eyes, low on the ground, highlighted by the fire. The eyes shone from an ill-defined black mass.

"My lords!" he cried, leaping back.

"Suffering gods!" exclaimed the man who'd made the fire.

The intruder was a huge panther, black as soot and coiled in a crouch.

Quivering in every limb, the horses reared and plunged, prancing to put distance between themselves and the panther. The men still mounted had to drop their weapons and concentrate on keeping in the saddle.

Egrin advanced, sword extended. "Light brands!" he shouted. "Chase it off with fire!"

There was no one to comply but Tol and the man who'd started the fire. Frantically they cast about for limbs or branches. But there was nothing large available.

Opening its huge jaws, the cat let out a bloodcurdling squall. Ivory fangs glistened. It crawled forward through the grass on its belly, sidling around Egrin toward the dazed Odovar.

Egrin rushed in and cut at it. The beast twisted to avoid the iron blade. A paw the size of a dinner plate lashed out.

Pearlescent talons, rimmed with dried gore, narrowly missed Egrin's sword arm. He leaped back, calling for aid.

The warrior who'd lit the fire was still vainly searching the grass for a tree branch with which to make a torch. Tol remembered a trick of his mother's. When wood was scarce at the farm, she'd burn bundles of grass. He pulled up enough standing grass to make a sheaf as thick as his wrist and lashed it into a tight bundle with another pliant stalk.

Egrin circled to his right, keeping between the bold panther and his liege. Whenever the cat rose to charge, Egrin shouted and rushed in first, slashing with his saber. Once he scored a bloody line across the taut black fur on the animal's flank. Hissing, the beast withdrew. Its eyes narrowed, focused now on Egrin instead of Odovar. Gathering his powerful rear legs under him, the panther sprang. Egrin stepped into the leap. Man and cat collided, and both went down.

The mounted warriors mastered their frightened steeds and, yelling wildly, they lowered their spears and tried to charge the panther. All they managed to do was get in each other's way. The cat's enormous claws slashed out, disemboweling a charger with one swipe. Dying, the horse pitched its rider headlong into the grass. The panther was on him in a flash, and the awful sound of fang shattering bone followed. Avoiding the warrior's hard helmet, the killer cat had bitten his face and crushed the man's skull.

Reeking of human and equine blood, the panther turned and roared defiance, hurling itself straight at Lord Odovar.

Egrin, back on his feet, shouted for Tol. The boy thrust his grass bundle torch into the flickering fire and brought it out blazing.

"To Odovar! Hurry!"

Tol ran to the beleaguered marshal, waving the torch. Odovar stumbled backward, away from the charging cat. When Tol was within reach, Odovar snatched the burning brand from him and flung it at the panther. It struck the creature square in the chest, but the black beast never faltered.

Odovar's face showed fear for the first time. No wild

animal, however hungry or enraged, could shrug off living flames. What sort of unnatural creature could this be?

Fangs bared and front claws extended, the cat seemed certain to rend the marshal to pieces. Odovar gripped his sword in both hands and drew the blade back. Suddenly, his right knee buckled and he fell heavily to that side, on top of the helpless Tol.

"Manzo! Spear!"

The warrior nearest Egrin tossed him his weapon. Egrin caught the long shaft in his right hand, tucked it under his arm, and thrust forward. He took the leaping panther just behind the left foreleg. Impaled, its massive claws just out of reach of Odovar, the fearsome cat fell to the ground.

Egrin drove the point in deeper. The panther howled and thrashed, rolling over on its back. The beast sank its claws into the shaft and dragged itself forward in order to reach Egrin. He could have dropped the spear and gotten clear, but Egrin neither faltered nor fled.

"A brave thrusssst!"

The words, hissed but clear, issued from the panther's throat.

"Unnatural beast, who are you?" Egrin demanded.

"A servant of my lord Grane," it gasped in reply. Slapping its right paw against the hardwood shaft, the cat hauled itself closer.

Egrin held his ground. "Whom do you seek?"

"Odovar of Juramona!"

As if summoned, Odovar came up behind the panther, saber in hand. Injured though he was, he severed the beast's head in one stroke. Egrin let go of the spear, and the cat's carcass fell in the grass, blood spurting from its neck in black jets.

"You found him," said the marshal, spitting on the dead beast. "May your master be as lucky!"

Tol and the warriors gathered around the monster. As they looked on, the panther visibly shrank to half its original size. Black fur sloughed from its face and paws, revealing unsettlingly human features and fingers.

"This is the creature Lord Grane set to track you, my lord!" Tol blurted.

"A half-beast, serving as a blood-hunter," Egrin said. "I've heard of them. Since men first walked the plains, they have lived among us, cleaving to the shadows. It's said they were created by the curse of an elf mage two thousand years ago, condemned to live neither fully human nor fully animal. Lord Grane must be a powerful wizard to subjugate such a monster to his will!"

Odovar's lip curled. "Foul beast. His head will decorate my hall. Bring it." Manzo recovered his spear and put the severed head—not quite feline, not quite human—in a leather bag for his master.

The men remounted. Tol found Egrin cleaning dark blood from his spear with a twisted tuft of grass. The boy watched him silently. He was awed by the warrior, having seen him stand his ground against the monstrous cat, wavering not at all even as the claws closed in.

Egrin looked up at him. "What is it, boy?" he asked. "Speak. Dawn is coming while we wait."

"Sir! Will we not camp and rest the night?"

"No time. Even now, Juramona may be under attack."

Egrin swung onto his horse. He held out a hard hand to Tol. Astride again, the boy admired the breadth of Egrin's shoulders and his cool, contained strength. How different he was from Tol's father, a lean, leathery man, short tempered, and suspicious of everything new.

Although his legs ached and his head swam with the terrors of the day, Tol soon found himself falling asleep. As Luin sank below the hills, he dozed, head bumping Egrin's back in time with the horse's plodding gait.

❦ ❦ ❦ ❦ ❦

Next Tol knew, they were cantering down a dusty lane, far from any place he'd been before. Tall cedar trees lined both sides of a road worn deep into the sandy soil. The company rode two abreast. Dawn had broken, and the new day washed the countryside in golden light. Tol marveled at that. Never in his life had he slept past sunrise.

He and Egrin were at the tail of the column. Lord Odovar was leading it. Riding next to the warden was Manzo. Although he was younger than Egrin—his face unlined—Manzo's brown beard was prematurely streaked with gray. His wide-set brown eyes scanned the area alertly.

The group clattered up the lane to the crest of a slight hill. The marshal held up a hand to halt his men.

On both sides of the road, beyond the ornamental cedars, lay tilled fields of a size Tol had never imagined. Plowed land stretched to the horizon, north and south. The enormous tracts dwarfed the little garden patches Tol's father had carved out of the wilderness. A bullock could toil all day in one of these fields, Tol thought, and never make a turn, just cut an endless furrow all the way to the where the sky and land met.

In between the plowed tracts were plots of fallow pasture, fenced with split rails and rubble stone. Strangely, no one was working the vast fields, and no herds grazed the pastures.

Lord Odovar signaled Egrin. The warden of Juramona brought his horse alongside the marshal's.

"Half a league from home, and it looks like the wastes of Thorin," said Odovar. "The Pakins doubled back on us, didn't they?"

"Seems so, my lord."

Odovar fingered the massive bruise over his left eye. "There's nothing for it but to go ahead. If Juramona's invested, we'll have to break through."

"With ten men, sir?"

Odovar glared. "Shall I ride away and leave my land to the bloody hands of Spannuth Grane?"

"If the manor is besieged, wouldn't it be better to stay clear and raise a force to lift the siege?" Egrin said carefully.

His master snorted. "You're too cautious, Egrin. Charge in boot to boot, shoulder to shoulder—that's how to deal with these rebels."

Paul B. Thompson and Tonya C. Cook

Tol could feel the tension in Egrin's posture, but the loyal warden merely replied, "It will be as you command, my lord."

"Form the men in a close column, and we'll go on."

Egrin passed the word to the others. Slinging their shields over their arms and couching their spears, they grinned at the prospect of battle. Only Egrin was solemn and silent.

"Troop, forward!" Odovar commanded. At a trot, they proceeded down the hill.

As they went, Tol noted signs of trouble. Hoes and rakes lay discarded in the fields, sharp edges and pointed tines facing the sky. Other items—a straw hat, a clay water bottle, a single shoe—were scattered about as though abandoned with extreme haste.

At the bottom of the hill, they crossed a stone bridge. Floating facedown in the stream was the body of a man, his back hacked and pierced many times. He was dressed in a homespun shirt and leather trews. The warriors glanced grimly at the body as they rode by.

Over the next rise they found more tokens of evil. A two-wheel cart was overturned, blocking the road. A dead ox still lay in the traces, and seed millet spilled out of the cart in a great drift. Black and purple hulls were trodden into the dust. Five bodies sprawled around the ruined cart, dead men in rough woolen cloaks and fleecy leggings. The hapless peasants, sent out with the seed for planting, had been sabered ruthlessly.

"This is what happens when cattle get in the way of warriors," Odovar remarked coldly.

Tol, swallowing hard, looked away to the vista below. A wide, shallow valley spread out in front of them, covered with cultivation and pasture. In the center of this rich landscape a steep conical hill of earth rose twenty paces high. Atop this mound was a great log house, tiered to match the contour of the hill on which it sat. The house was roofed with sod and pierced with many windows. Atop its highest point was a tall, slender pole bearing the red banner of the Ackal dynasty.

Clustered thickly at the foot of the mound were huts and

26

houses, so closely packed Tol could not distinguish where one ended and the next began. A stout wooden stockade surrounded the whole conglomeration. One gate was visible, facing them. The scene was shrouded in gray smoke, the outpourings of many hearths.

"The town gate is closed," one warrior observed.

"I see armed men on the ramparts," said another.

Lord Odovar steered his horse in a tight circle. "No sign of the Pakins," he said. "There must have been a swift raid, then they ran away. We'll enter Juramona."

"My lord, I advise against it," Egrin said firmly. "There's a third of a league of open ground between here and the gate."

"Do you see any enemies about?" Odovar retorted. He turned to the others and repeated the question even more loudly. The warriors could only shake their heads.

"Nor do I." The marshal's voice rose. "I tire of your weak-kneed caution, warden! This is not the time for idling about, poking under every bush for Pakins! I must resume my place and raise the Eastern Hundred in arms against the traitors! Why would you have me delay? Could it be you have Pakin sympathies?"

Egrin's face flushed. "My lord knows I am his loyal man, and always shall be!"

"Then ride on!"

Odovar spurred his horse and rode wide around the wrecked cart. Jaw clenched, Egrin followed his master.

"Whatever happens, boy, stay on this horse," Egrin said in a low voice. "If I should fall, grab on by the mane and hold on. Old Acorn will take you to safety."

Eyes wide, Tol nodded.

Odovar cantered briskly down the road, straight for the sealed gate. His men followed in ragged order, pennants whipping at the ends of their spears. At first nothing seemed amiss, then the flat, wavering sound of horns filled the air. Odovar slowed, Egrin and the rest behind him.

Everyone could see distant figures on the stockade, waving their hands and tooting horns.

"A celebration of your lordship's return?" suggested one of the riders.

Manzo, who had keen eyes, stiffened in the saddle. "I think not. Look yonder."

From behind the low stone pasture walls on either side of the road, men and horses popped up. A great many men, with a great many horses.

"Pakins!" shouted Manzo.

Odovar drew his sword. "Damned rebels," he snarled. "I hope Grane is with them! I owe him much I wish to repay!"

With a roar, he raised his saber high and spurred for the enemy. Without a plan or orders, the warriors followed their lord as best they could. Tol held on tightly, his aching legs jolting against Egrin's horse with every hoofbeat.

The rumble of approaching horses grew louder and louder. Shrill shouts rang out.

Old Acorn, Egrin's roan, shuddered violently and stopped. Another horse, dark brown and spattered with mud, scraped alongside. Its rider traded cuts with Egrin. Tol drew his leg back to avoid having it crushed between the horses. The enemy warrior, a rough-looking character with a drooping black mustache, noticed Tol cowering behind Egrin. The moment's distraction cost him his life. Egrin drove the brass handguard of his saber into the Pakin's face, drew back, and slashed the man from neck to navel. His quilted cloth jerkin was no match for the warden's iron blade. With an eerie screeching cry, he fell backward off his horse.

Lord Odovar laid about himself in a perfect fury, toppling four opponents with single blows. A Pakin in fancy spiked armor pushed in and rammed a bronze buckler into the marshal's back. Egrin urged Old Acorn into the press and stabbed Odovar's attacker under the arm, but the man's scale mail blunted the blow. Alerted, the Pakin cut at Egrin with a fine, gold-chased sword. Odovar tore the buckler from the nobleman's arm, and Egrin punched him in the face with his studded gauntlet. Nose gushing blood, the Pakin tried to break away. Egrin turned to face another foe, but Odovar was not granting mercy today. He chased the fleeing enemy a few paces and struck him on the back of his helmet with the flat of his sword. The fancily armored limbs flew up, the golden sword went sailing away, and down went Odovar's opponent.

Two of the Juramona guardsmen fell. The enemy was so numerous, they jammed together, inhibiting their own attack on the smaller Ackal contingent.

A tremendous blow knocked Old Acorn sideways; the horse lost his footing and went down. Egrin kicked free so his leg wouldn't be trapped under the fallen animal. Tol didn't have to bother. He was catapulted from the saddle like a stone from a sling.

He landed hard, on his back. Fortunately, he fell on a plowed plot, and the turned earth was relatively welcoming. No sooner had the shock of landing subsided than he saw churning horses' legs coming at him. It was Manzo, the guardsman, battling two Pakins. The mounted men whirled by in a welter of grunts, gasps, and curses. Tol scuttled away.

He saw Lord Odovar still mounted, battering a Pakin foe. There was no sign of Egrin at all.

Old Acorn trotted past, riderless. Remembering the warden's orders, Tol decided to follow the horse. He dodged through the melee, this way and that, avoiding Pakin and Ackal loyalists alike. Being a boy and on foot, he was ignored.

His toe caught something heavy, and Tol pitched onto his face. He kicked angrily at the snare and saw it was the gilded sword lost by the Pakin noble vanquished by Odovar. The weapon was easily worth more than his family's entire holding. Tol dragged it out of the dirt and hugged it close to his chest.

Where was Old Acorn? There! The roan was making for the town gate. The distance was great for a lone boy on foot, and the field provided no cover. Tol set off, dragging the tip of the golden sword in the dirt behind him.

Without warning, a hand seized his arm from behind and spun him around. Towering over him was the Pakin in spiky scale armor. The man's remarkably pale face was smeared with dried blood from his bashed-in nose.

"Peasant thief!" the noble said, his voice oddly inflected. "Give back what you have taken!"

Tol surprised himself by yelling back, "No!" and wrenching free. He'd taken only three steps before the man seized him again. He yelled for help, struggling futilely.

"You're past help now, boy!" The Pakin drew a dagger from his waist. It had an ugly forked tip. He raised it high.

Even as Tol stared in horror, the dagger flew from the Pakin's hand, knocked away by a whirling saber. Tol's head whipped around and he saw Egrin standing behind him.

"Give him the sword," said the warden. "I'll not slay a helpless man."

It sounded foolish to Tol, but he did as Egrin bid. The Pakin snatched the ornate hilt from the boy's hands. Tol stepped quickly from between the men.

"You are a Rider of the Horde?" the pale-faced noble asked, sizing up Egrin.

"Yes. I am the Warden of Juramona."

"Good enough to kill, then!"

The Pakin was of slender build compared to Egrin or Lord Odovar, but he had the speed of a striking snake. He traded swirling slashes with Egrin.

"You're a good man of arms," said the noble. "Join the side of strength—serve the Pakin Successor!"

Egrin thrust at his face and was deflected. "I will never lend my sword to a usurper."

The Pakin whirled in a circle, his broad, flat blade coming right at Egrin's neck. Egrin managed to block the cut, but the momentum of the blow drove him back. His guard went down, and the Pakin let out a cry of triumph.

"Life to the strong!" he shouted, the Pakin war cry. Extending his sword, he ran at the vulnerable warden.

Without thinking, Tol found himself on his feet and running toward the Pakin noble's back. He had nothing, not even a stick, so he threw himself at the man's knees.

The Pakin staggered. Cursing colorfully, he backhanded

Tol. His scale-covered gauntlet split the boy's cheek open and snapped his head back. Still Tol held on. Unable to pry the boy off, the Pakin twisted around and raised his sword. Tol clenched his eyes shut.

He heard a meaty thud, and a heavy weight pinned him to the ground. The slender Pakin nobleman had collapsed on him. Tol couldn't get free until Egrin dragged the unconscious Pakin off him.

"Are you all right?" the Ackal warrior asked.

Tol scrambled to his feet. He had a bleeding gash on his cheek where the Pakin had hit him—his head still rang from the blow—but otherwise he felt fine. He nodded in reply.

Horns resounded, and horsemen deluged the melee. The Juramona garrison, seeing their lord in peril, had sortied to rescue him. They quickly put the Pakins to rout, surrounding the exhausted men of Egrin's troop.

Lord Odovar rode up, looking remarkably fit after his ordeal. Battle agreed with him.

"So, Egrin Raemel's son! Alive but unhorsed, I see," he boomed jovially.

"Unhorsed, but not empty-handed, my lord." The warrior pointed to the fallen Pakin.

"Turn the blackguard over, so I may see his face," Odovar said. Egrin did so, and Odovar cried, "Vakka Zan! By Draco, you have true Pakin blood there!"

"A kinsman of the Pretender?" Egrin asked, scrutinizing his captive's slack features.

"His nephew, I believe. Bind him up, men. He'll make a pretty present for the emperor!"

Odovar's men tied Vakka Zan hand and foot, and threw him over a horse. Those of Egrin's troop who had survived formed up behind the marshal. The gate now stood wide open.

Manzo rode past. "Warden," he said respectfully, "you shouldn't walk. I'll fetch a horse."

Egrin held up a torn and bloody gauntlet. "No need. My legs work well enough for now. Old Acorn would take it amiss if I rode another animal." Manzo drew his dagger and saluted his commander.

Garrison and guardsmen rode on, leaving Egrin and Tol to walk the last hundred paces to Juramona. Tol moved ahead of the warden when the latter paused to pick up something.

"Boy," Egrin called. "Master Tol!"

He stopped. No one had ever called him "master" before.

"This is yours."

Egrin held out Vakka Zan's gilded sword, hilt-first. Tol gaped.

"Go on, take it. You earned it. To save my life you attacked an armed man bare-handed. I may have subdued Lord Vakka, but you made it possible. His sword is yours."

"Sir! It's too good for the likes of me—"

"Nonsense! My life is worth more to me than any blade in Ergoth. You saved me, and you'll have this reward and my thanks."

Tol took the heavy weapon from the smiling Egrin. With its point in the dirt, the pommel came up to Tol's chin. Blood-stained and mud-spattered though it was, the weapon was far and away the finest thing Tol had ever seen, much less owned.

He grasped the sword hilt in both hands and swung the blade up. It was weighted near the tip, the better to cleave through armored foes, and Tol had to step lively to keep his balance. He recovered, laid the flat of the sword on his shoulder, then looked up at the warden.

"Forward, my man," said Egrin. "Lord Odovar awaits."

C h a p t e r 3
The High Marshal's Will

When Tol entered the gate at Juramona, he felt he was leaving one world behind and entering an entirely new one. Never afterward would he experience such a head-turning, heart-pounding initiation. He forgot the bloodshed he'd just witnessed and the throbbing cut on his cheek, and all but forgot the gilt-edged weapon lying hard and heavy on his shoulder.

Juramona had begun life as a log fort, growing into a sizable town only after the lords holding it were named high marshals of the province. Some three thousand inhabitants, men and women of every size, shape, and color, dwelled within its wooden wall. Some were Riders of the Great Horde, born to the warrior class like Egrin, and these were striding about with long spears, helmets, and scaly breastplates, but most of the people thronging the streets were artisans or laborers, folks with greasy hands and dirty faces who crowded around to witness Lord Odovar's return. Some were not human at all. The boy spied a pair of bearded fellows no taller than himself, yet easily twice as broad.

Egrin saw him staring and said, "Traders from Thorin." In response to Tol's blank look, he added, "Dwarves."

Tol drew a breath and gazed anew at the pair. He'd heard tales of dwarves, but had never seen them in the flesh. These two were both black haired and well muscled. They held stout walking sticks, and their fingers glittered with jeweled rings.

The mounted warriors came to the foot of the high earthen mound in the center of Juramona and halted. Three men on horseback drew up to greet Lord Odovar. The one in the center wore a heavy brass chain around his neck, and it was to him the marshal spoke.

"Greetings, Morthur Dermount," said Odovar. He was leaning heavily on the pommel of his saddle, but though he was bruised and haggard, his voice was strong.

"Greetings to you, Lord Marshal. All Juramona rejoices at your safe return," Morthur replied.

Morthur Dermount had a thin nose, spade beard, and straight black hair cut severely away from his neck and ears. His dark eyes were hooded by black brows. Though not opulently dressed, he had the casual arrogance of one born to privilege.

"Your rescue was well timed," Odovar said sarcastically. "Another half hour and the Pakins would have finished us."

Morthur bowed his head. "I live to serve you, Lord Marshal."

Odovar's countenance flashed from annoyed to furious. "Impudent wretch! I know your game! If I had died out there, Juramona would have fallen to you, and only the Pakins would have my blood on their hands!"

"My lord, you do me an injustice," Morthur answered mildly.

"Justice is what I say it is," Odovar snapped. "Now make way! I want food and wine, and the attentions of a healer. Is wise Felryn about?"

"He will be sent for, my lord." Morthur and his escort moved aside, and Lord Odovar dismounted. He stomped up the wooden ramp into the great house on the mound.

The crowd slowly went about its business. Egrin called to him. Tol saw the warden standing a few paces away. The remnants of his troop sat on horseback around him.

Tol hurried to join them. They tramped down the winding lane, between a solid line of two- and three-story buildings, massively made of thick timbers and painted mud plaster.

Heavy shutters closed the windows to the weather, and atop the peak of each house was a colorful emblem, a talisman to protect the structure from ill fortune. Bird figures were common—brightly painted wooden roosters or wildfowl. A few wrought in copper were green with corrosion.

The street was muddy, though it hadn't rained recently, and Tol quickly learned why: Everyone in town threw his or her slops in the street. From the barber's soapy shaving water to the housewives' washwater and every townsman's chamber pot, it all ended up in the street, and Juramona, for all its wonders, smelled much the same as a compost heap.

The Household Guard lived in a large log house on the north side of the hill. On the roof peak was a great bronze eagle, the talisman of the guards. The house had two floors; the lower one was the stable for their horses. When Egrin and Tol walked in, they were greeted by a loud whinny.

"Old Acorn!" Egrin grinned broadly, patting his loyal steed's neck. "Trust you to make it home before any of us!"

The rest of the troops led their animals in and turned them over to stableboys. Saddles and tack were speedily removed. Each horse was led away to its own stall, and the boys fell to watering and feeding them. More than one animal had wounds from the skirmishes of the past two days, and an elderly man in a patched robe appeared to tend their injuries.

At Egrin's request, the old man first took a look at Tol's injured cheek. The cut had stopped bleeding, so after telling the boy to wash it well, the elderly fellow moved off to minister to the valuable war-horses. Tol followed the loud-talking warriors up the wide wooden stairs to the next floor.

The whole of this level was taken up by a single room. A spiderweb of beams overhead supported a steep thatched roof. From the beams hung brightly colored banners. One wall of the room held two wide fireplaces. Down the center of the room was an enormous trestle table, laden with victuals. Baskets of boiled nuts steamed next to heavy trenchers of roast venison. Capons, seared by fire, lay in piles between crocks of foamy beer. More boys toiled along the table, dispensing beer and food to the ravenous fighting men.

As warden, Egrin's place was at the table's head. He sat down, and a platter of venison was speedily put before him. A leather jack of beer appeared, and two sizzling capons. Egrin drew his knife to attack his dinner, then paused. He called Tol to him and proceeded to carve off half his portion of venison and push it to one side of the large trencher. Hacking a crisp bird in two, he added that to the serving and called for a cup. The small clay beaker he filled with beer from his own jack.

"Eat your fill," he said.

Although his head was swimming with hunger, Tol hesitated. The table's twenty-pace length was crowded with the Riders of the Great Horde, all talking, eating, and drinking. The serving lads ringed the room, staying back out of the way until called. None of them was eating.

"Go on. Eat." Egrin took the heavy gilded sword from Tol's hands, and leaned it against the table.

When his fingers touched the hot capon, Tol's reservations vanished. He tore into the bird greedily. Egrin couldn't know how rare a treat this was for the farmer's son. Perhaps four times a year he would taste red meat—and chicken or game birds only a little more often. Meat was for men, Tol's father always said. Women and children had to make do with broth and vegetables.

The capon was sweet and smoky, much finer than the stringy partridges or tough chicken he was used to. Tol put the stripped bones down and reached for the beaker.

He'd drunk watered cider once. Old Kinzen, herbmaster and healer to the hill farmers, had treated him for a cough with a decoction of sumac and willow in mulled cider, diluted by half with water. That drink had been bitter, but the warriors' beer was not. The first sip made Tol's tongue tingle, and the first swallow spread the sensation all the way down his gullet.

Tol's surprise showed plainly on his face. Egrin grinned at him.

"The second thing a Rider of the Horde learns," the warden said, loud enough for his comrades nearby to hear, "is to drink beer."

Red-faced from the liquid's spreading warmth, Tol asked, "What's the first?"

"How to fight." The men cheered.

Tol finished the capon and venison, then washed it all down with the last golden drops of beer. The world seemed to waver a bit, and he found himself sitting down without meaning to. Warriors looked at him and laughed.

"Our fare's too much for him," said Manzo, sitting across the table from Tol. Helmetless, Manzo's long brown hair was revealed to be as prematurely silvered as his beard.

"Is this the lad who saved Lord Odovar?" asked another man.

"The same. He saved me as well," Egrin said. They demanded to hear the tale. Pushing himself back from the table, Egrin related his fight with Vakka Zan, and how Tol interfered with the noble's fatal thrust. The raucous noise died as the Riders all listened, enthralled.

When Egrin finished, a blond-haired man farther down the table shouted, "A peasant boy did all that? Unbelievable!"

"By Draco Paladin, it's true," said the warden.

"Ah, he's got a rider's blood in his veins!" said Manzo.

"I'll wager his mother's mate doesn't know that!" the blond man quipped. That set the assembly to roaring.

The rest of the evening passed in a blur of loud voices and raucous laughter. Tol curled up on the oaken floor by Egrin's chair and slept deeply, weighed down by the toil of his journey, his rich meal, and the potent brew.

When he woke some time later, a tempest of snores filled the hall. Egrin and the other riders had fallen asleep in their chairs, slumped over the table or with heads hanging back, mouths agape. The shuttered windows admitted a dim gray light. Tol crept to the nearest one, carefully stepping over sleeping warriors. It was early morning, and the sky was thick with low clouds. He could smell rain coming.

Vakka Zan's golden saber lay across the sleeping Egrin's knees. Tol tried to take it without rousing the warden, but Egrin's senses were too keen. As soon as the heavy blade began to slide across his lap, he jerked awake and grabbed for the hilt.

Egrin scrubbed his face with one hand. "It's early. Why are you stirring?"

"Dawn is breaking. Isn't it time to wake?"

"For farmers maybe. Warriors sleep longer."

Egrin shifted the hilt to his shoulder and folded his arms over the blade. "G'night," he murmured, resting his head on his crossed arms.

Defeated, Tol tip-toed away. He decided to have a look around. Perhaps he could find some water—he was terribly thirsty and his injured cheek was stiff and aching.

He went down the wide steps, picking his way around guardsmen sleeping in awkward positions on the stairs. The stable below was quietly astir as boys went to and fro, filling mangers with hay and troughs with water. They ignored Tol, concentrating on their chores.

In back of the guardsmen's hall was a well. Two boys about Tol's age were hoisting a chain of buckets out, each brimming with fresh water. As soon as they set a pail down, another boy whisked it away.

"Spare some water?" Tol asked. "I'm dry as dirt!"

The tow-headed boy at the bucket chain shrugged. "Help self."

Tol raised the brimming bucket to his lips and drank deeply. The water was cold and tasted of minerals, much better than the creek water they drank back home, which too often tasted of mud or dead leaves. Twice every summer the creek dried up when the family needed it most.

After rinsing his injured cheek, Tol put the bucket down and thanked his benefactor. The second boy hooked the pail on the chain again and hauled away on the metal links, dragging the empty buckets over the flagstones and back down the well. Tol asked their names.

"I'm Narren," said the tow-headed boy. "He's Crake." Narren indicated his companion, who was dark-skinned, like the northern seafarers Tol had heard tales of. Crake absently waved a hand.

"Horses not fed, watered, and combed by the time the masters wake up, we all get beaten," he explained.

Narren nodded, confirming this.

"You joining us?" Crake asked, pushing the empty buckets over the lip of the well wall with his bare foot.

Tol had no idea what Lord Odovar or Egrin had in store for him. But before he could ponder it long, a clatter of horses' hooves out front was punctuated by the blare of brass trumpets.

Narren and Crake immediately abandoned the bucket chain and rushed into the stable. The other boys likewise ran about, clearing away stray buckets and brooms.

The front doors of the stable flew open, revealing eight riders led by Morthur Dermount. He wasn't smiling today. Black brows collided over his thin nose, and a purple vein throbbed visibly in his neck.

"Where is the warden? Roust him out, before I put a torch to this place and wake him myself!" he roared.

An older boy ran upstairs to fetch Egrin. On the steps, guardsmen steeped in beer stirred sluggishly, peering at the new day with bloodshot eyes.

"Why am I standing here in horse dung, waiting?" Morthur bellowed after several minutes. "Bring me the warden of the Household Guard!"

Egrin came down looking rumpled and cross. He drew himself up in front of Morthur and unsheathed his dagger blade in salute.

"My lord," he said hoarsely. "My apologies for the delay."

Morthur looked down scornfully from the height of his horse's back. "You sleep off yet another drunken carouse while I, a cousin of the emperor, am left waiting in the stables! It's intolerable, warden!"

"Yes, my lord. What is it you require?"

"The Lord Marshal tells me you captured a Pakin noble yesterday, one Vakka Zan to be exact." Egrin confirmed it, and Morthur added, "He is to be judged this morning. Lord Odovar would see him shortened by a head."

Egrin started visibly. "I thought the Lord Marshal intended to hold the Pakin as a hostage, or for ransom?"

Morthur sneered. "So thought I, warden. Vakka Zan is more nobly born than anyone hereabouts, save myself. Such blood should not be shed lightly, but the Lord Marshal has made his will plain." He moved to go, then turned back to add, "Oh, and Lord Vakka's sword. Fetch it to Lord Odovar at once."

Egrin glanced at Tol as he said, "Sword, my lord? It's mine as a trophy of single combat."

"I merely convey the High Marshal's commands," Morthur said irritably. "I, with the blood of emperors in my veins, reduced to carrying messages . . ." His hands tightened on the reins and his horse pranced under him. Egrin was forced to step back smartly to avoid its heavy hooves.

Morthur smiled thinly at the warden's quick movements. With a shout, he rode off, trailed by his retinue. Egrin watched them go, scratching his chin through his gray-speckled beard.

"Bad business," he said. "Bad business."

Tol remained behind when the other boys dispersed to their tasks. He came to Egrin's elbow. "I must give up the sword?" he said.

"Seems so, lad." Egrin scratched some more. "Or maybe not. You will accompany me to the High House to see the marshal. You shall carry the sword."

Feeling a mix of pride and apprehension, Tol asked, "Why me, sir?"

"To remind Lord Odovar not only what I owe you, but what he owes you as well."

He slapped Tol sharply on the back. "Make haste! If we hurry, we can reach Lord Odovar before Lord Morthur does. He's a lazy sort, and may visit two or three taverns before heading back to the High House."

"Why must we arrive before Lord Morthur?"

Egrin's eyes narrowed, but a hint of a smile revealed his good humor. "Showing a fool to be a fool is easy, but showing a fool to a fool may save a man's life."

❦ ❦ ❦ ❦ ❦

Glowering over the half-timbered houses of Juramona, the High House was almost a second town in itself. The seat of the Lord Marshal perched atop the man-made hill built by a thousand prisoners of war and had its own stable, armory, larder, and great hall. It was in this last that Lord Odovar conducted the affairs of his domain, subject to the will of his overlord and master, the emperor of Ergoth.

Tol arrived with Egrin, Manzo, and three other guardsmen. He rode behind the warden, Lord Vakka's saber held tightly in his sweating hands. They ascended a steep ramp made of logs into the lowest courtyard, then dismounted to walk up the spiral ramp that encircled the mound. Every structure on the hill had a flat, sturdy roof, manned by gangs of spearmen. The spearmen wore simple pot helmets and painted leather cuirasses over quilted jerkins. They were not Riders of the Great Horde, but hired men. Horseless, their only purpose was to defend the High House, for which they were paid in salt, meat, and bread.

The second-to-topmost tier was the marshal's hall. Egrin, Tol, and the guardsmen were held at the door until a lackey returned with Lord Odovar's permission for them to enter. It was granted, and Egrin marched in boldly at the head of his men.

Odovar was seated in a tall chair on a carpeted timber platform higher than the rest of the floor. He'd washed away the filth and blood of the past several days and wore a finely woven crimson robe and sash. Leather bands, sewn with red and blue gems, encircled his forearms, and a heavy gold chain rested on his chest.

To Odovar's left, on a lower bench, sat a handsome, well-fleshed woman. She was garbed in a white cloth that seemed to shine with its own light and, combined with her pale skin and light hair, gave her an otherworldly radiance. A large sapphire hung from a golden chain around her neck, and similar blue stones sparkled in her dangling earrings.

At the marshal's right hand stood a thick-waisted, bald man. He wore a stiff linen robe with a red velvet stole draped around his neck. His hands, like his belly, were big and soft-looking. A tight smile never left his face as he watched Egrin's group approach.

The walls of the great hall were plastered and white-washed, making the round room seem even larger than it was. Fires flickered in standing brass braziers on each side of the marshal's high chair, and heavy tapestries in bold, deep hues hung from the rafters behind the raised platform.

Egrin stopped abruptly, slapping his boot heels together and raising high his dagger. "My lord! I have come as you bid. How may I serve you?"

Odovar gave the pale woman's hand a squeeze and kiss, then dropped it. His forehead was swathed in a linen bandage, almost obscuring one eye.

"Where is Morthur?" he asked.

"I don't know, sir," Egrin replied. "He delivered your summons and departed. I came here straightaway."

"In some swill shop, no doubt," Odovar said, answering his own question, "or chasing a milkmaid around the dairy barns." His lady simpered, and the bald man clucked his tongue disapprovingly.

"I see you brought the Pakin's sword," Odovar added. He held out his hand.

Tol was reluctant to relinquish the weapon. Egrin nudged him, and Tol approached the high chair with arms outstretched, the gilded saber balanced across his hands. Odovar rose and took the sword. He swept it back and forth through the air, admiring its weight and the flashing glints from its gold chasing.

"A masterful blade," he said. "Made by the elf smith Exanthus, I'm told." He took the hilt in both hands and brought the saber down in a powerful chop. "Should sever the traitor's head with no trouble. What do you think, Lanza?"

He reversed his grip and offered the weapon to the bald man beside him. Lanza took it gingerly and scrutinized the fine filigree on the blade with a practiced eye.

"The hilt is typical Daltigoth, but the blade is Silvanesti work, right enough," he said. "You could probably cleave the altar stone of Solin with such an edge."

Odovar took the sword back. He seated himself again and leaned toward his lady, showing off the sword's exquisite inlay to her.

"My lord, I would ask a boon of you," Egrin said.

The marshal, only half listening, merely grunted. He chucked his lady's chin gently with the sword hilt, and she giggled, fluttering long eyelashes at him.

Egrin forged on. "My lord, I ask you to spare the life of Vakka Zan."

The whispered dalliance between Odovar and his lady died. The marshal turned his full attention to Egrin.

"What?" Odovar demanded. "Did you say spare the traitor?"

"Spare a noble hostage," Egrin countered.

Odovar leaped to his feet, hand clenched around the sword hilt. "How dare you plead for that rogue's life! You've gone soft on the Pakins, Egrin!" The marshal's voice rose to a shout. "I will exterminate this traitor. There will be no peace until every Pakin has his head removed from his shoulders! Vakka Zan will die, and the emperor will know he has a strong hand in the Eastern Hundred!"

The hard plaster walls echoed Odovar's shouts. His lady gazed up at him worshipfully, and bald Lanza nodded approval. Odovar resumed his seat with a forceful thump, his face flushed.

Egrin spoke quietly, trying another approach, "My lord, this is Tol, the boy who saved you from Lord Grane day before yesterday."

Odovar squinted from under his bandage. "Yes? So it is. As his reward, find a place for him in the stables or the cookhouse."

"Yes, my lord. You may not know it, but the boy also saved my life in the fight outside the town gates." Egrin related how Tol had thrown himself on Vakka Zan, saving Egrin from certain death. The tale seemed to please Odovar. His high color faded, and he smiled.

"A game lad indeed," he said. "I should put you to work in the High House."

Egrin glanced at Tol. "My lord, I must tell you—I gave the boy the Pakin sword. He saved me, and I defeated Lord Vakka. By right of combat, the Pakin's life belongs to me then, does it not?"

Odovar's massive hands closed into fists. "Greater things are at stake than the rights of single combat. The Pakin must die."

Egrin paused, giving his lord's words due consideration, then said, "Will you at least agree, my lord, the sword belongs to Master Tol?"

The marshal laughed shortly, unpleasantly. "Give a Silvanesti-forged blade to a peasant boy? What would he do with it? Plow a furrow?"

Egrin nudged Tol. The boy stepped forward. He was quaking inside, but as before his voice did not betray his fear.

"My lord, I gladly would give the Pakin sword to you—"

Odovar snorted. "My thanks, boy!"

"—in exchange for the life of Vakka Zan."

The marshal was out of his chair and down from the platform in one bound. "What knavery is this, Egrin? You bring a peasant brat to bargain with me, like some market day fishmonger? Saved my life or no, if I give the word his head will go on a spike next to the Pakin's!"

Tol's hard-won courage failed. He stepped back, trembling.

"The boy meant no harm, my lord," Egrin said quickly. "I told him what to say."

Odovar skinned back his lips in a broad, cruel smile. "I am not an ogre, after all. I accept your gift of the Pakin's sword, boy." He bowed his head mockingly to Tol. "And I, Odovar of Juramona, will not take the life of Vakka Zan."

Tol almost fainted with relief at the marshal's generosity. Yet the warden looked grimmer than ever.

"No, I will not take his life—you shall," Odovar announced, thrusting a finger at Egrin. "In the main square of Juramona, at dawn tomorrow." He handed the sword to Egrin. "You may borrow my Silvanesti sword to do the job."

Smoothing his crimson robe and tightening the sash at his waist, Lord Odovar resumed his seat. The great hall was still, save for the hiss of the braziers. No one moved or spoke for a long minute.

"Go," said the marshal at last, waving dismissal. "Practice your swing, warden. I don't want a botched job tomorrow."

The warriors saluted. As they withdrew, Odovar had one last spear to cast. "Bring brave Master Tol with you to the execution, warden," he called out. "We have him to thank for both sword and traitor." Egrin did not acknowledge the cruel command, so Odovar shouted, "That is my order!"

Egrin turned and saluted. "It shall be done, my lord."

The warriors and Tol remained silent until they had left the High House. Once on the streets of Juramona, Tol said, "I never meant to cause Vakka Zan's death!"

"You didn't," Egrin said grimly. "This is by the will of the High Marshal alone."

Tol lowered his voice so only the warden could hear him. "It doesn't seem right."

"Right is the word of the emperor, and through him, his princes, lords, and marshals. If you intend to live in Juramona, Tol, you'd better learn that truth straightaway."

Chapter 4
A New Life

Tol was lodged with the stableboys that night, given a berth in a bank of wooden bunks, a rough homespun blanket, and a clay cup from which to drink. The room was warm and smoky from the two banked fires, and alive with snores and snorts, coughs and groans. Crake and Narren were nearby, but sound asleep. Tol kicked off his unnecessary cover and tried to follow their example. Sleep eluded him. His mind wouldn't settle down.

Five days had passed since he'd left the onion field with Lord Odovar. On their journey here, the marshal had promised to send word to his mother and father. Things got so lively later on, Tol didn't know whether anyone had been dispatched to the farm after all. He didn't dare pester Lord Odovar about it. The marshal seemed all too easily angered.

Tol jerked awake, surprised to realize he'd fallen asleep. The boys' hall was quieter now. Glowing embers on the twin hearths had died, leaving the room fully dark and chillier than it had been.

Accustomed to living by the rhythms of night and day, Tol sensed dawn wasn't far off. With the sunrise, he remembered, would come the execution of Vakka Zan. He climbed down from the high bunk, threw his blanket around his shoulders like a cloak, and slipped outside.

The flagstone courtyard between the boys' hall and the stable was slick with dew. It wasn't actually raining, but a heavy mist silvered the morning in a fine, damp veil. After a drink at the well, Tol passed through the silent stable into the street beyond.

No one was stirring in Juramona at that hour. Following the directions Crake had given him the night before, Tol tramped down the noisome track to the town square, where the execution was to take place. It wasn't a very big place, nor was it a square—more a rough rectangle. On market days it would be thronged with hundreds of folk, eagerly trading. On this misty morning, there was nothing to see but a tall wooden platform and a few men sleeping on the ground next to it.

Tol approached. As he drew within a few paces, the man nearest him bolted to his feet in a clatter of arms.

"Stand off!" the man shouted, leveling a wicked-looking billhook at the boy.

Tol held up his hands. "Friend! Friend! I am lately come to Juramona with the warden of the Household Guard!"

"And his name is?" the soldier demanded.

"Egrin, Raemel's son."

The soldier raised the billhook and rested it on his shoulder. "Aye, that's him. A right good commander he is, too."

"Why are you men here?" Tol asked.

The fellow hiked a thumb over his shoulder. "Guarding a prisoner. He's losing his head this day."

Tol was surprised. Lord Vakka was already at the place of his execution? He voiced his curiosity, and the guard replied, "We marched him out here just after midnight. Lord Marshal's orders. 'No warm beds for traitors. Let 'im soak in the chill of night,' he says. So here were are, soakin' it up with him."

Beneath the tall platform Tol could make out a solitary figure huddled next to one of the center posts. The man's wrists were chained to the post and his head rested against them, hiding his face, but his fine head of colorless hair marked him as Vakka Zan.

The guard coughed nervously. "Uh, no harm's done of course—the Pakin is chained and no one could get to him but through us. Still . . ." He studied Tol from under shaggy brows, then continued in a lower voice, "You won't say nothing to the warden about us all sleepin', will you?"

Tol shook his head solemnly, then asked, "Can I talk to the prisoner? Only for a moment?"

The guard hacked and spat, pondering the request. At last he said, "Say your piece. But no touching, nor giving, or taking away anything. Understand?"

Tol swore to abide by the rules, and the guard moved off to roust his comrades from their slumber with the butt of his bill. Coughing and grumbling, the soldiers rose and shook off the clinging mist. Two set to work lighting fires in iron baskets beside the platform.

The Pakin prisoner stirred, raising his head. Tol approached him cautiously. Stripped of his fancy armor, Vakka Zan was revealed to be a slender, youthful man, somewhere between Tol and Egrin in years. Though disheveled and damp from his night in the square, he had remarkably refined, almost girlish, features. His hands and face were streaked with dirt and dried blood. A mighty greenish-blue bruise covered the left side of his jaw. Despite all that, he was a striking fellow. His hair was shoulder length and white, his skin very pale. His eyebrows and eyelashes were so white as to be nearly invisible. But his eyes were strangest of all: The irises were pink and the pupils, a deeper red. In the heat of battle, Tol had not noticed the man's oddly colored eyes.

"What do you want?" Vakka Zan said sullenly, interrupting the boy's silent scrutiny.

"Are you an elf?"

The Pakin noble laughed bitterly. "You're not the first to ask me that!" He shifted position, chains rattling loudly. "I'm no Silvanesti. There's a strain in the Pakin clan that's born without color in hair or skin. We're known as the 'White Pakins.'" Vakka Zan fixed the boy with his strange, pinkish eyes. "Have I satisfied your wondering?"

Tol nodded, missing the sarcastic tone. What he really wanted to say was hard to get out. Finally, he blurted, "I'm sorry you are being killed today!"

"You and me both." Vakka Zan leaned back against the post and cradled his chains in his lap, adding, "Why do you care? Aren't you loyal to the Ackals?"

Tol looked at the mist-slicked stones at his feet. "I helped capture you. I was the one who stopped you from killing Lord Odovar's warden."

The Pakin's eyes widened. His face remained blank for a few heartbeats, then contorted into a ferocious snarl. Screaming, he hurled himself at Tol.

The boy was so shocked he didn't respond until the white fingers were almost around his throat. With a sudden burst of self-preservation, Tol threw himself backward. The chains pulled Vakka Zan up short, but he hurled himself against them again and again, trying to reach the boy. Flat on his back, Tol scrambled away on elbows and heels.

Guards came running, shouting for quiet. When the Pakin refused to calm down, they pummeled him with the butts of their billhooks. He went down under their blows, but continued to scream threats at them all.

The corporal of the guards hauled Tol to his feet. "Sweet Mishas, what did you say to him?"

Tol stammered a reply, and the guard said, "So it's true, eh? You helped capture him." To his men he shouted, "Easy, boys. Don't kill him! Lord Odovar will have all our heads if the Pakin dies before his time!"

The heavy mantle of clouds had lightened, heralding the dawn beyond the rain. Massed, slow hoofbeats sounded on the stony street, and a contingent of the Household Guard, led by Egrin, appeared at the south end of the square. They were most imposing in their scale shirts and angular helmets. Egrin deployed them around the platform. While the riders moved into place, Egrin rode through the guards, who drew back out of Old Acorn's path. He halted beneath the edge of the platform.

"Stand up, my lord," he said to Vakka Zan. The Pakin noble tried, then slumped back to the ground.

"Get him up," Egrin said quietly. Two footmen dragged

Paul B. Thompson and Tonya C. Cook

Vakka Zan to his feet. At Egrin's order, a bucket of clean water was brought, and the Pakin noble was allowed to wash his face and hands.

"You're to die soon. I can't change that," Egrin said. "But there's no reason you have to perish like a pig, in mud and filth."

"Your time will come, all of you," Vakka Zan replied fiercely. "When word of this outrage reaches the true emperor, this entire settlement will be razed, and everyone inside will die a slow death!"

"The true emperor is our liege, Pakin III, who reigns in Daltigoth, not the charlatan you bow to," Egrin said.

"The throne in Daltigoth is held by a usurper, with no right to the Pakin name! His head will soon rot on the highest spike in the empire!"

A crowd of townsfolk was gathering, drawn by the promise of a rare spectacle. The mob parted as Lord Odovar arrived on horseback in full armor, with Morthur Dermount beside him. Trailing them, the marshal's retinue rode under a wide canvas awning supported by poles carried by mounted servants. Tol recognized bald Lanza and the marshal's plump, blonde lady.

"Your voice carries far," Odovar boomed at Vakka Zan. "But I doubt it will reach the Pretender in his squalid exile's camp."

The Pakin recovered his composure at the sight of his enemy. "It may reach Lord Grane," he said coldly.

Odovar's retinue shifted nervously, and the marshal flexed a gauntleted fist around his reins. The threat had touched a vulnerable spot. Grane had nearly gotten Odovar once, and was still at large with forces of unknown strength.

"Proceed with the course of justice," Odovar commanded. "Warden, are you ready?"

"At your command, my lord," said Egrin.

The chains were unwound from Vakka Zan, and the rivets of his shackles driven out. Burly footmen yanked his hands behind his back and lashed them with cord. Eight soldiers mounted the platform, taking positions at each corner and midway between. Facing outward, they presented their spears. Vakka Zan, followed by two guards, climbed the wooden steps to the platform's summit.

"Lanza, do your part," Odovar said.

The rotund man got down carefully from his horse and walked to the front edge of the canopy. The mist had become a slow rain, and he took care not to get his shiny pate wet.

"Great Manthus!" he intoned, lifting his hands high. His sleeves slid back, exposing hairy forearms. "See now our fair justice! Protect our Lord Marshal from all enemies, both of flesh and spirit! Disperse any curses laid upon him by the condemned or his blood kin, for he dies adjudged of the crimes of treason, rebellion, and the taking up of arms against his lawful sovereign! Hear us, O Manthus!"

So saying, he clapped his hands together thrice, then dipped first his right hand, then his left, into the voluminous pockets in his robe, bringing out dark red rose petals. These he slung in high, wide arcs. They fell on Lord Odovar, his horse, and the pavement around him.

Lanza nodded to his lord, and the marshal said, "Let it be done!"

In the center of the platform was a simple bench made of heavy planks. Without prodding, Vakka Zan walked to the bench and knelt behind it, facing Odovar and his retinue. He flung his long white hair aside and laid his head, right ear down, on the block.

Egrin mounted the steps. Tol's heart pounded. He saw why Lord Vakka had turned his head the way he did: so he didn't have to watch Egrin approach with blade bared.

Disdaining pomp or ceremony, Egrin shucked the scabbard from the gilded sword. Even in the dull light and drizzle the Silvanesti-forged blade sparkled like a fine jewel. The crowd of common folk strained forward against the ring of mounted warriors, eager to miss nothing.

Egrin did not wait. Taking the grip in both hands, he turned sharply on one heel and drew back the sword until the curved tip just touched the small of his back, then swung it down.

Tol did not close his eyes. Many around him did, soldiers included. He saw the gold-streaked blade flash through the air. Egrin let his knees bend deeply, putting his full weight behind the stroke. There wasn't the slightest hesitation or delay when blade met flesh. Silvanesti iron passed smoothly through the Pakin's neck and through the wooden bench beneath.

Egrin immediately recovered his stance and brought the blade up again. Simultaneously, the bench collapsed into two halves and Vakka Zan's head landed with a thump on the platform.

The crowd let out a spontaneous roar of approval. The cost of the Ackal–Pakin war had been high, in lives lost, in misery, and in grievous trade disruptions. One less Pakin seemed a fine idea to those watching.

Egrin descended the steps, the unsheathed sword held at his side. His hands were spattered with blood. More blood coated the blade. Without a word, he presented the weapon hilt-first to Lord Odovar. The two men's eyes did not meet, but Odovar took the sword by the handguard and tossed it to Morthur, beside him. Lips curled in distaste, Morthur held the Silvanesti sword for his liege lord. Crimson droplets fell from its tip.

Odovar turned his horse around and rode away. His entourage was slow to follow, as the long line of women and household retainers sheltering under the awning shuffled awkwardly around, trying to keep out of the weather.

Egrin's second-in-command, Manzo, brought Old Acorn forward. Tol stepped up and took the reins. He led the horse to the warden, still standing where he'd handed Lord Odovar the gilded sword. Egrin accepted the reins and laid a strong hand on Tol's shoulder. It remained there only a moment, then was withdrawn.

At Manzo's command, the Householders formed up and rode out. Next, the corporal of the footmen ranked his men and pushed the curious onlookers out of the square. Soon the only people left were Egrin, Tol, and the two men from the town charnel house, come to take the body away. Vakka's head Odovar had reserved for display in his hall.

After the body had been removed, Egrin mounted Old Acorn and departed. Tol ran after him, feet splashing in puddles.

The square was empty at last. Despite the rain, bloodstains remained on the platform for a long time.

❧ ❧ ❧ ❧ ❧

In spite of all the wonders he had seen, and the kindness and good fellowship of Egrin and the stableboys, Tol decided to leave Juramona. Lord Odovar's cruelty, matched by the viciousness of the condemned Pakin noble, left him feeling sick and disgusted. Life with his family, even amid the farm's ceaseless toil, was better than the wonders--and incomprehensible ways—of this town.

He had made the decision to leave by the time he'd returned to the boys' hall after the execution. The place was empty, as everyone was out working, but Tol huddled by one of the fires and dried his sodden clothing. The only food was the leavings of the boys' communal breakfast—dried-out oat porridge and some crusts of black bread. Tol ate all the porridge left in the pot and put what crusts he could find in a scrap of old cloth. He would need food for the journey.

The master of the boys, Zolamon, found Tol in the hall, and drove him out with shouts and buffets. He was given a wide wooden fork and set to mucking out the horse stalls with four other boys his size. The work was no worse than what he did every day at the farm, and he quickly outstripped his fellows, clearing two stalls to every one they managed. He welcomed the labor; it kept his mind from dwelling on Vakka Zan or, worse still, his severed head. He could've sworn that, as the head rolled free on the platform, the dead man's strange, pinkish eyes had shifted as though he were still alive and searching for someone. . . .

Zolamon returned. He was called "Big Stick" by the stableboys, and the origin of the nickname was obvious. He tapped a thick hardwood cudgel against his thigh as he strolled down the line of stalls, inspecting the boys' progress. Tol thought Zolamon would be pleased with what he'd done, but the taskmaster yelled at him just as he did the others. Still, he didn't hit Tol as he did two other boys, so Tol decided his work must have been satisfactory after all.

Supper in the boys' hall was a noisy, confusing affair, but what surprised Tol was the quantity of food available. Certainly not as rich as the capons, venison, and beer consumed by the Riders of the Horde, but the boys' stew and black bread were plentiful and filling. He'd never starved on the farm, but he never seemed to get quite enough to eat, either. And he seldom got real bread, only flat, hard disks of firecake, so even these coarse loaves were a treat. As he ate his fill among the raucous boys, Tol had no trouble secreting away several hunks of bread.

When supper was done, the healer arrived. Felryn served the marshal's entire household, from Lord Odovar down to the least stableboy. He was middle-aged, with curly black hair and dark bronze skin. Over a brown linen robe he wore a pantherskin tabard, tied with a heavy sash. His most striking feature was his hands. They were unusually large and powerful, with very long fingers. As he worked his way down the row of boys, those strong hands proved surprisingly gentle.

Reaching Tol, Felryn said, "You're new. What are you called?"

"Tol, my lord."

"I'm not your lord." He grasped Tol's chin and pushed his head back, peering into the boy's eyes. "I'm a physician. I work for my living, so don't call me 'lord.' "

"Yes, sir."

Felryn did not mention the cut on Tol's cheek. Instead, the healer said, "Show me your hands."

Tol did so, and Felryn grunted. "They tell me you cleared more stalls than three boys of long residence here. How is it you have no blisters?"

"I'm used to work," Tol replied. He glanced away at the

high slit windows. It was already dark and he was impatient to get away.

"Farm lad?" said the healer. Tol nodded.

Felryn lifted Tol's arms from his sides, prodded the muscles of his shoulders and upper arms, and asked his age. When Tol could only shrug, the healer said, "No matter. You're a well made lad. Where did you dwell before coming to Juramona?"

Tol's gaze strayed to the west window. "My family's farm is in the hills between the forest and plain," he answered.

Felryn pursed his lips thoughtfully. He took a ribbon of cloth from his sash, and bade Tol stand up straight. With another boy to help him, Felryn stretched the ribbon from Tol's feet to the crown of his head. From under the panther-skin tabard he drew a small board covered with wax. He made a few marks in the wax with a metal stylus then tucked the board away.

"Very good," he said, one large hand toying with the stylus. "I will see you again, Master Tol."

Felryn moved on to the next boy, whose hands were covered by blisters. The healer buttered them with a pungent salve that made the lad wince, then wrapped his palms with strips of rag.

When Felryn departed, the boys at last settled down. Weary older youths crawled into their low berths while the youngest boys banked the fires. Before long the first snores began, but Tol waited, making sure everyone was fast asleep.

Judging the time was right at last, he dropped soundlessly to the floor, his food bundle tucked under his arm. No one stirred as he padded outside.

Cold wind had scoured the rain away, leaving the heavens bright with stars. Tol pulled on the hide moccasins he'd been given in place of his farmer's clogs, then hastily wrapped his woolen leggings up to his knees. Ready at last, he straightened—and found himself facing a looming dark shape.

Even as he gasped in shock, the figure moved forward into a patch of moonlight. It was the healer, Felryn.

"Can't sleep?" Felryn asked, brown eyes crinkling in amusement.

Tol began to stammer excuses, but the healer waved them away, his expression becoming serious. "You want to go home, boy?" he said.

Tol admitted it, adding, "My family needs me on the farm."

"Mmm." Without warning, Felryn took him by the wrist and announced, "We must see the warden."

Worried, Tol tried to pull away, but Felryn held him fast and began to walk purposefully toward the Riders' Hall. Tol continued to stammer excuses and to try to free himself, but in no time they were climbing the wooden stairs to the upper story. Not wishing to embarrass himself in front of the Riders, Tol stopped his struggles as he and Felryn entered the hall.

The great room was dark but for a single candle burning at the head of the long table. Egrin sat alone there, the candlelight flickering over his face and the pewter mug on the table in front of him. He stared blankly at the mug, absently rubbing one ear, obviously lost in thought. Felryn's approach caused the warden to look up, but slowly, as though pulling his attention back from a great distance.

"Something amiss?" Egrin asked, frowning and getting to his feet.

Felryn halted by the table. "Master Tol is taking his leave of Juramona. I persuaded him to delay long enough to speak with you first."

The elder warrior looked down at Tol, and the boy colored in embarrassment.

"Why were you sneaking out in the middle of the night?" Egrin asked. Tol did not speak, so the warden added, "The Pakin's death shocked you, didn't it? Lord Odovar's word is law. His judgment was harsh, Tol, but the law must be enforced, or there is no law. You must understand that."

"Sir, my family will be worried," Tol blurted. "They don't know what happened to me. Lord Odovar has a lot of stableboys, but my family's got only me and my two sisters."

Egrin and Felryn smiled at each other, the lines in the

warden's face easing. "I never intended you should remain in the stables," Egrin said. "So, Felryn, how does he measure up?"

Felryn nodded gravely. "He is an excellent specimen, my lord. Fit for any duty suited to his age and size."

"Fine! Tol, how would you like to be my shield-bearer, my *shilder*? I'll train you in the way of the warrior. You'll learn to ride, and fight with sword, spear, and bow. Six springs from now, if you desire to leave my service, you can do so. You'll be free then to take any path you choose."

It was an amazing offer, all the more so because of Tol's humble origins. Most Riders of the Horde took on shilder from time to time, but they were always the sons of worthy retainers—not peasant boys.

"I can do anything I want six springs from now?" Tol asked.

"Aye, by then you'll be old enough to choose your own calling."

"Will I live in the hall with the stable hands?"

"No. Shilder have their own hall, within the walls of the High House."

Tol nodded, then walked slowly away, head hung in thought. His injured cheek ached, reminding him of his earlier brush with the life of a soldier.

"I'm not sure I can be a warrior," he said in a small voice, his hand coming up to touch his wound.

"Don't judge the life by the blood you've seen shed," Egrin said. "Anyone can be trained to kill. To be a warrior means much more than that. You'll also learn when *not* to fight. That's usually a far harder lesson to master."

After another silent minute, Tol turned and faced Egrin. "I would like to be your shield-bearer," he declared, "if my father agrees."

The warden smiled and clapped him on the shoulder. "Fair enough! Shall we go and ask him?"

❦ ❦ ❦ ❦ ❦

The next morning, they left Juramona before the sun had risen. Tol's farm lay four days' ride south and west, in the hills beyond the plain he'd crossed with Lord Odovar. Egrin and Tol rode Old Acorn. Accompanying them, somewhat to Tol's surprise, was Felryn, mounted on a sturdy brown horse.

The first three days passed uneventfully. Egrin explained the duties and responsibilities of a shilder, answering Tol's many questions. For his part, Felryn regaled the boy with a colorful account of the assassination of the previous emperor, Pakin II, and the subsequent fight for the throne between his son, Pakin III, and the Pakin Successor. Tol still found himself confused by the fact that the Ackal emperor, enemy of Pakins, was himself named Pakin.

"He chose that name to honor his murdered brother," Felryn said. "Pakin II had taken the name to reconcile the two factions." He sighed. "He failed."

Their third night out, they camped on the lee side of a hill, in the shade of a huge boulder. Tol, rolled up in a blanket provided by Egrin, fell asleep almost at once.

He dreamed, seeing himself and the others lying in a semicircle around their dead campfire. Something drew Tol's gaze upward, toward the star-sprinkled sky. He sensed a presence. Although he couldn't make out any shape, he felt that someone was staring down at them, an unfriendly someone. He sensed, too, that the formless, hostile watcher was coming closer, dropping directly down on his own sleeping body like a swooping bird—

Tol awoke, sitting up with a cry.

Egrin roused instantly, hand reaching for the sword lying next to him, and demanded to know what was wrong. Tol apologized and explained the dream he'd had.

"The evil was dropping down on me, like a hawk on a mouse."

Felryn put his head up from the depths of his own bedroll, muttering, "I like it not. Someone else has his eye on you, Master Tol."

"It was only a dream. Go back to sleep," Egrin said, settling himself again on his blanket.

"There's much stirring in the world, natural and unnatural, warden," Felryn said sourly. "Everything is a portent these days."

The healer's words spoiled Tol's rest for the remainder of the night.

The True Path

The next day they found the battlefield.

After their disrupted night, Felryn had arisen in a somber mood. What disquieted him he would not say, but as the morning progressed, signs of trouble appeared that upset them all. Thin columns of smoke rose in the distance. Crows and vultures wheeled overhead. Past noon the wind changed, bringing with it the unmistakable stench of death.

Egrin reined up. Felryn halted close beside him, glancing around with uneasy eyes.

"Where?" the warden asked.

Felryn fingered a deeply engraved white metal disk hanging from a cord around his neck. His face a blank mask of concentration, he pointed straight ahead.

They crossed a shallow creek and rode up the facing draw. The hills parted, revealing a broad, flat vale. From hill to hill, the valley was littered with the bodies of men and horses.

Egrin said nothing, merely touched his heels to Old Acorn's sides and rode slowly ahead. The war-horse was undisturbed by the sight and smell of corpses. Not so Tol. He clung tightly to Egrin. Although he turned his head from side to side to avoid the horrible spectacle, there was no escape. Death surrounded them.

Felryn's horse would not follow Old Acorn's lead through the battlefield. The healer had to climb down and hood the animal's eyes before it would advance. Even so, the terrified horse trembled in every limb, saliva dripping from its flaring lips, as it placed each hoof with care.

"Look well, Tol, and remember," said Egrin. "This is what victory looks like."

"What victory?" The boy's words were muffled against Egrin's back.

"These are Pakin dead. See the armbands, the banners?" The battlefield was littered with scraps of green cloth. "Those who win battles take their dead away with them. The defeated flee, leaving their men where they fall."

The carnage was many times worse than what Tol had seen following Lord Odovar's ambush. Egrin counted more than four hundred Pakins slain. He identified them as local levies, not of the warrior class. They were crudely equipped with leather armor, bronze-tipped spears, and the thick felt caps favored by men of the southern territories. There was very little metal among them—not much armor, no helmets. Here and there were scattered a few men of higher rank. They had been stripped to the skin, their valuable arms and armor carried away by the victorious Ackal warriors. None of their faces was familiar to the warden. Felryn agreed the men had been dead at least two or three days.

At the far end of the vale, Egrin found a mossy bank churned up by the hooves of many horses. Broken sabers littered the ground. He dismounted, felt the torn earth with his fingers, and studied the pattern of prints.

"This was not an ambush, but a pitched battle," he reported. "The numbers were even, but the Pakin levies were no match for warriors of a Great Horde."

"Imperial soldiers, here?" said Felryn, incredulous.

"Yes, see this sword hilt?" Egrin held up the stump of a shattered weapon. "That's the pattern used by the Daltigoth Silver Blades, one of four hordes quartered in the capital."

A horde was a fighting company made up of a thousand warriors. Each horde bore a proud and fearsome name, like the Silver Blades, the Ackal Bloods, or the Red Thunders.

"The fight started out there, on open ground. The Pakins charged, and the Imperial horde drew back, feigning retreat. Then they took the rebels in the flank, broke their formation, and drove them into this trap. Most of the Pakins died here." Egrin stood up and dusted his hands. "Basic tactics."

"I call it butchery," Felryn replied.

Tol listened openmouthed to Egrin's description of a battle he had not seen, then spoke up.

"These are the Pakins who ambushed Lord Odovar!"

Egrin regarded him skeptically. "How do you know?"

"Some of the men killed in the ambush, the Pakin ones, wore the same sort of hats. They, and the ones who came looking for Lord Odovar, had green cloths tied around their right arms, like these men. I remember wondering how right-handed men managed to do that."

Egrin studied the fallen rebels again. "I believe you're right. Good eye, lad!" A fresh thought struck him. "If these are the rebels who attacked the marshal, then Grane must have been with them. As far as I can tell he's not dead on the field, so he must be on the run. He may still be in the province!"

"Calm yourself, son of Raemel!" said Felryn, as Egrin mounted quickly. "No one knows what Spannuth Grane looks like under his helm. Any one of those stripped nobles could be him."

"True, but don't wager on it! Grane would not stand and fight if the battle was going against him. He ran away at the battle of Thingard, and again before the walls of Caergoth."

As he spoke, Egrin steered Old Acorn in a circle, clearly torn. Duty demanded he go after the traitor Grane, or at least ride back to Juramona with word of the Pakin defeat. But he had made a promise to take Tol home.

Felryn tried to resolve his friend's dilemma. "Warden, the blood is cold on the ground," he said. "If Grane abandoned his men as you say, then by now he's three days hard riding from here."

Egrin insisted Lord Odovar should be told.

The healer replied, "I'll tell him. You take the lad home."

Tol's farm was half a day's ride from there. Egrin promised to make straight for Juramona after speaking with Tol's father.

"On the way back, I'll cross country to the Caer road, in case Lord Odovar decides to sortie in search of Grane," the warden said.

"I'll carry your words to him. Farewell, warden. Be on watch, always."

"I shall. Fast journey, Felryn."

The healer thumped his heels hard against his mount's sides, urging the reluctant horse back across the awful battlefield. At the far end of the vale he turned and waved.

"He's a good man," Tol said, and he and Egrin waved back.

"The most honorable man in the Eastern Hundred."

"More than you?" blurted the boy.

The warden looked away to the horizon, absently rubbing one earlobe under his short helmet. His face was devoid of expression.

"I'm not honorable," Egrin finally said, "only obedient."

❦ ❦ ❦ ❦ ❦

The hills grew higher and closer together as they neared Tol's farm. Mud squelched under Old Acorn's hooves. The last of winter's snow had melted, leaving the high ground dry but the notches between the hills sodden.

They passed the place where Odovar had been ambushed. Scarcely twelve days had elapsed, but the site was much changed. The bodies were gone, either dragged away by wild animals or interred by pious farmers. Dead horses had been butchered for meat, and the trampled wreckage of battle scoured clean by scavenging homesteaders. Only memory and the scarred soil remained. A similar fate eventually would engulf the larger battlefield they'd seen.

It was dusk when they arrived at the onion field. Tol leaned to one side to see around Egrin. Neat hills of seedling onions had been planted despite his absence. That cheered him, but his pleasure quickly gave way to guilt. His poor mother must be mad with grief, wondering what had become of him! Perhaps they'd be so relieved at his return they wouldn't mind so much that he'd left the ashwood hoe in Juramona.

They followed the well-worn path over the hill. Beyond the crest, Egrin pulled Old Acorn to a halt.

"You'd best go in alone, Tol," the warden said, "Let them know I'm coming. A mounted man arriving after dark would frighten them."

Tol slid off the horse and made his way alone down the sandy slope. He took care to whistle a tune his father had taught him as a recognition sign.

The family hut was nestled tight against the facing hill, three walls of wattle-and-daub, with the hillside itself serving as fourth wall. A pigsty squatted to the side of the hut, and there was a brick cistern in the yard.

Tol's whistling abruptly ceased. No plume of smoke rose from the chimney hole—where was the evening's fire? And why were the windows shuttered and dark?

Tol licked his dry lips, thinking silence would be safer than whistling. He left the path and skulked along the row of hayberry bushes that lined it. His father had planted the thorny shrubs to keep wolves and panthers away. They were as tall as Tol and practically impenetrable. Hayberry thorns were a handspan long and tough enough to punch through boiled leather.

A horse neighed nearby, and Tol almost jumped into the thorn bushes. His family was too poor to own a horse, yet three were tethered to a post on the far side of the pigsty. Two animals were sturdy war-horses of no particular distinction, but the third was a splendid gray animal, trapped with gold-edged green silk that shimmered even in the twilight.

Green silk. Pakins!

Dropping to the ground, he crawled along the base of the thorn hedge. By the pigsty he found a heap of cold ashes, and many burnt bones. Where once there had been three yearling pigs in the pen, now only two remained, stirring restlessly at the sty's far end. Someone had obviously roasted the third.

He reached the hut at last, and pressed an ear to the wall. There was no sound from inside. All was deathly still.

Something cold and metal touched his cheek. Tol jerked in surprise and looked up. A very dirty, ragged-looking soldier stood over him, his iron saber pressed against Tol's face. On his upper right arm, the soldier wore a blood-streaked swatch of green cloth. Snarling, he seized Tol by the collar and dragged him bodily out into the yard.

"My lord," the Pakin soldier called out. "I caught this boy sneakin' around."

The door of the hut swung in, and a figure stood silhouetted against the brighter interior of the hut.

"Who is it?" said the dark apparition.

When Tol didn't answer, the soldier slapped him. "My name is Tol!" he said, rubbing his stinging ear. "I live here! With my family!"

The man emerged into the starlight. Instead of a face of flesh, the intruder's countenance was chiseled bronze, fixed in a hideous grin. Tol instantly recognized the armor and carriage of the man he'd met before at the onion field, the lord who had hunted Marshal Odovar and commanded the monstrous panther-creature. It was Spannuth Grane, leader of the Pakin rebels in the southern and eastern provinces.

"I know you, boy," Grane said, voice hollow inside his closed helmet. "You're the farmer's son. Where have you been?"

"Carried off by soldiers, master." Tol was surprised both by his own easy lie and that such a lordly fellow would remember him after their brief meeting. "I was made to work for them until a few days ago, when I ran away."

The leering bronze visor nodded slowly up and down. "Put him with the others," Grane said. A second Pakin warrior came out of the house, and together he and his disheveled comrade shoved Tol inside.

His family was there, huddled by the hillside wall—his father, Bakal, his mother, Ita, and his two sisters, Zalay and

Nira. His father had taken a beating: his face was bruised, and one eye was blackened and swollen shut.

Tol's mother whimpered with relief and tried to stand and take him in her arms. She was stopped short by a cord tied to her wrists and ankles.

The Pakin soldiers shoved Tol at his anxious mother. They sprawled in a heap on top of his sister Nira. Sorting themselves into sitting positions, they had a low-voiced but joyful reunion.

"How long have they been here?" Tol asked softly.

"Since sundown yesterday," muttered his father through split lips. "They killed our best pig, and mean to take the others—"

"Shut yer hole," one soldier snapped. Bakal prudently obeyed.

One man went back outside, to stand watch. Lord Grane shut the door and sat down in the only chair, Bakal's, by the cold fireplace. A lamp flickered on the hearth near his knee.

Grane removed his fearsome helm. Beneath it, he wore a close mail coif, so all Tol could see of his face was his nose and eyes. He did not resemble Vakka Zan, the White Pakin, for Grane's eyes were as black and cold as unburned coal.

"Is this all your brood, farmer? Are we to expect any more visitors?"

"This is all," Tol's father grunted.

With arms folded, Grane sat facing the cowering family. Tol kept his eyes downcast, even as he strained his ears to hear any sign that Egrin was coming. He heard nothing, and finally his curiosity would not be denied.

"Sir, what are you going to do with us?"

His father growled at him to hush, but Grane replied, "A fair question. Since you were brave enough to ask, I'll tell you. I shall tarry here awhile, resting. If you do not vex me, I shall spare your lives. When I depart, I shall resume the campaign of my master, the Pakin Successor, against the Ackal tyrant."

The carnage of the battlefield was still vivid in Tol's mind. "But your army's dead," he blurted.

The Pakin soldier snapped a vulgar word at him. Grane merely shrugged. "Ah, you saw the battlefield," he said. "A setback, I admit. My cavalry commander mistook Imperial troops for Odovar's local lackeys. He paid for his blunder with his life."

His escort sputtered, "My lord! Many a loyal follower of the true emperor died in that fight!"

"'Life to the strong,'" was Grane's ironic reply. He didn't even glance at his man.

"Are these your strongest, then?" Tol muttered, glancing around.

The soldier advanced, blade bared. "Shut up, whelp, or I'll feed you to your own pigs!"

"Sit down, Yarakin," Grane snapped. "The stableboy is baiting you, and you're swallowing it like a starving dog. Sit." Reluctantly, the anxious soldier complied.

Grane produced a short dagger with a sharply pointed, triangular blade. Tol's mother grasped his wrist in alarm, but the Pakin lord merely dug the tip into the chair arm, idly whittling.

"By daybreak we'll be gone, boy, so let us spend a quiet night, eh? Sleep, all of you. That is my order."

Tol's eyelids fluttered, and he yawned. The rest of his family followed suit.

"Sleep. Rest. Speak no more till sunrise . . ."

Grane's voice had taken on a gently insistent tone. Although his mind was racing, Tol felt himself growing more and more tired. His mother's grip on his arm slackened, and her head rested on his shoulder. Zalay and Nira sighed in unison, their heads drooping. His father yawned so widely his jaw cracked. The soldier Yarakin was already snoring, standing up, leaning on his spear.

"Sleep, all. Sleep. Close your eyes and visit the vale of dreams."

Grane was working magic, putting everyone to sleep! Tol tried to fight the spell. He was certain Egrin would come to their rescue, and he needed to be awake to help the warden.

But his efforts came to naught. He felt as though soft weights were collecting on his limbs and his eyelids. His head grew so heavy he couldn't hold it up.

"Sleep, stableboy. Sleep."

The last thing Tol saw was Grane dragging the chair away from the hearth, into the deep shadows behind the door. The Pakin lord sat down again and drew one of Ita's rag quilts close around his shoulders. The shadows swallowed him completely; only his greaves were visible, and light from the guttering lamp glinted on their rivets.

As sleep claimed him, Tol heard—or thought he heard—the deep voice of Grane, chuckling.

*   *   *   *   *

Light roused Tol. He cracked one eyelid. Slim bands of sunlight came through cracks in the shutters. In the beams, silent cascades of dust danced. Tol opened his other eye. Recognition returned as he looked around. His family, the Pakin soldier Yarakin, and Lord Grane slumbered on.

Tol shifted slightly, easing his mother's head from his arm. With his family at their mercy, the Pakins apparently didn't consider Tol a threat, and he had not been tied. If he could snatch Yarakin's spear before the warrior woke, he could perhaps hold him at bay until his father got free.

He listened hard, but heard no sounds from outside. Why hadn't Egrin come to save them? He was certain the warden wouldn't simply have ridden away, but he couldn't risk wasting this opportunity. Yarakin was slumped by the hearth, snoring gratingly. Tol crept toward him. When his hand closed over the spear, he tugged.

The movement unbalanced Yarakin. The soldier slumped forward, and sunlight fell on his face. His eyes opened.

"Ha!" he shouted, taking firm hold of the shaft. He dealt Tol a sharp blow on the thigh, then another in the ribs. Tol went down, dazed with pain.

"My lord, awake!" Yarakin cried.

Deep in the shadowed chair, Lord Grane did not move. Tol's family did. His father thrust away from wall and, despite his hobbles, butted the Pakin soldier in the stomach. Yarakin reeled back, stumbling over Tol, who was curled up on the floor in agony.

Tol's mother wept with terror, but his father and two sisters lost no time in falling upon the soldier as soon as he went down.

Tol could hardly believe his sisters would attack so fearlessly. Zalay, the eldest, butted Yarakin's face repeatedly with her head, and sturdy Nira sat on the hapless fellow's stomach, lifting herself a short distance and dropping her whole weight on him over and over.

Tol heard noises outside, men's voices, the ring of metal on metal. Swordplay! Still Lord Grane did not rise from his chair, speak, or assist in any way.

Seeing his father and sisters could handle Yarakin, Tol crept on hands and knees around the hearth, toward the motionless Grane. He took up a length of firewood. It was seasoned oak, and made a good club.

Tol abandoned stealth. He got up, let out a yell, and charged, firewood held high.

He brought it down hard, smashing into Grane's left knee. The articulated armor plates took the blow, and Grane's right boot fell to the floor. The quilt covering him fell away and, in a motion that scared Tol half to death, his armored sleeve fell from the chair arm, clanging against the floor. A dark powder streamed from the boot and Grane's sleeve.

Tol cupped his hand under the stream, filling his palm with cold grit. Black sand. The armor slowly collapsed as the sand poured out. Tol flung back the visor in time to see the empty coif sinking into the suit's neck. There was no one inside the richly gilded metal. Stunned, Tol stood there staring at the rapidly deflating suit of armor.

Yarakin broke free of his tormentors and made for the door, howling for help at the top of his lungs. He flung the door open and dashed outside. Immediately he gave an inarticulate yell and snatched the saber from his belt. Tol heard the clash of blades, backed by a chorus of neighing horses.

With Grane's helmet in hand, Tol ran to the door. The second Pakin soldier, the filthy one who'd caught him last night, lay facedown in the yard. Blood was pooling beneath him. Yarakin was trading frenzied cuts with a man in red-trimmed scale-mail. Egrin!

Yarakin jabbed at Egrin desperately. With power born of desperation, he managed to rake the tip of his sword down Egrin's left cheek. Blood flowed, and the warden of Juramona gave ground, backing toward Old Acorn, who stood by the pigpen fence.

Tol thought of lobbing the gilded helm at the Pakin, but he wasn't sure of his aim. The last thing he wanted was to hit Egrin.

Clutching the helm and yelling encouragement, Tol was startled to see his father come charging out of the house with Yarakin's spear in his hands. He caught the Pakin soldier from behind and drove the spear's bronze head in. Yarakin whirled, slashing at Bakal. The farmer leaped back, tripped on his unwound leggings, and fell against the cistern.

Blood streaming from his lips, Yarakin brought his saber up, but he'd reached the end of his strength. The sword fell from his hands, and his knees buckled. He was dead by the time he hit the ground.

Freed of their bonds, Tol's mother and sisters spilled out of the hut, all talking at once. They converged on Bakal. Fortunately, Yarakin's saber had barely nicked the farmer, making a shallow cut across his windpipe. A hair deeper, and he would have been dead beside his attacker. Ita bound the cut with a strip torn from her skirt, clucking worriedly yet proudly all the while.

Egrin shoved his weapon back in its scabbard and caught Old Acorn's reins. While the warden tied his horse to the sty, Tol held up Grane's helmet and cried, "Come inside, sir! Lord Grane!"

Egrin's hand went to his sword hilt. "Is he here?"

"Yes! No! Well, some of him is!"

Puzzled, the warden followed him into the hut. They examined the empty suit of armor from coif to boots. Every lacing was tied, every buckle fastened. Even the frog at the neck of Grane's cloak was still hooked. All that remained of the man inside was two hundredweight of fine ebon sand, drifted now around his sabatons. It looked for all the world like Grane had wafted away, leaving behind his fine armor filled with dust.

"I wish Felryn were here," Egrin said. With the blade of his dagger, he scooped up a small sample of the black sand into his belt pouch. "He might make sense of this."

Tol told of the sleep spell Grane had cast. Egrin nodded grimly. He'd realized Tol's peril fairly quickly the night before and had followed in after him, but just as he got close to the hut, he'd fallen into a strange sleep himself. The Pakin on sentry duty had been a victim of his master's sleep spell too. Fortunately, the sentry dozed in the shade, while Egrin had been awakened as the first rays of the rising sun struck his upturned face.

Outside, Tol's father had made a tidy pile of the two dead Pakins and their weapons. The dead men's metal and horses would bring a pretty price at the next trader's fair.

Egrin left the hut with Tol, and both regarded Grane's fine gray horse, still tied with the other two. The warden scratched his bearded chin in puzzlement. Lord Odovar would have to be told of these doings, and word sent to the emperor himself.

At his mother's urging, Tol introduced his family to the warden. Tol's family were awed that their son knew the warden of Juramona by name.

"You're Bakal, son of Boren?" Egrin said to Tol's father. "Those sound like dwarvish names."

The farmer shuffled his feet in the dirt. "Folks say that, but my father was a man like any other. We do come from the highlands near Thorin, but we had no dealing with dwarves."

"And you, good lady?"

Her cheeks colored. "I'm Ita, daughter of Paktan and Meri."

Tol's sisters, openly admiring the valiant warden, fetched him food and water. While Egrin refreshed himself, Tol brought water and fodder for Old Acorn.

Ita praised Egrin profusely for his care of Tol and his help liberating the farm.

"It's nothing, lady. Your son and I are comrades," Egrin said good-naturedly, clapping the boy on the back. "Saved my life, Master Tol did."

Still deferential, Bakal asked why the warden had come in the first place. Was he tracking the mysterious Lord Grane?

Egrin explained the proposal he'd made to Tol, that the boy return with him to Juramona and become his shield-bearer.

Ever plainspoken, Bakal asked, "Why, master? Why our Tol?"

Egrin held out his hand to the boy, who was holding a bucket of water for Old Acorn. "I've seen your son face danger," he said. "He's a brave lad, with a cool head and sharp wits for his age. He could go far." Egrin looked at his own calloused and scarred hands. "And he saved my life at great risk to his own. To become a shield-bearer is a great honor. This is my way of settling the debt."

Bakal pondered. Tol's leaving would mean a great loss of help around the farm, but Zalay and Nira were strong and willing helpers and soon would have husbands to help in the fields. The more he thought it out, the more convinced Bakal became.

"I'm for it," he said at last.

Thinking of Tol's departure, so soon after he had been restored to the family, set Ita to weeping. Egrin consoled her with talk of visits and gifts. Tol would earn a wage as a shilder, he explained.

Tol's father called the boy over. "This excellent sir wants you to be his shield-bearer," Bakal said. "What say you, son?"

"I say, yes!" he replied, and then ran to his mother, who was weeping harder now, and hugged her. He would have done the same to his father, but it no longer seemed like the thing to do.

His uncertainty lasted only a moment before Bakal put out his work-roughened hand. For the first time, father and son shook hands, in the way of men.

❦ ❦ ❦ ❦ ❦

Two days later, on the road to Juramona, Tol was swaying uncertainly on the back of Grane's gray horse. Egrin had left the other two Pakin horses and all the soldiers' gear with Bakal to sell, but he'd taken Grane's fine armor to present to Lord Odovar and had given the gray gelding to Tol. Scorched on the leather harness with a branding rod was the animal's name, Smoke. Tol could not read, but Egrin told him what the letters meant.

Tol wondered why Grane had run; how had he known Egrin was near? The warden shrugged, saying, "That sorcery of his may have warned him. He's escaped every time we've tried to take him. One day . . ." His words trailed off. Egrin's lips firmed to a hard, thin line. "One day, we'll get him."

The land was greening with spring. With the destruction of Grane's Pakin rebels, farmers, hunters, and herdsmen returned to their work, resurrecting the rhythms of everyday life. It was good to see, but Tol found himself unable to enjoy the sight. Something was nagging at his mind, a feeling that he'd left something undone, or unfinished.

It was not until they reached the village of Broken Tree that the niggling question was resolved. They stopped to have a farrier repair a loose shoe on Old Acorn. While they waited, the farrier shouted for his stableboy, telling the lad to pump the bellows and heat the forge fire.

Stableboy!

"Egrin!" Tol shouted.

The warden was haggling over price with the farrier. Tol's yell made both men jump and caused the farrier's lad to drop the bellows.

"Great Draco Paladin! What is it?" Egrin demanded.

"Grane! I know who he must be!"

The warden strode over to Tol, who was still mounted on Smoke.

"What are you talking about?"

"I know who Grane is! He as much as told me so himself at the farm! He called me 'stableboy,' more than once. Why would he call me that unless he'd seen me working in a stable? The only stable I ever worked in was the Household Guards', in Juramona! Grane must have seen me in Juramona!"

Egrin looked stunned. "The traitor's in our very midst. Still, we don't know who—"

Tol was shaking with excitement. "I know exactly who he is: Morthur Dermount!"

Egrin's frown broke and he laughed, unconvinced. "That fool of a feast-hall warrior? How could he be Spannuth Grane?"

"I saw his eyes! Grane wore a hood up to his nose, but I very clearly saw his eyes. They were black, just like Lord Morthur's, and he has the same thin nose and white skin!"

"It's little enough to recognize a man by," Egrin said. "Lord Morthur is an important man in Juramona. How could he leave and assume the guise of Grane without being detected?"

"The same way he left his empty armor in my father's chair."

Egrin lowered his voice. "Look here, Tol. You're a smart lad, but keep this to yourself! By the gods, you can't go 'round accusing a scion of the Dermount clan of being a traitor! A word from Lord Morthur, and you and I both would end in unmarked graves."

"But shouldn't Lord Odovar be told?"

"Yes, but let me tell him. Odovar despises Morthur, but even the marshal of the Eastern Hundred has to be careful who he brands a rebel."

Old Acorn finally had his new shoe, and they departed from Broken Tree. Egrin was not convinced by Tol's identification of Morthur Dermount, and he coolly refused to discuss it until they reached Juramona.

Once home, they found the town abuzz with news: The Pakin army in the Eastern Hundred had been defeated by Imperial troops under Lord Regobart, which Egrin and Tol knew already. Besides those killed in battle, hundreds of Pakin levies had scattered across the province. Lord Regobart, one of the greatest warlords of the empire, was hunting down the stragglers. He pointedly declined to invite Lord Odovar to join in the roundup, a snub which put the marshal in a towering rage.

Seeing—and hearing—Lord Odovar's fury as soon as they entered the High House, Egrin stayed clear of his liege. He sent word of his safe return, but lingered in the High House, keeping to the side and watching the flow of lackeys, servants, and petty officials. Tol asked him what he was waiting for.

"I think I should pay my respects to Lord Morthur," Egrin said evenly.

Tol's heart beat fast. "Will you face him, sir?"

The warden put a strong hand against Tol's back, and propelled him forward. "*We* shall face him!"

Lord Morthur was a cousin of the imperial house, a direct descendant of Ackal Ergot, first emperor of Ergoth. One did not antagonize so powerful a person with impunity. Tol's heart continued to hammer as they wound their way through the intricate passages and then mounted a spiral set of steps leading to the floor where Lord Odovar and other high nobles of the province dwelt.

Egrin walked up the door to Morthur's suite and knocked loudly on the carved oak panel. "My lord!" he boomed. "My lord, I must speak to you on important business!"

A lackey should have answered the warden's summons, but all was quiet within. Egrin drew his saber and delivered a mighty kick to the door jamb. Tol was appalled. He wished he'd never spoken of his fantastic theory.

Egrin slammed the door again with the sole of his heavy boot, and the wood splintered. Shouldering in, Egrin quickly surveyed the antechamber. It was in disarray. Sheets of parchment were scattered about. Caskets and chests had been flung open, and their contents—mostly clothing—had been tossed all around.

"Lord Morthur!" called Egrin warily. "Where are you?"

Silent as a ghost, the man they sought appeared in the doorway of a side chamber. Morthur Dermount was dressed in a smooth silk robe and velvet vest the color of ox blood.

"How dare you barge into my chamber!" he said. "You'll pay for this insolence, Warden."

Egrin extended his saber. "I don't think so, my lord Dermount. Or perhaps I should call you Spannuth Grane?"

By rights, Morthur could have denied the charge and rejected the warden's label. Instead, his gaze flickered to Tol, standing behind the warden, and he whipped his right hand out from behind his robe, revealing a long, thin court blade. He lunged.

Egrin parried, shouting at Tol, "Bar the door! Don't let the traitor escape!" Tol used all his might to drag a heavy chest in front of the broken door.

"Traitor?" Morthur said, laughing. "The blood of emperors flows in my veins—how can I be a traitor?"

They traded four fast cuts, neither man gaining an advantage. "You subvert the rightful emperor in favor of the Pakin Pretender!" Egrin declared.

"I worked with the Pakin claimant, true, but in no one's favor but my own."

"You have designs on the throne yourself? You must be mad!" Egrin said. Morthur was many generations out of the line of succession.

The sorcerous noble made practiced, wicked thrusts at Egrin's eyes. More than once Tol thought the stalwart warden would be blinded or killed, but each time Egrin fended off Morthur's blade.

"There is only one truth in this world," Morthur said, panting. "Power belongs to the one strong enough to take it!"

So saying, he drew back suddenly and swept the empty air before him with his sword. Magical sparks fell from the narrow blade. Then voices called from the stairs. The tramp of many heavy feet resounded. Tol heard Egrin's name being called. He jumped off the chest and shoved it aside, flinging open the door.

"Here! We're here!" he cried. "Hurry! Help!"

A line of soldiers came storming up the steps. Morthur was inscribing an intricate pattern in the air with his sword, and Egrin could only watch helplessly. Although he strained mightily, grunting with effort, his feet were rooted to the floor.

Felryn led a squad of soldiers through the open door. He snatched the medallion from his neck, uttered a swift, incomprehensible sentence, and hurled the bright metal disk into the room. There was a clap like thunder, and Tol was thrown down. When he regained his senses, Felryn was standing over him. The healer drew him upright with ease and set him on his feet.

Lord Morthur's suite was now filled with a fine haze, like smoke, but without any odor of burning. Egrin was down on one knee, shaking his head to clear it. Of Morthur Dermount, also known as Spannuth Grane, there was no sign.

"He has escaped?" Egrin asked as the soldiers helped him stand. He was uninjured, only stunned.

Felryn shrugged. "I had to choose: save you two or stop Lord Morthur's flight," he said simply.

Egrin asked Felryn how he'd known to come to Lord Morthur's rooms with troops.

"I've been scrying, watching the boy," Felryn admitted. "When I saw you standing before Lord Morthur's door with a drawn saber, I knew there'd be trouble."

They thoroughly searched Morthur's rooms, finding a collection of magical scrolls, and a wax tablet impressed with the seal of the Pakin Pretender. No one could read the strange glyphs on the tablet, but there was more than enough evidence left behind to confirm Morthur's duplicity.

Curiously, Lord Odovar refused to believe his second was Spannuth Grane. He accepted the proof of Morthur's complicity with the Pakins readily enough, but his pride would not let him admit that the cunning foe who had ambushed his

Paul B. Thompson and Tonya C. Cook

troops and nearly killed him was the pleasure-seeking fool he knew as Morthur Dermount. Still, from that day forward, no one ever again mentioned the names of Morthur Dermount or Spannuth Grane to the marshal, on pain of his violent displeasure.

Chapter 6
The Emperor's Summons

Two score horses pranced and chivvied, their hooves sending up clouds of dust. Sword blades flashed, and unwary riders toppled from their mounts to the ground.

Juramona's shield-bearers were getting their first lessons in formation riding. It was no simple matter, the eager boys learned, for forty horses and riders to stay together, charge, and fight as one. They collided at every turn, and lost their seats at the first exchange of blows. Clad in quilted jerkins and leather helmets, armed with blunted swords, theirs was no game for children. Unhorsed boys staggered out of the melee with bloody noses and missing teeth.

Mounted on Old Acorn, Egrin watched the boys whack at each other and fall hard. Beside him under the only shade tree on the practice field, Felryn was astride a swaybacked mule named Daisy. The healer alternately chuckled or gasped at the boys' antics. He knew he was in for a busy time later.

"I don't see Tol," said Felryn, scanning the press of boys and horses. "Where is he?"

"In the thick of things, as usual," Egrin observed.

A riderless roan galloped from the fray and in the gap it left the two men glimpsed Tol. His helmet was gone, and his neat queue had come undone, leaving his long brown hair flying. He laid about on all sides, unhorsing a boy with every blow he landed.

"He's very strong, isn't he?" said Felryn. "I see now why you let him lead the teaching. Has the makings of a fine warrior."

"He's already a fine warrior. He has the makings of a great one," Egrin replied.

Just then Tol received a violent blow on the back, and the warden shouted, "If he remembers to watch behind him!" Felryn could not help but laugh.

The farmer's son had grown into a powerful youth, not as tall as some, but broad in the chest and shoulders, and muscled beyond his size. Although Tol's father had denied it, both Egrin and Felryn still wondered whether there might not be some dwarf blood in Tol's past.

Tol had more in his favor than mere strength. Being a peasant's son, he remained humble and unafraid of hard labor. Most shilder were the sons of Riders of the Horde, and a few could boast truly noble parentage. These young lords thought themselves too good to clean the older men's armor or scrub the floors of the Householders' Hall. Tol's cheerful compliance with such mundane duties galled them. That he enjoyed the favor of the warden and officers of the guard further annoyed them. Things might have gone hard on Tol had he not been so formidable. He thrashed a few bullies in bloody bare-knuckle brawls, and that put an end to his troubles. No one picked on Tol more than once.

The companions of his leisure were not his fellow shield-bearers, but former stableboys or sons of village tradesmen. Narren, the tow-headed boy who'd given Tol a drink of water his first morning in Juramona, had become a foot soldier in Lord Odovar's employ. Tol's other close friend, Crake, had forsaken arms altogether and now played a wooden flute in a tavern. Through him Tol learned the follies of drink, and made the acquaintance of barmaids.

The exercise swiftly became a free-for-all, all notion of organization lost, every boy battling every other. Disgusted, Egrin was about to put a stop to the fight when a low, bleating note echoed from the nearby walls of Juramona.

"An alarm?" asked Felryn.

Egrin shook his head. "A recall." He stood in his stirrups and shouted. "Form column of fours! We return to Juramona! Everyone keep your place—I'll be watching!"

Two guardsmen led the column of boys back to town. Egrin frowned at the passing youths.

"What do you think?" he asked.

"They're good boys," the healer said. "They'll find the knack—"

"No, the recall. Can you sense anything?"

With his long, strong fingers, Felryn grasped the image of the goddess Mishas he wore around his neck. Creases appeared in his forehead.

"You're right . . . trouble," he muttered. "Conflict. The source is not clear, but it comes from afar."

Egrin grunted. "Well, Tarsis has been quiet too long, I guess."

The tail of the column passed, and he and Felryn fell in behind the last four boys.

❦ ❦ ❦ ❦ ❦

Juramona had grown along with Tol. It now boasted four thousand inhabitants, the largest imperial town between Caergoth and Hylo. Prosperity had come with the end of the civil war between Ackal and Pakin factions.

After Lord Morthur Dermount, alias Spannuth Grane, had disappeared, the Pakin Pretender was hunted down and slain while to trying to escape across the sea to Sancrist Isle. Lord Morthur was proscribed by the crown, and a bounty was placed on his head. Rumor had it he'd fled south, to find shelter in the city of Tarsis, Ergoth's trade rival and some-time enemy.

A messenger awaited Egrin at the Householders' Hall. The lord marshal commanded his presence. Egrin, his two lieutenants, and Tol, his shilder, went at once to the High House.

Entering the audience hall, Egrin saluted Odovar. "My lord," he said. "I am here. What is your will?"

Five years of peace had not been good to Odovar. From a burly, impetuous warrior he'd become a fat, sluggish ruler, with either a mutton joint or a tall tankard always in one hand. Dark whispers said the crack on the skull he'd received from Grane had changed him. Once he'd been harsh, but fair. Now he was cruel. Known before as a man of rough good humor, he had become suspicious and bitter.

Belly bulging over his thighs, he sat in his marshal's chair, his children at his feet. Emea was a pampered nine year old who conducted herself as though she were empress of all Ergoth. Four-year-old Varinz was a good-natured boy, but overfed and lazy. On either side of Odovar were his two principal advisers—his consort Sinnady, and bald Lanza, priest of Manthus.

"Eh? Egrin? Took your time getting here, didn't you?" Odovar said, gasping slightly.

"I was in the field, training the shilder," replied the warden evenly. "I came as soon as I heard the horn."

The marshal gave a grunt and reached down beside his chair for his tankard. He swallowed a long pull of beer, then burped loudly. Varinz giggled.

"Looks like we shall have some action at last," Odovar proclaimed. "Too much peace has dulled our swords and widened our backsides!"

Egrin remained prudently silent, as did the rest of the assembly.

With another grunt, Odovar returned the tankard to its place by his chair. When he was upright once more, he said, "Call in the visitor—no, not the kender! The imperial courier!"

A lackey bobbed his head and hurried away. He returned shortly with a distinguished though travel-stained noble who wore the red livery of the imperial court. A mature man, he had a magnificent mane of iron-gray hair and a long, pointed beard. He saluted by striking his metal shod heels together.

Odovar waved a flabby, beringed hand. "Repeat your message for my warden."

The courier turned and repeated his heel-clanging greeting.

"Are you Egrin, Raemel's son?" he asked. At Egrin's nod, the courier smiled slightly. "I served with you in the late Emperor Dermount III's campaign on the north dales."

Recognition flickered across Egrin's face. "Yes! You're— Karil—Kanel?"

"Kastel, son of Furngar." The two men clasped arms as comrades and the courier said, "The years have treated you very well, son of Raemel. You seem unchanged."

"Get on with it!" Odovar rumbled petulantly.

Kastel stiffened, resuming his formal manner, and said to Egrin, "There is to be war, my lord. His Imperial Majesty requires the high marshal of the Eastern Hundred to raise a force of four hordes, to be sent at once to join the army of Crown Prince Amaltar, now encamped at Caergoth."

"Are we riding to Tarsis?" Egrin asked.

"No, warden. Our foes are the forest tribesmen of the Great Green. For many days they've been raiding the countryside south of Caergoth, stealing cattle, burning farms, and carrying off imperial subjects as captives. Worse outrages followed. Sixteen days ago, they attacked a hunting party and killed an imperial cousin, Hynor Ergothas. The emperor means to teach them a sanguinary lesson."

The courier turned to Lord Odovar. "What is the fighting strength of your garrison, my lord?"

Odovar plainly didn't know, and referred the question to Egrin.

"Two thousand, two hundred horse, plus six hundred ninety foot," the warden said.

Kastel shook his head. "Not enough. His Majesty expects four thousand horse."

Odovar laughed, his swollen belly bouncing. "Well, shall I put peasant spearmen on horses and call them Riders of the Great Horde?" He glanced at Tol, who stood a pace behind the warden. Tol kept his eyes down and his expression blank.

"If we recall retired warriors from their estates in the country, we might make up another two hundred horse, my lord," suggested Lanza.

"Fine. Order it so," said Odovar.

Onlookers in the assembled crowd murmured; such a move would be highly unpopular. One of the wise policies of long-ago Emperor Ergothas II had granted large tracts of virgin land to warriors of the Great Horde who had served the throne long and well. These retired soldiers had carved out enclaves, built fortified manor houses, and put the land to work, adding greatly to the wealth and prosperity of the empire.

In a louder voice meant to override the muttering, the marshal added, "How many shilder have you, warden?"

"One hundred six, my lord, but they're barely half-trained."

"They can finish their training on campaign. Nothing like real war to harden boys into men." Again he laughed.

Lanza did the figures. "Three thousand, one hundred ninety . . . and six."

"Best I can do," Odovar said to the courier. "Convey my compliments to the crown prince and inform him three hordes will join him at his camp."

"Yes, my lord." Kastel bowed, unhappy. He would have to relate the unwelcome message to the emperor.

"Begin the preparations at once," said Odovar with a wave of his hand. He groped for his tankard again.

"What about the other petitioners, my lord?" asked Lanza carefully.

The marshal snorted in his brew. "Fool kender! Run them out of Juramona!"

Kastel frowned at this casual dismissal. "My lord," he said, "the kender of Hylo are the emperor's vassals too. As they owe him their allegiance, so does he owe them protection. May I not hear what concerns them?"

Odovar's face—always slightly flushed—grew even redder, quickly acquiring a near-purple hue. Lady Sinnady recognized the unhealthy rage that was now so quick to build in him. She leaned toward him, patting his hand and murmuring soothingly. Following her example, the marshal's children hugged his knees and did their best to jolly him out of his anger.

It worked, for now. His choler subsiding, Odovar said in a low voice, "Bring in the kender."

A side door opened, and sentries waved in the new arrivals. They were fashioned like humans, except for their small stature and pointed ears. One had his long brown hair in dozens of tiny braids, each with brightly colored wooden beads worked in. These clattered noisily whenever he moved his head. His companion's lighter, sand-colored hair was pulled to the top of his head and fell to the middle of his back in a single horsetail. Both kender wore homespun shirts over buckskin trews, and vests stitched in bright colors and decorated with painted beads.

"Hiya," said the braided one. "Is this a ceremony?"

His partner thumped him soundly in the gut. "Hold your tongue, Rufus. These guys are important." Spreading his hands wide and skinning back the sleeves of his shirt, he added, "Nothin' up my sleeve!"

Tol didn't understand the gesture, but the kender went on without explaining.

"Me, my name is Forry Windseed." Tossing his thick hank of hair to one side, he gestured at his braided companion. "This ugly joker is my brother-in-law, Rufus Wrinklecap."

The braided kender, spread his hands also and shook out his sleeves. "Not *the* Rufus Wrinklecap," he added. Without pause he said to Sinnady, "That's a nice sapphire you got there, ma'am. Really sparkles in this light."

Windseed shook his head so that his beaded braids clattered and clashed. "Not a sapphire," he said authoritatively. "Blue topaz."

Wrinklecap's snort was eloquent. "Topaz my a—"

"Explain yourselves!" thundered Lord Odovar, interrupting the high-pitched disagreement. Everyone present flinched, even Egrin, but the kender merely grinned.

"I bet he could kill it single-handed," said Wrinklecap. "Did you smell his breath? He could knock ol' Xim out with that—"

Odovar, face once again purple with rage, stood, and drew the sword hanging from the back of his marshal's chair. The sight of sharp iron brought the kender at last to the point, so to speak.

"There's this monster, you see . . ." resumed Windseed.

"Called XimXim," his partner prompted. His Hylo accent made it sound like "Zeem-zeem."

"We know the beast," interjected Egrin. "The empire has sent warriors and mages to battle XimXim some eight or nine times."

"I know of eleven instances myself," said Kastel. "No survivors returned from any of them. Eleven expeditions, one hundred-twenty men slain without result. No one even knows for certain what the monster looks like." He explained that the creature's very name was a testament to his mystery; the kender had dubbed him XimXim because of the sound he made in flight: *zimm-zimm-zimm*.

"I've always thought it must be a dragon," murmured Lady Sinnady, paling at the thought.

"It's most unlikely, ma'am. Since the defeat of the dragons two and a half centuries ago, no such beast has been seen in these parts," Kastel answered.

"XimXim has been quiet for years. I thought him dead or gone away," said Odovar. He sat down heavily, resting his sword across his knees. "What's the foul creature done now?"

Windseed said, "In the spring he crossed the Ragtail River and destroyed the village of Skipping Trace—"

"It was the Froghead River," Wrinklecap corrected.

The marshal forestalled yet another disagreement by raising his sword again. The kender contented themselves with trading narrow-eyed looks, and Wrinklecap continued.

"Anywho," he said, "XimXim moved into the caves above Skipping Trace, and there he sits, eatin' kender right and left just like boiled eggs—crack, snap, gulp."

Both kender seemed amazingly untroubled by the terrible events they were relating. They stood side by side, hands clasped behind their backs, rocking lightly from heels to toes.

"If nothing's done, all of western Hylo may be depopulated," Lanza said, frowning.

"An alarming prospect," murmured the marshal, though he was suddenly smiling. The kender stopped rocking.

Kastel's face was serious. "My lord," he said, "the empire has trading rights in Hylo town, and in the ports of Windee and Far-to-go. Something must be done to protect life and property."

Odovar drained his tankard dry, and bawled for more. "You can't have it both ways, sir! Either my warriors go to fight the foresters, or they ride to Hylo. Which do you want?"

The great hall was quiet. In the stillness, the marshal's son started hiccuping. At a wave from Sinnady, a lady-in-waiting scooped him up and hustled him away.

"The kenders' request is valid," Egrin said thoughtfully, "but an imperial order takes precedence, does it not?"

"It does," declared Lanza, patting his forehead with a small white cloth. The robes of his office were heavy, and he suffered in the summer heat. The kender seemed fascinated by the beads of moisture trickling down his bald pate.

"Then this foolishness is a waste of time!" Odovar said, glaring at the kender. "My order stands. Prepare the hordes to ride to Caergoth."

The kender opened their mouths to protest, and the marshal added quickly, "When the campaign against the forest tribes is done, I'll send someone to look into your monster problem. I have no warriors to spare until then."

The courier stroked his pointed beard thoughtfully. "My lord, could you not send someone now to discover the nature of the threat? Perhaps your seneschal?"

Lanza's eyes widened in horror. "Me? Hunt a monster?" His mellifluous voice rose to a squeak.

"You need not fight XimXim, merely stalk and observe him."

"Do it, Lanza," said Odovar, bored with the whole discussion.

"My lord, please! I cannot abandon my duties as priest and seneschal, and I am not a young man! Travel is so difficult. My health—"

"You eat better than I do, and little less," snapped the marshal. "Go with the kender! Take a pair of footmen with you to ward off danger. Find out exactly where—and what—this monster is, and report back here. That is my order!"

Lanza could only bow his head and withdraw, but the expression of terrified dismay remained on his sweaty face. The kender followed him, talking rapidly to each other.

"Poor man," Egrin said under his breath.

"You fear the monster will get him?" Tol whispered.

"I fear that after two weeks among the kender, he may prefer XimXim's company!"

♥ ♥ ♥ ♥ ♥

The atmosphere of the town quickly changed. Heralds were dispatched to outlying estates to call the retired gentry to arms, and everyone in Juramona set to work preparing for the campaign, each doing his or her part to serve (or exploit) the situation. Unlike Odovar's expedition against the local Pakin rebels five years earlier, this was to be a real campaign, shoulder to shoulder with hordes from all over the empire. In command of all would be Crown Prince Amaltar, eldest son of Emperor Pakin III.

Riders of the Great Horde mustered in the square where Vakka Zan had lost his head years before. Each rider had to provide his own arms, two horses, a shilder, and provisions for ten days. There weren't enough shilder in training to accommodate every warrior in Juramona, so servants and stableboys were pressed into service.

Foot soldiers, chiefly the guards who manned Juramona's wall and kept the gates of the town and High House, assembled in a side street. They were not considered very important in the scheme of war-making. Their chief job on campaign was to march with the supply train and protect it from bandits or enemy raids. Commanding them was Durazen the Lame, also called One-Eyed Durazen.

Once a Rider of the Horde, Durazen had not earned his injuries in battle. Blind drunk on a boar hunt, he'd fallen from his horse into a hayberry hedge. His leg was badly broken and he'd lost an eye to a hayberry thorn. No longer fit for mounted warfare, he had been given command of Juramona's foot soldiers.

Besides actual fighting men, hundreds of ordinary folk in town prepared to go to war as well. Sutlers, blacksmiths, and healers, as well as quacksalvers of every stripe, packed their bags and waited to follow the warriors. A ponderous civilian wagon train formed up outside the wall. It was laden with everything from spare spearshafts to barrels of brown beer.

Tol had imagined war as a grim business, with hard-faced warriors gazing at the horizon, watchful for a cunning enemy. In truth, the preparations seemed more suited to a festival or fair. He saw his friend Narren among the footmen and Crake among the sutlers. Tall and lean, his heavy scale hauberk hanging from his shoulders, Narren looked calm as he leaned on his spear and listened to Durazen, mounted on a sturdy cob, rasp out marching orders. Crake, reclining on a canvas tarp covering a wagonload of beer, played dreamy airs on his flute. Tol knew Crake's hunting bow would be stowed in the cart as well. Although he liked his ease and his pleasures, Crake never took chances. He wouldn't dream of going into harm's way unarmed.

Lord Odovar appeared on the back of a black charger. Sleek and powerful as he was, the animal looked strained by the massive burden he had to bear. Rumor had it the marshal weighed twenty stone—without his arms or armor.

"Poor beast," Egrin said tersely, echoing Tol's thoughts. "He won't last five leagues. Odovar will be in a wagon before we reach the river Caer."

Tol gave his own horse an affectionate pat. He still rode Smoke, the horse left behind by Spannuth Grane at Tol's family farm. Smoke had proved to be a strong, clever beast, and Tol valued him greatly.

The whole of the army mustered outside the walls of Juramona, covering the pastures and road. Drovers lashed at unruly bullocks, and competing carters shouted and shook fists at each other as they jockeyed for position. Children and dogs ran among the files of stolid footmen who sweated in their mail jerkins. It was a sultry morning, heavy with the promise of more heat.

Odovar made a short speech that few heard, and even fewer remembered. He rode forth with his private bodyguard to the front of the three columns of horsemen. The center column was the horde known as the Plains Panthers, veterans of the civil war between Ackal and Pakin. The left wing, the Firebrand Horde, included the landed gentry and men of rank and wealth in the province. The right wing, the honor wing, was led by Egrin. Behind him rode eight hundred twenty-seven horse, including Tol and his shilder comrades. Though not a properly constituted horde, the right wing was given the name Rooks and Eagles, signifying their mixed nature—which combined youth and vigor with age and experience.

"Ho, you men!" Manzo called. "Bring out the standard!"

Two veteran warriors pushed their way on foot to the head of the column. Between them they carried the Eagle of Juramona, carved from the trunk of an ancient oak and painted in lifelike colors. It was twice the size of a normal bird, and as the men held it, a large pole was inserted into the base between its clawed feet.

"Too bad there's no rook to go with him," a shilder remarked.

Egrin waved his hand in a circle like a conjurer. Grinning, the warriors turned the eagle around. Rather than the same brown and gold coloring, the bird staring out from the reverse had been painted black. It was cleverly done. Viewed from one side, the figure was a soot-black rook; from the opposite side, a noble eagle.

Egrin's own remarks to his men were very brief. Lifting his dagger high, he invoked the bison-headed god of battle, declaring, "May Corij ride with you all!"

The elves of Silvanost were known to sing as they marched, and the dwarves of Thorin went to battle blowing horns and beating enormous brazen gongs. It was traditional for the hordes of Ergoth to ride in silence. They spread out across the land like a flood, and the wordless, inexorable block of saber-wielding horsemen brought great fear to its enemies. The countryside ahead of an advancing horde emptied of travelers, traders, bandits, and brigands. Game animals fled the massive onrush of metal and men. For leagues in advance of an Ergothian army, all was still and empty. Farmers abandoned their fields and bolted themselves in their huts. Even insatiably curious kender stayed clear of the army's leading elements, but they were drawn to the long, winding baggage train behind it as ants are drawn to a trail of honey.

Juramona was located ten leagues north of the headwaters of the Caer River's twin branches. Working from maps drawn in the Silvanesti style, Egrin chose as his line of march a trail that arrowed south, toward the confluence of the two branches. The other two segments of Juramona's army swung east, a longer but easier route. They would skirt the tip of the river's eastern fork, then angle south-southwest for Caergoth. Egrin's route required fording the river, but it cut a full day off the journey, insuring his men would arrive at the crown prince's camp before the other two columns.

The land between Juramona and the great confluence was friendly territory, though devoid of settlements and nearly empty of people. Fine weather favored their advance. Towering masses of white clouds rose up like fortresses in the air, separated by clear blue. Gently rolling grasslands provided plenty of fodder for their animals, and Egrin sent his shilder ahead of the main body to scout the line of march.

After two days' travel, Tol found himself nearing the confluence in a group of six shilder under the command of Relfas. The red-haired youth was the youngest son of the noble and wealthy house of Dirinmor. Relfas's patrol was charged with finding a likely fording place. Relfas had split up his small band, ordering the shilder to reconnoiter singly.

Tol rode over a stony hilltop and saw the meeting of the two river branches below. Converging from either side of the bluff, the western and eastern streams formed the mighty Caer, which flowed by the walls of Caergoth. Cattle were watering on the western bank. Herders moved among them, swatting slow beasts with long willow switches.

Tol's presence did not go unnoticed. Dogs barked an alarm. The herders spotted Tol silhouetted against the sky and took fright. They drove their animals from the water, hurrying the beasts west over the next hill, and were out of sight in a trice. They knew warriors of any allegiance meant danger. Under imperial law, hordes could confiscate any provisions they needed from the local population. They were supposed to pay for what they took, but in practice few did so.

Though the herders couldn't know it, their cattle were in no danger from Egrin's men. The herd was on the west side of the river, and Egrin's force was riding east. It was fortunate they didn't need to ford the western branch. The West Caer was narrow here but deep and very swift. Huge square boulders, gray as beaten iron, dotted the surface of the water and broke the flow into foam. The sound of rushing water was loud.

Tol was about to descend the hill on the east side when something caught his eye. It was a ruin of some sort. He could see worked stone protruding from a tangle of ivy: cut blocks still layered one atop the other, and the stumps of massive columns, all of the same dark gray stone as the boulders in the river. Curious, he directed Smoke off the well-worn trail for a closer look.

As he drew nearer, Tol saw the ruins were very old indeed. The stonework was extremely weathered and had lain undisturbed for countless centuries.

The vines soon grew too thick for him to proceed further on horseback, so he dismounted and tied Smoke to a convenient sapling. slashing his way through the undergrowth with broad swipes of his saber.

What he'd taken for a foundation stone turned out to be the stump of an enormous column, so wide he could have lain across it and still had room to spare at head and heels. The waist-high column had a spiral groove as wide as his hand cut into it. Up close he could see it was made of bluestone. Farm boy that he was, Tol despised the pale blue rock. Turned up in a field, the hard stone could easily break a hoe blade or plow. Old Kinzen, the root-doctor in Tol's neck of the woods, called the blue rock *Irdasen*—stone of the Irda.

Those long ago masters of the world, called "the beautiful Irda" by storytellers, had supposedly been kin to the gods. Yet they had fallen into evil ways and been destroyed by their own corruption and black desires.

Tol circled the broken column. Tumbled among the choking weeds were more fragments of bluestone. Great blocks as big as a tall horse were cut with dovetail mortises and tenons of impossible size. These Irda must have been giants, or else had giants to do their building for them.

A piercing whistle signaled Relfas's recall. As Tol turned to go, the glint of metal halted him. The reflection came from a circular hole in the underside of an upturned block. Thinking he might find an ancient coin, he probed the hole with the tip of his saber. It was only elbow-deep, and seemed snake- and spider-free. He pushed back the sleeve of his ring mail shirt and eased his gloved hand inside. He found what he sought— metal, hard to the touch—and withdrew it from its stony hiding place.

It was a circlet made of three kinds of metal braided together like a woman's hair—a dark reddish metal intertwined with silver and gold. As thick as his smallest finger, it fit easily in the palm of his hand. The circlet's two free ends were joined by a spherical bead of the odd red metal. On the bead was etched a complex pattern of angular lines and curving whorls. Completely filling the center of the circlet was a piece of black crystal.

If this was a relic of the Irda, it had to be uncounted generations old. Yet it was completely unblemished by tarnish or corrosion. Its strange markings flashed in the sun like the facets of a gemstone. It was surprisingly lightweight, not heavy as might be expected of gold or bronze.

Tol held the circlet up to the sun and squinted through the center. The crystal did not blot out the bright orb of the sun, merely darkened the distant fire to a bearable level. Tol thought the crystal must be glass rather than a black gem like jet or night jade, because it was flat and dull, not shiny at all.

The whistle sounded again, and Tol slipped the ancient artifact into his belt pouch. He untied Smoke's reins from the slender elm tree, mounted, and galloped up the hill to meet his comrades.

Relfas, his freckled face red from heat and sheened with sweat, grumpily asked why Tol had taken so long to return. Tol pleaded the noise of the river's rush as the reason he hadn't heard the recall at first.

"Well, we found a crossing," Relfas told him. "The warden's sent word we're to join up, right away!"

The Rooks and Eagles rejoined at the ford Relfas's scouts had located. Everyone made it safely across, and the quick splash through cold water was welcomed by men and horses alike.

Because their wing of the army was so far ahead of the others, Egrin called an early halt to the march, well before sundown. They pitched camp and fortified it with a ring of sharpened palings to prevent surprise cavalry attacks. When the hedge was finished, Egrin ordered more riding drill for the shield-bearers. Groaning and complaining after a full day in the saddle, the youths went off to practice formation riding and mounted sword fighting until well past dark.

When the shilder fell onto their bedrolls at last, they slept like dead men. So tired was Tol, he forgot to show his strange artifact to Egrin, or to ask Felryn if he could divine its purpose.

Chapter 7
High and Low

East of the river, the Rooks and Eagles found clear signs they were not alone. They crossed wide areas of grass trampled flat by scores of cart wheels and hundreds of horses. Once they turned south, the evening sky ahead was illuminated by massed campfires; by day, stragglers and coveys of camp followers dotted the countryside.

Before noon on the fourth day out from Juramona, Egrin halted the horde and called in all his outriders. He climbed a convenient stump and addressed the youthful contingent among his soldiers.

"Lads, we'll soon be joining up with warriors of the Great Horde. There are things you should know. The empire is wide, and those who serve the emperor come in all shapes, sizes, and colors. You'll see many who dress differently, and bear strange arms. Don't be distracted! Listen to your orders, don't converse with strangers. You'll be offered every sort of vice you can think of, and many more you haven't yet imagined. No one expects you to behave like priests, but beware! Nothing is free. If an offer sounds too good to be believed, then believe it not. Pay up front for what you want, or you'll pay a far higher price later."

"Sir, what about the enemy?" called out a youth in the rear ranks.

"Your commanders will have an audience with the prince

and his advisers, and we'll know more after that. All I know myself is the enemy is said to be forest tribes, living in the Great Green. They've raided imperial lands around Caergoth, looting, pillaging, and carrying off captives."

"Are they men?" asked Tol.

"Can't say. We're near enough Silvanesti land, there might be wild elves, Kagonesti, among our foes."

Egrin got down from the stump and mounted Old Acorn. The Rooks and Eagles formed into a compact column and resumed their southern course.

Evidence of movement was all around them. Tol saw so many dust clouds he stopped counting them. Trampled grass became common, and the thickening stands of trees shielded sight but not sounds. All around them they heard the creak of harness leather, the fall of horses' hooves, and the thump of wagon wheels. On ridges, the silhouettes of riders, all heading south, could be seen. One band in particular caught the attention of the shilder—a group of dark-skinned men in breechcloths and wicker breastplates. Each carried a short bow and a sheaf of throwing spears—javelins, Manzo called them. They never overtook the Juramona horde, but merely dogged their heels. Their ghostly presence got on Relfas's nerves, and he asked permission to chase them off.

"Think you can?" asked Egrin.

"Give me twelve horse, and I'll banish them!" Relfas vowed.

"Take your choice, but no bloodshed, mind you." To Tol, riding near him, Egrin said, "Will you go?"

Tol thought for a moment, then said, "No, I'll stay with the column."

Relfas picked twelve of the best riders among the shilder and led them off to chase the lightly clad riders away. Waving their sabers, they charged across the dusty plain. In a markedly unhurried manner, their quarry cantered behind a nearby hill. Relfas divided his eager group, sending four shilder out wide to cut the riders off, and leading the remainder behind the hill.

Tol twisted in the saddle, straining to see what was happening. Dust rose from behind the hill, but no horsemen appeared. A short while later, Relfas returned, his puzzled and dejected troop behind him.

"What happened?" Tol demanded.

"They vanished!"

Egrin, Manzo, and the other veterans laughed.

"Of course they vanished! Those are men of Alkel!" Manzo exclaimed, naming a province far to the west, on the shores of the sea. "They're called Wind Riders, and it's said they can disappear from sight—man and horse—in broad daylight."

"You might have told us," Relfas grumbled.

"Lessons are best learned by doing," Egrin told the youth. "The Wind Riders serve the emperor as we do. They trail us for sport."

Under the glaring noonday sun, the Rooks and Eagles emerged from a grove of hardwood trees onto a broad ridge. The air shook with the sound of hoofbeats, a ceaseless, rolling thunder. From the top of the ridge, they saw an awesome panorama spread out beneath them. Egrin halted the column and let the shield-bearers take it in.

The plain below was filled by a huge city of tents—hundreds and hundreds of them—tall, wedge-shaped tents in the southern style; conical canvas huts common to the Eastern Hundred; and vast, flat-roofed beehives called Daltigoth tents. Temporary corrals were sprinkled throughout the tent city. Most were filled with milling horses, but more than a few contained fat bullocks to feed the multitude. There was no fence of sharpened stakes around the camp. The site was so vast, there wasn't enough timber available to surround it.

Smoke ascended from a thousand fires, and brightly colored banners hung limply from their poles in the hot, still air. Red was the dominant color, with gold a close second. In addition to the banners, horde standards were thick as daisies in an upland meadow. Egrin pointed out some famous ones: the crossed iron thunderbolts of the Red Thunders, the gap-toothed brass skull of the Deathriders, and the white onyx ox head representing the Bulls of Ergoth. Standards of nine different hordes encircled a huge tent in the center of the camp. With the addition of Lord Odovar's three hordes, some twelve thousand warriors would be assembled to enforce the emperor's will on the foresters.

"Raise our standard!" Egrin commanded. Men and boys cheered as the pole was lifted.

Egrin ordered them forward and called for another concerted cheer. "Let them know the men from Juramona have arrived!" he cried.

Chanting *Jur-ra-mo-na!* the newest horde in the emperor's service descended the ridge to the camp. At the time, amid the noise and chaos of the vast assemblage, their entry was barely noticed. Only much later would many claim to have seen the Rooks and Eagles arrive.

🦅 🦅 🦅 🦅 🦅

Lord Odovar reached the encampment just after dawn on the next day with the balance of his army, completing the force poised to invade the forest known as the Great Green. Egrin, accompanied by his lieutenants and Tol, sought out his commander. They found Odovar reclining in the back of an ox-drawn wagon. The marshal's breathing was labored, his right leg propped on a roll of canvas.

"My lord, are you ill?" asked Egrin.

"Ill enough," the marshal groaned. "That cursed horse collapsed on me two days ago. Threw me to the road and sprained my right knee. Useless beast! I had his throat cut."

An empty flagon dangled from Odovar's fingers. Without being asked, a dusty servant filled it with beer from a wooden bucket.

"Can you walk, my lord? Prince Amaltar will expect us to present ourselves soon."

"Damn the protocol," Odovar grumbled, but he knew Egrin was correct. He called for help. Two sturdy footmen dragged him off the back of the wagon. Wincing, he tried to put weight on his right leg. It crumpled, and only with considerable struggle did the soldiers prevent the marshal from landing on his cherry-red nose.

Felryn ordered a crutch made from a pair of spearshafts. While the men saw to the erection of the tents, Odovar and the commanders of his three hordes prepared for their audience with the Crown Prince of Ergoth. Durazen the One-Eyed would not be going. As captain of the footmen, his position was too lowly.

The leader of the Plains Panthers was a taciturn warrior named Pagas, whose misshapen nose was the result of a blow from a centaur's axe. Pagas had the hard look of a seasoned fighter, allied with a surprisingly high-pitched voice, a side-effect of his deformed nose. He spoke as little as possible, since the sound of his voice undermined his fierce appearance.

Unique in the army, the wealthy gentry of the Firebrand Horde elected their leader. He was an old campaigner named Wanthred. With his silver hair and full beard, lacquered shield, and old-fashioned studded mail, he cut a far more impressive figure than the wheezing, corpulent Odovar. Yet, he, Pagas, and Egrin waited loyally for their marshal to lead them, hobbling, to the crown prince.

Nervously, Tol wrapped and rewrapped his sweating hands around the pole displaying the ceremonial banner of Juramona. Lord Odovar had tapped him to carry the triangle of scarlet cloth as they marched through the bustling camp to the imperial tent. Tol could hardly believe his good fortune. He, son of Bakal the farmer, was going to see the heir to the throne of Ergoth!

The sprawling army camp resembled a barely contained riot. Men and women dashed back and forth between tents, shouting, laughing, or screaming. Some were done up in armor, while others wore light linen shifts, such as well-born folk slept in. A few revelers of both sexes crossed Tol's path, naked as newborn babes. Unclothed women were still a mystery to Tol, and he almost tripped over his own feet while trying to remedy that gap in his education.

A torrent of smells assailed him—some delightful, some foul. Cooking spices and incense mingled with the odor of horses and unwashed flesh. Pipers warred with drummers and lute players, while a cacophony of sutlers' cries strove to overbear them all. Traders strolled along the tent line, loudly hawking their wares: beer, wine, nectar from Silvanost, roast meat, trinkets and trifles, amulets to heal wounds, ointments to sooth saddle sores, linen scarves, woolen leggings, silken smallclothes, and a host of other goods.

The nearer they got to Crown Prince Amaltar's dwelling, the calmer the camp became. The wide lanes were patrolled by pairs of footmen in polished cuirasses, with battle-axes on their shoulders. Tol saw three such guards subdue a drunken warrior who'd wandered too close to the imperial enclave. The drunk was a brawny fellow, but the guards clubbed him quickly to the ground and dragged him away.

The men of Juramona paused to allow the burdened guards to cross in front of them. Odovar, taking a deep pull on the flagon he carried, said, "There you see the folly of vice, young Tol. Take heed." The marshal belched.

Tol inclined his head. "Yes, my lord."

Directly ahead was the enormous imperial tent, ringed with banners and standards. At the entrance, armed guards halted Odovar's party with crossed weapons.

"Who would enter the house of Amaltar, first prince of Ergoth?" demanded the watch commander, a towering warrior with an elegant, drooping, dark mustache. "Name yourselves!"

"I am Odovar, marshal of the Eastern Hundred, and these are the masters of my hordes!" For a moment, the old bark returned to the marshal's voice.

"I am Wanthred, son of Orthred, lord of Six Pines."

"Egrin, son of Raemel, warden of the Household Guard."

Pagas was unhappy at having to speak, but said firmly in his high voice, "Pagas, son of Janjadel, master of the Plains Panthers."

The watch commander nodded. "Disarm, my lords."

The men were taken aback. Odovar spoke for all. "You ask Riders of the Horde to surrender their swords? Why? We are free and loyal men!"

"It is the will of Crown Prince Amaltar. He remembers too well the fate of his uncle, Emperor Pakin II, assassinated in his own hall by 'free and loyal men.'"

Everyone knew the evil tale. The late emperor had been widely admired for his skill in ending the civil war and preserving the empire. For this he'd been dubbed "the Conciliator." In spite of his successes, a cabal of lords from within his own house had murdered him, touching off the rebellion that had sent Odovar into battle and ultimately brought him to the onion field and Tol.

Although they understood Prince Amaltar's caution, the Juramona men still felt it was unseemly to ask warriors to give up their swords. However, the watch commander's iron gaze was steady on them. Odovar glared back.

Egrin broke the impasse by unbuckling his sword belt, and handing it to the nearest guard. One by one they submitted. Even Tol had to surrender his saber. But where his betters had taken affront, he found the requirement curiously pleasing. In this small way, he was his masters' equal, considered as dangerous as these accomplished warriors.

They entered the tent and left the coarse outside world behind. Under their feet was a thick carpet the color of old wine. The tent's side walls were a loose weave to let in the daylight. From deeper within the structure, hidden by the interior cloth walls, an oddly cool breeze wafted over the startled warriors.

Odovar paused, eyes closed, leaning on his crutch. The others hovered behind him.

"What is it, my lord?" asked Wanthred, concerned.

"Nothing . . . a memory from long ago." Odovar looked at the flagon in his hand as if seeing it for the first time. He flung it out of the tent.

"When I was not much older than you, boy," the marshal told Tol, "I was taken before Emperor Dermount III. I received my honor dagger from his own hands. He was served by a corps of magicians who surrounded him with sweet, cool air like this. Strange how one remembers small things from so long ago."

Easing Felryn's makeshift crutch out of his armpit, Odovar leaned it against the tent wall. "I'll not go before Dermount's grandson a cripple," he vowed. He squared his heavy shoulders, his face white from the pain of standing unaided.

Egrin signaled Pagas, and the two warriors took up positions close on either side of Odovar. The marshal glared at them.

"Peace, my lord," Egrin said. "Grant us the honor of walking by your side."

Odovar's cheeks took on new color as they bolstered him. "Right," he growled. "Follow me!"

The cloth corridor wound ever inward in a left-hand spiral. At one point the men of Juramona heard gentle, tinkling music. Further along the curving path, they found a wind chime stirring from the cool outward flow of air. Shards of clear crystal hung on pale threads fine as hair. The crystals touched lightly, playing the tune. Tol was delighted. He had never seen such a thing.

A small room opened in front of them. In it, a mixed group of warriors awaited the crown prince's pleasure. There were seafarers from the north, black-skinned like Tol's friend Crake, and dressed in white silk and peaked iron caps; barechested Wind Riders, their skin painted with mystic signs; Imperial Guards, with clean-shaven chins, and wearing crimson cloaks; and a lone kender. Dressed in fringed buckskins, the kender was telling jokes to the assembled warriors, who were laughing uproariously.

An Imperial Guardsman with gold chevrons on his helmet saluted by clanging his iron-shod heels together.

"Lords of the Eastern Hundred? You are expected. Follow me."

He held open a flap, and they passed through into a larger room, likewise carpeted from wall to wall. An assortment of dignitaries and favor-seekers waited here, sipping wine from golden goblets and conversing in low tones. All wore civilian dress. Three were dwarves with elaborately curled beards and rich, heavy robes of black and gold brocade. A singular trio, two men and a woman, were dressed in billowing trews, wide sashes, vests, and flat cloth hats. Tol had seen merchants in Juramona dressed in similar fashion and knew the three hailed from the city of Tarsis, far to the south of Odovar's domain.

The Tarsans fell silent as the Juramona men passed by. The woman's eyes, Tol noticed, were the deep, rich color of honey. She was twice his age and exuded an air of worldly charm he could sense as clearly as he smelled her perfume. She didn't lower her eyes, like the girls in Crake's tavern did, and her frank perusal made him uncomfortable. He looked ahead and tried to ignore her knowing gaze.

Once they were in the next room, their escort said, "You've just seen Hanira, ambassador from Tarsis."

"The lady?" asked Odovar, and the guardsman nodded. "I'd heard Tarsan women share rule in their city—a foolish indulgence," the marshal said firmly.

"But a handsome woman," said Wanthred, stroking his silver whiskers.

"And ruthless, they say," murmured the guard.

This third chamber was like the one they'd just left, a waiting room for those seeking an audience with the crown prince. Folk even more exotic to Tol's eyes were gathered here—a gaggle of six little men, bald as eggs but bearded. All were talking at once and waving little wooden tablets at each other.

"Gnomes. A delegation from Sancrist Isle," said their guide.

The gnomes were shorter even than kender, coming barely up to Tol's waist. Their skin was a warm brown, and all had large noses and curly white beards. Their clothing was as peculiar as their appearance: each wore cloth trews stitched to a sleeveless top, with straps crossing over the back and buttoning at the shoulders. Squares of cloth were sewn to the front of these garments, and the squares bulged with slivers of chalk, snarls of string, and oddly shaped metal instruments.

". . . it's as simple as hydrodynamics!" said one gnome in a rapid, high-pitched shout.

Odovar looked questioningly at the Imperial Guardsman, but he only shrugged and said, "Gnome-speak."

Leaving the babbling little men behind, the Juramona delegation and their escort entered a fourth room. It was the largest of all, ten paces wide at least, and the ceiling rose twice the height of a man. A buzz of conversation permeated the room, which was crowded with richly dressed folk of many nations and races. By this time Tol was growing accustomed to exotic strangers, but his mind reeled at the spectacle overhead.

At the peak of the canvas roof a flock of birds circled. They were shaped like geese, but weren't like any birds Tol had ever seen. They were transparent! Solid and clear as spring water, their wings wafted up and down as they endlessly rounded the room, sending a cool downdraft over the assembly. As they passed beneath them, Tol saw the transparent geese were dripping water from the flapping wings. A droplet fell on his cheek. It was very cold. At last he understood—these birds were made of ice!

To one side, a quartet of serene-looking men stood, eyes closed, lips moving silently. The man on the end twirled a silver bead on a thread, each revolution matching exactly the motion of the ice-birds overhead. Dressed in white homespun robes with red jackets and red sash belts, each man wore a thick silver medallion on a chain around his neck. They were Red Robes, mages of the Order who served the gods of Neutrality.

The Imperial Guard led them out of this room. The Juramona men passed through a wide curtained doorway and beneath a series of wooden arches, each one wider and grander than the last. At each stood a pair of armed guards with spear and shield. This close to the Royal Presence, Tol was relegated to the back of the delegation, behind Lord

Wanthred. Voices and music filtered back to him, and the splash of running water. He strained to see over the old noble's broad shoulders.

"Wait here," their escort said. He stepped forward, and spoke in a low voice to a richly draped man of middle years. This fellow had a big nose and leaned on a gold-capped staff.

"Ah, yes, bring them ahead," the big-nosed man said. His face was scrubbed pink, and his fingernails gleamed like mother-of-pearl. He was the cleanest man Tol had ever seen.

Lord Odovar announced himself and his vassals, and the man nodded.

"I am Valdid," he said, "second chamberlain to His Highness. My lords, attend upon me."

He turned away, the hem of his blue brocade robe flapping, and they followed him into the heart of the tent-palace.

It was a single great room, thirty paces wide, filled but not crowded with warlords, courtiers, favored guests, and diplomats. Tol's gaze was caught by a white-robed figure surrounded by a dozen attendants in light, etched armor plate. By their slim, angular features and upswept ears, he realized he was seeing Silvanesti elves for the first time.

He had no time to stare, for fresh wonders were ahead. A carpeted platform rose from the center of the room. Tripods with unlit braziers flanked four corners of a heavy wooden chair, which was padded with leather and carved with the arms of the House of Ackal. The prince's throne was empty.

Tol looked this way and that, trying to decide which of the many lordly men present was the prince. Perhaps the tall, muscular noble in burgundy velvet? He wore a silver circlet on his brow. Or maybe the rather portly lord speaking to the elves in a musical tongue that must be their own language. Or could he be the handsome blond fellow, only slightly older than Tol, laughing in a group of young women?

Valdid, the second chamberlain, went down on one knee. "Your Highness," he said, "the marshal of the Eastern Hundred is here with his warlords."

None of Tol's guesses was correct. Crown Prince Amaltar was perched on a folding stool, a scroll in his hand. He was dressed in a simple robe of midnight blue silk, cinched at the waist by a wide leather belt. A jeweled war dagger was thrust through the belt, the only visible weapon in the room. The prince's black hair was cut shorter than the fashion, barely brushing his collar, and unlike all the other men present he sported neither beard nor mustache. Around his neck on a fine gold chain he wore a woman's golden torque, set with a pair of rubies—said to be a memento of his deceased mother.

Putting down the scroll he held, the prince's dark eyes inspected the Juramona men as they knelt before him.

"Long life to Your Royal Highness and to your noble father. Death to all enemies of Ergoth!" Odovar cried. The fighting men and many of the women present echoed the marshal's sentiments, but the foreigners merely looked on, quietly amused.

"Rise, loyal vassals," said Amaltar.

Grunting from the task of raising his bulk on a sprained knee, Odovar managed to stand without help.

"How long has it been since I last saw you?" asked the prince.

"I last met Your Highness eleven years ago, after the battle of Torgaard Pass."

"That's right! You gained the pass from the Tarsans with a picked force of fifty men, as I recall."

"Your Highness favors me by remembering," Odovar said, bowing his head. "Alas, we did not hold the pass for long."

"No matter." Amaltar gestured to the stool he'd vacated. "Take your ease, my lord. Your leg obviously pains you."

Odovar colored. "I cannot sit in Your Highness's presence!"

Amaltar's pleasant demeanor vanished. "You can if I order it. Sit, marshal."

Odovar slumped onto the stool, stiff leg extended, embarrassed both by the breach of protocol and by how obvious his need for it was.

The prince snapped his fingers, and a light camp table was carried over, its top covered with scrolls. At another imperial command, four nobles, each the commander of a horde, unrolled a large parchment and held it open by the corners. It was a grand map of the vicinity, drawn in vibrant colors. The blue Caer River snaked across the landscape. Caergoth, three leagues away, appeared as a black ring on the west bank of the river. The only spot on the map devoid of color was the forest itself, east of Caergoth. A line of green delineated its boundary, but within the border no features were depicted.

"The Great Green, my lords," Amaltar said. He waved a beringed hand across it. "One hundred and fifty leagues end to end, varying from eighteen to thirty leagues wide. We know the dimensions and fringes of the forest thanks to our own surveyors—and our friends the Silvanesti." He nodded to the listening elves. "But the interior a day's ride beyond the border is as hidden to us as the far side of the red moon!"

A line of scribes stood behind Amaltar, ready to note any imperial utterances. Four waited with styluses poised, while the fifth was writing, rapidly but discreetly, recording every word the prince said.

Amaltar smote the map with his fist. "Since the days of Ackal Ergot, this region has sheltered brigands, runaways, rebels, and savages. My uncle, Emperor Pakin II, thought he could pacify the forest tribes with gifts and soft words. All he gained for his efforts was the worst series of raids since the founding of the empire. The foresters have continued to block our attempts at eastern expansion, and in their latest raid they murdered my cousin Hynor. No asset to empire was Hynor, but the killing of imperial relatives cannot be allowed to pass."

"The foresters respect nothing but force, Highness, and heed nothing but cold iron," Odovar said staunchly. His fellow warlords murmured agreement.

"That's why we are here," said the prince. "We will harrow the Great Green like a farmer does a patch of weeds. Any pests we don't destroy will be forced to flee over the mountains." With one finger, he traced a line across the unknown land, east to the north–south course of the Kharolis range.

"Is that our limit, Highness?" asked the black-haired noble in burgundy who wore the silver circlet.

"It is, Lord Urakan. When your men reach the western slopes of the mountains, they'll have ridden far enough."

Prince Amaltar went on, specifying goals for the invasion. Ten hordes would enter the Great Green in five different locations. They would move parallel to each other as they drove into the woods. Two hordes would remain outside, to guard against sallies by the tribesmen and to catch anyone who tried to escape back into Ergoth.

The three Juramona hordes would not be fighting together. The Firebrands, under Wanthred, would fight alongside another horde from southwest Ergoth, the Corij Rangers. The Rooks and Eagles and Pagas's Panthers, with Lord Odovar, would enter the Great Green through a large meadow known as Zivilyn's Carpet.

Amaltar called on the flaxen-haired, white-robed Silvanesti. The elf glided to the map table, trailed by his entourage. This included several dark, painted faces—elves of the woodland Kagonesti race.

The prince said, "My good cousin, Harpathanas Ambrodel, speak of your experiences."

The tall elf bowed slightly to the heir of Ergoth. "I have fought my way through the great forest seven times," he said. His voice was mellifluous and pleasing, though it carried a definite air of command. "Each journey brought new battles against new foes. You will find humans, Kagonesti, and, occasionally, ogres."

The assemblage stirred at the mention of ogres. Harpathanas spoke again, calming his listeners.

"Most ogres never leave the high slopes of the mountains, far to the south," he said. "Single marauders sometimes stray north to the lowlands, but not often."

The Silvanesti smiled thinly, showing narrow white teeth. "Humans are the most numerous folk in the forest, as they are elsewhere. The forest humans live in tribes, as humans did centuries ago on the plains. The sizes of the various tribes are hard to measure. At one skirmish my archers had to contend with two hundred human fighters, but I believe more than one tribe was arrayed against us. I would say a typical tribal war party would include ten to fifty warriors, including women. They fight alongside their men."

The handsome young warlord laughed at that, tossing back his long blond hair. "I look forward to meeting them!" he said.

"Be careful what you wish for, Lord Tremond. Forest women are ferocious in combat and collect the heads of any foes they vanquish," Harpathanas replied gravely.

"And sometimes they take other parts," said one of the Kagonesti. Rough laughter encircled the table. None of the elves joined in.

At Harpathanas's behest, a Kagonesti left his entourage and stepped forward to describe forester weapons and tactics. The Kagonesti's muscular build and tanned face, painted with red and blue loops and lines, seemed at odds with his attire—a plain yet good-quality dark green robe.

"They are good archers," said the Kagonesti, "but use only short bows, which may not penetrate iron plate armor. Their favorite tricks are deadfalls and pit traps, which they also use against wild beasts. Take care when pursuing tribesmen who flee too easily. They are likely leading you into a trap."

"Do they use metal?" asked Wanthred.

"Such metal as they trade for or take from their victims. Elsewise, they use flint weapons."

Odovar leaned an elbow on the map table. "What about the forest elves? Will we have to fight them?"

Harpathanas and his Kagonesti retainers exchanged glances.

The painted elf replied, "Some of my woodland brethren have mated into human tribes, and some humans have likewise joined Kagonesti bands. These mixed groups will fight you. The pure Kagonesti bands will not, unless trapped and forced to give battle, but there are few west of the mountains anyway."

The war council continued well into the afternoon. Tol strove to absorb everything, but late in the day he began to think over the crown prince's plans. Amaltar accepted as fact the notion that Ergothian cavalry could fight in the forest, and none of his warlords objected, but Tol wondered. As a very minor member of the imperial army, he had no right to question his masters. That night in the tent he shared with Relfas and four other shilder, he expressed his doubts.

"It seems wrong," he said. "How can mounted men fight in thick woods? The foresters go about on foot, I'm told. They fight from behind bushes and from treetops. How will our hordes come to grips with them?"

Relfas, tipsy from cheap Kharolian wine, shrugged broadly. "Don't worry so mush—uh—much. Ol' Egrin will see us through," he said blithely. "The warriors of Ergoth will defeat the rugged—rag—uh—ragged root-eaters! You'll see!"

The other boys cheered his bravado, and Relfas added, "I'm going to clip the ears off the first tribesman I kill and wear them home as trophies."

"I want one of those woods-women," said Janar, also befogged with drink. "Simpler than courtin' the girls back home!"

They all laughed, but Tol didn't feel merry. When his comrades staggered out to find more wine, he remained in the tent. By the light of a tallow candle, he prepared his armor, honed his saber and spearheads, and continued to brood over the morrow.

Chapter 8
The Harrowing

Wanthred's Firebrand horde departed at first light the next morning, after taking leave of Marshal Odovar. Shortly thereafter, the remaining two hordes from Juramona left the imperial encampment. They arranged themselves in a formation suitable for moving through enemy country. Out front in a wide arc were lightly armed skirmishers, provided with horns of different sizes, each of which sounded a distinctive note. A hundred paces back was the main body of the Eagles and the Panthers, in a compact mass moving ahead at a steady walk. Next came the Rooks, three hundred shilder ranging in age from fifteen to eighteen. Although without rank, the shield-bearers acknowledged several chiefs of their own: Relfas, by his noble blood a leader; Janar, blond, genial and popular, and widely rumored to be Lord Odovar's natural son; and Tol, who owed his station to his strength and fighting skills.

Trailing them was the baggage train, forty-four carts and wagons drawn by oxen. These bore everything needed to keep the hordes in the field, from a rolling blacksmith's shop to kegs of Lord Odovar's favorite beer. Marching alongside the baggage wagons were two columns of foot soldiers, four hundred thirty men commanded by Durazen the One-Eyed. Last of all was the rear guard, two hundred veteran warriors from Juramona chosen for their steadiness and courage. It was their job to reinforce a successful attack, or form a last defense in case of disaster. Command of the rear guard was given to Egrin's old comrade Manzo.

Hordes ate on the move, falling back in groups of ten to the provision wagons. Cooks handed them skewers of meat, roasted over pots of coals. Two skewers per man was the daily ration, plus a stone-hard biscuit, all washed down with a jack of *salat*—beer cut with water.

On their first campaign, the shilder were excited, keyed up for a fight. They laughed too much and talked too loudly. The summer heat, wide clear blue sky, and verdant open meadow-land made for a general feeling of being on a grand adventure.

Lord Odovar ignored the boys' high spirits until the army had forded the Wilder River. Now within a few leagues of their goal, the marshal sent a rider back to silence the noisy shilder.

"Why so stern? No one knows we're coming!" Relfas complained, as the warning messenger galloped back to the front.

"Think again. We're probably being watched even now," Tol replied, eyeing the dark smudge on the horizon that was the edge of the Great Green.

"How do you know?" Janar asked.

"It's what I would do. Even if the foresters don't expect an invasion, they must have sentinels to watch for travelers and merchant caravans to plunder."

His reasoning sobered the boys. Their chatter steadily declined as they rode inexorably closer.

Midmorning of the next day, the Juramona hordes ascended a rise and beheld their destination at last.

Zivilyn's Carpet was an enormous open meadow, a full league across, bordered by the forest on three sides. Summer's heat had turned the hip-high grass brown, but the meadow was thick with flowers. Enormous drifts of white daisies, blue cornflowers, and yellow running roses covered the field, tossing their heads in the mild breeze. Even more startling were the islands of tall sunflowers sprouting from the turf. They grew in thick clusters as high as a horse's back, and their flat brown faces were as wide as trenchers. A steady mix of bees, butterflies, and other insects crisscrossed the meadow, feasting on the abundant pollen. Beyond the lake of flowers, the distant forest was a dark green wall, as solid and featureless as a cliff face.

Before noon, Odovar halted his men. The baggage carts formed a square near the eastern end of the vast meadow. Footmen fell to erecting a palisade around the square, and Odovar called in his scouts and skirmishers. Sweating hard, the marshal nonetheless sounded more like his old self when he addressed his lieutenants.

"We will enter the woods at once," he told them. "It's important we strike the tribes without delay, before they can unite. I will lead the Panther horde personally. Egrin, you'll remain here till the sun is at your back; then you will enter and follow on the track we make."

Again Tol was surprised. Divide the hordes? Wouldn't it be better to keep them together? He studied Egrin's face, but couldn't tell if the warden was frowning from the sun in his eyes or from his disapproval of the plan.

"What about the rear guard and the shilder?" asked Manzo.

"Form your men with Egrin," said Lord Odovar. "The boys will remain here, with the baggage train."

Many of the shilder openly groaned when they heard that, and Odovar barked, "Those are my orders! Do any of you infants care to dispute with me?"

More temperately, Egrin said, "You boys will be our reserve. If we get into a serious fight, you'll be called to join in."

"There won't be much fighting," the marshal snorted. "I expect the savages will run for the mountains as soon as they hear us coming."

The other warriors hailed this bold boast, but Egrin seemed unmoved. As the hordes sorted themselves out, he took Tol aside.

"Note this well," he said quietly, ignoring the tumult around them. He mashed a common jackberry, a bitter and unpalatable fruit, in the hollow of his left hand. After smearing the juice on his ring, he pressed the ring against the back

113

of Tol's hand. The emblem of Egrin's house—a crescent moon—remained, printed in dark berry juice.

"If I send for you, the messenger will have this mark," the warden said. "Otherwise, ignore any call you get to join me. The enemy we fight are not honorable warriors. They're plunderers and scavengers, and may resort to all manner of tricks. If anyone tries to summon you to my aid without this mark, kill them, or beat them to get the truth. Is that clear?"

Tol nodded gravely. Egrin clasped arms with him, not like master and student, but man to man. The youth was poignantly reminded of the day he'd left his father's farm to join the ranks of the shilder, when his father had gripped his arm just that way.

Odovar and Pagas led the Panther horde into the Great Green. It took quite a while for the thousand mounted men to penetrate the green wall of bushes and saplings. For a long time after the last Panther disappeared from sight, Tol could hear them crashing through the undergrowth.

Egrin sat on the ground by his horse, reins loosely tied around his wrist, regarding the forest with a silent frown. Tol asked if he was troubled by the coming expedition, but the warden denied it. The dense woodland, he said, reminded him of his youth. He offered no further comment, but found a rose in the trampled grass and idly plucked its saffron petals.

Time passed. The sun reached its zenith. Most of the soldiers made a quick meal of cold meat and hard biscuit. Egrin remained where he was, sitting by Old Acorn, as the sun began to move westward. At last, he stood and mounted the roan. Without a spoken order or horn call, the men of the Eagle horde did likewise, sorting themselves into squadrons of twenty. Egrin placed a peaked iron helmet on his head, adjusting the chin strap to a comfortable fit. He wrapped the reins around his left hand, thumped Old Acorn's flanks, and started toward the trees. The Eagles followed him without fanfare or fuss.

Watching from a wagon, Relfas sniffed. "Our warden is no gallant, is he? He lacks Lord Odovar's style."

"He's a great warrior," Tol objected.

Janar waved the chunk of biscuit he held, saying, "Fighting is one thing, leadership another. I agree with Relfas—Egrin has no sense of glory!"

They often talked this way, and Tol never could understand their thinking. Surely the measure of a warrior was how well he fought, not how well he dressed or bellowed commands? To his mind, Egrin was worth a dozen Odovars. The marshal was brave enough, but impatient, even rash. In a battle between equal hordes, one under Egrin and one under Odovar, Tol would ride with Egrin, no question.

The Eagles were swallowed by the forest in less time and with much less noise than the Panthers. Once they were gone, a pall fell over Zivilyn's Carpet. The sun declined further and the brightness of the day was swallowed by deep shadows. The bustle and noise that had accompanied the full camp gave way to the nervous quiet of those remaining. To many of the youths it seemed as though they had been taken to the edge of the world and abandoned.

Tol left his shilder comrades to hunt up Narren and Crake. He found the former off-duty and playing knucklebones with other footmen behind the healer's wagon. Tol joined the gaming for a time, lost a small amount, and quit.

"Seen Crake?" he asked, as Narren's fellows raked in their winnings.

"Probably napping in the wine cart." Narren often accused others of vices he wanted to commit himself.

In fact Crake was awake, though comfortably ensconced with his feet propped up on the driver's box of his wagon. The young flutist was enlarging the holes in his instrument with a slim, sharp blade. He hailed Tol's arrival.

"A new flute?" Tol said.

"Naw, an old one. They get soft, you know, from spit and breath blowing through them," Crake explained. "The wood swells, changing the pitch, so I have to open up the holes to keep things in tune."

Tol climbed in beside his friend. He pulled off his helmet,

running his fingers through his sweat-sleeked hair and glorying in the fresh air. For a moment he envied Crake's pleasant life, and told him so.

"It isn't bad," the youth replied. He dipped a hand below the driver's box and brought out a half-full wineskin, offering it to Tol. It was politely declined, and Crake set it aside. "But there's a lot of ugly work in tavern life, too."

Tol prompted him to go on.

"Dealing with drunks is the worst. How would you like to wrestle nightly with besotted soldiers who think they're the emperor's champion swordsman? If you tap one with a persuader, then you have to drag his arse outside, and nothing weighs more than a lifeless body. But leave the fellow on his feet, and he'll either take a swing at you, or heave his supper on your shoes." Crake blew a random note on the flute. "Some life, eh?"

Tol gazed into the woods. The low, westerly sun washed the Great Green with bloody light, yet the brilliance seemed to penetrate only a few steps into the forest.

"I wonder what it's like?" he said. "Battle, I mean."

"Loud, I imagine. Sweaty. And scary."

"Do you suppose they're fighting now?"

Crake laid the flute on his chest, and gave his friend a thoughtful look. "You really do wish you were with them, don't you?"

"Better than waiting here, doing nothing."

"That's where you're wrong, my friend," Crake said, and smiled, a quick flash of teeth in the gathering dusk. "We're not doing nothing. I'm tuning my flute, and you're daydreaming."

He pulled the stopper of the wineskin and let it dangle on its cord. The potent aroma of red wine filled the air between them. Crake took a drink, then passed the skin to Tol.

"And now you're drinking," he said wryly. "That's not nothing, either."

* * * * *

Tol thought he was too excited to sleep that night, but nodded off on his bedroll before the campfire had burned down to embers. Night passed peacefully until a firm hand prodded him awake.

"Eh, what is it? Who are you pokin', Janar, you dolt—"

"Wake up, boy. There's trouble." The voice belonged not to Janar, but Felryn. The healer looked worried.

Tol bolted upright. "What trouble?"

Felryn hushed him and said softly, "Not here. In the woods."

He beckoned the puzzled youth to follow. They went to Felryn's wagon, a large, canvas-roofed vehicle drawn by six oxen. Inside, the air was hot and heavy, laced with musky incense. At the far end of the wagon was a small altar to Mishas inscribed with arcane symbols of the wizard's craft. A thick candle burned on one side, and several pewter talismans lay beside the steadily burning light. Tol and Felryn squeezed in, and the healer closed the flap.

"First, I must anoint you," the healer muttered. "So as not to offend the gods."

He took tiny brass vial and shook out a few drops of clear oil on his fingertips. He dabbed the oil first on Tol's forehead, then his chin, and finally both cheeks. As the liquid warmed, Tol detected a faint, spicy aroma.

"I was consecrating talismans for the protection of Lord Odovar and his warlords," Felryn said. "Nothing was going well. I broke my stylus, and the sacred candle went out twice . . ." He frowned. In the candlelit gloom, his form seemed to merge with the shadows. His strong face resembled a mask carved out of smooth, dark wood.

"Bad omens, but I put them down to nerves. I was nearly finished with the dedication of these two medals to Corij when there was a flash of fire, and this happened." He held up the two medallions: they were fused together, edge to edge.

"What does it mean?" Tol asked, head swimming a little from the overpowering aroma of incense.

Felryn closed his long fingers around the ruined medals.

"The air here is heavy with magic. There are powerful spells being cast, not far away—spells against our people—and, I fear, much danger for Lord Odovar."

"Who's casting these spells? Foresters?"

"No, not the local shamans; their power is drawn from the realm of Zivilyn. There are stronger forces stirring." When Tol looked alarmed, Felryn stared at him silently for a few seconds, rubbing the fused talismans between his hands. "I will see what I can see," he said at last.

He pulled the silver Mishas medallion from beneath the neck of his robe. Clenching it in one hand and the fused Corij talismans in the other, he closed his eyes, lowering his chin to his chest. Tol held his breath, waiting to see what would transpire.

The silence deepened. One by one the night sounds from outside—the chirrup of crickets, the muted call of an owl, even the whisper of wind in the long grass—all ceased. Soon, Tol realized he could no longer hear even his own breathing. The lack of sound was absolute, pressing against his ears like a thick blanket. He could feel himself gasping for air, his mouth wide, but still heard nothing.

Felryn began to tremble. When at last he spoke, although his voice sounded flat and toneless, Tol felt a huge surge of relief. Any sound was welcome after the dreadful, smothering silence.

"Great forces are at work. They do not originate in the forest—though that's where they're working," Felryn intoned. "Lord Odovar faces death—a trap, an ambush!" His eyes sprang open, wide and worried. "And so does Egrin!"

Tol's hands clenched into fists. He wanted to shout questions, demand more information, but he feared distracting the healer from his vision. So he waited.

After a pause, Felryn closed his eyes again, and continued: "Six leagues from here is a stream, bent like a horseshoe, in a deep ravine. A large tree lies across it, like a bridge. The marshal cannot advance on horseback across the ravine. He dismounts and starts over the log on foot. The log breaks when he's halfway across; it has been sawn through, save for the last bit on top. Odovar falls into the stream. It's only chest-deep, but with his bad leg he can't get out."

Eyes still shut, Felryn turned his head, as though looking at something in the scene he described.

"Arrows fly—the foresters are all around." Felryn's voice lost its toneless quality, and he exclaimed, "Men struggle to reach Lord Odovar, but all who try are slain! The enemy is in the trees . . . they have good bows. The marshal is hit! He brandishes his sword and calls for a charge. But the mounted warriors have no room to maneuver among the closely growing trees. They are felled from all sides by arrows and thrown spears. Egrin—"

The healer grimaced, moving his head left and right, searching, then reported, "I cannot see. Something impedes my sight."

Tears oozed from under Felryn's tightly clenched eyelids—red droplets—blood, not water. He opened his eyes and inhaled deeply. Immediately the oppressive silence ended, and the familiar nighttime sounds flooded back into Tol's grateful ears.

"I will rouse Durazen and seek his counsel!" he said, gripping Felryn's arm. "He's the senior warrior in camp."

The healer slumped wearily against the side of the wagon, but he assured Tol he was well. Tol left him and ran to the center of the square, shouting Durazen's name. Soldiers and shilder sat up all around, but he didn't see the commander of the footmen.

Narren suddenly came running, wearing only a breech-clout and clutching a blanket around his shoulders. He had a war dagger in his free hand.

"Tol! Come quick!" he panted. "It's Durazen!"

Tol raced through the roused camp. In the far corner, Narren stopped and stood over an unmoving figure on a bedroll. For a moment Tol thought Durazen must be dead or drunk, but Narren kicked the blanket aside to reveal not the commander's body, but a bundle of grass and vines, cunningly lashed together to resemble a man.

"Torches!" Tol yelled. "Search the camp! Find Durazen, or anyone who doesn't belong here!"

By now the whole camp was in an uproar. Brands blazed; shilder and foot soldiers searched the camp, even turning out the civilian wagons. Durazen could not be found.

No one slept for the rest of the night. At dawn, the nervous shilder and foot soldiers greeted the sunrise with relief, though there was still no sign of their missing commander. And with Durazen gone, there was no clear leader among the footmen or shilder.

Tol, mounted on Smoke, addressed the assembled warriors and civilians. He told them of Felryn's vision of an ambush.

"We must find Lord Odovar and Warden Egrin," he declared. "I need at least a hundred men to do it. Who's with me?"

"We can't leave camp," Janar protested. He was only half-dressed, his broad chest bare and blond hair askew. "Our orders were to stay here."

"The marshal is in trouble—he may be dead already!"

"We don't know that," said Relfas skeptically. "Felryn is an admirable healer, but I've never heard he was a seer."

Tol turned to the older man for help. Felryn said, "I am a priest of Mishas, chosen by the goddess to serve the marshal of Juramona. If she grants me visions of my charges, you can believe them."

The shilder remained unconvinced. "We should send a few riders to contact Lord Wanthred and the Firebrands," Relfas countered. "That would be the wisest course."

Many relieved voices supported this plan. Tol's frustration grew.

"If Lord Odovar is to be ambushed and cut off, every hour is precious," he insisted. "For the honor of the empire and the safety of our comrades, we must *do* something!"

On and on they wrangled, until a delegation from the foot-men interrupted. Relfas disdained to discuss strategy with mere foot soldiers, but Tol went to speak to them.

"It's Durazen. We found him," Narren reported. Tol looked

relieved until Narren added, "He's dead, Tol. Come and see."

Shilder, civilians, and foot soldiers streamed out of the camp behind Tol. Narren led them to the extreme eastern end of the meadow.

"Boys from the cook wagon went out a little while ago to collect tinder for their fires," Narren explained. "Instead they found this."

Forty steps from the edge of the woods, the crowd halted as though they'd all been turned to stone. Lashed to an oak tree, his hands bound behind him, was Durazen. The shaft of an arrow protruded from his throat, effectively pinning him to the tree trunk. His belly had been cut open, and his entrails wound around the tree.

The forest folk had not simply killed the commander of the Ergothian camp. They had sacrificed him to the spirits of the trees in which they lived.

The sound of retching behind him broke through Tol's shock. He had to clear his throat twice before he could speak. Even then his voice was hoarse.

"Cut him down," he rasped. No one moved. Dazed, he drew his dagger and did the job himself. Felryn knelt by the body, examining it closely.

"Why did they do this?" Tol asked, stunned by the method of the old warrior's death.

"To propitiate their ancestors' spirits—and to terrify their enemies," Felryn answered tersely.

Tol stared at the bloody tree. Was Lord Odovar going to meet a similar fate in the forest? And Egrin?

His name, sharply spoken, called him out of his horrified daze. Narren and the footmen had gathered around.

"We'll go with you, Tol," Narren said. "We'll find Odovar and the warden, and pay back the savages for what they did to Durazen, too!"

Tol surveyed the foot soldiers' hard faces. Aside from Narren and a few others, they were generally older than the shilder, some as old as thirty. Of humble birth, they were used to being looked down upon by Riders of the Horde. None of that mattered now. Their blood was up, and they would take the battle to the devious enemy in their own way: on foot, face to face.

"Pick a hundred men, Narren, no more. Each man is to bring food and water for two days, his sword, dagger, helmet, a pair of spears, and breastplate. Everything else stays behind—we have to move fast," Tol said. He looked up at the mid-morning sun. "We'll leave as soon as you're ready."

Narren took off running, to do as Tol said. All the way back to camp Relfas, Janar, and the other shilder harangued Tol, warning him not to go. He was disobeying orders, they said. He was inexperienced. He was risking the lives of the ignorant footmen who chose to follow him.

Tol ignored them. Finally, Relfas quieted the others and said, "So be it! If Tol wants to throw his life away, that's his choice. At least he won't weaken the Rooks doing it!"

Considerably more than a hundred footmen lined up to follow Tol into the forest. He sent a third of them back, not wanting to leave the camp's defense so weakened. Among the volunteers, he was surprised to see Felryn and Crake. The healer refused to be left behind, insisting that, as his auguries had stirred them up, he felt responsible for the expedition.

To Crake, Tol said, "You're not a soldier. You don't have to do this."

"None of your men has a bow. You'll need one," Crake said with a shrug. Flashing a smile, he added, "Just don't try to order me around, all right?"

Before they set out, Felryn took Tol aside and showed him the arrow that had been removed from Durazen's throat. Made of ash wood, blackened with soot and fletched with crow feathers, it would be nearly invisible at night. It was obviously forester workmanship, except for its head, which was a sharp triangle of bronze. Common knowledge held that the foresters used flint heads.

"Also," Felryn added, "the cuts on Durazen's body were too smooth and even to have been made with stone blades. He was cut with metal."

"Where would the forest tribes get metal?" Tol said. "Taken from those they've slain?"

"Perhaps. Or perhaps the foresters have found someone to supply them," Felryn suggested darkly.

With a minimum of fuss and no noble speeches, the rescue expedition slipped into the woods. The trees closed in behind them, and Zivilyn's Carpet was quickly lost from sight.

Chapter 9
The Place of Bones

The Great Green was denser than any forest Tol had ever seen. Ancient trees stretched lordly limbs up to the sky, blotting out the sun. The glare and heat of day gave way to a sort of muted twilight. Gray lichen clung to the trunks, and thick carpets of moss filled the space between gnarled tree roots. Not only were there majestic oaks and broad maples, but several of the truly gigantic vallenwoods united to form a leafy canopy under which lesser plants could not grow.

By the time they'd gone ten score paces into the forest, the Ergothians found the way clear of the clinging growth that first had hampered their progress. The forest floor was covered by a thick bed of dead leaves, broken here and there by islands of mossy boulders. The soft light and great tree trunks made it impossible to see much more than a dozen paces in any direction. A thousand savages could be hiding within a stone's throw and they'd never know it, Tol thought. He wondered how Odovar's and Egrin's hordes had gotten anywhere on horseback in this maze.

The forest was still as death. No birds sang, and there was no game in sight, not even a rabbit. The weird silence brought out a kind of nervous tic in the soldiers. Every few steps, each man would pause and look around, certain he was being observed by hostile eyes. Even Felryn succumbed to the sensation.

124

Without asking permission, Crake slipped away from the soldiery. For a flute player who spent most of his days in a tavern, he was remarkably stealthy, moving ahead of them through the leaf-litter with hardly a sound.

A shrill whistle brought Tol's band to a halt. He continued forward and found Crake crouched by a pit dug in the center of the trail. Sharpened stakes lined the bottom of the pit. Their points were darkly stained.

More traps, all likewise sprung, were found—snares dangling in the air, deadfalls tripped, more of the stake-filled pits. A few traps held dead horses, and there were plain signs Odovar's men had fought back: tree trunks defaced by sword cuts, blood spattered on leaves, scraps of shredded buckskin. Still, there were no human bodies, living or dead. That mystery played on the soldiers' already taut nerves.

When the rescue party topped a slight knoll they beheld an even more startling sight. A series of vines had been stretched between trees directly across their path. From the vines hung skulls, more than a hundred of them. Their missing lower jaws gave them an especially horrible aspect: they seemed to be silently screaming.

The soldiers shifted uneasily, drawing closer together. Their muttering was loud in the silence. Even the veteran campaigners among them were powerfully affected by the sight.

Felryn took a small vial from his belt pouch. He flung droplets from the vial at the screen of skulls. A musky, sweet aroma surrounded the men.

His banishing oil used up, the healer gripped Tol's arm. "It's woodland magic," he said. "A display meant to cause fear."

Tol swallowed hard. "It works well."

Felryn examined the nearest bones with professional detachment.

"Human, elf, human, human—and judging by the size of those two, kender, or perhaps gnome," he said. "And they've been here for years. Bones don't get this dry overnight."

Tol felt a flush of anger drowning out his earlier horror. "Cut them down! Cut them all down!" he commanded, drawing his saber.

The task helped dispel the last traces of the Ergothians' fear. When the way was clear, Tol sheathed his saber and the rescue party moved on.

At the top of the next rise, behind a tangle of bracken, they found a distinct path worn into the mossy earth. It was the first real trail they'd seen, and as it ran along their line of march, Tol decided to follow it. Wary of traps, the Ergothians paralleled the trail on either side, moving single file through the closely growing trees. Crake alone chose to walk down the worn path, bow in hand.

Crake suddenly stopped. Keeping his right hand low, by his side, he waved for everyone else to halt as well. The Ergothians knelt in the leaves.

The young flutist nocked an arrow very slowly, hands still held low. Raising the weapon swiftly, he loosed the arrow at a high angle. There was a screech, and something heavy came hurtling down from the tree tops.

"Tol! Now!" Crake shouted.

Trusting his friend, Tol rose with his sword in the air. "Have at them!"

They ran forward with no thought of stealth. Ahead, the path passed between a pair of tall boulders, and more waist-high rocks formed a barrier between the pair. Shouting the name of Juramona, the foot soldiers leaped onto the rocks. On the other side, still scrambling to grab their weapons, were several dozen foresters.

Tol dropped into the midst of the shocked tribesmen. Though he'd never attacked anyone with lethal intent before, the heat of the moment seized him, and he slashed forward without mercy. In such close quarters, most of the Ergothians abandoned spears and drew swords too, hacking at the unprepared enemy. The foresters fought back as best they could with wooden spears, stone axes, and clubs.

Tol struck a spear from the hands of an older man, then

followed this with an underhand cut. It caught the tribesman under one arm and sent him reeling. Tol leaped over his fallen foe, not even bothering to see if he was alive or dead. He ran the next man, a painted half-elf, through, then spun around and recovered his blade. As the foot soldiers battled below him, Crake stood atop a convenient boulder, picking off enemies with his bow.

The fight was quickly over. Not one of the foresters escaped. The Ergothians, flushed with battle fever, were dazed as the fight ended abruptly. They gathered in the center of the camp and surveyed the carnage.

"I can't believe we were able to steal up on them," Tol said, panting. His mouth was searingly dry, his voice little more than a croak. One of the older footmen passed him a waterskin.

"They had a sentinel," Crake said. "I shot him from the path."

"Odovar must have come this way," Narren observed. "The fools thought the danger had passed. Only one man on watch? Stupid!"

Twenty-eight foresters had been killed in the skirmish. Eight were half-elves—and four were women. As the elf Harpathanas Ambrodel had warned in Prince Amaltar's camp, the women had fought as hard as their men, and died just as bravely. The Ergothians had lost not a single man, though five had received minor wounds.

One tribesman still lived, though he was wounded. He had long blond hair pulled back in a queue, and a short beard. His ears swept up to blunt points. Some of the men, eager to avenge Durazen, were ready to cut the injured half-elf's throat. Tol forbade it, though the footmen grew angry.

The awful scene of Durazen's death would live in his dreams for a long time, but Tol stood firm. Looking at the fair-haired prisoner, the face of Vakka Zan came back to him. Tol adamantly refused to allow them to kill the captive.

One or two might have disputed the decision with force, but they were drawn away and calmed by the rest. Tol called for Felryn.

The healer examined the wounded forester, reporting the fellow had a sword cut on his calf. He applied a herbal powder and tied up the wound with a scrap of soft leather.

"It'll hurt like a bite from the Dragonqueen, but he should live," Felryn said.

Questioned, the green-daubed man would not reveal even his name. Felryn gave the ends of his leather bandage a tug. The tribesman's face whitened.

"Nara," he finally grunted. "Name's Nara."

There was no time to waste on interrogation. The forester's comrades might even now be massing a force to counterattack the Ergothians. Over Felryn's protests, Tol put him in charge of the half-elf's safety. Without the healer's protection, Tol knew the other soldiers would likely finish the prisoner.

Uncertainty gnawed at Tol. As he walked along the row of slain tribesmen, he wondered if he had made a terrible mistake disobeying orders and coming into the forest. Like a hunter trembling after taking his first buck, he was sickened by the sight of death. His hands were shaking, and his eyes stung with tears.

Narren came up beside him, also gazing at the enemy bodies. Tol clenched his jaw, forcing the lump back down his throat. He would not shame himself by weeping at a time like this.

"Why do they color their faces?" Narren asked. He'd taken off his helmet, letting his fair hair blow free.

"To look fierce?" Tol suggested. "Or to better hide in the greenwood?"

His own words sparked a thought, and Tol turned abruptly. He clamped a hand on Narren's arm.

"That's it! That's how we'll get through!" he exclaimed. Narren's confusion was plain, so Tol added, "We've been fortunate so far, don't you see? The Panthers and the Eagles must have drawn off most of the tribesmen in these parts—the best armed, the ablest fighters. That's why we've encountered only these ragged scavengers. If we go on, we're sure to run into more fell warriors."

"What of it?" said Narren. "We came to find our comrades. We've no choice but to walk the way in blood."

Tol managed a smile. The plan forming in his mind chased away his earlier doubts. "Odovar, with two hordes at his command, foundered, so how can we hope to get through with only a hundred? We can't, unless . . ." He looked again at the lifeless half-elves and their verdant skin. "Unless we become foresters too!"

❦ ❦ ❦ ❦ ❦

It was easily done. Among their scant possessions, the slain tribesmen had small bags of paint, compounded from boar grease, leaves, and sap. There wasn't enough pigment for the entire Ergothian band, but the veteran soldiers didn't much fancy the idea of painting themselves up anyway. Tol and thirty-two of the youngest soldiers shed their armor and smeared their faces, arms, and hands with paint. As best as possible they copied the markings Nara bore, for extra authenticity.

The day was well advanced by the time they finished, and night would fall early under the shield of leaves. After a quick, cold meal in the boulder-ringed camp, the Ergothians set out again. Tol and his painted comrades led the way.

They detected signs of activity. More paths, leading off in various directions, were discovered. A faint smell of smoke drifted on the breeze, and twice they heard the distant pulse of drumbeats. At dusk, the drums grew louder.

By Felryn's estimate, they'd come some five leagues from Zivilyn's Carpet. Everyone was weary, but no one asked to stop. Night had truly fallen when they reached a small clearing. Tol signaled for the company to kneel in the shadows at the edge of the clearing. He called for Felryn.

Stars shone overhead in a clear circle where the trees had been cleared. The white moon was just peeping over the trees. In the center of the clearing stood a single white column. It was two paces tall, a handspan wide, and shone brightly in

Solin's light. The column stood on a low base of dark stone. Indistinct objects lay in heaps around its base.

"An altar," Felryn explained softly. "There is power here, much greater than the simple fear-spell at the wall of skulls. This is a consecrated spot, though from this distance I can't tell to which god it belongs."

Tol took a deep breath and stood up. Felryn grasped his wrist, hissing, "What are you doing?"

"I'm a forester," Tol replied coolly. "I'm not afraid to be seen here."

He walked into the clearing. No alarm was given, so he advanced boldly to the white column.

The pillar was eight-sided, its top cut off on a slant. A smooth yellow gem was inset in the angled top. Around it and all down the sides of the column were finely carved hieroglyphs. Tol knew the writing was not Ergothian.

He squatted to examine the objects piled up around the pillar. To his surprise, he saw they were pieces of bronze weaponry—arrowheads, spear tips, knife and sword blades. All looked newly made and unblemished by corrosion.

Taking a spearhead to show Felryn, Tol started back toward the trees. Before he was halfway there, he was brought up short by a sharp command.

"You! Stop!"

Tol froze, then slowly turned. Out of the darkness strode two figures, one in a maroon cloak, the other wrapped in black. Like apparitions, they entered the narrow stream of moonlight and the silvery beams glinted off the bronze helmet worn by the maroon-cloaked fellow. He was a Silvanesti warrior in full array; of the other figure all that could be seen was the hooded sable cloak that covered him to his toes.

"What are you doing, half-breed? The Isaren Glade is a sacred place, and that bronze is not for you!" the elf said. The haughtiness of his expression matched the arrogance of his tone. Arms folded into voluminous sleeves, the hooded one said nothing.

Even as he wondered what a Silvanesti was doing so deep in the Great Green, Tol affected what he hoped was a rustic woodland accent and replied, "Uh, sorry. I didn't think anybody would notice one bit o' metal gone."

The elf knocked the spearhead from Tol's open hand. "This belongs to Chief Makaralonga!" he snapped. Spotting the saber hanging over Tol's shoulder, he said, "An iron blade! Where did you steal that? Give it to me!"

Tol glanced over his shoulder at the trees—but couldn't see any of his men. They were in hiding.

"I said, give me that iron blade!" he said, shoving Tol roughly.

"As you wish!"

Tol abruptly whipped his saber out and cut at the elf. He felt the edge scrape along the Silvanesti's cuirass. Exclaiming in his native tongue, the elf warrior leaped back, groping for his own sword. He blundered hard against his comrade, and the man's black hood fell back, revealing a familiar face.

Morthur Dermount!

Tol's heart raced. What was a Silvanesti doing in the Great Green, and in the company of the empire's most wanted fugitive? The man also known as Spannuth Grane had not been heard of since he'd disappeared from Juramona years earlier.

The elf whipped out his sword, as Morthur Dermount laughed. "No need for such exertions, Kirstalothan. I'll down him for you," he said. Fingering a length of slender copper chain, Morthur began to speak in the sing-song voice that Tol remembered from that night at his family's farm.

Tol backed away a pace and threw a desperate glance at the trees. What was Felryn waiting for? Where were his men?

Even as Morthur continued to chant and finger the links of the chain, Tol realized he wasn't feeling the heavy, irresistible sleepiness. Morthur's look of consternation brought a fierce grin to his face as he lifted his sword again and launched himself at the Silvanesti.

No sooner had their blades met than six of Tol's green-faced men burst from cover and joined in the fray. They bore the Silvanesti down. Black-garbed Morthur backed out of arm's reach and dashed for the trees.

"Get him! Stop him!" Tol cried.

Four men raced after Morthur, but they soon returned empty-handed. The treacherous sorcerer had easily eluded them in the dark.

"It was Morthur Dermount!" Tol told Narren, who was sitting on the Silvanesti's back.

The name meant nothing to Narren and the other foot soldiers; they had long forgotten Odovar's former lieutenant. Grinding his teeth in frustration at having let the criminal escape, Tol snapped, "Spannuth Grane!"

That evil name all recognized. Felryn declared Grane had been the source of the evil magic that he'd detected. Yet he no more than the rest could say what Grane might be doing here, and with a Silvanesti warrior to boot.

They dragged the unconscious elf back to the trees. Bound and gagged, he became their second prisoner.

Felryn examined the white column. He declared the writing to be Dwarvish. According to the inscription, he said, this place was called the Isaren Glade, and was dedicated to the smith-god Reorx.

He added, "Yet elves don't worship Reorx. Neither do the forest tribes. Perhaps someone merely wants us to think dwarves have been here. As for Lord Morthur—" Felryn shook his head. "There's more at work here than meets the eye."

As the foot soldiers discussed the strange doings among themselves, Felryn said quietly to Tol, "He cast a befuddlement spell on you. Didn't you feel it?"

Tol said he hadn't, and thanked the healer for his protection. Felryn stared at him silently for a moment. "I did nothing," he finally said, but Tol could offer no explanation for the failure of Morthur's spell against him.

With renewed care, the Ergothians passed through the mysterious glade after first hiding all the bronze weapons in some nearby bushes.

Back in the trees again, they began to hear movement. More than once Tol spied dark figures gliding through the woods alongside them. He kept his hand on his sword hilt, but no one else bothered them. The strangers must assume he and his party were foresters.

Eventually, the trees grew more slender and undergrowth appeared between them. As they made their way through the brush, they saw a glow ahead. Loud masculine voices rang out—Ergothian voices!

Narren started to push past Tol, but was held back.

"If we are near, now is the time for patience," Tol whispered. Narren agreed reluctantly.

Keeping the unpainted soldiers in the rear, Tol and his disguised comrades pushed forward. The ground sloped upward. They could hear the gurgle of a stream and smelled smoke. Parting the last barrier of brush, Tol beheld an astonishing scene.

Ahead was a large knoll, rising sharply above the surrounding land. The sides and rear of the knoll dropped into a steep ravine, through which a creek coursed. Across the open end of the knoll, large logs had been piled to create a low, zigzagging bulwark. Two bonfires blazed behind the fallen trees. Hundreds of Ergothian warriors and a similar number of horses were crowded together around the fires. All the warriors were dismounted, swords drawn and spears ready. The dead—foresters and warriors both—lay in heaps on both sides of the bulwark.

They strained every muscle trying to make out Lord Odovar, but could not find him. Tol did spot Egrin, slouched against a boulder, and his heart leapt with relief.

"The warden lives!" he said. In eager whispers, this news was passed back from the disguised soldiers to the rest of the footmen.

Outside the fitful light of the bonfires lurked hundreds, perhaps thousands, of tribesmen. Both groups of combatants were plainly exhausted.

"We'll wait for sunrise," Tol told his people. "We can't

attack now. Our own comrades might fight us. At dawn, one side or the other will attack again, and that's when we'll strike."

No one had a better plan, so the footmen settled down in the dark to wait. Tol was amazed. He and his troop were surrounded by foresters, but none paid them any heed. Aided by darkness, they hid in the midst of their enemy. He couldn't imagine falling asleep, poised on the very cusp of danger, with myriad questions about Silvanesti intruders and Morthur Dermount racing in his head, but sleep he did. Exhaustion finally got the better of him and he slumped against the base of an oak tree.

¥ ¥ ¥ ¥ ¥

A high-pitched scream tore his eyes open.

Swarms of foresters came howling out of the woods, waving clubs, axes, and spears as they charged up the knoll. The Ergothians under siege braced for the onslaught, a bristling hedge of spears lining the length of the improvised wall. Ten paces from the bulwark, the foresters paused to hurl spears and stones. Armor was no protection against a fist-sized hunk of granite, worn smooth in a tumbling creek. Ergothians went down, faces bloody, under the barrage.

Tol kept his men hidden, watching the battle develop. He saw the attack for what it was—an obvious feint, an attempt to wear down the defenders with noise and thrown missiles.

"Footmen to the front," he called softly. The undisguised soldiers worked their way forward.

"When the foresters attack the barricade, form up and hit them from behind. Shout 'Juramona' to let our countrymen know who we are. Those of us in paint will stay in the woods and cut off any reinforcements moving up against you."

It was a dangerous plan. The footmen were outnumbered. If the tribesmen stood their ground in the face of the footmen's surprise rush, the Ergothians could be overwhelmed. Although the risks were plain, no one spoke against Tol.

Every soldier was aching to come to blows with the enemy.

They did not have long to wait. The bombardment of the bulwark ended with the foresters scrambling back down the hill into the trees. Two breaths later, a mob several hundred strong erupted from hiding, screaming and running up the knoll. The first wave reached the line of felled trees and climbed over, only to be impaled on Ergothian spears. Still the wild-eyed tribesmen pushed on, shrieking like fiends, climbing over their fallen comrades, and letting their weight bear down the deadly spears.

For a moment Tol took in the horrible panorama: tribesmen naked to the waist, wielding a stone axe in each hand; women warriors, their long hair woven into braids, lofting arrows over the throng; painted Kagonesti and half-elves with slings and spears; and the grim, bloodied faces of the trapped Ergothians, finding three fresh foes behind every one they felled.

The veteran footmen were led by Caskan, one of the soldiers who had wanted to execute Nara. They fell upon the rear of the forester mob. Chaos reigned as the tribesmen struggled to turn and meet this unexpected blow. Behind their bulwark, the embattled Ergothians were plainly astonished, but took new heart from the recognized rallying cry. The rest of Tol's band, those painted like foresters, slipped sideways through the trees, watching for any fresh threats.

A gang of tall, rugged-looking humans emerged from the ravine and moved to strike at the rear of Caskan's band. Tol let them collect in a tight mass for charging, then hit them before they got clear of the trees.

Shaken at being attacked by men they had taken to be allies, the buckskin-clad humans retreated, before recognizing their new enemies and counter-attacking ferociously.

With difficulty Tol wounded a foe a head taller than himself, leaped over a prostrate forester, and traded cuts with another tribesman. This one had a magnificent head of golden hair, a thick beard, and eyes the color of a summer sky. He wore a brass circlet set with crudely cut gems, and carried an ancient straight sword of the kind used in Ergoth a century past. Three times Tol's age, he was still a powerful man. The youth's hands stung every time their blades met. If the golden-haired warrior had thrust with his straight blade, he might have killed Tol, who was no duelist. Fortunately for Tol, his untutored opponent chose to fight as if he had a saber, slashing overhand again and again.

The press of the fight propelled them both to the edge of the ravine. Below, the stream was stained with blood and littered with bodies. The blond tribesman delivered a mighty blow at Tol's left shoulder, which the boy deflected by using both hands on his sword hilt. Pressing forward with all his strength, Tol slid his curved blade down his enemy's straight one until the iron tip drove deep into the older man's shoulder.

The forester was strong. He did not lose his grip on his sword even with a span of cold metal in his flesh, but as he backed away from the thrust, he did lose his footing and pitched backward into the ravine.

Tol slid down the muddy bank after his foe. He planted a foot on the fallen forester's chest and shoved. Golden hair sank beneath the muddy water. Tol held him down, knocking the sword from his hand. When bubbles ceased coming from the warrior's lips, Tol let him float to the surface.

"Yield!" he cried, digging the tip of his bloody saber into the man's bearded jowls. "I will spare your life!"

"Traitor half-breed!" sputtered the beaten forester. "Makaralonga yields to no man of ill faith!"

Makaralonga. The Silvanesti warrior captured at the Isaren Glade had invoked this man's name. He was a chief!

Tol swiped a sleeve over his face, scrubbing away paint. "I'm no forester," he announced. "I am Tol, shilder to Egrin, warden of Juramona!"

Makaralonga blinked through sodden strands of hair. "A grasslander!"

"Yield, and you shall be honestly treated." Tol stepped back, drawing a deep breath into his aching chest.

Above, Tol's charge had broken Makaralonga's attack, and Caskan's footmen broke the foresters' latest attempt to storm the knoll. When Tol emerged from the ravine with Makaralonga at sword point before him, a wail went up from the foresters. Although they still outnumbered the Ergothians ten to one, they lost heart at the sight of their chief in the enemy's hands. They began to back into the underbrush, but their retreat became a rout when Ergothian soldiers flung themselves on the horde's surviving horses and charged after them. The log barricade was dragged down and horsemen thundered down the knoll. They sabered scores of fleeing tribesmen, following them into the trees in their eagerness to pay back their tormenters.

Tol prodded Makaralonga to the broken bulwark. Waiting there was Egrin. Wan and bloodied, he still sat proudly on Old Acorn.

"By the gods, Tol! How did you get here?" Egrin exclaimed.

Tol told him quickly of Felryn's vision and how they'd mounted a rescue.

The warden looked over the scattered members of Tol's little host. "Footmen? You entered the forest with two hundred footmen?"

"One hundred," Tol corrected. "Half remained behind to guard the encampment."

Egrin shook his head, but put aside his astonishment to stare at the man Tol had captured. On learning the fellow's identity, the warden was amazed anew. "The chief of the Dom-shu!"

"I am," said Makaralonga proudly. "I yielded to this warrior on the promise of my life." He grimaced, clutching his shoulder where Tol's sword had cut deeply. "You raise bold fighters in your country, horse-rider."

"So it seems," Egrin said, staring at his shilder. He was torn. He didn't know whether to upbraid Tol for disobeying orders and entering the forest, or praise him for his astounding success. In the end, he simply ordered him to secure Makaralonga inside the bulwark, then had horns blown to recall his vengeful warriors from their pursuit of the fleeing tribesmen.

At the crest of the knoll, they found Lord Odovar. The foolhardy, courageous marshal had been laid beneath a broad elm tree, arms crossed reverently on his chest. His armor was deeply scarred, and he bore many terrible wounds.

"He died fighting like a bull," said a nearby warrior, badly wounded himself in an earlier fight. "The savages tried four times to capture him, wading out with nooses and nets, but hip-deep in water, Lord Odovar slew so many they drew back and rained arrows on him until they killed him."

The hardened warrior put his head down and wept, and Tol grieved for the loss as well. So much had happened to him since that day in the onion field when he'd first met Lord Odovar. After the terrible head wound he'd received from Grane, the marshal had grown into a harsh and impatient man, yet he represented Tol's first taste of a wider world, the world beyond the narrow confines of farm and family. Staring down at the still form, Tol silently thanked Odovar of Juramona for giving him the chance to make a better life for himself.

"A good death!" Makaralonga declared. "I would wish for the same."

Tol blinked away his tears and looked up at the brawny chief. "Yet you surrendered. Why?" he asked.

The chief of the Dom-shu tribe, favoring his wounded shoulder, sat down heavily on a slab of sandstone.

"I could see you are a great warrior. There is no shame being beaten by a man like you."

Later, when Makaralonga saw Tol scrubbed clean, the chief was surprised at his conqueror's obvious youth, but showed no shame at having been captured by one so young. In fact, the knowledge only made him prouder.

"This one will be known to the gods some day," Makaralonga declared. "And when they speak his name, they will say, 'His first victory was over Makaralonga of the Dom-shu.'"

C h a p t e r   1 0

Hostage of Victory

E grin and Pagas led the survivors of the Panther and Eagle hordes out of the Great Green. Collecting their people and baggage from Zivilyn's Carpet, they rode back to Caergoth to report the death of Lord Odovar, their sighting of the traitor Morthur Dermount, and not least of all, their repulse by the surprisingly well-armed and well-led forest tribes.

The news they brought was not unexpected—nor warmly received. Elsewhere, too, the war was not going as Prince Amaltar and his advisers had anticipated. Wanthred, leading the Firebrands alongside the Corij Rangers, had been attacked on three sides at once. His men had to resort to setting part of the woods ablaze in order to stage a fighting withdrawal under cover of the flames. The pillar of smoke from the conflagration could be seen all the way back to Caergoth.

Further south, two hordes under the dashing Lord Tremond had fared better. They penetrated deeply into the wilderness, sacking a dozen small settlements and taking hundreds of prisoners. In the shadow of his success, blame for Odovar's and Wanthred's failures was laid squarely at the feet of those two commanders.

Tol was present when Egrin disputed this injustice before the prince. Lord Urakan, the general of all the armies of the empire, angrily dismissed Egrin's explanations. Urakan, looking nearly as regal as the prince himself in the burgundy velvet robes he favored, berated the accomplished warrior as if Egrin were a blundering neophyte, using abusive language Tol had never heard before. Behind the enraged Urakan, Crown Prince Amaltar slouched silently on his high-backed throne.

When Egrin tried to point out the hidden dangers of the Great Green, Lord Urakan cut him off.

"You failed, that's all that matters!" Urakan stormed, black brows drawn down in a ferocious scowl. "Odovar let the foresters hoodwink him into an obvious trap, and you failed to extricate him!"

"My lord. Your Highness," Egrin said to the general and the prince, "it is true Lord Odovar did not take adequate precautions against ambush. He was a loyal and formidable warrior, but not a skilled tactician. However, it was because of one of Lord Odovar's chosen men that we were able to fight our way back with valuable information and captives."

With a bow to the prince, Urakan said dismissively, "A shield-bearer claims to have seen Lord Morthur Dermount in the forest. The prisoners Warden Egrin brought out of the forest, Highness, are hardly compensation for the shame of our losses!"

Egrin did something unprecedented; he bypassed Urakan, his superior, and spoke directly to the prince.

"Your Highness, our two captives are of considerable importance. One is the chief of a major tribe in the northern forest. The other is—well, he may have dynastic importance."

"How dare you!" Urakan's face went purple with rage at being disregarded. His hand reached for the hilt of his sword, but he was wearing no weapon in the presence of the prince. He declared, "I will have satisfaction for this insult!"

"You'll have no such thing," Prince Amaltar said, sounding bored. He gestured for the burly general to stand aside. "Warden, bring the prisoners to me, and I will judge for myself."

"They await Your Highness's pleasure," Egrin said, bowing. He snapped his fingers, and the two captives were hustled in.

Makaralonga hobbled forward, weighted down with heavy

chains on his wrists and ankles. Despite his disheveled appearance—his garments muddy and bloody—his expressive face and noble bearing were still impressive.

Slightly behind the forester chief was a second prisoner, likewise shackled, but with his head and shoulders covered by a canvas hood. Two guards guided the hooded captive, while a second pair kept an eye on Makaralonga.

The chief stopped beside Egrin. He openly gawked at the elaborate tent and richly dressed folk around him. When he spied Tol in the crowd, he bowed his head gravely to the young man. He did not bow to Prince Amaltar, much to Lord Urakan's anger.

"Are you the chief of the grasslanders?" Makaralonga asked.

Amaltar smiled thinly. "I am his first-born son."

"Ah! As the chief of the Dom-shu, I will treat only with the chief of your people."

"Impertinence!" Urakan fumed. "By the gods, your head will decorate a pole above this tent before nightfall!"

Prince Amaltar, accustomed to the quick temper of his general, ignored him, and said to Makaralonga, "I regret my father, the emperor, cannot be here to deal with you, Chief. In his place he has sent me."

Makaralonga acknowledged this with a shrug. Tired of standing in his heavy chains, he gathered the links in his hands and sat down on the thick carpet.

Chamberlain Valdid gasped at the forester's liberty. Before he or Lord Urakan could object, Amaltar gestured to the second prisoner.

"You said this man's capture had dynastic importance, Warden. Let's see his face."

"As you wish, Highness. But he is not a man."

The hood was whisked off, revealing the Silvanesti warrior captured in the glade sacred to Reorx. Dazzled by sudden daylight, the elf blinked and squinted. His blond hair was lank and unwashed, his face smudged with dirt, yet his bearing was one of haughty disdain.

A loud murmur rose from the crowd behind Tol. Lord Urakan was stricken speechless by the sight of the Silvanesti.

"What does this mean, Warden?" demanded Amaltar, shaken at last out of his habitual calm.

"This elf, Kirstalothan by name, was taken in arms at a place called the Isaren Glade, near where Lord Odovar and I were ambushed. He was found in company with Grane, who evaded capture. In the glade was a shrine dedicated to Reorx, and these 'offerings.'"

At Egrin's signal, Tol and Narren approached, carrying two sacks. These they dumped on the carpet at the prince's feet. Bronze arrowheads, spear points, and blades clattered out.

Amaltar asked to see one of the objects more closely. Valdid picked up a spearhead and handed it to the prince. Amaltar examined it closely.

"Chamberlain," he said, "we had reports of foresters using metal, didn't we?"

Valdid bowed to his lord. "Yes, Highness. Bronze arrowheads and the like were sent to us by several commanders, from all parts of the forest."

The prince lifted a hand. "Send for Harpathanas Ambrodel, envoy of the Speaker of the Stars," he commanded.

Valdid dispatched two heralds to the task. Prince Amaltar descended from the dais, tapping the spearpoint against his palm. He stood nose to nose with the elf warrior.

"You've been trading weapons to the forest tribes, yes?" he said, dark eyes narrowed. When the elf did not answer, the prince shouted, "Haven't you?"

Kirstalothan averted his face and said nothing.

"What part did Morthur Dermount, alias Spannuth Grane, have in this plot?" Still the stubborn elf would not reply.

Amaltar stepped back. "Take him away and make him talk. I must know all about this!"

Hood replaced, the hapless Silvanesti was dragged out. No sooner had he departed than Valdid's heralds returned. They held a hasty whispered conference with the chamberlain. Valdid's face reddened.

"Let me guess," Prince Amaltar said, anger in every syllable. "Harpathanas is no longer in camp?"

Valdid sputtered, "His tent is still pitched alongside yours, Highness, but no one is within! My heralds report that none of the Silvanesti has been seen since yester eve."

Amaltar hurled the spear tip to the floor. "Is there no end to the treachery of elves?" he cried. "I see now why the Speaker's envoy made so many perilous trips through the Great Green to visit us—he was distributing arms each time!"

"So it would seem, Highness," said Egrin. "I'll wager they hired Morthur Dermount to obscure their deeds with his magic."

Amaltar went to the warden and took him by the shoulders. "You've done well, Egrin. By your service, you've opened our eyes to a deep and dangerous plot."

"I thank you, Your Highness, but the honor of this service is not mine."

Egrin held out his hand to Tol, kneeling with Narren by the piles of bronze weaponry.

"This lad, my shield-bearer, led the men who captured Kirstalothan and brought back the evidence of Silvanesti perfidy," the warden said. "He also defeated the chief of the Domshu in single combat and made him Your Highness's prisoner."

Amaltar regarded Tol with unconcealed surprise, ordering him to stand. Although the shilder was little more than half the prince's age, the two were of a height. Amaltar studied him for a moment, then said, "You shall be rewarded."

"Thank you, Your Highness," Tol said nervously. "But I was just one of a larger band of willing warriors. My deeds were no greater than theirs."

Egrin described Tol's rescue of the two beleaguered hordes with a hundred footmen.

Amaltar openly stared. "Who are you, boy? From which line do you descend?"

"No line, Your Highness. My father is a farmer, as was his father, and all the fathers before him."

The crowd of nobles, courtiers, and foreigners whispered amongst themselves, making much of Tol's humble origin. As their titters and ugly comments came to his ears—"peasant upstart" being the kindest of the lot—his embarrassment vanished. He straightened his back and glared at the gaudily dressed idlers around him.

Prince Amaltar returned to his throne. He held up a hand for silence.

"You have served the empire well, Master Tol, and the empire does not forget. Three days hence, I shall confer on you the rank of Rider of the Horde, with an award of five hundred gold crowns."

Turning to Valdid, the prince said, "Let it be written in the chronicle that Tol of Juramona was raised this day to the rank of warrior, with all mention due that honorable position. Draw five hundred crowns from my personal cache to give to him."

"Yes, Highness," said Valdid as the scribes busily took down the prince's edict.

The audience was over. Tol stood dazed. The bronze weapons were cleared away for shipment to Daltigoth, where Prince Amaltar would place them and the story of their origin before the emperor. It could mean war with Silvanost. At the very least, it meant a temporary halt to the campaign in the forest. Faced with such a well-armed force, a radically different strategy was required.

Guards lifted Makaralonga to his feet. Hearing the chief's chains clank, Tol's attention snapped back to the here and now.

"Your Highness!" he said with newfound boldness. "What will become of the chief?"

Lord Urakan frowned at the shilder's presumption and said, "He will lose his head! That's the fate of all those who lead wars against the empire!"

"Must it be so, my lord? Chief Makaralonga is an honorable foe. He surrendered to me because I promised to spare his life."

"His life belongs to the empire," Urakan snapped.

Prince Amaltar sighed deeply. A liveried lackey placed a golden goblet of wine at his side.

"I'm afraid my imperial father will insist on his death," he said, sipping wine. "It is the law of the realm."

"Then, Highness"—Tol stepped up to the foot of the dais—"as part of my reward, may I be his executioner?"

The tumult around Tol died. Everyone from Egrin to Valdid betrayed open surprise.

The prince's black brows rose. "Strange request," he said. "Why do you want to do it?"

"I captured him, Highness. If he must die, let it be by my hand, with the same sword I used to defeat him."

Silence reigned in the assembly. At last, the prince smiled and waved a hand at Chamberlain Valdid.

"Put that in the scrolls too," Amaltar said. "I give the task of executing the captured Dom-shu chief to Master Tol, in token of his service to the empire."

And so it was that six days later Tol found himself standing alone before the fighting men of Juramona, dressed in new leather armor and a brilliant white mantle. The three hordes—Firebrands, Panthers, and Eagles—and the shilder company, the Rooks, were drawn up on a hillside outside the imperial camp at Caergoth. They were awaiting the arrival of Crown Prince Amaltar. A south wind blew, piling clouds into gray pinnacles, promising much rain. Tol wore his empty saber scabbard, and an equally empty sheath for his war dagger. Even here, in the open air, the crown prince would allow no weapons near his person.

An honor guard two hundred strong thundered out of the camp. All rode white horses with bright crimson trappings. In their wake came more than a hundred mounted courtiers in their finery of velvet and silk, polished leather and thick brocade. Behind the courtiers were eight richly bedecked young women, each in her own chariot drawn by a pair of horses. The open, two-wheeled carts, the preferred mode of travel in the capital, were ill-suited to rough ground, and the women clung to their drivers as they bounced along. The eight women were Amaltar's wives—polygamy was another custom reserved to persons of the highest rank.

The honor guard split into two sections, drawing up on each side of Tol. Courtiers formed a living avenue for the imperial party, and the chariots bearing Amaltar's wives rattled down the line. They drove past Tol, pivoted, and stopped on the slope between him and his comrades.

At last, with the stately deliberation acquired by long practice, Prince Amaltar cantered up on his black horse. He rode well, and looked at ease in the saddle. That, like the crown of Ergoth, was his birthright. His ancestors, back to the great and terrible Ackal Ergot, had lived and died on horseback. In the words of the poet, the first conquest an Ergothian warrior had to make was "the kingdom of the saddle."

Amaltar reined up. His personal entourage, including Lord Urakan and Chamberlain Valdid, fell into place behind him. All looked solemn and serious, save for Urakan. His beetling black brows met over his nose in a deep scowl aimed directly at Tol. The youth realized that although he might have won the gratitude of the prince, his deeds had annoyed the noble general in some unfathomable way.

"Tol of Juramona!" Valdid's voice rang out over the whipping wind. "Advance to your sovereign lord, His Royal Highness Amaltar Ackal of Ergoth!"

Tol stepped forward smartly, striking his heels together as Egrin had taught him.

"Kneel," Valdid told him. Tol did so, and the chamberlain intoned the ritual questions: "Are you a free-born man, bound to no other lord or state? Do you swear allegiance to the House of Ackal in the person of His Imperial Majesty Pakin III and his son, Prince Amaltar?"

Tol recited the answers he'd learned from Egrin. "I am a free-born man. I renounce all loyalties to any lord but His Majesty Pakin III, and his duly anointed heir, Prince Amaltar."

"Arise, Tol of Juramona!"

Tol stood. The prince held out an empty brass scabbard, chased with the red ribbons signifying the House of Ackal. "My eye is on you, Master Tol," Amaltar said, placing the scabbard across Tol's upraised palms.

"I shall strive to prove worthy, Your Highness." Tol hung the new scabbard from his baldric.

That should have concluded the ceremony, but Amaltar broke tradition. He drew his own dagger and presented it hilt-first to Tol.

"A personal token of my gratitude," he said in a low, friendly tone.

Breathless with surprise, Tol took the weapon. It was magnificent—a chilled iron blade filigreed with gold, set in a cross-shaped hilt of burnished brass with a ruby adorning each tip. The handle was wrapped in silver wire. The pommel was a golden dragon's claw grasping another ruby the size of a hen's egg.

Courtiers and imperial wives strained to see what had passed from the prince's hand to Tol. More disciplined, the honor guard and the Juramona hordes kept their faces front, but their eyes were full of curiosity.

Prince Amaltar turned his horse and trotted away, his entourage trailing behind him in strict order of precedence. The last man in the party was Amaltar's valet, who gave Tol two heavy suede bags. Tol grunted under the weight of five hundred crowns.

The imposing array of chariots, horsemen, and soldiers departed in a swirl of hooves and flashing jewels. Once they were gone, a roar rose behind Tol. Grinning, he turned to see Narren leading the footmen in a hearty cheer of approval. They broke ranks and engulfed him, shouting, shaking him, and pummeling his back with painfully vigorous enthusiasm.

Tol pressed the bags of gold on Narren. "A crown to every footman in the guard," he shouted in his friend's ear. "And don't forget Crake and Felryn!"

Word of this generosity spread through the crowd like oil

on a fire. The cheers became louder, and two stout soldiers hoisted Tol on their shoulders. They paraded him around in a circle until Egrin and the mounted commanders broke up the celebration.

"Well done, lad," said Wanthred. "A coup worthy of my own youth!"

Pagas, laconic as always, contented himself with clasping Tol's arm and nodding his approval.

"We owe our lives to you twice over, Tol," Egrin said. His remark plainly puzzled the youth, and he added, "If you hadn't come to rescue us, we might all have been slaughtered. And if you hadn't captured the elf and the forester chief, we would have been disgraced before the whole of the empire."

Egrin added, "And now we've been ordered home."

Pagas and Wanthred were surprised, so much so that Pagas broke his silence and piped, "By whose command?"

"The new marshal of the Eastern Hundred. By Prince Amaltar's order, subject to the emperor's approval, our new marshal is Enkian Tumult, lord of the house of Mordirin."

The name meant nothing to Tol, but Pagas's and Wanthred's faces hardened with concern. Wanthred fell to stroking his silver beard, which he did only when deeply troubled.

❧ ❧ ❧ ❧ ❧

There was much celebrating in the Juramona camp that night. Tol's elevation and his sharing of the crown prince's bounty did much to lift the spirits of the men demoralized by their losses in the forest.

The only group not happy were Tol's own comrades, the shilder. Because they had elected to obey orders and stay behind at Zivilyn's Carpet, they had done no fighting and so shared none of the glory. The success of the lowly foot soldiers who had accompanied Tol added further gall to their cup. Tol's rival Relfas was bitterest of all.

Tol did not revel late into the night with the rest. He slipped away from the bonfire where the footmen were drinking and singing. His mind was not on the celebration but on the unpleasant task he faced at sunrise—the execution of Chief Makaralonga.

He walked slowly through the darkened periphery of the camp, deep in thought. Whatever happened, he was determined to spare Makaralonga's life. Since the brutal death of Vakka Zan years ago, he'd had a horror of executions. Moreover, he'd given his word to Makaralonga that the chief would be spared if he surrendered. Imperial law or not, Tol intended to keep his word, but he couldn't simply let the tribesman go. Lord Urakan was expecting Makaralonga's head, and if it wasn't forthcoming, Tol's own head could easily take its place on the roof of the Imperial Palace.

"Your thoughts are loud."

Tol flinched. Deep in the shadows stood Felryn, leaning against a wagon. The healer added, "You're pondering how to spare the life of the forester."

"So you divine thoughts, too?"

Felryn shook his head. "No. It has been plain on your face since supper."

They walked together outside the ring of wagons. Tol poured his feelings into the healer's sympathetic ear, finishing with a plea for help in saving the chief.

"Why ask me? Egrin is your mentor, is he not?"

Tol drew in a breath and let it out slowly. "Egrin is a good man," he said carefully, "but he will not go against the law. I saw Lord Odovar use Egrin's sense of duty against him when he forced him to execute Vakka Zan. He can't help me. But perhaps you can."

Felryn smiled, acknowledging the wisdom of Tol's reasoning and thinking to himself how much the callow farm boy had matured. He extended a hand. He did not clasp forearms, warrior-fashion, but took Tol's hand in his own large one and shook it, as one priest to another.

"I will help you," he agreed.

* * * * *

The morning brought a sky leaden with thick coils of black, rain-heavy clouds. A warm wind rushed through the camp, upsetting carefully stacked spears, rattling the tents, and awakening every man. Close on the heels of the wind came the first drops of rain. In moments the sprinkle was a deluge. The lashing torrent soaked through the oiled canvas panels of the tents, droplets falling in a steady indoor shower. In these miserable conditions, the Juramona hordes struck camp.

Tol and Felryn rode to meet the warden. Between their horses Makaralonga trudged, his hands tied. A thick halter wound around his neck, the end of the rope held in Tol's hand.

Tol saluted with Prince Amaltar's dagger. "I am prepared to carry out the imperial order," he said, having to spit water and blink rapidly against the pouring rain.

"Why are you here, Felryn?" Egrin asked.

The healer indicated a large pot he had balanced on the pommel of his saddle. "Lord Urakan wants the chief's head sent to Daltigoth," he said. "This pot contains salt and medicinal oils. I'm to insure the head survives the trip to the capital."

"We'll do him in by the Wilder Green," Tol said. In answer to Egrin's inquiring look, he added, "The chief must die, but it doesn't have to be here, a spectacle for all to see. The Green is a fitting place of execution for a forest chief."

Egrin, his thoughts impossible to read, nodded. The Wilder was a small woodland several leagues east which bordered the river of the same name.

Tol and Felryn rode eastward, drenched all the way by rain. When the trees of the Wilder Green came into sight, Makaralonga broke his silence at last.

Lifting his bound hands toward the dark sky and continuing rain, the chief exclaimed, "Chislev herself weeps for your treachery! I knew a grasslander would never keep his word! So be it! When my blood flows, it will be a curse on you, Tol of Juramona. My curse on your faithless head!"

They ignored him, and he tried to plant his feet. However, Smoke continued to move ahead and Makaralonga was jerked forward. He had to content himself with raging at them as they rode stolidly onward through the rain. Once, he tripped, and Tol let go of the rope lest the chief be strangled. Immediately, Makaralonga jumped up, ready to run.

Tol drew the new saber Egrin had given him in a private ceremony. "Can you outrun a horse?"

Makaralonga's broad chest heaved as he panted with the force of his anger. He abandoned his attempt to flee, but glared as Tol recovered the halter. Abruptly, his frustration and fury shifted to Felryn and the vessel he carried.

"My head will not fit in that cabbage pot!" he snapped.

"Probably not," Felryn replied, "but after a few weeks in the salt, it'll shrink down very nicely."

A dozen paces from the edge of the forest, Tol stopped. He dismounted, never letting go of the rope around Makaralonga's neck. Felryn likewise got down, clutching the clay pot close to his chest.

"Kneel," Tol said to the chief.

"I won't! I am a free man! Kill me on my feet!"

So saying, Makaralonga bolted. Tol put out a foot and tripped him. He sprawled in the dripping grass.

Tol put the sharp edge of his sword under the chief's chin. "Stay still, or this will hurt!" he said severely.

Makaralonga closed his eyes. He felt a slight tug, then the blade came away from his throat. Stiffening, he awaited the return swing, the rending of his flesh, and the outpour of his life's blood on the sodden ground.

"Get up," said Tol. "You're free."

The chief's eyes flew open. It was true. The halter had been cut from his neck, and Tol sliced through his bonds with a single stroke of the jeweled dagger.

"What trickery is this?" Makaralonga demanded.

"I never intended to kill you. I asked Prince Amaltar for the task so I might free you instead."

Makaralonga looked from Tol to Felryn and back again, too astonished to take in what he was hearing.

Tol sheathed his dagger. Felryn put the clay pot down and

removed its lid. The pungent smell of spices erupted, reaching their noses in spite of the continuing drizzle.

Felryn pulled on a leather gauntlet, then stuck his hand into the pot. He lifted the heavy object inside. Golden oil streamed down the face of a dead man.

"By the Blue Phoenix! It's my head!" Makaralonga exclaimed, staggering back in shocked disbelief.

From braided locks to yellow beard to broad nose, the severed head looked exactly like the chief. Felryn returned it carefully to the pot and replaced the lid.

"How is it possible?" Makaralonga asked.

"Our masters in Daltigoth expect a trophy. We could not disappoint them," Tol said. "Felryn used his magical skills to alter the appearance of another man—a victim of war."

"His suffering was already over, and now, so is yours," said Felryn.

He clapped the chief on the shoulder and hauled himself onto the broad back of his horse. Makaralonga threw his arms around Tol and hugged him fiercely.

"Forgive me, noble foe! I thought you would kill me to please your masters!"

Tol struggled to breathe in the ardent embrace, his face crushed against the larger man's chest. "All right, all right! I always meant to keep my word!"

Zivilyn's Carpet, and the edge of the Great Green, lay another six or seven leagues east. Makaralonga would have to tread carefully to evade capture and reach his forest kingdom safely. Capture would mean death not only for him but for Tol as well, if his failure to behead the chief became known.

Makaralonga looked down at Tol, the rain running down his face.

"Henceforth, you are my son!" he declared. "I will make peace with your people, for your sake!"

Tol hadn't expected this. "Very well," he said. "Send some of your people to Juramona, and we'll make a pact of peace. Don't come yourself! Remember, you're supposed to be dead."

Makaralonga's face split wide in a grin. "I shall be the best of corpses, brave son Tol! You shall know me as *Voyarunta*—'Uncle Corpse'!"

He sprinted to the trees. Before plunging in, he turned and waved at his deliverers. Tol raised a hand in farewell, and Makaralonga vanished into the woods.

"Do you think he'll keep his promise?" asked Felryn as they rode away.

"A man like him lives by his word," Tol said.

❦ ❦ ❦ ❦ ❦

Chief Makaralonga was indeed as good as his word. Before summer was out, a party of eleven tribesmen made the long trek from the Great Green to Juramona. They evaded Ergothian patrols up to the very gates of the town, and there asked to see "the mighty lord Tol."

Egrin and a guard of twenty horsemen, including Tol, came out to meet the delegation. The Dom-shu were impressive folk, each strongly built and at least a head taller than the "grasslanders" who greeted them. They wore close-fitting tunics of pale buckskin and boarskin trews, embellished with beads and shells. They carried knives and bows, but on drawing near to Juramona had unstrung their weapons to show their peaceful intent.

Most striking of all were the leaders of the party, two women. One was a strapping blonde with waist-length hair. The other was an equally towering creature with bobbed brown locks.

"We are Dom-shu. We come in peace from our chief, Voyarunta," said the blonde woman.

From his place in the ranks, Tol grinned. Makaralonga had remembered to use his new name, the one with the double meaning.

She continued. "I am Kiya, eldest born of the chief, and this is my sister, Miya. We have come to make peace between the Dom-shu and the grasslanders of Juramona."

Egrin rubbed his bearded jaw in puzzlement. He was quite in the dark.

"I will take you to Lord Enkian, marshal of the Eastern Hundred," Egrin said. "He commands here."

"What of the great lord Tol?" said the brunette giantess, Miya.

All eyes in the mounted guard turned toward Tol, and Egrin pointed him out.

"Greetings, husband!" Kiya exclaimed. "We are your new wives!"

There was perfect silence for the length of four heartbeats, then all the Ergothians (save the red-faced Tol) burst out laughing. The Dom-shu did not understand what amused the grasslanders so, but they were good-natured enough to join in the merriment.

Tol urged Smoke forward, halting him in front of the two female foresters. He decided not to dismount. The sight of them towering over him would only provoke more laughter.

"I asked for no wives," he said sternly, when the hilarity subsided.

"It is the wish of our father, Chief Voyarunta," said Miya. Her dark hair was cut shorter than Tol's own, but her brown eyes were softer and her face more round than her sister's.

"We were told the great lords of the grasslanders keep more than one wife," Kiya added. "Is this not so?"

"Yes, but—"

"It would be a grave insult to the Dom-shu to refuse us," warned Miya.

Egrin came to the flustered youth's rescue. "The great lord Tol is overwhelmed by your chief's offer," he said. "Give him time to adjust to the magnitude of his good fortune. In the meantime, please be our honored guests in Juramona."

The Dom-shu strode into town between two lines of riders. Their appearance drew crowds along the route to the High House. Solitary wanderers and traders were common in Juramona, but fierce tribesmen from the Great Green had never been seen here before.

Bringing up the rear of the little column, Egrin and Tol went over the situation in hushed tones.

"Don't be hasty," Egrin said. "If it brings peace to the frontier, accepting the Dom-shu's offer seems a small price to pay." He smiled. "Besides, what's wrong with having a wife?"

Tol's voice rose. "*Two* wives? I don't want to get married!"

"Nonsense. It's time you settled down with a wife . . . or two," said Egrin, chuckling. More seriously, he added, "I was married when I was your age."

Tol was so surprised he reined up. The warden never spoke about his past, and Tol had never dared question the older man.

"Really?" the boy said. "Where is she now?"

Egrin's face was solemn. "Her soul went to the gods many years ago. That is past. What will you say to Marshal Enkian?"

Tol watched the last of the Dom-shu disappear around the curve of the street leading up to the marshal's residence. He gave a helpless shrug. "What *can* I say?"

❦ ❦ ❦ ❦ ❦

Enkian Tumult, Lord Mordirin, was descended from Mordirin Ackal, fifth emperor of Ergoth. That unfortunate autocrat had been dethroned by his wife, Empress Kanira, and imprisoned in the Imperial Palace for the rest of his days. The children of Mordirin Ackal were proscribed for a century. When civil war broke out between the Ackals and Pakins, the ruling clan needed all the allies of royal lineage they could muster, and so readmitted the Mordirins to the imperial fold. The Mordirin line no longer had any claim to the throne, but constituted a powerful and wealthy clan in their own right.

Enkian was the physical and temperamental opposite of the late marshal. Where Odovar had been hearty, impetuous, and harsh, Enkian was cool, calculating, and ascetic. Burly Odovar would have made two of Enkian, who was tall but lean, and, like Prince Amaltar, pale skinned and dark of hair and eye.

Enkian had the high forehead and sharp features of the Ackals, and an equally sharp and calculating mind. According to the wags in Juramona, Odovar had been twice the warrior Enkian was, but only half the ruler.

Enkian did not laugh when Tol's so-called wives were presented. He thanked them sincerely and promised to hold a lengthy parlay on the subject of peace. Reassured, the Domshu allowed themselves to be ushered into another room, where their presence was celebrated with beer and many haunches of venison.

Alone with their liege, Egrin and Tol stiffly awaited the verdict on the Dom-shu. The marshal sat in a characteristic pose, fingers folded together under his chin as he considered the matter.

"The women will stay," he said at last. When Tol looked distressed, he added, "Not as your wives, Master Tol. We'll keep them as hostages to the Dom-shu's future good behavior."

Egrin bowed. "Wisely chosen, my lord."

"You won't imprison them, will you, my lord?" asked Tol.

"That wouldn't be friendly, would it? No, they shall be guests of the Eastern Hundred, and provided suitable quarters. You shall live with them, Master Tol, and keep a close eye on them."

Again the youth looked alarmed. "What if they expect me to be a husband to them?"

"Carry a sword at all times," replied Enkian dryly. He did not smile at his own joke, but asked, "Can either of you fathom why the Dom-shu would choose this time to make peace? We invaded their land and executed their chief not two months past."

Egrin said, "Perhaps that's why, my lord. The foresters respect strength. Considering what's happened, maybe they understand the empire must be dealt with, not opposed."

He was referring to the severance of relations between Ergoth and Silvanost, which had come about once the elves' scheme to arm the forest tribes became known. Trade between the two nations had been cut off, and Silvanesti prestige had suffered a grave reverse among all the nations of the west.

Enkian sat back in his chair thoughtfully. "You may be right, warden," he said. "It seems the empire has much to thank you for, Master Tol. We must find a proper place for you in the ranks of the Great Horde. Have you considered what you would like to do?"

This very question had occupied Tol's thoughts fully in the weeks since his return to Juramona. He had discussed his future with everyone close to him—Egrin, Felryn, Crake, Narren, even Pagas and old Lord Wanthred. He could ask for assignment to any spot in Ergoth, to any horde in the emperor's service. Ambition required that he choose a position close to the seat of power in the capital, Daltigoth, or at least on a frontier where danger paved the road to fame. A picked band of warriors was hunting Morthur Dermount in the Great Green—joining them would put him squarely on the path to advancement in the empire.

He took a deep breath. "I wish to remain in Juramona, my lord. And"—he glanced sideways at Egrin—"I would like Durazen's old command."

Enkian was startled. "Why would you want command of the foot guards?"

"I learned in the forest a warrior's worth lies not in how he arrives at a battle, but how he fights once there. I believe foot soldiers can fight and win as surely as any horsemen, my lord, given the right training and leadership."

The new marshal shook his head. "You're a fool, boy. A lucky fool. What you did in the Great Green was a fluke, a chance favor granted by the capricious gods. It gave you an opportunity few men ever see—imperial notice, a crown prince's gratitude. Yet here you stand, throwing the opportunity away."

Enkian stood, plainly disgusted. "Elevation or no, you're still a peasant, not a true Rider of the Horde. Very well. Walk with your footmen, if you wish. I shan't stop you."

Hardly a gracious start to Tol's first command, but having gotten what he wanted, Tol was happy. He kept his pleasure hidden, not wishing to annoy the haughty marshal further.

He accompanied Enkian and Egrin to the Dom-shu banquet. There, he sat between Kiya and Miya, who ate prodigiously but drank little. After sundown, they followed him to the Householders' Hall. When he explained no women were allowed to pass the night inside, they squatted just outside the door, resting their heads on their knees. Tol hesitated, thinking he should try to locate better quarters for them. The blonde, Kiya, waved him away impatiently, so he left them there.

The next morning, that's where he found them, waiting for his return.

A Dangerous Man

Two horsemen, trailworn and dusty, cantered down the road. A group of men working on the south bank of the river saw the riders before they heard them. The noise from saws and the pile-driver drowned out all other sounds. The workers called a warning to their commander.

It was spring, the seventh year of the reign of Emperor Pakin III. Tol and the men of the Juramona Foot Guard were building a new bridge across Three Kender Creek. The old bridge, indifferently constructed by local folk, had been swept away by a winter torrent. It connected Juramona to the heartland of the empire, and Lord Enkian had charged Tol and his corps of foot soldiers with the important task of replacing the bridge.

Tol knew the job was not meant as an honor. True warriors—those who rode in an imperial horde—were above common labor. Still, Tol took the task cheerfully, so cheerfully in fact Lord Enkian wondered if there was some hidden advantage in the job his calculating mind had missed. Tol explained that two years of peace had left his men little to do but chase cut-purses and fight the occasional house fire in town. Rebuilding a bridge would strengthen their backs and toughen their hides.

The answer was as honest and straightforward as Tol himself, and the calculating Enkian could not believe it. He sent a personal spy, Tol's old shilder comrade Relfas, to keep an eye on things.

Tol had hired a builder, a dwarf by the name of Tombuld, to lay out the new bridge and oversee construction. Tombuld had erected much larger structures across high valleys in the Khalkist Mountains, so a single span across Three Kender Creek didn't present much of a challenge. His design called for a simple cantilever bridge, supported on each end by stout stone piers. Tol and his men had been at work for six days when the pair of unknown riders appeared.

Tol climbed out of the creekbed. Shading his eyes against the morning sun, he watched the horsemen approach.

In the two years since he'd rescued the Juramona hordes in the Great Green, Tol had grown stronger without gaining very much in height or girth. As a youth, his physique had been intimidating. As a man, it was deceptive. Of only modest height, all his power was in his shoulders and legs. He was agile rather than brutishly strong. Succumbing at last to masculine vanity, he'd grown a beard, though he kept it closely trimmed.

"Turn out the watch," he said, not raising his voice.

Sixteen sturdy soldiers left their work and divided a stand of arms between them. They fell into a double line on Tol's left. Drilled by Tol in his new ideas of fighting on foot, the men extended their spears in unison, presenting a formation both precise and dangerous. All they had to do was swing across the road and the way would be blocked by a hedge of spears.

The riders slowed, then stopped. Through the dust, Tol could see they wore complete coats of ring mail beneath sleeveless linen gambesons.

"You there," called the rider on Tol's right. "Is the way passable?"

"Yes. If you go carefully, you can cross," he answered. The new bridge rails were spanned by temporary planks. "Are you messengers from Caergoth?"

The horsemen were startled. "Yes, we are. How did you know?"

"Your armor is too extensive for our local hordes. That, and the fineness of your tack speaks of the city."

The rider grinned, pushing back his wide-brimmed iron hat to reveal a sunburned nose. "Sharp eyes! Are you a warrior?"

"I am a Rider of the Horde."

"Why do you work in your shirtsleeves, like a common drudge? Are you being punished?"

Tol shrugged. "The bridge needed rebuilding. My men needed to sweat."

"You provincials have strange ways!" commented the sunburned fellow. He patted the leather case around his neck. "We have dispatches for the marshal of the Eastern Hundred."

"You'll find him in the High House in Juramona."

Tol called for water to be brought for the messengers and their horses. He introduced himself, and again the men looked surprised.

"Your name is known to us! You slew the chief of all the forest tribes in single combat!" said the message-bearer with the sunburned face.

Tol only smiled, for the tale had grown in the telling.

Tombuld came bustling across the bridge planking, growling at the men for shirking. Tol waved the dwarf's objections aside, pointing to the imperial couriers.

"Well, send 'em on their way and get back to work!" Tombuld said, tugging on his long beard in frustration. "Bridges don't build themselves, you know!"

Watered, the horsemen went on their way, muttering between themselves about "impudent dwarf artisans." Fortunately, the crotchety Tombuld did not hear them.

Tol ordered everyone back to work. Down in the gully, he resumed toiling alongside his men, filling the stone pier with rubble and mortar.

"Why couriers? Is it war?" Narren asked him.

"I doubt it," Tol replied. "War would bring more than two messengers for Lord Enkian. Besides, no recent traveler on the road has mentioned war."

The only menaces Tol could think of were the elusive monster XimXim, still at large in Hylo though quiet for some time, and Spannuth Grane, who was presumed to have fled the Great Green for parts unknown.

Two years earlier, Lord Odovar had sent his seneschal, the priest Lanza, to report on XimXim's depredations against the kender. Lanza entered a cave above Hylo city and was never seen alive again. Later, some kender found his head, hands, and feet, all neatly severed and left in a tidy heap at the foot of the mountain. After all this time and many hundreds of deaths, there was still no one who could say just what XimXim looked like, or even what kind of creature he was. People heard him in flight or saw his distant silhouette against the clouds, but to go closer meant certain death.

A rumor had reached Juramona that a powerful sorcerer had quelled XimXim, but no one knew if it was true. After Odovar's death, Lord Enkian paid scant attention to the monster and did not bother to confirm the story.

As for Grane, imperial bounty hunters had scoured the Great Green for him, but never found so much as a hair. Some of the finest trackers in the empire had vied for the glory and gain to be had from collaring the renegade, but he had escaped them all, vanishing like a morning shadow at midday. No new plots or rebellions had surfaced, and many had begun to believe the high-born sorcerer dead. No, thought Tol, as the riders passed, the empire was almost sleepy with calm.

Tol's soldiers worked until twilight on the new bridge, then returned to their camp overlooking the creek. In his tent Tol found Kiya and Miya waiting for him. Kiya had made supper, and Miya was waiting to scrub the day's dirt off him. Although they were spouses in name only, Kiya and Miya took their responsibilities seriously. The Dom-shu women never left Tol's side, refusing to remain in Juramona when he was away.

"Strip, husband! A healthy man must be clean!" Miya said. She held up a boar-bristle brush that could scour verdigris off a copper kettle.

"I can wash myself!" he thundered. To Kiya, he said, for the hundredth time, "Let the camp cook prepare our food! It's his job!"

Long ago he'd learned quiet answers didn't impress the Dom-shu sisters. They respected him only when he was as forthright as they. Respect did not, however, translate into obedience.

"It isn't right for a stranger to cook for a woman's husband! Mates can cook for each other, but it isn't proper for strangers to do so!" Kiya replied, also for the hundredth time.

In truth, the three of them got along well together. They occupied a spacious timber frame house in Strawburn Lane, near the potters' kilns. Little more than a ruin when Lord Enkian gave it to them, the house had been filthy and infested with rats, but the Dom-shu women quickly set things right. Miya crawled under the house with a club and killed or evicted all the rats in a single morning, while Kiya fumigated the interior with burning sulfur, and scrubbed walls, ceiling, and floors till they shone. Confounding village preconceptions about tribal people, the sisters were scrupulously clean and kept the house that way, too. Woe to any visitor who walked in with manure on his heels! Regardless of rank, the miscreant was likely to find himself pitched headfirst into the street and barred from entry again until he cleaned his boots.

Rather than wives or hostages, it seemed to Tol that he'd acquired a pair of brawny, bossy sisters. Their first night in the new house, he'd been relieved (if a bit surprised) when the Dom-shu women prepared a bed for themselves by the fireplace—in a room away from him. They explained that he was not the lover they dreamed of, but they were content to do as their father ordered, and live with a great warrior and serve him. He didn't know whether to be relieved or insulted.

But Kiya proved to be a fine archer and an excellent hunter. Disdaining to buy meat from merchants in town, she ranged the pastures and woodlands around Juramona, taking rabbits, deer, and grouse. Unfortunately, she insisted on cooking what she caught. She could reduce a toothsome venison roast to a

163

blackened cinder seemingly in moments.

Unlike her woods-roving sister, Miya took quickly to town life. She visited the markets daily and became known as a fearsome haggler. Tol saw traders fold their stalls and flee, though the day was not yet half over, when Miya appeared in the market square. She reduced the dreaded silver merchant Cosen to tears by her persistent bargaining, obtaining a silver earring she wanted for much less than his asking price. She also became known as the only human in Juramona who could trade with kender and not end up picked clean.

Now, having fended off Miya's deadly brush, Tol was saved from indigestion when Relfas arrived at the tent. The young noble demanded to speak with him. The sisters shouted at Relfas to go away, but Tol accompanied him outside.

Relfas sported a full red beard and flowing mustache. His polished armor and faultlessly clean cape and boots stood in sharp contrast to Tol's humbler, sweat-stained attire. Relfas demanded details of the encounter with the imperial couriers. The story was quickly told, and the young noble frowned in thought.

"I wonder what they want?" he said. "Perhaps I should return to Juramona."

"Why don't you? All you're getting out here are blisters on your backside from watching us work." It was true, but Relfas reacted to the jibe with ill-concealed contempt.

Before Tol could reenter his tent, he witnessed the clattering arrival of a dozen riders from Juramona. Leading them was Egrin's chief lieutenant, Manzo. In the past two years, the premature graying of Manzo's hair and beard had become complete. His old man's coloring sat oddly on his still-young face, yet it also lent him an air of gravity.

"You are recalled," Manzo said to him. "I am to bring you to Lord Enkian at once."

"Is it war, then?"

Manzo shook his head. "Couriers came today with messages for the marshal, messages bearing the imperial seal. He read them, and sent me to fetch you and your men. Prisoners from the town dungeon will be sent to finish work on the bridge."

Tol began to ask more questions, and Manzo added brusquely, "Make haste! I was bidden to have you in the High House well before dawn."

Tol had two hundred men working on the bridge. Tired from a long day's work, they nonetheless shouldered their axes, mallets, and shovels, and formed for the march home. Without complaint, Kiya and Miya packed Tol's things and took their place in the marching order. Left behind were the civilians: Tombuld, two dozen expert craftsmen, and the blacksmith who was making nails. They would remain at the bridge and complete the project with the prisoners.

Tol's mind whirled in a riot of speculation as he marched home. Manzo offered him a horse, but he politely declined. As long as he was with his men, he went on foot, as they did.

❦ ❦ ❦ ❦ ❦

They reached Juramona after midnight. The Dom-shu sisters made for Strawburn Lane, while Tol wearily climbed the hill to the High House. Torches blazed in every sconce in the timber citadel. A caravan of wagons waited in the square, and servants dashed up and down the halls, carrying clothing and supplies to the wagons. Short of full-scale war, Tol could not imagine what crisis had provoked such feverish activity.

Lord Enkian, in full marshal's panoply, was in the audience hall. He had refined its furnishings, as he had done with the rest of the High House. The tapestry behind the marshal's dais was new and showed the empire's founder, Ackal Ergot, receiving a golden crown from the hand of the god Corij himself. To the usual banners hanging from the rafters had been added the crimson and black standard of the Mordirin line. Brocaded draperies covered most of the formerly bare, whitewashed walls. Numerous braziers on high tripods blazed, filling the hall with light.

When Tol entered, the marshal was snapping orders to

Egrin and his subordinates. He saw Tol and waved him forward.

"We're leaving in the morning," Enkian declared flatly. "I want one hundred of your best footmen to accompany the wagons as guards. You will lead them."

"Yes, my lord. Ah . . . sir?"

Enkian had turned away to give more orders to his seneschal, an elderly, crippled warrior called Zabanath. He turned back with an impatient growl.

"May I ask, where are we going, my lord?" Tol asked.

"This is an affair of state. We are going to Daltigoth." He lowered his voice, adding, "Your presence was specifically requested by Crown Prince Amaltar."

Tol was thunderstruck. Daltigoth, first city of the empire! As Caergoth was a city many times the size of Juramona, so Daltigoth was many times greater than Caergoth. He knew a few people who'd gone to the capital to seek their fortunes: His old friend Crake, for example, had departed more than a year ago after a dispute with a tavern patron left the other fellow dead. One step ahead of arrest, Crake had lit out for the city. Tol had received no word from him since, and he sorely missed the flutist's company.

Tol left the hurly-burly of the High House and assembled his tired men in the street outside the Householders' Hall. There was no need to pick the hundred best. They were all excellent—loyal, tough, and willing fighters—so he let them volunteer. When they learned the destination was Daltigoth, several demurred immediately.

"The city's full of wizards," said one soldier warily. "I hear they fly around the streets, casting spells on unwary folk!"

Another gave a disgusted snort, saying, "The emperor wouldn't allow that! I heard tell they got houses faced with pure gold, and towers of stone so high eagles nest in the rafters."

They wrangled about the supposed wonders of Daltigoth until Tol called for quiet. Those who wanted to go drew lots, and soon he had his hundred. Narren, he was pleased to note, was among those who made the cut.

The soldiers staying behind packed the supplies for the trip while those who were going fell into their beds to catch what little sleep they could before departure. When dawn finally broke, Tol was shaken awake not by one of the Dom-shu sisters, but by Egrin himself.

"Come, Tol," the warden said. "Walk with me."

In the next room, Kiya and Miya were stirring. An awful smell assailed Tol's nostrils, probably Kiya's breakfast. He pulled on a rough woolen cloak and followed Egrin outside. The warden led him around the corner of the house to a deserted alley, then turned suddenly and laid a scarred, strong hand on Tol's shoulder.

"I want you to be careful!" he admonished with unusual verve. "There are many dangers, many vices in Daltigoth for a young man. Swear to me you'll be careful!"

Tol smiled, scratching his bearded chin. "You said the very same to us before we entered the prince's camp in Caergoth two years ago. And I'm not a child, you know."

"It doesn't matter if you're twice as old as Zabanath! The temptations of an army camp—even an imperial one—are nothing compared to what you'll face in the capital. And you not only have to avoid them yourself, but lead your men away from them, too."

More curious than afraid, Tol asked, "What sort of temptations?"

Egrin looked away, obviously remembering some past adventure. "All the usual ones—drink and debauchery are there in mortal abundance. More subtle are the dangers from the young nobles of Daltigoth. They consider it vital to their reputation at court to fight duels and kill as many opponents as they can. Any excuse will do, so beware! And there are foreigners of every race, and thieves, footpads, procurers, cheats, liars, and killers for hire. Sorcerers abound, both licit and illicit, and they can ensnare the unwary in all sorts of dangerous schemes."

It all sounded very interesting to Tol, but the concern in his mentor's voice led him to say, "Aren't you going with us, Egrin?"

"No. Lord Enkian must make the journey, so I am appointed to govern the Eastern Hundred in his place."

That cast a damper on Tol's enthusiasm. Egrin was his second father. Not in seven years had he been separated from the warden by such distance.

"I will be on my guard," Tol said earnestly. "Besides, the giant sisters won't let me come to harm."

"You'll take them?" asked Egrin, not displeased.

"We're supposed to awe them with the might of the empire, aren't we? What better place for that than the capital?"

Despite the young man's assurances, Egrin fell into a melancholy mood. He knew no one came away from Daltigoth unchanged. The idea consumed him so thoroughly he could not bring himself to see the caravan off.

The sun had cleared the nearby hills and flooded the valley with golden light when Lord Enkian and an escort of two hundred horse rode out of Juramona. Behind them came the train of twenty-two wagons, guarded by the foot soldiers.

Tol marched his contingent through streets filled with well-wishers. His men were all commoners, well known to the ordinary inhabitants who turned out to see them on their way. Traders in the crowd were no doubt pleased to see Miya among the departing contingent. Along the way, Tol spotted healer Felryn and his disciples from the temple of Mishas, Lord Wanthred and his retainers, and many familiar faces of former shilder who had not become full-fledged Riders of the Horde. He felt a twinge of sadness at not seeing Egrin, however.

Outside the walls of Juramona, Enkian reined up, hearing, behind him, the crowd's cheers for the lowly foot soldiers. No such display had accompanied his departure. He did not care whether the peasants he governed approved of him, only that they obeyed as was proper, but their obvious affection for Tol still sparked a flame of jealousy in his cold heart. Lord Enkian's lean, dark face set in hard lines, and he spurred his mount to a brisker pace. It would be a long way to Daltigoth, especially for those on foot.

❦ ❦ ❦ ❦ ❦

The spring weather was fine as the marshal's caravan wended its way down the high road south to Caergoth. Red bud and dogwood trees bloomed in purple and white profusion, and goldenrod covered the hillsides in drifts of yellow.

When they reached Caergoth's stone walls, Tol's soldiers and the wagons remained outside while Enkian and his mounted escort spent the night within. The evening was unusually warm, and traders hurried out from the city to peddle luxuries to the soldiers. Miya snared a wine merchant and wrung a cask of pale Silvanesti wine from him at a bargain price. Tol had his first taste of "nectar," as the elves called it, and decided he should stick to beer. The expensive and potent drink went down with deceptive ease.

Gossiping with traders, he learned more about their precipitous trip to Daltigoth than Enkian had revealed. A guild of powerful sorcerers had long desired to erect a great tower in the capital. The tower (and the buildings surrounding it) would constitute a kind of school of magic, where wizards of various orders could gather in safety and discourse with their fellows on the practice of their art. Several construction attempts had failed due to the Ackal-Pakin wars, but the time had finally come to lay the cornerstone of the Tower of Sorcery in Daltigoth.

To maintain his prestige before the great assembly of wizards, the emperor had summoned his principal vassals to the capital to attend the ceremony. Pakin III was determined to stand at the head of an imposing array of nobles, each of whom had hordes of trained warriors backing him. The message to the magicians would be plain: Tower of Sorcery or no, true power resided in the hands of the emperor of Ergoth.

No one could refuse the emperor's call and keep his position. As head of one of the provinces farthest from the capital, the marshal of the Eastern Hundred had one of the longest journeys to make, but that made his timely presence all the more imperative.

That night, lying in the shadow of the wall of Caergoth, Tol gazed at the heavens, wondering what Daltigoth would be like. Kiya and Miya slept peacefully, one on either side of him, each in her own bedroll. So far they seemed neither excited nor anxious about the trip, taking every development in stride. On their arrival at Caergoth, the sisters spared the encircling walls and jutting towers a moment's look, then went back to arguing with a sutler over a length of soft doeskin they wanted for gloves. Tol tried to impress them by telling them Daltigoth was much larger than Caergoth.

Miya asked, "Is it as big as the Great Green?"

He had to admit it was not. The forest covered an expanse one-third the size of the whole empire. So the sisters had shrugged, Kiya saying, "Daltigoth is not so big, then."

Tol glanced at the sleeping women. He wished he could be so serene. His thoughts churned for the remainder of the night, spoiling his rest and making the next day's march a long and weary chore.

❧ ❧ ❧ ❧ ❧

Southwest of Caergoth, they reached the great imperial road, Ackal's Path. Unlike the dirt track from Juramona, this road was broad enough for three wagons to drive abreast. Slightly higher in the center than on the sides, it was paved with stones pounded into a bed of sand. The Path, begun under Ackal Ergot, had been completed almost a century later under Ackal III. It was a magnificent feat, but legend held that when it rained, the paving stones turned red from the blood of the thousands of prisoners who'd died building the road.

For two days the caravan from Juramona drove along, pushing through the thick commercial traffic streaming between the two greatest cities in the empire. Lord Enkian and his mounted escort rode straight down the center of the road, sending traders' carts into the ditches and trampling any on foot who were slow to get out of the way. Tol's blood boiled to see such high-handed treatment. He slowed his pace, allowing his foot guards and the supply wagons to fall farther behind the marshal's party. He didn't want to be identified with Enkian's brutal progress.

On the morning of their third day out from Caergoth—about halfway to the capital—Tol and his men broke camp, took to the road, and found it deserted. After the constant activity of the previous days, the silent emptiness was unsettling.

Tol scanned the sky and horizon. The terrain was open on both sides of the road—low rolling hills and widely spaced trees. A few hawks wheeled in the bright blue sky, but there was no sign at all of other travelers.

Even the stalwart Dom-shu sisters were unnerved. For the first time since leaving Juramona, Kiya strung her bow and hung a quiver of arrows on her back. Miya armed herself with a staff, which was as thick as her wrist and as long as she was tall.

Tol divided his men into two groups, placing half on the right shoulder of the road and half on the left. Between these marching columns the ox carts proceeded. Tol and the sisters walked alongside the lead wagon.

The sun rose higher. At last they came to the place where it seemed Enkian's troop had passed the night. They found hoofprints in the windblown sand on the north side of the road, fresh horse droppings, and trash left behind by the marshal's escort. Though this was reassuring, they still could not account for the continuing lack of other traffic.

Before noon, Miya spotted a man on horseback ahead. He was sitting motionless in the road, watching their approach. His head was bare, and he was draped in a long, dark cape. When he didn't move from their path, Tol held up his hand and halted the caravan. He arrayed a dozen soldiers in front of the caravan, telling them to stand fast with spears ready.

Tethered to the second supply wagon was a horse Egrin had thought to provide for Tol before their departure from Juramona. Tol mounted the animal and laid a spear on his shoulder. As he trotted toward the mysterious rider, the Dom-shu fell into place on either side, running swiftly on bare feet.

There was no point in telling them to stay with the wagons, so Tol simply rode on. Several paces from the stranger—well beyond sword reach—he reined up.

"Greetings," he said. "I am Tol of Juramona. We're on our way to Daltigoth. Will you give way, sir?"

The staring man said nothing. He was clean shaven, with short brown hair. Tol couldn't tell if he was armed. Everything below his neck was covered by his voluminous brown cape.

Tol repeated his request, and the man raised a hand clear of the folds of his garment. A large golden ring shone plainly on his gloved forefinger when he extended his fist toward Tol.

There was a clatter on Tol's left. Miya, her staff falling to the pavement, dropped like a stone. Kiya's arm went over her head to her quiver before she too collapsed.

Tol thumped his heels into his horse's flanks, but the poor beast shuddered and went down. Tol managed to slide off its rump so as not to be trapped beneath.

Sorcery! The man had put the sisters and his horse under some spell. But why wasn't he affected?

The stranger was obviously wondering the same thing. He clenched his hand into a fist again, and Tol thought he saw a flicker of blue light spark from the sapphire set in the golden ring. Yet, though he braced himself, still Tol felt nothing. A quick glance over his shoulder showed him the whole of his guard, the drovers on their wagons, and the oxen too, all lay inertly on the road. They'd been felled where they stood, all affected by the strange man's wizardry.

Gripping his spear, Tol charged the man. The fellow whipped his cloak back, revealing a mail shirt beneath, and drew a quite ordinary iron saber from his waist.

Tol caught the blade on the wide spearhead, whirled it in a small circle to disengage, then thrust at the rider's chest. The man's horse reared, flailing the air with its legs. Tol crouched low, wary of the heavy hooves.

Iron whistled past his ear, and Tol swung the butt of the spear in a wide arc. He caught his attacker in the ribs.

The fellow grunted under the blow, but his mail shirt protected him.

Tol fell back and assumed a spearman's ready position. For two years, he and his foot soldiers had trained, learning by trial and error the best methods of battling mounted foes. The two things a lone man on foot had to remember were *keep moving*—his two feet were nimbler than a horse's four—and *get into reach*. Tol had had his men's spearshafts lengthened by four spans. With spears that long they could reach the face of an enemy mounted on the tallest horse in the world.

When the rider showed reluctance to press his attack, Tol lifted his spear to shoulder height and ran at him, shouting. The man tried to fend off the spear with his sword, but the saber was too light to turn the big spear away. Tol rammed the spear tip into the man's chest. It snagged in his cloak and tore through, skidding off his armor. Although the point did not penetrate, the momentum of Tol's charge knocked the man off his horse. He fell heavily to the pavement.

In the blink of an eye, Tol had a knee on the fallen man's chest and a dagger at his throat.

"Yield!" he said, pressing the dagger's point slightly into the man's neck. It was the finely jeweled weapon given to him by Crown Prince Amaltar.

"Kill me, and your master will die an agonizing death!" rasped the man.

"Speak plainly, or die!" Tol declared. He dug the dagger in just below the man's chin. Blood welled around the keen point.

"The marshal of the Eastern Hundred is our captive!"

"You lie! He rode with two hundred Riders of the Horde!"

The man's eyes shifted toward the caravan. "How many lie insensible there?" Point well taken. "If I fail to return, your marshal and all his warriors will be slaughtered!" the man added.

Tol stood, dragging him to his feet. "You'd better pray no such thing happens," he said coldly. "If it does, your death will be an agonizing one!"

Dagger firmly against his captive's throat, Tol marched him along until they recovered the stranger's horse. Tol tied his hands, shoved him onto the horse, and mounted behind him.

"Take me to Lord Enkian," he said, pressing the dagger behind the man's right ear. Sullenly, his prisoner complied, guiding his horse off Ackal's Path. Tol looked over his shoulder at the Dom-shu sisters and his footmen, still slumbering, and prayed for their safety in his absence.

They rode north, into the hills. Progress was slow as Tol watched ahead, reading signs and tracks, always alert for ambush. Up a dry creek, the man pointed with his chin to a gap between two knolls.

"There. You'll find your people there."

Without another word, Tol used the heavy pommel of his dagger to knock the stranger senseless. Once the limp man fell to the ground, Tol traded the dagger for a saber. He wrapped the reins tightly around his left hand, took a deep breath, then thumped his heels on the horse's flanks. The animal sprang forward.

He rounded the curve of the dry streambed, sand flying from the horse's pounding hooves. A single sentinel perched atop a boulder tried to challenge him, but Tol cut the man's legs out from under him without slowing. He left the fellow bleeding to death on the rock and plunged on, taking another curve at full gallop.

He came upon four conical tents, a picket line with half a dozen horses, and a small campfire around which sat four men in leather brigantines. His arrival brought them to their feet in a hurry. Two, armed only with axes and small round bucklers, tried to stave him off while the other pair sprinted to their horses. Tol drove straight through them, making for the unguarded end of the picket line. He slashed it, shouting wildly to spook the horses. The animals broke and ran.

A strange sensation of heat played over Tol's head, like warmth from an unseen bonfire. Tol whirled and spied a new threat. Striding out of the largest tent was a man in full armor, his face covered by a weirdly grinning visored helmet.

Although years had passed since he'd last seen that horrible visage at his family's farm, it was all too familiar.

Spannuth Grane!

The armored man drew a very long, two-handed straight sword. Tol steered his horse toward him. Grane—if indeed it was he inside the familiar armor—held up his right fist. A massive ring gleamed on one mailed finger. Again Tol felt a fleeting kiss of heat on his face, but nothing more. However, all four of the fighting men he'd faced when he first entered the camp now lay insensible on the ground. Grane's first attempt to hex Tol had felled two; his second attempt downed the others.

Tol crouched low and leaned forward in the saddle, boring in on the armored man. With a flash of polished metal, the fellow brought his blade up, striking Tol's saber hard. Hand stinging, Tol kept his grip as his horse thundered by.

He made a second pass, and this time his sword skidded off iron shoulder plates. His foe did not cut at him, but with brutal efficiency stabbed the horse. The animal went down, shrieking, and pitched Tol to the ground. His head rang with the hard impact, and he lay stunned. Bronze sabatons crunched in the gravel, coming for him.

Get up, get up! Egrin's voice seemed to echo in Tol's head, shouting as he had when berating clumsy shilder. *Why are you lying there like a poleaxed pig? Your head's still attached, isn't it?*

Tol rolled away in time to dodge a killing stroke. He got to one knee, and discovered to his joy that he still held his saber. It was too light to take direct blows from his opponent's great blade, but it was better than fighting bare-handed.

"Spannuth Grane! I know you!" he yelled.

The sword halted in mid-swing. Calling his enemy by name had earned Tol a brief respite. "Who are you?" the man asked, voice muffled by the visor.

Tol stood up. "Tol of the Juramona City Guards."

"Guards? You mean the footmen?" Lord Morthur Dermount laughed in his helmet. "You fight well for a hireling!"

"Where is Lord Enkian?" Tol demanded.

"He will join you in death soon!" The sword came up again.

He attacked, raining heavy blows like a hammer breaking stone. Tol's knees quavered under the onslaught. He ducked a vicious sideswipe, saying desperately, "You're lost, my lord! Your powers have failed you!"

Morthur laughed loudly, but checked his swing. "What do you mean, meddling stableboy?"

"You tried to hex me in the Great Green, remember? I didn't collapse. Your hireling left every man and beast from Juramona sleeping in the road, everyone but me. Now you have felled your own men. Why not me?"

Morthur gave his words thought, but the respite was short-lived. Up came the terrible sword.

"I'll divine the answer from your bones!" he roared.

He forced Tol back with savage thrusts, scything his sword upward in terrific two-handed uppercuts. Their blades collided, and when the force of Morthur's attack shivered down his arms, Tol spun away under the impact. Thinking Tol was going down, Morthur stepped in, dropping his left hand as he prepared to bring his blade down for the final overhand slash.

Tol continued his spin, rotating in a complete circle on the toe of his right foot. He brought the curved edge of his saber down on Morthur's right wrist. Iron cut through bronze scale and leather, into the flesh of Morthur's arm, and then through bone. His hand, and the sword it still gripped, fell at Tol's feet.

Morthur staggered back, screaming. He clapped his left hand over the stump of his right, trying to staunch the coursing blood. Tol took careful aim. He thrust the slim saber into the gap between Morthur's visor and the gorget at his throat. The high-born sorcerer uttered a horrible gurgling groan. When Tol recovered his blade, Morthur fell to the ground.

Breathing hard, Tol planted a foot on the man's cuirass and flipped the visor up with the tip of his sword. Morthur Dermount's pale face, thin black brows, and slender, almost delicate nose had not changed much in seven years. Now, his black eyes were open and lifeless.

Men came stumbling out of the tents. Tol shouted defiance and prepared to fight in spite of his exhaustion. With enormous relief, he realized he faced Lord Enkian and four of his lieutenants. Morthur's death must have released them from the spell that had held them captive.

"Tol!" said the marshal hoarsely. "How did you get here?"

Tol explained the wagon caravan's encounter with the magic-wielding rider. "His spell didn't work on me for some reason," he finished. "I captured him, and forced him to bring me here. I found . . ."

Tol stepped to one side and gestured at the dead man.

Enkian looked from Morthur Dermount to Tol, and back again. "In the name of Draco Paladin," he breathed. "You bested him!"

The marshal ran thin hands through his hair, trying to take it in. He said, "We were stopped on the road. Next I knew, I was in this tent, awake but unable to move. I heard Morthur conferring with someone I couldn't see. A well-born man, I think—his speech was refined, though I did not recognize his voice. Morthur said he would use magic to take on my appearance and replace me at the conclave in Daltigoth!"

Tol wondered what Morthur had hoped to gain from such a deception. The marshal couldn't say, but neither of them doubted the dead sorcerer had intended treachery of the blackest kind.

They found nothing of interest in the camp, only the normal supplies and a small bag of Ergothian coins. When Morthur's four henchmen came to, they found themselves looking down the blades of Enkian's lieutenants.

"They'll tell us plenty," the marshal said grimly.

Before long, riders from Enkian's escort found them. Awakening from the spell, they'd immediately set out in search of the marshal and had followed the tracks to Morthur's camp. Enkian sent them to sweep the countryside for any more of the sorcerer's minions.

Tol squatted by Morthur's severed hand. The golden sapphire ring it wore seemed identical, though larger, to the one worn by the first man Tol had fought, the lone rider on the high road. The wide gold band, incised with angular symbols, held a single sapphire larger than the ball of Tol's thumb. Within the oval stone, sparks seemed to flicker.

"Why was I alone unaffected by his spells?" Tol mused.

"Thank the gods you were," said Enkian. "None of us would be breathing now if Morthur's evil scheme had succeeded."

He picked up the bloody hand and wrenched the ring free, offering it to Tol. "Morthur was my cousin, but you deserve the spoils of combat," he said.

Tol accepted the ring and put it in his belt pouch, where it kept company with a few silver coins and the ring of braided metal and black glass he'd found in the Irda ruin above the Caer River two years earlier. No one in Juramona had been able to say what the artifact was or what it meant, not even the wise Felryn. His only advice had been to get rid of it, since relics of the cursed Irda were likely cursed, too. For once Tol hadn't heeded the healer, but carried the ancient relic as a cherished token of his first campaign.

When Tol, Lord Enkian, and his entourage returned to the wagons on the Ackal Path, they found everyone there also awake and unharmed. Kiya and Miya, Narren and the foot guards, and the wagoners and their beasts were all well. Whatever spell Morthur had used, it seemed to have no lasting ill effect.

Lord Enkian ordered the body of Morthur Dermount put in a keg of vinegar to preserve it. The marshal intended to present the corpse to the emperor, as proof the long-hunted traitor was at last dead.

Tol's rescue of the marshal had a profound affect on Enkian's view of him. The marshal had always regarded Tol as a peasant favored above his station—good fodder for the city guards, but hardly the equal of warriors born to ride with the Great Horde. His successes in the Great Green, Enkian felt, should be attributed to luck, nothing more. A caprice of the gods had allowed him to capture the Silvanesti agent,

Kirstalothan, and the Dom-shu chief. He was nothing special.

However, his own rescue and the death of Morthur Dermount changed all that. During the rest of the journey to the imperial capital, Lord Enkian turned the incident over and over in his nimble mind. He kept arriving at the same conclusion.

Tol of Juramona was a very dangerous man.

Chapter 12
The Center of the World

A cold drizzle had been falling all night and day. The paved road made traveling easier, but there was no shelter for those on foot. Tol tramped along at the head of his men, cloaked to the eyes, his whole body soaked. There seemed little prospect of getting dry short of Daltigoth.

The Juramona delegation reached an enormous stone bridge spanning the eastern tributary of the Dalti River. Twice the width of the road, the bridge was nonetheless clogged with anxious and irritated travelers. Horses, mules, oxen, and people struggled in the chill rain, trying to force (in both directions) three hundred carts and wagons through a space meant for a third that number. On the walls along both edges of the bridge, men of high rank stood, shouting orders at the teeming mob at their feet. They might as well have tried to command a cloudburst; no one paid them the slightest heed.

Lord Enkian was losing his temper. Normally cool-headed, his impatience at the delay was exacerbated as he was pressed on all sides by soldiers, traders, emigrants, and foreigners of every race. He was about to order his riders to draw swords and force their way through when he spied Tol and waved him over.

"The whole world comes to Daltigoth!" Tol had to shout above the melee.

The marshal was not amused. "The doings of peasants and

180

riff-raff do not concern me. I must enter the city before night-fall. I may have come the furthest distance, but the emperor will not be told Enkian Tumult was the last of his lords to arrive!"

"Perhaps if you took only a few retainers you could work your way through."

"The Marshal of the Eastern Hundred does not enter the imperial capital like a Caergoth clerk, with only a handful of lackeys at his heels! I will enter with my full escort!" Enkian fixed him with a hard, unfriendly eye and added, "See to it, Tol. Disperse the mob."

Tol knew better than to ask how he was to cleave through a crowd of harmless, quarrelsome folk without causing dangerous panic or bloodshed. "I shall do my best, my lord."

He wended his way back to his motionless men. Miya and Kiya, in grass capes and hats, offered him a steaming cup of cider. The resourceful sisters had found someone in the supply wagons with a charcoal burner. Tol sipped the warm brew gratefully.

"What are our orders?" Narren asked.

Tol regarded his friend over the rim of the cider cup. "Lord Enkian says we must part the crowd for him, but how? We can't go through with leveled spears!"

"Too bad that Morthur Grane fellow is dead," Miya said. "He could magic these folk asleep, like he did us."

Her words sparked an idea. Tol dug in his belt pouch and fished out Morthur's sapphire ring. He was about to slide it on his finger when Kiya stopped him.

"Don't. It is an evil ring."

"How evil can it be? You only slept. Truly evil magic would have killed you."

Kiya was adamant. "There are worse things than death."

He ignored her and pushed the ring onto his finger. Holding out his hand, as he'd seen Morthur do, he waited. Nothing happened.

"Maybe there must be words spoken," Narren suggested.

The crowd rippled, forcing Tol's group to step lively to keep their balance on the wet pavement. Kiya climbed on a wagon wheel and peered over the heads of the mob.

"More warriors arrive," she reported. "Their banner has two blues—one dark, one sky."

"The Marshal of the Northern Hundred," said Tol, removing the ring from his finger. Lord Enkian would be pleased to know he was at least ahead of them.

Miya took the ring from him, and Kiya barked, "Sister! Beware!"

The younger Dom-shu grinned, saying dismissively, "Faw, grasslander magic. This ring is as lifeless as its former owner. And it's pretty!"

She slid the ring on over her gloved finger. It was a loose fit.

"A very fine stone," she said smugly, and brought her hand up to admire the jewelry. She had to clench her fingers into a fist to keep the ring from sliding off and being lost in the mud underfoot.

Without a sound, Narren and Kiya collapsed, along with fifty or sixty of the nearest people. Tol caught Kiya, staggering under her weight. He propped her back against the wagon, as the ox team sighed and laid down in their traces.

A momentary hush fell over the crowd, then a woman screamed. In a circle twenty paces across centered on Miya, every living thing had dropped unconscious. Men and women, a cart full of gnomes, two kender (their hands still in others' pockets), horses, oxen, a poulterer's caged chickens— all lay inert. Only Tol and Miya remained upright.

Cries of "A curse!" "Poison!" "Plague!" began, low at first, then rising in volume. Panic erupted as those not stricken struggled to escape whatever baleful influence had struck so swiftly. Carters lashed their beasts, turning away from the bridge. Ahead, terrified folk trapped on the bridge leaped into the Dalti. Fortunately, though the river here was deep, it was also placid.

"Put your hand down!" Tol said sharply to Miya.

Startled by the efficacy of the magic ring, she complied immediately.

A shout went up from the west bank as the bottleneck broke open. People on horseback, in wagons or carts, and on foot burst off the end of the bridge and fanned out across the riverbank. Over the heads of the stampeding crowd, Tol could see Lord Enkian, vainly shouting orders at his mounted escort. No discipline could be maintained in such a rout. The marshal and his retainers were swept away by the rushing tide of people and wagons.

Tol took Morthur's ring from Miya and put it away. Once the ring was safely tucked into his pouch, his comrades began to stir.

Miya squatted down by her groggy sister. "I hexed you!" she announced happily. "You went down like a rotten elm!"

"Shut up," Kiya growled.

The others roused too. By the time they had collected themselves and shaken the wagon drivers awake, the great bridge was temporarily clear of traffic.

Tol looked back at the eastern shore. The men of the later-arriving marshal of the Northern Hundred were scattered to the horizon. It would take them half a day to regroup. To the west, toward Daltigoth, Lord Enkian had vanished from view. At least the stampede had driven them in the right direction. Despite the strangeness of their success, Tol couldn't help but grin.

"Men of Juramona, forward!" he called to his foot soldiers. The rain still fell, but the day now seemed brighter.

❧ ❧ ❧ ❧ ❧

The peninsula between the two branches of the Dalti was low and flat, covered by a patchwork of rich farmland. Imperial roads had been built on causeways above the fields, orchards, and pastures, so traffic to the capital would not damage the lush cropland below. Already the neatly ruled plots of black earth were streaked with fresh green sprouts. The paved causeways were wide enough for one wagon to pass another unimpeded. Tol was amazed to see the hard stone was rutted with the imprint of the hundreds and hundreds of wheels that had passed over it.

To the southwest the sky lightened, clouds thinning and rain easing. When they came to the west fork of the river, the Juramona contingent was relieved to see ten broad bridges spanning the waters. Traffic streamed freely across the gleaming white stone bridges toward the city, now only nine leagues away.

A rider in Enkian's retinue was waiting on the far shore to collect the baggage train, and Tol's escort. As he led Tol to where Lord Enkian waited, in a grove of pines alongside the Ackal Path, the rain finally ceased.

Tol saluted the marshal. Enkian pointedly did not ask how he had broken the bottleneck on the eastern bridge. "I want the baggage train to stay close behind us from now on," he said. "The streets of Daltigoth teem with thieves, and I don't want to lose any property before we reach the Imperial Palace."

The only way for Tol's foot soldiers to keep up with horsemen was to ride, so he divided his men, ten to a wagon, and bade them climb aboard. He and the Dom-shu sisters rode in the lead wagon.

Enkian's escort removed their wet cloaks and donned clean, blood-red capes. They fixed scarlet horsehair plumes to the combs of their helmets and to their horses' bridles. Finery in place, they set off.

The valley opened before them. Like the peninsula, it was bursting with abundance. On the north side of the road were endless rows of fruit trees—apple, cherry, pear, and a host of others. The rain-freshened air was scented with the perfume of the flowering trees.

On the south side of the road, the valley floor was dotted with herds of shaggy red cattle. Hundreds grazed behind stout timber fences. All bore the same brand on their hips: a curved line with a simple cross at one end. Parver, the wagon driver, explained that the saber symbol was the emperor's own brand. The entire vast herd belonged to the lord of all Ergoth.

An arrow-straight canal paralleled the road. Long stretches of it were banked with slabs of granite. According to Parver, the Dalti river had been diverted into the canal, which ran all the way to the city. Rafts and barges (some visible as he spoke) traversed it to the main river, and thence all the way to the Gulf of Ergoth and the sea.

They rolled past a monumental pillar engraved with many lines of hieroglyphs. Atop the marker was the bust of a stern-looking man with a square-cut beard and a tall, conical helmet. The glyphs identified him as Ackal II Dermount, son of Ackal Ergot and the builder of this section of the road.

More statues appeared along the imperial way, each at least four times larger than life: emperors, empresses, famous generals, and heroic warriors. Miya and Kiya were quite fascinated. In the forest, only gods merited images, and the women asked if the sandstone and marble effigies were the gods of Ergoth. Tol, whose rudimentary reading skills were overtaxed by the flowery language beneath the names on the memorials, lied a little and said they were.

They came abreast of two rather ominous statues whose heads had been struck off, the names on the bases effaced. Tol didn't need labels to guess these had been images of Pakin Zan and, most probably, his son Emperor Ergothas III.

As they passed the last of the statues, the sky suddenly cleared and sunlight flooded down. Tol could see a distinct line of light and shadow on the ground behind them. The sky overhead showed the same sharp delineation; the gray clouds did not thin gradually, but rolled solid as a ceiling up to a line beyond which was only clear, brilliant blue sky and gentle spring warmth.

The wizards of Daltigoth must be great indeed to command the clouds and hold back the rain, Tol mused.

The sunlight illuminated a great mass of mellow white stone rising ahead from the surrounding fertile fields. Daltigoth, capital city of the empire, filled the valley from the canal in the east to the foothills of the Harkmor Mountains on the south and west. Tol and his people were still two leagues away, yet the city spread from horizon to horizon, blotting out everything else. A constant haze hung over it—smoke from a prodigious number of inns, taverns, temples, and family hearths—but this faintly blue pall did not dim the gleaming expanse of the imperial city.

The first things Tol noticed were the towers. A profusion of lofty pinnacles jutted skyward, in every shape and color. About half boasted high, pointed roofs covered in green copper or gray lead. The rest were flat-topped with crenellated parapets, like the wooden watch towers of Juramona. A few towers—the very tallest, gathered in a group at the center of the city—were made of a polished white stone, and their conical roofs were gilded with pure gold. Seeing them flash in the sun, the Dom-shu sisters finally lost their tribal stoicism and began to point and exclaim with excitement.

The gray stone city wall came into view. It was many times the height of Juramona's wooden stockade, yet even this prodigious barrier was dwarfed by a truly massive white curtain wall that encircled the inner grouping of those tallest, gilded towers.

Other roads converged on the Ackal Path. From his perch on the wagon seat Tol could see streams of mounted warriors approaching on every side. Thousands of fighting men surrounded them, each with a crimson plume attached to his polished helmet. Tol recognized hordes from every far-flung corner of the empire—from the borderlands of the north, the great cattle estates of the south, and the woodlands in the east. Each contingent bore its own banners and standards. Every color in the world was represented, and the standards depicted creatures mundane and fantastic—serpents, panthers, wolves, great birds, griffins, and even dragons.

In spite of this mighty and glorious panoply, Tol knew his party was the equal of any. Ahead of the creaking wagon, Lord Enkian and his escort rode at a stately walk, the breeze filling their crimson capes. Arrogant and conniving though the marshall might be, at that moment Tol was proud of him, proud of Juramona, and proud to be a part of the magnificent procession making its way to Daltigoth.

Looking beyond the marshal at their intended destination, Tol saw the Ackal Path led straight to a massive fortified gate in the outer wall. He could scarcely credit his eyes—the gate alone was a hundred paces high, twice the height of the wall it pierced. Huge, terraced columns flanked the entrance, the arch of which was heavily carved with weathered figures intertwined in complex ways. The gate's swinging doors were only half the height of the arch, but were still quite impressive. Tol asked the knowledgeable Parver about the fantastic portal.

"It's called the Dragon Gate. The great hero Volmunaard fought a black dragon, Vilesoot, on this spot," said the wagoner. "The gate was erected to commemorate Volmunaard's defeat of the evil beast."

"A man beat a dragon?" scoffed Kiya, and Miya snorted her disbelief.

The garrulous driver raised his eyes heavenward. "By Draco Paladin, it's true! He dealt Vilesoot a deathblow, but Volmunaard died too, consumed by the monster's vitriol."

Closer, they could see the frieze encircling the Dragon Gate, which told the story. Volmunaard, twice life size, rode out from Daltigoth in old-fashioned banded armor. Pictures showing his battle with the dragon were carved sequentially around the arch. The last detail on the right side of the gate showed the dragon dead and the hero perishing in a cloud of Vilesoot's acid-breath.

As three great roads converged here, the structure was not wide enough to handle the traffic flowing in and out of the city. Tol resumed his seat by Parver as the wagon entered the shadow of the monumental portal.

The gatehouse was a small fortress of it own, garrisoned by bored-looking men in dusty iron breastplates and short kilts. Tol nodded to them. A few returned the gesture. They were commoners, foot soldiers like his men.

As he wondered how even a gang of men could close such

ponderous metal-clad gates, he saw the answer: an ogre. Twice Tol's height and twice his girth, the ogre stood just inside the swinging doors of the gate, wearing an iron collar affixed to three heavy chains secured to the stone city wall. A human with a sharp goad stood by him, ready to prod the hulking creature into action.

Tol was amazed that an ogre would work for humans, chained and guarded though he was. Parver sagely pointed out the reason for the ogre's acquiescence: His eyelids were sewn shut. To control their powerful captive, the Ergothians had blinded him.

Once inside, the caravan from Juramona became embroiled in a fresh snarl of traffic. Tol quickly quashed Miya's suggestion that she use Morthur's ring again. Fortunately, Lord Enkian hadn't been stopped long before a gang of guards charged out of the Dragon Gate armed with cudgels. They waded into the crowd and, with well-placed blows, got things moving again very quickly. It was a harsh but effective tactic, and Tol had the feeling it happened often.

He ordered his men off the wagons. Spears in hand, the footmen kept gawkers and pilferers back as the caravan crawled through the streets at a slow pace.

Tol tried not to stare at all the sights; he was on duty now, with the good reputation of Juramona at stake. Still, it was impossible not to notice the tall dwellings lining both sides of the street, four and five stories high. At street level were artisans' shops, vegetable sellers, sausage and cheese vendors, bakers, petty diviners, and wineshops. Where two roads met, larger establishments loomed: full-fledged taverns, inns, and houses of healing.

"What noise!" Kiya called, still riding on the lead wagon. "Why does everyone talk at once?"

Tol had once thought Juramona noisy and impossibly busy. As a boy riding into town behind Egrin, he'd nearly panicked at the commotion. Yet compared to Daltigoth, provincial Juramona was quiet as a cemetery. The sheer number and variety of people to be seen were amazing. Lowly beggars in dirty rags jostled with prosperous merchants in leather and high-born ladies in sumptuous velvet. The wealthy went about with armed escorts and haughty retainers, parting the crowds of half-naked seamen, gnomes, dwarves, and kender who the filled the wooden walks lining both sides of the street and spilled into the roadway. A cacophony of languages assaulted the ear.

Rolling past a whitewashed inn called The Four Winds, Tol saw two shaggy male centaurs involved in a raucous conversation with a red-bearded dwarf and a handsome black-skinned woman. The woman was dressed in leather breeches and a leather tunic, with a knife nearly as long as a sword hanging at her waist. Her thick braid of hair reached nearly to her knees. He hadn't realized he was staring until the woman turned and regarded him with hands on hips and a measuring expression in her eyes. Flushing, Tol looked away—

—and found that he himself was the object of several other pairs of eyes, unfriendly ones. Three men were idling in the doorway of the inn. Lean types, with scarred faces and tight-fitting clothes, they each wore slender swords hanging from leather baldrics. Egrin's warning about duelists came to mind, and Tol shifted his gaze quickly ahead.

After what seemed an age, the caravan at last reached the high white wall they'd seen from the valley. This turned out to be the boundary of the inner city. From ground to parapet, the wall was covered with low-relief carvings—coronations, entire battles, and enormous images of the gods, with Corij, Mishas, and Draco Paladin predominating. Within the wall were just two households: the emperor's palace and the college of wizards. The future Tower of Sorcery would rise from the grounds of the wizards' enclave.

The caravan halted before a closed gate in the inner city wall. Guards handsomely bedecked in black iron armor and scarlet tabards came out to confer with Lord Enkian. The exchange went on for some time, with much nodding and pointing from the guards. At last, Enkian sent the bulk of his entourage away, to be quartered in local inns with warriors from other provinces. Tol, his footmen, and the wagons remained, waiting.

Enkian waved Tol forward. He jogged to the marshal, followed as always by the Dom-shu sisters.

"Master Tol, your men are to seek accommodation in the Canal Quarter, by the river," Enkian said.

"Are any hostels set aside for us, my lord?"

"No, but all lodging houses in Daltigoth are required to accept provincial troops wherever they can fit them in. Your room cost will be borne by the Juramona treasury, but food and drink are at your own expense."

Not exactly a generous arrangement, Tol thought, knowing his men would grumble, but it was better than sleeping in the street. He saluted smartly and made to leave. Enkian cleared his throat, halting his departure.

"You, Tol, are to enter the Inner City with my retinue—by the crown prince's order."

He stifled an urge to whoop. Kiya tugged his sleeve, prompting him to ask, "And the Dom-shu, my lord?" Two years he'd lived with them, and he still couldn't bring himself to call them his wives.

"Oh, bring them. I daresay they can bed in the scullery or kitchens. Take the wagons with my baggage to the Riders' Hall and see to their unloading."

Enkian's baggage filled four of the twenty wagons. Tol split the guarding of the rest of the wagons between the escort riders and his footmen. When all the wagons were emptied, their drivers would be paid off and dismissed.

Thinking it unmartial to enter the palace grounds in an ox-drawn wagon, Tol walked ahead of the four bearing Enkian's baggage. Kiya strode along on his right, Miya on his left. The imperial guards, with their black armor, red scarves, and brightly polished poleaxes, watched the trio curiously as they passed through the gate.

"This is the heart of the empire," Tol murmured to the sisters. "Mind what you say and do!"

The inner city wall was enormously thick—Tol counted

sixteen paces before they emerged into daylight again. On the other side, he stopped, blinking in surprise. Surely this was the most amazing place in all the world!

Stretching before them was the Imperial Plaza, a courtyard seemingly larger in area than the whole town of Juramona. It was paved, not with ordinary stone, but with small colored blocks arranged in beautiful patterns. Red granite, blue slate, and buff limestone framed the great mosaic images rendered in chips of turquoise, agate, onyx, coal, and shell. Here, where Tol had entered, was a panorama depicting Ackal Ergot's victory over the Pakitene tribes two centuries earlier. He could easily spend hours staring at the vibrant, colossal pictures.

As awesome as the plaza was, the landscape of the inner city was even more breathtaking. To the left of the gate stood the Imperial Palace, a complex of buildings and towers which had grown up over the years into a massive single structure. A great staircase rose from the plaza to the main doors, pausing twice in broad landings large enough to drill an entire foot company. The palace gates were sheathed in gold, and the hundreds of windows in the thick stone walls were equipped with gilded shutters. Expanses of sloping roof were sheathed in hammered lead plates, and rainspouts shaped like openmouthed dragons perched on the corner of every gutter. Towers even taller than the inner wall shone white in the sun, while the rest of the inner city lay wreathed in the shadow of its own wall.

On Tol's right, in a graceful park of trees, was the college of wizards. More modest and elegant than the palace, the college itself was a four-story building shaped like a squared horseshoe. Each floor of the building was faced by a colonnade, the columned walks overlooking a courtyard at the center. In that courtyard, just visible above the trees, a complicated wooden scaffolding rose. Tol realized the platforms must surround the site of the future Tower of Sorcery.

Two other buildings were visible from Tol's vantage in the Imperial Plaza. One was a large timber frame hall directly ahead. Judging by the warlords entering it, this was the Riders' Hall, where the emperor's chief vassals were lodged. The other building was just inside the gate, a severe three-story stone structure with a flat roof. It had the look of a stronghold, and Tol took it to be the barracks of the Imperial City Guard.

The vast plaza teemed with activity. In addition to guards and servants in imperial livery, there were lords and ladies of the court strolling about in the latest city fashions—the women wearing tall hats shaped like curly rams' horns, their bright gowns with long trailing hems; the men in richly colored cloaks; and both sexes dripped with gems. People in plainer dress, with little or no jewelry, Tol took to be members of the sorcerers' college. Enormous wolfhounds bounded across the mosaic pavement, chasing a leather "fox" dragged by a fleet servant boy. When the wind stirred the trees in the college garden, flower petals took flight and collected in sweet drifts around statues and along walls.

Miya prodded him in the back. "If you don't close your mouth, birds will nest on your tongue," she said.

Tol shut his mouth with a snap. "Wagons, forward!" he ordered, lowering his chin to hide his flushed face.

He had the laden wagons draw up at the Riders' Hall for unloading. From the hall came an army of lackeys, clad in matching leather jerkins and baggy trews. They swarmed over the Juramona wagons like ants and emptied them in short order.

Taken aback by the swiftness of the operation, Tol looked at the lead wagoner and shook his head. Parver grinned and doffed his cap, exposing his bare, sun-browned pate.

"Watch yourself, young master," he said, as the wagons departed.

Tol was uncertain what to do next, but the Dom-shu sisters were looking at him expectantly. He squared his shoulders and mounted the steps to the Riders' Hall, Kiya and Miya following. At the top, guards at the doors barred the way.

"Only Riders of the Horde may enter," said one. The nasal of his helmet mashed his nose flat and made his voice sound odd.

"I am a rider, Tol of Juramona. These are my wives."

"You arrived on foot—you can't be a rider," said the second guard.

Tol tried to convince the guards, but their logic was inflexible and unanswerable: He'd arrived on foot, therefore he was no rider; if he was no rider, he couldn't enter the Riders' Hall.

Tol and the Dom-shu withdrew to the bottom of the steps.

"We could rush them," Kiya murmured, brown eyes narrowing as she studied the foe.

"No, no fighting!" Tol hissed. "Lord Enkian will vouch for us. I'm here at the order of the crown prince himself."

"Lord Enkian may not come out for hours," said Miya.

"And I'm hungry," added Kiya.

Tol looked across the plaza at the wizards' college, then at the palace. He was much less unnerved by the pomp of the royal residence than by the unknown mysteries lurking in the sorcerers' garden, so—

"To the palace," he said.

The sisters gave him identical questioning looks, so he winked, saying, "The food's probably better there anyway!"

Unfortunately, when they drew nearer, they realized that the monumental entrance to the palace was patrolled by no less than three dozen guards, half of whom were mounted. If Tol couldn't bluff his way past the guards at the Riders' Hall, it seemed unlikely he and his Dom-shu companions could wander into the Imperial Palace unchallenged.

Striving to look like he belonged there, Tol walked boldly down the alley between the palace's west wing and the inner city wall. It was a rather pretty shaded lane, though the palace loomed overhead like a mountain of marble and gold. Trailing red roses spilled from terraces over their heads, and to their ears came the sweet music of pipes.

The palace wall slanted in, mirroring the lozenge shape of the surrounding curtain wall. At the rear of the imperial enclave, the gentle, rose-scented atmosphere gave way to smoke and noise. Here was where the real work of the enormous household went on—smoky kitchens, a smithy, and wagons waiting to haul away the offal and slops. Cooks, servants, and artisans scurried to and fro. A few glanced at Tol and the Dom-shu, but no one paused long enough to challenge them.

Following her nose, the hungry Kiya walked up a ramp, leading the other two into a fantastic kitchen. Four great hearths were roaring. Turbaned cooks stirred cauldrons and basted a savory phalanx of chickens and ducks roasting on an iron rack. Whole oxen rotated on spits turned by gangs of boys nearly naked against the searing heat. A lordly white-robed cook raised a dipper the size of a wine keg and basted an oxen, drenching the simmering carcass in golden butter.

"By my ancestors!" Kiya exclaimed. "All I prayed for was a joint to gnaw and a tankard to wash it down!"

A burst of laughter erupted behind them. Under a low-beamed ceiling, some kitchen workers were gathered around a long trestle table. They passed trenchers laden with capon and round loaves of bread, tops snowy with flour.

Kiya grinned happily. She beckoned Tol and Miya to follow, but only her sister did. They eased themselves up to the table. Miya cracked a joke and set the workers roaring. The Dom-shu were made welcome.

Tol found he was simply too excited to eat. He wanted to see more of this fantastic place and to present himself to Prince Amaltar. After all, the prince had personally requested his presence in the inner city.

He left the Dom-shu sisters in the kitchen and slipped between the blazing hearths until he reached a cooler, quieter room beyond. Here, utensils were stacked on shelves from floor to ceiling: silver trenchers, pewter cups and bowls, forks and table knives. Tol kept moving. With no idea where he was going, or where he'd end up, he followed a narrow corridor in the general direction of the center of the palace.

He came to a pair of heavy velvet curtains. Parting them, he stepped out into a wide hall. Oil lamps burned in wall sconces, but the corridor was dim. Trying not to seem furtive, Tol walked down the hall toward a lighted chamber ahead.

"—worthless imbeciles!" someone shouted—a male voice, very angry. Tol heard the unmistakable sound of a blow against flesh. He halted.

"It's bad enough the city is flooded with provincial nobility, but now the palace reeks of country gentlemen, too!" Another ugly impact, followed by a grunt of pain.

"Gracious prince," a second voice gasped, "I do but obey the will of your imperial father!"

Intrigued, Tol peeked around the corner. The next room was an antechamber where three corridors intersected. An atrium allowed sunlight to penetrate, illuminating the scene. Groveling on his face was a richly dressed man of middle years. Standing over him was a younger, taller man with a fiercely upswept mustache and hair the color of a sunset. His scarlet robe was weighed down with huge golden medallions, and belted with a wide black leather strap.

"How dare you invoke my father against me!" said the strange noble, driving his booted foot into the cowering man's ribs. The man rolled away from the blow, and Tol saw his face. He was Valdid, chamberlain to Crown Prince Amaltar, the same man who had guided Lord Odovar and his lieutenants into Amaltar's presence at his camp outside Caergoth.

"Prince Nazramin," the chamberlain managed to say, "I will keep the conclave guests away from your quarters—"

"And my garden too!" snarled the prince. "If I find anyone in my sanctum, I'll slit their worthless throats."

"It shall be done, Your Highness."

"Cross me, you fool, and I'll have your hands cropped off!"

Prince Nazramin stalked out of the room. Tol shrank back into the shadows. Valdid scrabbled on the floor a bit, retrieving his gold-capped cane, and used it to brace himself to his feet. Tol remained hidden, not wishing the older man to know that the prince's cruelty to him had been witnessed.

After straightening his robe and smoothing his hair, Valdid limped away, but Tol hesitated still, worried now what else he might blunder into. Perhaps he should find his way back to the kitchen.

Turning to go, he glimpsed a set of steps ahead. Sunlight filtered down the plain stone stairwell, beckoning him upward, teasing him with thoughts of the marvels he might find. He hesitated only a moment before giving in to his curiosity.

At the top of the steps he found himself on a columned walkway between two wings of the palace. Below was a sea of rooftops and chimneys. Above were more walkways and soaring towers. He heard a hum of voices at the end of the walk and moved cautiously toward the sound. Several times servants popped out of side passages, bearing linens or trays of empty wine cups. They glanced him at him curiously, but no one questioned him. Prompted by their stares, he suddenly realized that he still wore his saber and dagger. Even the smallest weapons were forbidden in Prince Amaltar's presence, and here he was loose in the Imperial Palace, girded for battle!

Casting about for a place to store his weapons, he noticed a passage on the right. A light curtain screened it. The curtain stirred gently near the floor, teased by a draft. Tol swept the curtain aside and ducked in.

He wasn't in a passage, but a niche, about six steps deep. And he was not alone.

Seated on a marble bench was a girl with an open scroll in her hands. A circle of daylight fell on her from a small skylight. At Tol's entrance, she looked up with a gasp of surprise.

"Forgive me," he said. "I didn't know anyone was here."

"I forgive you," replied the girl. "No one knew I was here."

She looked to be somewhat younger than Tol—fifteen perhaps, sixteen at most. Her straight dark brown hair was waist-length and parted in the middle. She wore it loose, but looped behind her ears. Her pallor proved she didn't spend much time outdoors. That, coupled with her simple gray gown, led Tol to conclude she was a servant, hiding to avoid her chores.

"Weapons are forbidden in the palace—are you an assassin?" she said calmly, gesturing at his sword.

"No!" He unbuckled his belt and stood the saber in the corner. Adding his dagger, he straightened his tunic and said, "It was a mistake. I didn't mean to come here armed. I'm from—I'm from the provinces."

"Obviously. Well, I hope you don't get caught. Even without weapons, you'll be flogged for entering the private wing of the palace."

The sound of voices came to his ear, and he exclaimed, "Someone's coming!"

She listened a moment, then said, "No. That's only the Consorts' Circle in the empress's garden." She waved a hand vaguely behind her, adding with a grimace, "Wives of the emperor, princes, and high lords of the court—they gather there daily. Chatter, chatter, chatter. What a bore!"

He smiled. Looking at the scroll in her lap, he asked, "What's that you're reading?"

"The Chronicle of Balif. Do you know it?"

He said no, and she explained that Balif was a Silvanesti noble and general who had lived during the time the elf kingdom was established. He helped found the Sinthal-Elish, the great council that chose Silvanos Goldeneye as first Speaker of the Stars. Balif could've been Speaker himself, she said, but chose instead to support Silvanos.

"Why?" Tol asked. Having read little himself, he knew nothing of the history of the Silvanesti. The only elf he'd ever met was the one he'd captured in the Great Green.

She pushed an escaping strand of hair behind her ear again. "He was shown his future by a sorcerer named Vedvedsica, and realized he could never be Speaker of the Stars," she explained. "Elves are very concerned with how they look and sound. Balif learned he would be stricken by a loathsome curse. In the end, it was so awful, he had to flee the country under cover of darkness."

Tol heard voices again, this time unmistakably male and growing louder. The heavy tramp of booted feet was plain in the corridor.

"The armed man entered this passage, sir!" a voice whined.

The booted feet halted seemingly just outside Tol's niche. "Search the side passages!" ordered a stern voice.

Tol flattened himself against the wall, his saber within reach. If it came to being arrested, he wondered if he should fight rather than meekly submit.

A gauntleted hand grasped the curtain screening the niche. The girl let out a high-pitched scream.

"Stay out!" she cried.

The hand was withdrawn. "Beg pardon, my lady. Who are you?"

"Princess Carafel! Don't come in—I'm not clothed!"

Tol blinked and swallowed hard. Had he been sharing the niche with a daughter of the royal house?

"A thousand pardons, Princess!" said a deeper, more imposing voice. "It's Draymon, captain of the guard. We are searching for an armed man seen in the palace."

"Do you think he is in here with me?" the girl said shrilly. "Go about your business, Lord Draymon, or I shall mention this incident to my father!"

"My humblest apologies, Highness. We'll continue our search elsewhere."

Tol crept to the curtain and listened. He heard the heavy footsteps diminish with distance. Turning to the girl, he found her shaking with silent laughter.

"Are you really Princess Carafel?" he asked, intimidated.

"That soaphead?!" She rolled up the scroll. "I'm Valaran, fourth daughter of Lord Valdid and Lady Pernina. Most people call me Val."

He sighed with relief. "I'm Tol of Juramona," he said. "Most people call me Tol."

Valaran smiled. She had an intriguing smile, with a dimple just under the left corner of her mouth. It made her look even younger than he'd guessed. Her eyes were green, like the weathered copper roofs of Daltigoth.

"You'd better get out of here, Tol of Juramona," she said. "Draymon may yet wonder what a royal princess would be doing in here unclothed."

"How do I get back to the kitchens? I left my friends there."

She slid off the high bench, showing a bit of pale calf as she did so. Unselfconsciously, she smoothed her gown and retied the pearl-beaded sash around her waist. Plainly dressed or not, Tol knew he wouldn't have mistaken her for a housemaid if he'd noticed that expensive sash. She was shorter than he, but only barely.

"I'll lead you to the kitchens. You'll have to leave your sword and knife here," she said, and handed him the thick scroll. "If anyone stops us, you're escorting me to the temple library."

Tol nodded. Valaran lifted the curtain and peeked out. Satisfied no one was around, she waved Tol out. They went quickly down the corridor. Her step was light and fast. Tol commented on her confident navigation of the confusion of twists and turns.

"I should know the way; I've lived here forever!"

Her vexed tone made him smile. She was rather pretty. If she were a little older, he would be tempted to court her. He was a Rider of the Horde after all, he reminded himself, appointed by Prince Amaltar himself.

"Why were you in that cubbyhole?" he asked.

She frowned, crinkling her nose. "They don't like to see me reading. Sometimes the ninnies of the Consorts' Circle snatch the scrolls right from my hands!" She adopted a nasal, mocking tone: "'Reading isn't good for women. If you're smarter than a man, he won't like you.'"

"That's not true. Nothing's more boring than an empty head." He glanced at her. "Why did you save me from the guards?"

Once a passing trio of servants moved out of earshot, she said flatly, "If they'd found you with me, I would've been whipped."

Tol's buoyant mood collapsed. She'd done it merely to save herself. He suddenly remembered the ugly scene he'd witnessed between the angry prince and Valdid. The hapless chamberlain was Valaran's father. If such beatings were common in the Imperial Palace, he couldn't fault her for wishing to avoid one. Her next words restored his good humor.

"Besides, you're the first provincial to make it this far into the palace. You've got nerve." She favored him with another dimpled smile, adding, "Or you're stupid. I can't tell yet. Anyway, I like to talk to people who have experienced the world outside the city. I want to hear everything about the world—and you."

He stopped in his tracks. "You want to see me again?"

"Certainly. How else could we talk?"

They resumed walking, and Valaran said sternly, "You can't come here, though. Are you lodging in the Riders' Hall?" With nothing else definite, Tol nodded. "Good. We can meet in the wizards' garden—at the fountain of the centaurs. I go there to read sometimes. The mages don't mind."

"I don't know what my duties may be," he said doubtfully. "If I am free, I'll come."

"I'm usually there four marks before sunset," Valaran said, explaining that time in the Inner City was marked by the procession of the highest tower's shadow across a set of lines carved into the inner wall.

They had reached the sweltering kitchens, and Tol's adventure was over. He wanted to say something gallant, as he imagined a seasoned warrior would do, but Valaran didn't linger for his goodbye. She plucked the scroll from his hand and darted away. Opening the fat cylinder of parchment, she was soon engrossed once more, reading as she walked.

Kiya and Miya were still seated at the table. Red-faced from wine and heat, they hailed their wandering companion. He sat down heavily between them. Miya pushed a plate of seared chicken in front of him, and filled a clay cup with dark red wine.

"Have some grub," she said, sounding more rustic than usual. "It's good! They treat you right here!"

Tol thought about his close call. Whether she'd been saving

only herself or him, Valaran had a quick wit and courage enough to face down an irate captain of the guard. He looked forward to seeing her again.

He clinked his cup to Kiya's, then Miya's. "That they do," he said.

Chapter 13

The Centaur Fountain

T ol passed the early part of the night sleeping in the doorway of the Riders' Hall. It was late when Relfas found him, shaking him roughly awake and demanding to know what he was doing there.

"No one would let me in," Tol said sleepily.

Relfas grasped his hand and hauled him to his feet. "Where are your bruising tribal women?"

Tol yawned. "The palace kitchens. I told them to stay there."

Within, the Riders' Hall was much like the barracks at Juramona, only grander. Where the provincial hall used wood, the Daltigoth building used finely cut stone. Tol followed Relfas up a narrow stair to the topmost of four floors. The youngest and least senior of the empire's elite warriors bedded down here, while older and more favored men occupied larger quarters on the lower floors. Settling himself on a bunk in a back corner, Tol fell asleep again in an instant.

Day began early. The young nobles turned out and ate a hearty breakfast at the long table in the center of the hall. They were served by a gaggle of scarlet-clad boys. As in its Juramona counterpart, women were not permitted even as servers in the Riders' Hall. The married lords had to sleep apart from their wives, who were comfortably housed in the vast Imperial Palace.

Once fed, Tol's comrades fell to preparing their finery for the upcoming conclave. Sharp smells of polish, saddle soap and oil filled the hall. Shield-bearers from the city's hordes assisted the warriors. The ceremony surrounding the laying of the cornerstone for the Tower of Sorcery was to take place in four days, when the moons Luin and Solin would meet in the constellation of Draco Paladin, the great dragon-god.

It didn't take Tol long to prepare, for he had little in the way of possessions, and his sword and dagger were still in Valaran's hands. He had only to polish his leather boots, belts, and braces, and to scrub the tarnish from his armor. A pair of Daltigoth shilder offered to do the work, but Tol politely declined. He said he preferred to take care of his own equipment, the better to know its condition. The two youths departed, smirking at the funny ways of provincials.

His chores completed, Tol was at loose ends by midday. He slipped outside, determined to have a look around the Inner City.

The great plaza was being cleaned in preparation for the ceremony. An army of drudges moved across the mosaics, wielding brooms, while a smaller band of lackeys scooped up the piles of dust they left in their wake and hauled them away. A company of the Inner City Guard paraded across the entrance to the palace, relieving the men who'd stood watch since midnight. No courtiers or high officials were stirring yet in the square.

Inevitably, Tol made his way to the garden surrounding the wizards' college. It was too early to meet Valaran—the sunclock on the inside wall showed it was six marks till sunset—but he was decidedly curious about the sorcerers.

The garden at the wizards' college was surrounded by a low stone wall, decorative rather than defensive. There were neither gates nor guards, just a simple flagstone path leading into a deserted garden. Tol felt uneasy when he entered its shaded calm, but Valaran had said the mages didn't object to visits. Besides, if they were concerned about trespassers, surely there would be guards.

Newly leafed trees closed overhead, blotting out the sky. Fallen flower petals had drifted across the path, their perfumed thickness deadening his footfalls. A clear, musical tinkling wafted on the breeze, conjuring the memory of the wind chime he'd seen in Prince Amaltar's tent at Caergoth.

He passed three stone pillars, each half again as tall as the one before it. For a moment he thought he saw inscriptions on them, but when he ran his fingers over the cold granite, the surface was smooth.

Voices whispered behind him. Tol snatched his hand back and whirled, but saw no one. The breeze died, and the chiming sound ceased. The canopy of leaves was still, blocking out the sunlight. Shaking his head at his nervous imaginings, he continued his slow progress through the beautiful grove.

Another path intersected his at a right angle. He looked left and right, wondering which way to go. For an instant he thought he glimpsed pale gray robes disappearing behind trees in both directions.

Disconcerted, Tol decided he'd gone far enough. He turned to retrace his steps, but discovered to his shock the path behind him had disappeared! Where moments before he had trodden on gray flagstones, there was now a thickly growing cluster of oak and elm trees.

His hand dropped to his hip, seeking the comforting handle of his saber. Of course it wasn't there; Valaran still had it.

Tol turned around—and received yet another shock. The intersecting path was gone as though it had never been.

"Magic," he muttered, glancing nervously over one shoulder, then the other. He went on, having no path to lead him back.

He soon came upon a four-sided clearing filled with blooming red roses. The flower, he knew, was sacred to Manthus, god of wisdom. The path led directly to the sea of blooms and thorny stems, so he was forced to wade knee-deep through crimson flowers. Thorns made little impression on his stout leather trews, but the aroma of roses filled the air in overwhelming strength. Coughing, he held a kerchief over his nose and pushed on. The flagstone path resumed on the other side of the clearing.

Ahead, he could see the colonnades of the wizards' college. Off to his left was the rough wooden scaffolding he'd glimpsed on his arrival at the Inner City. Just now it was deserted.

Using the scaffold to keep his bearing, Tol left the path and was able to navigate through the closely growing trees without too much trouble. He emerged in a sunny, diamond-shaped courtyard directly in front of the wizards' college. A number of robed clerics and sorcerers were sitting on stone benches around the courtyard. When Tol came into view, they stood up and gaped at him in alarm. The closest ones hurried away, as if he were some ravening fiend come to attack them.

A woman in white robes approached. Hollow-cheeked, she was very advanced in years, her hair completely white. She stood very straight, though, and did not lean on the tall staff in her hand.

"Who are you? How did you get here?" she asked sternly.

"Forgive me, lady," Tol said, bowing his head. "I mean no harm. My name is Tol of Juramona."

When he raised his head again, other robed figures stood behind the woman. A rotund, red-faced man asked, "How did he get so far?"

"I don't know, Oropash," the woman replied. "Helbin, was the Wall of Sleep properly invoked?"

"The wards were properly placed. I saw to it myself," answered a more youthful man at her right hand. His sand-colored hair was tightly curled, as was his thin mustache. "No one could possibly have gotten through!"

The old woman looked from Helbin to Tol and back again, white eyebrows rising significantly. Young Helbin flushed.

To Tol she said, "Come here, young man. Don't be afraid. I am Yoralyn; come to me."

Tol's feet crunched on the bright quartz gravel. He wasn't afraid, but many of Yoralyn's colleagues obviously were. He halted several paces from the startled mages and spread his hands.

"I'm not armed," he reassured them. "I'm visiting Daltigoth with my liege lord, Enkian Tumult, marshal of the Eastern

Hundred. We're here at the emperor's command, for the laying of the cornerstone of the great tower."

Yoralyn consulted a smooth sphere of amethyst in her hand. "He speaks the truth," she said. "His aura is as innocent as a child's."

"Then how did he penetrate the Wall of Sleep?" demanded the rotund mage, Oropash.

The younger sorcerer, Helbin, advanced and stared Tol in the eye. He was tall and vigorous-looking, more like a warrior than a priest. Over his robe he wore a loosely draped mantle of faded red silk. Each of his fingers bore a ring. He extended one hand, palm out, and waved it in front of Tol.

"I perceive no sensation of power," he muttered. "I sense no counterspell or amulet, but there must be a reason! An ordinary person could not pass through the barrier without succumbing to its influence!"

Their agitation, and the speculative gleam in Yoralyn's pale blue eyes, unnerved Tol. "I'm sorry," he said, backing up a step. "I'm not sure what happened. But I'll go at once—"

"No, stay," said Yoralyn. "Come this way."

Helbin and Oropash stood aside, allowing Tol plenty of room to pass. The two sorcerers, fearful but curious, followed Tol as he trailed the old woman to a nearby fountain. A silver stream spewed from the mouth of a dragon statue in the center of the pool. The statue was three paces tall and carved from a single block of emerald.

As he passed, Tol realized the fluid flowing from the statue's mouth wasn't water, but quicksilver. A droplet splashed out of the pool onto the low marble wall surrounding the fountain's basin, and then, like a living thing, the silver globule rolled up the stone slab (against the slope, Tol noted with astonishment) and dropped back into the pool.

More sorcerers joined the procession. They emerged from other side paths or simply appeared out of the air on the grassy lawn. Scores had congregated by the time Yoralyn halted at the foot of the ramshackle scaffolding. Inside the scaffolding, a single course of masonry had been laid, enormous cyclopean stones two paces high and as wide as a tall man could reach.

Yoralyn regarded Tol silently with a disconcertingly piercing stare. He stammered, "I'm truly sorry if my coming has caused a problem."

"It has, Tol of Juramona. We defend the Vale of Sorcery with a special conjuration, intended to keep out all those not of our orders. Yet you wandered in without apparent difficulty. Moreover, none of us seems to have felt the disruption of our solitude. We find that gravely disturbing. Who are you?"

Tol gave her a brief account of his coming to Daltigoth.

"So, you're the one who slew Morthur Dermount?" Helbin said at the end of the tale.

Tol acknowledged this, saying, "He gave me no choice but kill or be killed."

"No blame attaches to you," Yoralyn assured him. "Morthur was a wild mage, an unregulated practitioner of the black arts. He was trained by rogue elements of the Red and Black Robes. It's a pity we couldn't have discovered the names of his mentors, but . . ." She shrugged, then said, "You possess his ring, do you not?"

Reluctant to part with so powerful an object, Tol simply nodded.

"We would like it returned to us. It is not lawful for an untutored person like yourself to use it."

"Must I give it up? Lord Enkian awarded it to me as a spoil of victory. It does not work when I wield it." He described his inability to use Morthur's ring at the Dalti bridge and told of Miya's success.

A sustained murmur went through the crowd. Helbin and Oropash held a hushed conversation with Yoralyn. At length she silenced the group with upraised hands.

"Master Tol, we have no quarrel with you. You seem a good and honorable man. Something is amiss, however. Your immunity to Morthur's soporific spell, and to our protective enchantment, is unheard of and most troubling."

"You must give us Morthur's ring," Helbin said, and it was more an order than a request. "There may be something in it that helped you defeat our wards."

Tol didn't want to comply. The large sapphire ring was his prize from a hard-fought struggle. "I care nothing for the ring's power," he argued, "but I would like to keep it. Lord Morthur—or Spannuth Grane as I knew him—did much harm to me and my people, and his ring is the only trophy I have."

Helbin seemed disposed to overrule him, but Oropash said reasonably, "Let us study the ring during your visit here, Master Tol. Once we've delved into its secrets, you may have it back."

Tol looked to Yoralyn, who nodded in confirmation. Satisfied, he loosed the lacings of his belt pouch to produce the ring.

A fresh wave of agitation rippled through the throng of mages.

"You have it with you?" Yoralyn exclaimed.

Tol paused, two fingers buried in the pouch. "I do. What's wrong with that?"

Turning to her fellow wizards, Yoralyn declared, "I did not sense the ring's power on the boy. Did anyone here?"

From the fresh consternation on every face, it was obvious no one had. Helbin asked for the ring, extending a hand. Tol dropped it on his open palm. The mage closed long fingers around it. His eyes shut momentarily, then sprang open.

"The ring is consecrated to Nuitari. It is potent still!" Helbin exclaimed.

"You must give it back to him immediately," Oropash said quietly.

Helbin did so, and Tol, his eyes wide, returned the ring to his pouch.

Eyes firmly closed, Oropash said, "I cannot see the ring when the boy possesses it!"

"Nor can I!"

"It vanishes as soon as it touches his hands!"

Every sorcerer in the glade began talking at once. The disorder of their thoughts caused strange displays—a cloud of coal-black butterflies appeared over one mage's head; another's lost all color and took on the appearance of a snow sculpture; flames played about the feet of a female mage.

"Calm yourselves!" Yoralyn cried.

The manifestations instantly dissipated. The sorcerers quieted, looking chagrined at having lost control.

Yoralyn came to Tol, tightly clutching her staff with both hands. Up close, he noticed the staff wasn't wood, but some kind of animal limb, covered in greenish-black hide.

"The ring, please."

He again took it out and gave it to her. She handed it to Helbin and seized Tol's large hand in her dry, gnarled fingers. Her grip was powerful, and Tol didn't struggle against it.

"Where are you?" she whispered. "I cannot find you. You are here in my hands, but invisible to my inner eye!" She released him abruptly. "I would know more of this," she said, more kindly. "Will you return and speak with me again?"

"If you wish, lady. I will be in Daltigoth and at your service, until the foundation ceremony is done."

Yoralyn addressed the assembled wizards. "Go back to your studies. I will see to the stranger. The source of his immunity to magic will be found, I promise you."

"I will assist," Oropash offered, with a gracious bow.

"As will I," put in Helbin. He regarded Tol with open hostility.

The other mages slowly dispersed. When only Yoralyn, Helbin, and Oropash remained, Tol asked the woman where he could find the fountain of the centaurs.

"Centaurs? Oh, you mean the Font of the Blue Phoenix," she said. "It faces the end of the west wing, yonder. Why do you seek it? Are you a devotee of the god?"

Tol colored a little. "I was told to meet a friend there."

Yoralyn's wrinkled face showed amusement for the first time. "Oh, you seek Valaran."

"You know her?"

"No one else from outside comes to the Font of the Blue

Phoenix." She folded her arms. "But it is a sacred site, not a trysting place for young lovers."

"We just met," Tol protested. "She wants me to tell her about life in the provinces!"

"And what do you want from her, Master Tol?"

Her pale blue, almost white, eyes bored into his own, forcing him to give serious consideration to her question. Valaran was a strange girl, educated and observant, not like his hearty companions Kiya and Miya. Although they had met only once, she had made a strong impression. Her openness and cleverness in saving him from discovery intrigued him. But what did they really have in common? Why should he seek her out?

"I want to know her better," he decided aloud.

"I suppose you do," Yoralyn said cryptically. "Very well. It's not as though we can keep you out. In the future, please enter the garden Valaran's way: Keep to the path along the wall of the Inner City; it will lead you without fail to the Font of the Blue Phoenix. For a few hours each day we leave an open passage in the Wall of Sleep there, just for her."

Tol thanked her. Before leaving, he said, "I lodge in the Riders' Hall. Summon me, and when duty permits I will come." He bowed awkwardly and hurried off to the fountain.

Helbin clenched his hand around Morthur's signet. "I will purge the ring," he said.

Yoralyn nodded, and he departed. She turned to Oropash.

"Have the boy watched," she ordered. "I would know what Master Tol does, and with whom. Use your best spy."

Oropash's round face showed alarm. "Is he dangerous?"

"I cannot tell," Yoralyn said. "If his immunity to magic is a wild talent, then he's an aberration, nothing more. But if he's an agent of a rogue mage, even an unwitting one, he may be the most dangerous person in Daltigoth. In either case, we must know the truth. See to it at once."

"It shall be done."

❦ ❦ ❦ ❦ ❦

The Font of the Blue Phoenix proved to be a beautiful shrine to the god of nature. A veritable mountain of jade rose up from a shallow pool forty paces wide. A golden disk hovered over the gemstone island, fixed in place by no visible means. All around the circumference of the basin, droplets of water fell from open air, an endless rain from a cloudless sky.

Surrounding the central isle of jade were life-sized figures of animals—horses, dogs, rabbits, deer, ancient elk, wild oxen, a crouching panther, wolves, eagles, crows, vultures, and doves. All were rendered in a startlingly lifelike fashion. Had they not been in various colors of marble, Tol might have taken them for living creatures.

Also clustered around the jade pinnacle were representations of the world's sentient inhabitants. Although elves, men, ogres, dwarves, gnomes, and kender were all present, a trio of rearing centaurs stood higher than the rest, providing the inspiration for Valaran's name for the fountain.

Tol circled the pool and saw other, more legendary beings: *bakali,* the lizard-like minions of the Dragonqueen; bull-headed minotaurs; and other strange creatures for which he had no names.

It was still too early to expect to see Valaran. Tol sat to wait for her on the sculpted marble rim of the fountain and pondered his meeting with the mages. Did they think him immune to magic? Grane's spell had put him to sleep quickly enough in his family's hut years ago. Of course, the fellow's conjurations had failed in the Great Green and on the road to Daltigoth. Although he pondered these contradictions long and hard, he couldn't find any answers. Growing bored finally, he reclined. The patter of falling water, the stillness of the clearing lulled him, and he dozed, one arm laid across his eyes.

He dreamed, and his dreams were strange indeed. In one of them he was ranging over the hills of his homeland, hunting with a bow in his hand. Far ahead, Kiya and Miya called to him to hurry. Suddenly, a plump brown rabbit broke cover and dashed in front of him. He loosed an arrow that found its mark. Running forward in triumph, he found a marble statue of a rabbit, pierced by his arrow. Blood trickled from the wound, staining the white stone.

A cold wind gusted over him. With dreamtime swiftness, the landscape changed from green hills to an unfamiliar bleak winter clime. He was alone. Kiya and Miya were nowhere to be seen. Mountains filled the horizon.

Suddenly, Tol knew a menace was behind him. He spun about, sword instantly in his hand. All he could see was a figure silhouetted against the sky, far away. It was a man—a man who meant to kill him.

Something cold touched his face. Tol flinched and struck out. He rolled off the fountain ledge and awoke when he hit the grass. In a flash he was up, ready to fight.

Valaran regarded him quizzically. In one hand she held his sheathed dagger. Slung over her shoulder was his saber and sword belt. The weight of it dragged down her pale yellow gown, exposing a smooth and slender shoulder.

"That's a fine greeting," she said. "I bring your stupid heavy knife and sword, and you throw a punch at me."

Breathing hard, Tol lowered his fists. "You shouldn't sneak up on me."

She dropped his dagger and shrugged off his saber, letting it fall heavily to the grass. In her other hand she carried a canvas satchel. Tol bent over the pool, scooping cool water to his feverish face. Valaran seated herself on the edge of the fountain and watched him.

"I've already learned one thing about country people," she said. "They don't have any manners. Do you know how hard it was to sneak out of the palace carrying that big sword? And I wasn't even certain you'd be here."

He took her hand and bowed low, as he'd seen noblemen do. "Thank you, my lady," he said fervently. "How can I repay you?"

She jerked her hand free, but he saw a touch of color come to her cheeks. "Now you're being silly."

Valaran opened her satchel. It was full of books. She read

aloud the wooden tags affixed to the ends of the scrolls. "*A History of Sancrist Isle, Customs and Practices of Balifor, Genealogy of the House of Pakin.*" She looked up at him—her green eyes were striking—and added, "But I'm glad you came today."

Tol smiled. "Really?"

She looked down at the scrolls. "Really. I've read all these before"—his smile froze into a frown—"and I hate being idle when I can learn something. Please tell me absolutely everything about yourself."

Tol was charmed anew. Despite the plain appearance she cultivated, and her sharp tongue, there was something very winning about Valaran. She didn't seem quite so young today. Her shape beneath the fine yellow linen was proof of that.

Tol did as she bade. He told her of his early life, his family, of farming, and, as modestly as possible, how he'd saved Lord Odovar from Pakin rebels. She listened, silent and attentive, until he described the capture of Vakka Zan.

"I'm a Pakin, you know," she told him calmly, then smiled at his astonishment. "Much removed, of course. My great-great-grandfather, Ersteddin Valdid, married the youngest sister of Pakin Zan. My great-aunt, Darali, was set to marry the Pakin emperor Ergothas III, but he died before the arrangements were complete."

"Is being a Pakin held against you here?"

"Not really. My father has always been loyal to Prince Amaltar. He was the prince's tutor for many years, and now he's his chamberlain."

It was Tol's turn to listen. Valaran spun a fantastic story of dynastic marriages, palace politics, suicide, murder, and madness. Tol found it appalling, but Val recounted it with great verve, even pride. She spoke of the assassination of Emperor Pakin II, providing much more detailed insight than Tol had previously heard.

"A courtier, Lord Bathastan, and three subverted servants slew Pakin II in front of the entire court. They stabbed him with daggers."

"What happened to the assassins?"

"Tortured. Killed." She said it as calmly as Tol might have said, "Hungry. Ate dinner."

Conversation lagged. Valaran leaned down to close the satchel at her feet. Her long hair fell forward, sunlight giving the brown mass a red sheen. Sitting up, she regarded him thoughtfully.

"What do you want—?" they both began in unison. Laughing, Valaran gestured for Tol to speak first.

"What would you most like to do?" he asked.

"See the city," she replied immediately.

That puzzled him. "But you live here."

"I'm never allowed outside the palace grounds. Oh, when I was two my mother took me to a healer in the Old City, but I don't remember it."

Tol was astonished. "You've left the Inner City only once? How old are you?"

She feigned offense. "Rude question! Or it would be if I were one of the empty-headed lackwits in the Consorts' Circle. They'd faint at such impertinence. I'm seventeen years and two months old. What about you?"

"Country folk don't reckon time as closely as city people do, but I think I'm over eighteen now—maybe nineteen."

An idea came to him of a sudden, and he jumped to his feet. "Valaran, let me take you outside! I've been wanting to see some of the city myself."

She regarded him skeptically. "You don't know your way about. We'll be like two blind kender with our hands in each other's pockets."

"My men, the Juramona foot guards, are quartered by the canal somewhere. I'll tell Lord Enkian I'm going down there to visit them."

Valaran stood slowly, green eyes shining. "Aren't you afraid? I'm forbidden to go out without my father's permission. We'll be punished if we're caught."

"A warrior does not fear reprisals, only failure," he said gravely. This made her chuckle, the rich sound bringing a grin to his face.

They concocted a plan. Although prohibited from leaving the Inner City, Valaran had a fair amount of freedom otherwise. Her father would not miss her if she went out after supper. Tol would meet her at sunset, by the palace kitchens. He was sure Kiya and Miya would help him smuggle her out.

Valaran shook his hand like a comrade, then hurried back to the palace to prepare for her illicit foray. Tol waited a bit, then left the Font of the Blue Phoenix, nightmares and magical immunity forgotten.

🦅 🦅 🦅 🦅 🦅

The Dom-shu sisters were not disposed to be helpful.

When Tol arrived at the kitchens after making excuses to Lord Enkian—who, frankly, cared not a whit if he left—he found Miya and Kiya chafing to get out in the city themselves. The idea that one sister should stay behind so Valaran could masquerade as her was flatly rejected.

"Why should we do this for a stranger?" grumbled Miya.

"You'd be doing it for me," Tol said, annoyed. "I ask little of you. Can't one of you oblige me in this?"

They wrangled awhile, then the sisters agreed to gamble for the right to go with Tol and Valaran. He imagined they would match for it, or do evens-odd, but instead Kiya found four big butcher knives and leaned a chopping block against the wall as a target.

"Nearest each corner wins," said Kiya. Miya agreed with a grunt.

Holding the iron point between her thumb and forefinger, Kiya hurled one knife after another at the block. Her throws were formidable; each knife came within a finger's width of its intended corner. Miya frowned and worked the big blades free. Standing beside her sister, she gripped the knives by their oily wooden handles rather than the blades. Her first three throws were no better than Kiya's, but the last imbedded in the very peak of the chopping block's upper right corner. Miya whooped in triumph.

"Don't fret, sister," she said. "While you're here, get the palace cooks to teach you how to make real food instead of dragon-bait!"

Kiya responded with a pungent metaphor, so Tol stepped between them. "My thanks, Kiya," he said, giving her a brotherly hug. "I owe you a favor."

The Dom-shu slipped on the sandals Tol had insisted they wear in the capital, then stole outside. In moments Valaran arrived. She wore a dark blue hooded cloak that covered her from head to toe.

Immediately, Kiya noted a snag in their plans, saying, "She's tiny; she'll never pass for me."

Valaran was more than a head shorter than the lofty tribal women.

"I have it!" Miya said, smacking a fist into her palm. "Husband, get on the other side of her!"

Tol winced at being labeled the mate of the Dom-shu, but he stood on Val's right while Miya flanked her left. At Miya's command, they grasped Valaran's elbows and hoisted her up.

"Light as a bird," declared Miya.

Valaran vowed they were crushing her arms, but Tol said, "Be easy. We just have to get past the guards."

"But I have no feet!"

It was true. The hem of Valaran's cloak now floated above the ground, and no legs or feet were visible below it.

"The dark will hide that," Tol said, and the three of them bid farewell to Kiya.

They headed down the lane to the south gate. As it was used only by victualers and tradesfolk, the guards there were surprised when the trio appeared before them. The guards' poleaxes clashed together, barring the way.

"Who goes there?" snapped the sergeant of the guard.

"Tol of Juramona and his wives."

The soldier held up a shielded candle. Yellow light fell on their three faces. Valaran did not arouse suspicion by trying to avert her face.

"I know you, sir," said the guard. "You command the footmen of Lord Enkian, do you not?"

"That's right," said Tol. Valaran didn't weigh much, but the burden was starting to tell. His arm quivered with the strain and he fought to keep his voice normal. "I'm heading down to the canal district to visit my men. I have Lord Enkian's permission."

"Ah, you're a Rider of the Horde, sir, you don't need to prove anything to us!" They withdrew their arms, and let Tol and the women pass. "But tell us some time how you bested Lord Morthur, will you, sir?"

"Surely," Tol said, flattered. "I shall."

They moved away from the gate, careful not to seem too eager. Out of sight of the friendly guards, they set Valaran on her feet.

"You're becoming known," said Miya. She looked back in the direction of the gate. "I should have asked them for money."

Tol opened his mouth to protest such dishonorable behavior, but Valaran pulled at his hand. "Let's go! I want to see everything!"

The road descended a steep hill, curving slightly to the right. Valaran threw back her cloak to free her arms. She started to lower her hood, but Tol stopped her.

"No sense announcing who you are," he warned. He cautioned Miya to refer to their companion only as Val.

Valaran had studied a map of the city and she announced this avenue was called Bran's Way. It was lined on both sides by two-story warehouses—brick at ground level, timber above. Here were kept all the stores for the Inner City, as well as tribute and trade from every corner of the empire. Torches burned on iron stanchions outside the door of each warehouse, and well-armed watchmen stood guard, each with a halberd on one shoulder and a brass alarm bell in his hand.

Not until they reached the first crossing street, called Saddler's Row, did they encounter traffic. Carts and wagons, single riders on horseback, and a modest crowd of pedestrians moved in either direction. Far down Saddler's Row the lighted doorways of taverns and theaters beckoned. Miya and Valaran were ready to go that way, but Tol insisted they at least try to find Narren and the Juramona soldiers.

The closer they came to the canal, the brighter the lamplight and the thicker the crowds. Valaran was enchanted. She stopped to listen to a slanging match between a pushcart vender and a woman who apparently didn't have the price of a grilled sausage. Words were getting quite heated as Tol dragged her away.

"Wait!" she pleaded. "She just called him the three-fathered son of a pox-riddled goatherd. I want to hear his response."

"Keep moving! We'll end up in the middle of a knife-fight," Tol said.

Farther along, they came across two gnomes, pink-pated fellows with silky white beards, who had set up a table at the edge of the street. They were demonstrating an apparatus of their own design. Four flattened glass globes turned on spindles, while a rack and pinion allowed them to move backward or forward, up or down.

"With the new Solar-Optical Domestic Stove Lighter, you'll never have to buy fire again!" proclaimed the green-clad gnome. They were so alike only their clothes set them apart.

"My estimable colleague is correct," said the other gnome, who wore brown clothing spotted with gray patches. "The Solar-Optical Domestic Stove Lighter is clean, dependable, reliable, safe—"

"Sounds like the perfect husband," said Miya.

The small crowd chuckled appreciatively. Ignoring the interruption, the gnome in green resumed his spiel. "Throw away your flint and steel! Forsake dangerous and smelly tinder boxes! The Solar-Optical Domestic Stove Lighter makes all those old-fashioned items obsolete!"

"Excuse me," said Valaran, stepping up to the table. "Do I understand from the name this device uses sunlight to ignite fires?"

Both little men first looked surprised, then immensely pleased. "Just so, lady, just so!" said the brown-shirted gnome. "It's so nice to meet an educated person so far from home."

"Thank you. However, I see one grave problem with your invention."

Twin looks of approval changed to displeasure, and Valaran added, "How does it work at night?"

If she'd slapped the gnomes, she could not have stunned them more. The gnome in green faced his colleague and punched him on his cherry-red nose.

"Imbecile! How will it work at night?"

"Who are you calling imbecile?" retorted Brown. "I have a diploma from the Institute of Higher Gnomish Engineering—"

"I wipe my nose on your diploma!" Green shouted. "I dribble gravy on it too! How can a stove-lighter work without the sun?" A new thought seized him, and he shook with emotion. "Or when it rains?"

Brown attacked Green, and the two gnomes rolled on the ground, locked in a furious embrace. When they fetched up against the table, its folding legs collapsed, sending their invention crashing to the pavement. Instantly, scavengers converged on the broken device, ransacking the gnomes' goods while the two fought on.

Tol and his party moved past. Miya, looking back at the melee, said, "They're crazy. Why use that big thing when flint and iron fit in the palm of your hand?"

By the canal, boats and barges were tied up for the night. The streets were crowded, and waterfront taverns were doing a roaring business.

Valaran's head swiveled left and right as she tried to take it all in. Catching Tol's eye, she smiled, dimple dancing at the corner of her mouth.

As they strolled along the plank quayside, Miya said quietly, "We're being followed. Since the gnomes' table. Stocky fellow, dressed in black. I can't make out his face."

Tol chanced a glance. He saw no one of that description,

but trusted Miya's woodland instincts. They were acute, even in the city.

Sword and dagger reassuringly in place, Tol kept his expression pleasant for the girl's sake. "Let's find Narren and the men," he said. He took Valaran's hand, and was pleased when she didn't pull away.

They visited four inns before they found the Juramona company. The fourth spot was called The Bargeman's Rest, and it was a sprawling place, combining dock, boathouse, wineshop, and hostel.

Standing on his toes to see over the crowd, Tol spotted Narren and five of his men leaning on hogsheads, drinking from the short tin cups favored by Daltigoth's tapsters. Narren hailed him. Tol elbowed his way through the press, drawing Valaran after him. Miya hung back a few steps, watching their backs.

There was much cheering and back-slapping as Tol was reunited with his comrades. Narren spoke for all when he said, "Who's the kid, Tol?"

Valaran flushed scarlet. "Mind your tongue, rascal!"

Tol cut her off by squeezing her hand tightly. "This is a friend—Val."

"Want a drink, friend Val?" said Narren, offering her a cup.

She would have taken it, but Tol got it first and drained it down. Out the side of his mouth he said to her, "Better keep your wits about you here!"

Miya sidled up and spoke in Tol's ear. "He followed us inside. Over there, by the pile of rope."

This time Tol saw him. Dressed in black as Miya had said, the stranger seemed to blend into the dark corner.

Cutpurse? Thief? Crimper? Drunken idlers on the canal often found themselves kidnapped and put aboard outgoing barges, forced to work off the price of their passage. This fellow looked too well-heeled for such lowly work. Tol made a swift decision. Straightening his sword belt, he told Miya to keep Val out of the way.

"Narren, Gustal, with me," he said. The three of them

wedged their way through the noisy crowd, straight for Tol's black-garbed shadow.

The fellow didn't react to their obvious approach, even when they effectively boxed him in against the wall. Instead, the stranger pushed the hood of his cape back slightly from his face, revealing he was masked. A fitted black cloth covered his entire head, leaving only dark eyes visible.

"Gentlemen," he said, voice muffled as it came through a thin slit cut in the hood.

"You've been following my friends and me," Tol said. "Why?"

"You're mistaken. I often come here."

"Who are you?" demanded Narren. "Why do you hide behind that mask?"

The fellow shrugged. "I'm no one. My face is my own concern."

Tol dithered. Miya had seen the stranger follow them here, but perhaps he was telling the truth. Perhaps his presence was nothing more than a coincidence.

The stranger put two fingers in a pocket on the front of his tunic. Tol and his friends tensed, but he brought out only a silver coin.

"Have a pitcher on me," he said. "No hard feelings?"

Before Tol could accept or decline, Gustal cut him off. Somewhat the worse for drink, Gustal said belligerently, "I say we yank that hood off, get the truth out of him!"

Gustal made a clumsy grab for the mask. In a flash, the stranger's hand went beneath his cloak and came out holding a long, thin dagger. Swift as a striking snake, he drove the blade upward into Gustal's belly and then withdrew it, all in one smooth, practiced motion.

Astonishment bloomed on Gustal's ruddy face. He sagged to his knees and fell heavily against Narren, sending them both sprawling. By the time Tol looked around for him the stranger had slipped away.

"He's dead!" Narren cried, pulling himself from beneath Gustal's weight.

Tol already knew by Gustal's staring eyes it was true. The suddenness, the pointlessness of the death shocked and sickened him, but he had to put aside his feelings. Even as Narren spoke, a woman nearby saw blood flowing and she screamed. The inn erupted.

"Juramona!" Tol yelled, trying to rally his men to his side.

Close to a hundred bargemen, stevedores, serving women, and assorted jetsam of the canal district filled the inn. They didn't take kindly to being manhandled out of the way as Tol's soldiers fought to come to their commander's aid. What started with shoving and oaths quickly developed into a brawl. Stools and wine jugs flew.

Tol leaped onto a table, scanning the melee. He saw Miya pull Valaran to the far wall. By tribal custom, the Dom-shu woman would defend Tol's guest even at the cost of her own life.

Narren shouted, "There he goes!"

Tol followed his pointing hand and saw the hooded stranger running down the quay. He jumped down from the table and started to give chase. Narren tried to follow, but was tripped from behind and swallowed by the fracas.

The man had a head start, but Tol was soon treading on his heels. The masked killer spun around. Torchlight flashed on his deadly blade. Tol parried quickly, and the murderous weapon was knocked away to splash into the canal. The hooded man vaulted nimbly over a boat upturned on the shore, and produced another dagger.

"Go back, Master Tol," the stranger said, scarcely panting from his exertions. "Look to the chamberlain's daughter, or she'll burn!"

Tol risked a glance at The Bargeman's Rest and was horrified to see fire spreading over its roof.

"Who are you?" he demanded. "How do you know me?"

The stranger shook his head. "Nothing happens in Daltigoth that I don't know about. I've no orders to kill you, but I will do what I must, if you try to interfere with me."

Tol hesitated, torn between his desire to avenge Gustal's death and the need to make sure Valaran was safe.

"If you love the girl, go to her!"

With those words, the hooded stranger melted into the darkness. Wasting no time on fruitless regrets, Tol shoved his sword into its scabbard and raced back to the burning inn.

The fire watch had arrived on the scene. They formed a bucket brigade from the canal to the blazing inn. Tol sorted through the crowd until he found first Miya and Val, then Narren and his men. Soot-stained and bruised, the Juramona footmen had managed to clear the room after an overturned lamp set the rope stores afire.

Impulsively, Tol took Valaran in his arms and kissed her. Surprised, Valaran stiffened for a moment, then responded in kind.

Miya shook her head. "Kiya will be so mad! A gnome fight, wine, a tavern brawl, a fire, and our husband kisses the skinny girl—she missed everything!"

Chapter 14

The Tower

A hush fell over the multitude.

The great mosaic plaza of Daltigoth's Inner City was completely filled, from wall to wall and palace door to garden grounds. Every contingent was in its place. The marshals of the empire and their retainers stood with their backs to the Riders' Hall, facing the center of the square. All were dressed in their finest martial attire. Helmets gleamed in the bright sunshine; spearpoints and scale-mail glittered. Standards of every province hung from their poles—limply, as no wind stirred.

Across from the warlords of Ergoth were the residents of the Imperial Palace—the emperor's wives, children, and relatives—as well as courtiers and their families. All wore their best raiment: smooth silk, weighty brocade, soft, stifling velvet. Every color known to nature, and a few the gods had never imagined before today, was in that crowd. Red predominated, as befitting a ceremony presided over by the reigning dynast of the Ackal line.

Behind the imperial household crowded those who served them, from the highest valet to the humblest dustman. They were but a smudge of drab gray and brown in comparison to the bold rainbow presented by their betters, but every servant sported a scrap of crimson: from swatches tied on their arms, to scarves or headbands, to the discarded piece of frayed red ribbon binding a scullery maid's hair. Even the imperial cooks wore red cockades pinned to their starched aprons.

Also assembled, at right angles to the warriors and imperial household, was the college of wizards. The Red Robes were divided, flanking the slightly smaller number of White Robes in their midst. All presented a solemn face for the occasion. A few wore gold or silver ornaments, but the leaders of the orders were dressed plainest of all.

Every eye was fixed on the doors of the palace. Ranging down the steps in full panoply were the Imperial Guards, three ranks deep. Every man wore a new scarlet cape and feather plume on his helmet. Even the shafts of their pole arms were painted red. At the bottom of the broad steps the mounted guard was arrayed in a double line, facing each other five paces apart. Sabers bared and laid against their shoulders, the Horse Guard's iron cuirasses had been polished until they shone like mirrors. Elite of the elite, the greatest warriors of the empire, every man was a noble, equal in rank to the provincial marshals.

On plinths to either side of the palace steps were musicians. Both groups were composed of drummers, cornetists, pipers, and sistrumists. The drummers stood behind a half circle of waist-high goatskin drums, the same sort played a thousand years earlier by the tribes who had first settled Ergoth. In front of the drummers were the cornetists, equipped with both brass instruments and gilded rams' horns. The pipers played the more recently invented brass flute, brought to Ergoth from the gnome island of Sancrist. Lastly, sistrum players—men naked to the waist and wearing the horned heads of buck deer—rested the staffs of their brazen rattles on their feet, awaiting the order to play.

Every eye was on the palace door—every eye except Tol's. From his place at the rear of the Juramona delegation, his attention was focused on the gaudy crowd opposite. He searched the courtiers for Valaran. Not given to extravagant dress, she was impossible to spot.

He hadn't seen Val since returning her to the palace two

days ago, following their misadventure in the city. He'd managed to slip away to the fountain of the centaurs each day at the appointed time, but she did not appear. He wondered if his bold kiss had frightened or offended her. Neither of the Dom-shu sisters had any sympathy for his fretting. Kiya, peeved at having missed their wild night in the city, told him simply to "be a man." Miya's equally unhelpful advice was, "If she's meek enough to be scared away by a kiss, she's not worth your trouble."

At some hidden signal, drums and brass horns sounded. The crowd stirred, and Tol turned his attention to the palace. The tall, gilded portals swung inward. The drums began a steady cadence, augmented by the jangle of sistrums. Out the palace door marched a standard bearer, holding a golden sun disk, symbol of the emperor. Four honor guards followed, in cloth-of-gold mantles and gilded helmets. They carried enormous two-handed swords, unsheathed.

A new, less impressive figure emerged before the honor guard reached the steps. Bare-headed and in clad in wine-colored robes was the emperor's eldest son and heir-apparent, Crown Prince Amaltar. Aside from the golden torque around his neck and the jewel-studded circlet on his brow, he was one of the most modestly dressed nobles in the square. He descended the steps with dignity, keeping an interval of five steps behind the honor guard.

Next came eight women archers in white robes, carrying unstrung bows. These were the prince's wives, chosen for him from among the highest families in the empire. They also functioned as Amaltar's ceremonial bodyguard.

Behind the archer-wives came a host of small children, offspring of the various imperial princes. They too were dressed in white, and carried baskets of pink and white dogwood petals, which they scattered on the steps and mosaic pavement. Their floral tribute exhausted, they slipped through the ranks of the Horse Guards and joined the rest of the imperial household.

When Amaltar, the standard bearer, and the honor guard reached the end of the lane made by the Horse Guards, they stopped. The chiefs of the Red and White Robes bowed their heads to the prince, and Amaltar moved to the side, looking to the open doors of the palace. He was ringed by his wives.

The drumming ceased. A fresh hush fell over the Inner City. The cornetists put down their new-fangled brass instruments and took up their rams' horns. The silence was shattered by a deep, bleating note from the sixteen cornets. It was an ancient call, as old as humanity, and echoed within the high stone walls as no other sound made that morning. Tol felt a lump grow in his throat.

Warriors next to him murmured, "The emperor . . . the emperor . . ."

Pipers began playing a slow march, and the rest of the musicians joined in. Innocent of honor guards or consorts, Emperor Pakin III strode out the palace door.

A spontaneous shout went up from ten thousand throats: "Long live the emperor!"

Tol found himself shouting with the rest. He was so moved by the great ceremony, he couldn't help himself.

The emperor was a big man, much like Egrin in size and apparent age. Unlike his clean-shaven son, Pakin III wore a full warrior's beard, iron gray and neatly trimmed. A white silk mantle, edged in crimson and with golden tassels, hung from his shoulders. His tunic and kilt were red velvet, so dark it looked almost black. At his throat he wore a chain of heavy golden medallions. From his brow the crown of Ergoth flashed, two gilded horns amid a ring of stylized solar rays. His rider's soft boots and leggings were made of the finest doeskin. In the crook of his left arm was the imperial scepter, an ivory baton inlaid with one hundred flawless rubies. The orbs on the ends were single rubies, each the size of a ripe apple.

Pakin III did not acknowledge the shouts. Having paused at the top of the stairs, he squared his shoulders and began to descend. Hurrahs gave way to general cheering. Warriors held high spears or swords, ladies waved handkerchiefs, and children threw fistfuls of red rose petals in the emperor's path.

Only the wizards remained composed, stolidly waiting their time.

The procession wasn't finished. In the emperor's wake came the empress, slow-moving and beautiful, and Pakin III's other sons. The only one of the four Tol recognized was red-haired Prince Nazramin, draped in black and gold. Behind them walked ambassadors from foreign lands and vassal states—burly dwarves of Thorin, gnomes from Sancrist, richly draped merchant-princes from Tarsis, and even kender delegations from Balifor and Hylo. Tol was surprised to espy six Silvanesti, cool and aloof, following the ragtag kender. There were no centaurs or ogres. Centaurs were too frag-mented and nomadic to maintain diplomatic relations, and the ogres were eternal enemies of all humankind.

The emperor reached the center of the plaza, the center of the Inner City. Prince Amaltar and his retinue went down on their knees, and the standard bearer lowered the banner of the empire to Pakin III's feet.

Now the priests and mages bowed in unison to their host and temporal master. Pakin III held out his scepter, and the musicians finished their playing with a flourish.

From far across the crowded square, Tol heard the emperor's voice ring out: "Send forth the high mages of the White and Red Robes!"

Four sorcerers stepped forward, two from each order. One of the White Robes Tol recognized as Yoralyn. Once emperor and wizards met, the crowd edged forward to better view the proceedings. Tol, however, could see nothing but the heads and shoulders around him.

"What's happening?" he asked.

"The emperor and the high mages are exchanging greet-ings," explained Lord Enkian, standing in front of Tol. Though he could see little better, he had been informed how the ceremony would unfold. "Small gifts will be exchanged, then the wizards will bring forth the cornerstone."

Sure enough, after some polite byplay, the assembled sor-cerers parted, and a gang of forty-four muscled laborers crept into view, dragging a sledge bearing an enormous block of stone. The cube was four steps wide on every side, and it was all the workmen could do to ease the monstrous stone forward. Chanting in unison to synchronize their effort, the sledge gang slowly advanced. Pakin III waited, imperturbable, as the cornerstone approached at barely a crawl.

The sun was well over the wall by now, and in the still air Tol was sweltering. Packed shoulder to shoulder, the high and mighty of the empire likewise waited—and sweated.

At last the great stone thudded to a halt before Pakin III. He said words Tol couldn't hear, and touched the stone with his scepter. Tol sighed inwardly. If they had to stand here until the work gang shifted the stone all the way to the tower site, they'd still be waiting when night fell!

Fortunately, that wasn't the plan. Having sanctioned the construction of the new Tower of Sorcery, the emperor withdrew to the palace steps. Prince Amaltar followed. The empress and the foreign representatives fell back among the Horse Guards. Pakin III halted on the steps and once again raised his imperial baton to the wizards.

The high mages were joined by their assistants, and the rest of the Red and White Robes filled in behind them as close as possible. All the mages linked hands. A low, steady murmur filled the plaza, punctuated by the beat of a solitary drum. The chant grew in volume and intensity. Out of nowhere, a cold blast shivered through the Inner City, causing a grateful moan to arise from the sweat-drenched onlookers. Fallen blossoms, now brown around the edges, rose in a whirlwind from the sorcerers' park.

The stone block rose into the air, bobbling above the sledge like a cork in a basin of water.

Tol's mouth fell open in shock.

The chanting increased in volume, until it was echoing off the city walls. All the mages now raised their joined hands high, rapidly shouting their incantation. Tol tried to isolate the words, but they were meaningless to him, perhaps another language entirely.

Compelled by the will of twelve hundred sorcerers, the block soared into the air. Courtiers and hardened warriors alike gave vent to their surprise as the stone cube lofted skyward, light as a feather. When it was level with the top of the Inner City's wall, it paused, hovering.

The elder mages shouted a single sharp syllable. They repeated it slowly, over and over. The cornerstone began tumbling in place. In counterpoint to the elders, the balance of the college of wizards chanted a different spell, just four words which they repeated endlessly. The rotating block drifted in a straight line toward the tower site. It skimmed just over the treetops. When it reached the proper place, the chanting stopped. The white stone block stabilized thirty paces off the ground. Slowly, very slowly, the elders lowered their hands. Following their movement, the cornerstone sank below the treetops. Though it was lost from the sight of those in the plaza, the wizards maintained the gentle descent of their arms. When at last their hands were at their sides again, the block was in place. Four of the eldest sages collapsed, completely drained by the effort.

That was not the end. Yoralyn and the remaining elders came together in a much smaller circle, facing inward. They each thrust their right hand into the middle of the circle until their fingers touched. The drifting cloud of flower petals ceased whirling and began to coalesce at the tower site. A second ring of mages closed in on Yoralyn's, and then a third. The pastel column of petals formed a cylinder rising from the trees to well above the Inner City wall.

Thunder rolled out of the cloudless sky. A second chill blast swept through the plaza. The assembly gasped as the column of flower petals seemed to solidify into a tower a hundred paces tall, with minarets halfway up its length and a tall, conical roof.

"What theater," Lord Enkian snorted. "A tower made of cherry blossoms? They'll have to work in stone if they expect that thing to stand!"

His cynical words jolted Tol, but could not lessen the

impact of the enthralling spectacle. Although the grand ceremony was at an end, the magically crafted phantom tower remained, shining white against the clear blue vault of sky.

Unhurriedly, the emperor re-entered the palace, followed by the crown prince, the empress, princes of the blood, guards, and standard bearer. The foreign ambassadors remained in the square, and as the Horse and Foot guards withdrew, the mass of onlookers flowed together. Tol sensed Lord Enkian moving away to leave and managed to tear his gaze from the cherry-blossom tower.

"My lord, will you be needing me?" he asked the marshal.

"Need you? No, not till tonight for the grand banquet. We are to sit at the crown prince's table. See to it you are there, on time and without arms! Clear?"

Tol saluted, jostling people in the thick crowd. "I shall be there, my lord."

He slipped away, anxious to continue his search for Valaran. He saw any number of ladies, lovely and unlovely, dark-haired and blonde, but none was his newfound love. As he was buffeted back and forth by the surging crowd, he despaired. Where was Valaran?

A strong hand grasped his elbow and held on. He tried to see who'd grabbed him, but the unseen stranger twisted his arm so he couldn't move.

"Don't struggle," said a low voice close to his ear. "This is your friend from the quayside."

The hooded killer from the tavern! "What do you want?"

"Come to the Font of the Blue Phoenix today. You'll be met."

"Met by whom?" Tol tried to break the killer's hold, but failed. "When?" he asked, exasperated.

"You know who, and you know when."

The iron grip vanished. Tol spun, but the fellow was quick—and lost in the throng of people.

The fellow must have meant Valaran and her customary visit to the fountain four marks before sunset. Yet how could the murderer know of Tol's rendezvous with Valaran, unless she'd been forced to tell him? Fear and fury filled Tol.

He would keep the date. If Valaran were harmed in any way, the hooded stranger and any who aided him would pay severely. This Tol vowed as he remembered his man Gustal, victim of his last encounter with the smooth-voiced killer.

🦉 🦉 🦉 🦉 🦉

All Daltigoth took on a festival air that afternoon. The streets were full of people celebrating the beginning of the new Tower of Sorcery. They gathered in huge crowds outside the Inner City, gazing up at the vast surrogate tower. Most cared not a whit about the magical orders or their progress, but gladly seized upon the ceremonial day as an excuse for revelry. People danced in every street, and wine flowed.

Tol consulted with Narren about his coming meeting. Narren agreed the masked killer was hardly the sort of go-between a gently raised girl like Valaran would use, so the meeting was likely a trap. Narren also agreed Tol had no choice but to go. In the end, his only practical advice was that Tol should wear a mail shirt under his jerkin, to fend off back-stabs and thrown knives.

When the sun dipped into the foothills west of the city, Tol clasped hands with Narren and bade him farewell.

"May the gods go with you," Narren said. Grinning, he added, "Better yet, may the Dom-shu sisters go with you. They're the equal of any masked strangers!"

Tol took his leave without comment. He had no intention of involving Miya and Kiya—and risking their lives, too.

The vast palace square was nearly empty when he arrived. The guards at the gate knew him by sight now, and waved him through. In the plaza was a line of head-high iron tripods; each would hold a burning torch after nightfall. The double line of tripods ran from the palace steps to the edge of the wizards' garden.

Tol entered the west end of the garden, hurrying to reach the fountain on time. To his surprise, he spotted couples strolling

"Listen to me, Master Tol!" said Yoralyn. "Long, long ago, in the time the bards call the Age of Dreams, the mighty Irda flourished in a power and glory that not even the empire of Ergoth can match. Created by the Dragonqueen herself, they feared neither mortal being nor god. To protect themselves against the powers of Light and Neutrality, they made these nullstones—some as large as the Imperial Palace! Thousands of small ones, like yours, were used in every building the Irda erected. Most have been lost or destroyed in the terrible wars since the Irda fell. I am ninety and five years old, and this is the first I've ever seen."

Yoralyn paused to draw a deep breath, staring into Tol's eyes. "Do you understand?" she asked. "Nullstones are extremely rare now and, because of what they can do, much sought after by those few who know their power. The emperor himself does not possess such an artifact! There are forces abroad in the world who would level an entire city to obtain an Irda nullstone. If it becomes known you have one, you'll be hunted and hounded to your death, along with everyone you care about!"

Her words hung in the air, sharp as daggers. Tol was amazed to think he'd been carrying such a thing for two years, unrecognized, in his pouch. It certainly explained his odd immunity to magic, as well as his inability to make Morthur's ring work for him. But should he get rid of it now, when he'd only just learned of its power?

"Can it be destroyed?" he finally asked.

"Smashing or melting it should do it. Nullstone metal is not as hard as ordinary iron, and the band's power resides not in the metal itself, but in the wholeness of shape and the spells laid on it in construction," Helbin said.

There was silence again as Tol pondered this information.

"Yes, destroy it," Yoralyn said, reading the uncertainty in his face. "It will be the death of you if you don't."

He bowed to them. "I will take care of it. Will you pledge to keep this a secret among us?"

She put out her bony hand, and Oropash and Helbin

clasped it. "We swear not to speak of this to anyone else," Yoralyn intoned. The two men echoed her oath.

Tol saw the torches in the plaza had been lit, as twilight had fallen. With hasty politeness, he took his leave. "My thanks for all your advice and wisdom. I must go. The crown prince expects me to dine at his table tonight."

When Tol had departed, Oropash rubbed his sweating palms together. "Will he do it?"

Yoralyn said, "No, I do not think so."

"He'll suffer then," Helbin said darkly.

"Yes, he will." Yoralyn glanced at the towers of the Imperial Palace, jutting above the darkening trees. "But if that young man manages to keep his artifact a secret, he will transcend his suffering, and one day he may sit upon the throne of Ergoth."

"Tol has no such ambitions," scoffed a voice from the deep shadows. A black-garbed figure moved out from the trees. He wore a close-fitting hood.

"Why are you lurking there?" Yoralyn demanded angrily.

"You asked me to come, lady," the hooded man replied.

"What do you know of Master Tol or his ambitions?" asked Oropash contemptuously.

The masked man put a hand to the back of his neck and untied the string there. With a flourish, he whipped off his hood, revealing ebon skin and closely trimmed curly hair. "Tol and I were boys together in Juramona. We were friends once. I know him as well as anyone."

Yoralyn's hand gripped her staff tightly. "Crake, is it true—did you kill in our service?" she said, voice grating harshly.

"A necessary act, lady."

"Necessary!" Oropash's round face reflected his obvious disgust.

Crake looked from the horrified face of one mage to another, and he shrugged. "I did it to preserve the secret of our relationship."

"I made a mistake to hire you," Yoralyn said. "You are released from our service. Never come here again!"

She departed with haste. Oropash followed her, but Helbin lingered.

"You say you were once a friend of Tol's, yet you're willing to fight him, kill him, perhaps. Why so, Crake?"

"That's my business. I didn't become what I am by giving away advantages," Crake said.

"What are you? A soulless spy? A mercenary?"

"We all must live as the gods decide."

Helbin gave up trying to understand. Shaking his head, he followed his compatriots.

The sky had darkened to dusk. Crake watched the stars emerge for a moment, then brought his attention earthward again, looking the way Tol had taken only moments before.

No, his old friend was not ambitious. But Crake himself certainly was.

❦ ❦ ❦ ❦ ❦

Tol strode along the pebbled path, his thoughts racing in many directions. The fear that something might have happened to Valaran had ordered his thoughts at last. He would declare his love to her, tonight. He would find her father and ask permission to wed her. As for the Irda nullstone, he would not destroy it. No, it would be his secret forever. Only a few people back in Juramona even knew he had it: Egrin and Felryn hadn't recognized it, and no one else had seen it, not even Narren.

A shadow slid out of the shrubbery ahead. It ghosted to the middle of the path, blocking his way.

Neither moon was up yet, but by faint starlight Tol could see that the person wore a cloth hood, completely covering his head. Immediately, Tol drew his saber.

"Very good," stated the hooded man. "You never were one for useless banter."

"This time you won't get away so easily. I owe a debt to the man you killed."

"Old, forgotten history. We have new business, you and I. The artifact, please."

He held out his hand. Tol swung his blade at it, but cut only air.

"Betraying your masters now?" asked Tol, inching closer.

"I live by what I know," the fellow replied. His hand dropped, then rose again gripping a long thin dagger, like the one he'd used on Gustal. "I'd rather not have to use this. Give it over."

"Never!" Tol cried, lunging.

The man twisted out of reach of Tol's blade, then flipped his dagger at Tol's face. Tol batted it away with his sword hilt. By the time he recovered his stance, however, the black-garbed killer had melted into the darkness.

Tol cut a swath through the air in a complete circle, striking nothing.

"Would you really skewer me, Tol?"

He stiffened.

The killer emerged from the shadows to one side of Tol. He tossed the hood at Tol's feet, lifting his face to the feeble starlight.

"Crake?" It came out as a gasp. "By Corij, I thought I recognized your voice—is it really you?"

"Been a long time, Tol," he said with heavy irony.

Tol's head reeled. "So you've become an assassin?"

Crake's dark eyes narrowed. "Not an assassin—a man of work. Your soldier friend shouldn't have laid hands on me."

Tol shouted, "Gustal was drunk! You could have brushed him aside! You killed him for nothing, Crake!"

"We're not boys anymore, Tol, and Daltigoth isn't Juramona." Crake shot back with equal heat. For a moment Crake's eyes grew distant, as memories flickered there. He presented the point of another dagger.

"Last chance," he said. "Give over the nullstone."

Tol couldn't believe he was facing Crake with a sword in his hand. Crake and Narren were his oldest friends, starting from the very day he arrived in Juramona. When Crake fled town under a cloud for having killed a man at the tavern, Tol never doubted it had been done in self-defense. Now, two years later, the man facing him seemed an utter stranger. A deadly, intent stranger.

"I won't hand it over," Tol said tersely. "Not while I live."

In answer, Crake flung a dagger. Caught unaware, Tol couldn't even get his sword up in time to deflect the knife. It thudded hard against his breastbone, but no blood appeared. The dagger fell to the gravel with a metallic clang. His mail shirt had saved him.

Tol brought his saber down in a long, wide cut. Crake fell back with a grunt, a diagonal slash on his chest. Blood welled from a shallow wound.

Tol had no time to celebrate. Crake commenced a whirling, two-handed attack, a long dagger in each fist. Tol parried shakily, then gave ground to avoid the flashing blades.

By now he was off the garden path, on the dewy grass. Crake stopped his windmill attack and came on, daggers held low.

They traded cuts and parries, Crake's lightning moves against Tol's strength and longer blade. Still, the young soldier was forced to retreat.

But Tol had a second blade, too. Breaking contact just long enough to step back a few paces, he drew Amaltar's gift dagger with his left hand.

"You're good," said Crake, voice steady. He wasn't even winded. "I thought you'd have given it up by now."

"Foot soldiers must stand and fight. Can't outrun horses, you know."

Crake's hands came up and he threw both daggers at the same time. Tol knocked down the one whizzing at his face, but couldn't prevent the other from burying itself in his left thigh. Crake drew another dagger, advanced a step, then stopped, dumbfounded.

Tol showed no signs of going down. In fact, while holding his saber at full extension, he grasped the handle of the dagger and yanked it from his leg.

Crake folded his arms, tapping the point of his last dagger against his chin. "I see this task calls for more iron," he said. "Another time."

"No," Tol said through gritted teeth. "One of us will not leave this garden alive!"

Crake shrugged, turned, and ran. Tol pursued, leg wound or no. Blood sluiced down his injured leg, staining the grass. By sheer force of will, he kept up with the fleeing man. Crake knew of the nullstone. He couldn't be allowed to escape with that knowledge.

Unnerved by Tol's implacable pursuit, Crake erred. He blundered into the torchlit plaza. Several hundred guests of the emperor had gathered there before the banquet. They looked on in astonishment as the black-clad Crake, bleeding from a long cut on his chest, entered the circle of firelight.

Guards came running. Crake tried to double back into the shadowy garden, and there was Tol. More consternation broke out when Tol appeared, sword and dagger in hand. Not knowing who was who, guards swarmed out of the barrack by the main gate. They swiftly ringed both men. Hundreds of swords were drawn.

"Keep off!" Crake yelled. "Out of my way!"

He drove straight at Tol, his thin dagger piercing Tol's forearm. Tol hardly felt it go in, but his hand immediately went slack. His saber clattered to the mosaic.

Tol threw himself backward, pulling his arm off Crake's blade. Again, his childhood friend was amazed at Tol's stamina. Switching to an overhand grip, he darted in, aiming for Tol's throat.

Imperial guards were closing in. One shouted, "It's Tol of Juramona!" and the rest voiced shock that the crown prince's favorite was dueling at the very steps of the Imperial Palace.

Tol struck with Prince Amaltar's dagger. The broad blade caught Crake's thin one, and Tol used his superior strength to throw Crake back.

"Hey, Juramona! Have this!"

A sword came winging through the air. Tol snatched it with his right hand, forcing his weak fingers to close on the handle. His attack was awkward because of the injury to his left arm, and Crake skillfully turned the plunging blade aside with his dagger. However, the sword had distracted his attention. With a mighty thrust, Tol buried his own dagger in his opponent's belly all the way to the burnished brass hilt. Crake gasped as their bodies thudded together.

Eye to eye, they stared at each other for a silent, frozen moment.

"Well done," Crake gasped, and fell backward, Tol's blade still in him.

Tol's leg and his strength failed. He collapsed beside his former friend.

Chapter 15

Longer Name, Shorter Life

He awoke in daylight, in a bright sunny room with a ceiling so lofty he could scarcely believe it. He was lying in a big bed between cool linen sheets, naked but for a breechcloth. He felt no pain, but was terribly weak.

The room was enormous. Sunshine poured in through a phalanx of windows four stories high. Other beds lined the walls, but all were empty. Someone close by made a noise, a little cough just loud enough to be heard. Tol slowly turned his head and beheld Valaran, seated in a tall wooden chair alongside his bed. She had an open scroll spread across her lap.

"You're awake! Good! If you'd slept much longer, I would've run out of things to read." She got up and held a beaker of cool water to his lips. He drank gratefully.

"I can't believe it," he said hoarsely. "What is this place?"

"The Hall of Healing, in the palace. How do you feel? Better?"

He allowed he did, and she awarded him one of her smiles. It vanished when she said, "You certainly know how to embarrass a girl!"

His confusion was plain, so she explained. "Last night you were carried into the palace, bleeding profusely. All you could say was 'Valaran, Valaran,' over and over. Draymon, commander of the Imperial Guard, sent for me. Father demanded a full explanation!"

242

He apologized, but she shrugged impishly. "It made for a lively evening. After I told mother and father how I knew you, they heard about the murderer you killed. The story is all over the Inner City."

Tol said sharply, "Crake's dead?"

"Yes. The guards were agog over your fatal thrust."

Tol closed his eyes. He had killed Crake, one of his first friends, the free-spirited flute player whose skill with a bow had saved Tol's life in the Great Green. The pain that flared in his heart was nearly overwhelming. Although he and Narren were friends, Tol had always been closer to Crake. Shilder were given few days away from training, but during his early days in Juramona, Tol had spent much of his free time with Crake's family. They had lived in Juramona for four generations. How could he bring them such black news—that their son was not only dead, but had died an assassin, and by Tol's own hand.

"I'll let you sleep," Valaran said, her voice penetrating his misery. She was rolling up a scroll on Silvanesti geography.

"No!" The word came out more harshly than he intended, but above all, he wanted her to stay. She ceased making preparations to leave.

The import of her earlier words suddenly sank in, and he realized an entire day had passed. "I missed the banquet! Prince Amaltar and Lord Enkian will be furious!"

"Well, it was quite an affair," Val said, "thanks to you. Everyone was talking about you, Tol, even the emperor. The featherheads in the Consorts' Circle were livid!"

He blinked several times, having trouble keeping up with her rapid changes of subject. "Why?"

"Because a dashing warrior from Juramona swooned on the palace steps, calling *my* name."

Although her tone was mocking, she was blushing. Tol gazed at her face, his own misery eased by the light he saw in her eyes.

"I missed you after our excursion into the city," he finally said. "You didn't come to the fountain. I thought you were angry with me."

"Why should I be angry?"

"Because I kissed you."

"Oh." She toed the silk slippers from her feet, letting the dainty footwear drop to the floor. She drew her bare feet up beneath herself, a very childlike posture. "I didn't object, did I?"

He agreed she hadn't.

"I couldn't get out of the palace for two days. Father had everyone practicing day and night for the banquet."

Careful of his injured left thigh, Tol turned on his right side, the better to see her. "Practice for what?"

"Our introduction to the crown prince. My two unmarried sisters and I were formally presented to him at the banquet."

"But surely you've met him before? Seen him around the palace and such?"

Valaran looped fine hair behind one ear. "Of course, but my father has been trying to arrange marriages for us for some time. The crown prince, being crown prince, gets first choice of all eligible ladies."

"Which one of your sisters did he pick?"

"Me," she said, smiling. "All the nobles and ladies were talking about your fight, and how you called out for me. I suppose that influenced him. He's never taken much notice of me before."

Tol felt as though his wound had been re-opened with a red hot iron. "It can't be," he whispered.

"It's true. I am to marry Crown Prince Amaltar at the next fortuitous conjunction of Solin and the constellation of Mishas."

Tol sat up abruptly, almost losing his sheet. Pain lanced through his leg. "You can't! I love you, Val!"

Her breezy manner evaporated. She hugged the geography scroll to herself and looked away. "I can, and I will," she said. "It's my duty, to my family and the empire. The crown prince has publicly chosen me. I can't decline. To do so would ruin my entire family."

"Don't you love me?"

Her green eyes returned to his face. "Yes, I suppose I do."

"Then we'll leave Daltigoth—leave Ergoth altogether!"

She stood quickly. "No! Aren't you listening? Can't your dim provincial mind understand? If I humiliated the crown prince, my father would lose his head, and the rest of my family—mother, brothers and sisters, my nieces and nephews—all would be sold into servitude! Everything we own—land, servants, goods—would be forfeit to the crown. Everything!"

His eyes stung with tears. Closing them, he said, "Isn't true love worth it?"

For an instant anger flared across her face, but compassion won out. "I'm sorry, Tol. I'm not some country lass who can leave the family farm for your sake."

Tol wondered how he'd ever thought her too young for him. Just now, she seemed immeasurably older and worldly-wise.

She started to leave, but he caught her wrist and held on. "So you'll marry the prince. Will you then be empress one day?"

"Oh, no. When Amaltar succeeds to the crown, one of his wives will be designated empress, but I'm not from the first rank of nobility. That's why my father was so pleased I was chosen. The union will greatly improve our family's standing at court."

Tol released her. He could not take it in, could not understand the logic of it. Not only was the girl he loved being taken away, but she was wedding a man with many wives already.

Her cool hand rested on his forehead. "Don't despair," she said calmly. "We might still see each other. Amaltar does not love me, nor I him."

He shivered, whether from anticipation, or fear, he wasn't certain. "How can we be lovers if you're married to the heir to the throne of Ergoth?"

Misunderstanding, she hastened to reassure him. "It shouldn't be too difficult. Ardent Amaltar is not. He's a cold cipher of a man, who'd rather hatch a scheme than woo a lady. Once we're married, I doubt I will see him much more than I do now. Oh, I'll be expected to have his children, but not for a while. We can be together if we're discreet."

He didn't know whether to weep or laugh. Born and raised in the Imperial Palace, Val had lived her entire life surrounded by intrigue, marriages of state, and affairs of convenience. He wondered if she truly loved him, or loved only what he represented—the adventure of being with an outsider, someone rough, notorious, and perhaps dangerous.

Seeing him frown, Valaran put out a hand and touched his cheek. As she looked down at him, green eyes bright and a half-smile on her face, his doubts fled.

If Valaran would have him, he would be there. No other course was possible. She was a wound from which he would never recover.

❦ ❦ ❦ ❦ ❦

Tol was up and walking in a few days. At first the only patient in the Hall of Healing, he had company from his second day on. A guard injured in a fall, a cook with burned hands, and the ten-year-old dyspeptic son of a courtier soon occupied other beds. They were kept well away from Tol, and they all received visitors. He did not. He was surprised Kiya and Miya did not come to see him, and stricken when Valaran did not return. Not till he was able to walk again did he discover why he'd been left so alone.

He hobbled past the long line of beds to the double doors and managed to swing one open. Barring the way were four of the Inner City Guard, bearing halberds. Politely, Tol was ordered back from the door. When he asked why he couldn't go out, the corporal said only, "Orders."

"Am I under arrest?" Tol asked, leaning his weight against the edge of the door and feeling extremely grubby next to the sleek, alert guards.

"Arrested persons go to cells, not the Hall of Healing," replied the corporal.

Tol decided that meant he wasn't under arrest. He asked if anyone had come to see him while he slept.

"No one can be admitted to see you."

Tol was perplexed. "Why not?"

"Orders."

Exhausted, he gave up. Returning to his bed, and ignoring the petulant complaints of the injured cook, Tol spent a feverish day trying to unravel his confusing situation. Evidently he was in trouble, but for what offense? The killing of Crake, though it weighed heavily on his heart, clearly had been an act of self-defense.

Inevitably his mind returned to Valaran. Betrothed to the crown prince, she was no longer just a girl in the palace, hiding in alcoves or stealing off to gardens to read. Wounded and weak, he'd given his feelings away. Prince Amaltar and Lord Valdid must know all, which would explain why he was being kept isolated.

These mental exertions left him in a sweat, spoiling his rest. Two days after his conversation with the guards, he was hollow-eyed with anxiety. The arrival of Lord Draymon, captain of the Inner City Guard, seemed to confirm his fears his life would soon be over. They must have decided to execute him for presuming to court a high-born lady.

"Arise, Master Tol," said Draymon. "His Imperial Highness requires your presence." Tol studied the captain's face for clues to his fate, but saw only professional indifference.

Two palace valets had come with Draymon, and they laid out a complete set of clothes for Tol—not his usual soldier's togs, but a handsome ensemble of crisp linen and gray leather, trimmed in imperial red.

"What's going on?" he asked, keeping his voice even despite his fears.

"Crown Prince Amaltar requires your presence. Be quick. His Highness does not like to be kept waiting."

Tol pulled off his sick-room shift and dressed. He was unfamiliar with some of the fancier items, but the valets smoothly fitted, buckled, and buttoned him into the outfit. Save for his lank hair, he looked quite the gentleman when they were done. Bypassing the new pouch they'd provided, he tied his old, rain-spotted one, containing the Irda nullstone and Morthur Dermount's sapphire ring, around his waist.

Lord Draymon led the way. Tol's thigh still gave him a twinge, but he was on the mend, thanks to the skillful ministrations of the clerics of Mishas. They had applied healing poultices to his wound, drawing the soreness out and speeding the healing. Even so, he had trouble keeping up with the long-limbed captain's stride.

The four soldiers by the door fell in step behind them. The ominous tramp of their booted feet made Tol all the more certain he was going to meet a dire fate. He questioned Draymon again.

"You know what I know," said the captain. "I am to bring you to the Hall of Audiences."

The public side of the Imperial Palace was quite spectacular. Everything was constructed on an enormous scale. Ceilings were ten paces high; walls were faced with tapestries or polished marble paneling; and intricate mosaics covered the floors. Lord Draymon conducted Tol through a series of corridors and antechambers before halting before a monumental double door that extended from floor to ceiling.

"Prepare yourself," he said quietly. Tol's heart contracted to a hard knot, but he squared his shoulders and thrust his chin out. Come what may, he would not dishonor himself, his mentor Egrin, or the good name of Juramona.

The massive doors swung inward. Draymon and the guards struck their heels together and strode inside in perfect step.

The audience hall was a very long room with a high, arched ceiling. All along Tol's right were lofty windows, open to the summer air. Light streamed in through the towering arches, softening the harsh bas-relief sculptures of emperors, warriors, and generals, wrought far larger than life size on the facing wall. Like Amaltar's tent outside Caergoth, the hall was alive with courtiers, favor-seekers, warlords, and foreigners. Loud laughter rang out from the back of the hall, where a group of richly dressed young men were tormenting a hapless servant, pushing him from side to side as he desperately tried not to spill the tray full of goblets he carried. With them, seated on a tall chair by the wall, was Prince Nazramin. In a posture eloquent of arrogance and disdain, he sat with one long leg thrust out, ignoring the inconvenience it posed to all who passed by. At his feet lay a huge mastiff, its coat closely clipped to reveal heavily muscled limbs. Scars on the dog's chest and front legs showed that he was a fierce battler. Nazramin gave Draymon and Tol a brief sidelong glance, then kicked his dog's rump. A loud growl erupted from the beast, and its brown eyes followed the two men with a chilling fixity.

A portly little man, not very old but bald as an egg, sidled up to Draymon, bowing.

"Who shall I say has arrived?" he asked in a light, lisping voice.

"Tol of Juramona," the captain barked as though speaking to raw troops. "We are expected by His Highness!"

The round little man wasn't at all impressed. "You will wait. I will announce you," he said, bowing. He scurried away.

Tol asked who the fellow was, and the captain said, "Graybardo, fifth—or maybe sixth—chamberlain to the prince. Vain little weasel . . ."

Graybardo came hurrying back, quite red in the face. "This way, this way!" he said. "Hurry, please! The prince doesn't like to be kept waiting!"

The armed guards remained at the door. Draymon unhitched his sword belt and handed it to his corporal, then he and Tol followed on the anxious Graybardo's heels. They made an imposing pair, cleaving through the crowd like a couple of wolfhounds through a flock of brightly plumed birds.

Prince Amaltar was concluding a conversation as they arrived. Facing him was a delegation of three richly dressed Tarsans, two men flanking a woman. She was tall and raven-haired, wearing a tunic and trews of sky-blue silk. Her face and figure were at odds with the masculine cut of her clothing. Staring at her seductive profile, Tol had the feeling he'd seen her before.

Paul B. Thompson and Tonya C. Cook

"Gracious prince, those are the wishes of the Syndics," she was saying, her voice smooth and rich as honey. "May I convey to them your answer?"

"Lady Hanira, decisions this weighty must be considered at length. My imperial father needs to be told of your proposals, and the Council of Companions must be consulted," Amaltar replied coolly.

The ambassador from Tarsis bowed like a courtly swain. "I shall remain in Daltigoth four days," she said. "I pray the gods counsel you to an answer before I must depart for home."

She turned with a flourish and glided away. Onlookers gasped at the woman's impertinence, turning her back on the crown prince. Her male comrades departed in the proper fashion, backing away, eyes lowered.

As Hanira swept by, Tol remembered her now from the tent at Caergoth—how she had stared so boldly at him. In passing, she did so again, and Tol thought he saw a flicker of recognition in her honey-colored eyes.

With the Tarsan delegation gone, Amaltar beckoned Draymon and Tol forward. He took a silver goblet from a tray borne by a waiting lackey.

"Draymon. Good, I'm glad you're here. Welcome, Master Tol." Amaltar suddenly seemed all kindness, but Tol was not relieved by his reception. Too often he'd seen Odovar or Enkian sentence prisoners to death with a smile and a gentle word. Those who exercised power often learned to put a soft face on their harshest rulings.

"That woman!" Amaltar exclaimed, once he'd drunk from the goblet. "She has more"—he checked himself—"more *nerve* than all the men in the Council of Companions." He set the empty goblet on the tray. The servant promptly whisked it away. "Do you know, she had the impudence to present an ultimatum! To me, crown prince of the Ergoth Empire! We sent a note to the Syndics of Tarsis, complaining about the high taxes they charge on goods they import from the empire. And what do you think their reply was? They're doubling the tariff again!"

"Will there be war?" asked Draymon carefully.

"We shall see. Many crave war with Tarsis, if only to cleanse their influence from Hylo and the north." Shifting his attention, the prince said, "You seem to be healing well, Master Tol. Doing better than the other fellow, eh?" Amaltar leaned forward and adopted a confidential tone. "You know," he added. "My informants tell me this Crake had killed twenty-four opponents single-handed, including ten city guards. Tell me—how were you able to best him, Master Tol?"

Tol found such numbers impossible to credit, but he kept a calm face. "I was lucky, Your Highness. I lost my sword, but someone threw me another."

The prince shot a glance at Draymon, noting the captain had colored like a handmaiden.

Amaltar smiled. "You're just the sort of man I need. Skillful and lucky—an unbeatable combination." He cast about, and not seeing who he wanted, shouted, "Valdid? Where's Lord Valdid?"

Valaran's father shouldered through the crowd behind Tol. "Here, Your Highness! I have the casque. I had to hunt all through the imperial stores to find it."

Under one arm Valdid carried an old wooden box, the corners of which were reinforced with tarnished bronze medallions. He presented the dusty box to Prince Amaltar, who set it on his lap and raised the lid.

"Come forward, Tol of Juramona."

Tol glanced at Draymon for elucidation. The captain of the guard was staring straight ahead and said nothing. Tol took a step closer to the prince, and was commanded to kneel. He sank to one knee.

Amaltar handed the box to Valdid and rose to his feet. When the crown prince stood, all conversation in the hall died. Tol felt several hundred pairs of curious eyes fixed on the back of his head.

"For outstanding service to the throne of Ergoth, by exposing Silvanesti plots in the Great Green and the capturing the chief of the Dom-shu tribe; for the defeat and death in single combat of the traitor Morthur Dermount, and for ending the career of the arch-criminal known as Crake, I, Amaltar Vorjurn Ackal Ergot, first-born son of His Imperial Majesty Pakin III, do hereby bequeath upon Tol of Juramona the Order of the Silver Saber!"

From the box, Amaltar lifted a heavy silver chain from which hung a thick silver disk. He draped this around Tol's bowed head.

"I meant to give this to you at the great banquet," the prince whispered, "but you were having too much fun in the courtyard to attend, eh?" Too stunned to reply, Tol gazed at the heavy silver medallion resting on the breast of his borrowed finery.

Amaltar stood back, and Lord Valdid indicated to Tol he should stand and face the throng. He did, and they broke out in applause.

Lord Draymon stepped forward and offered his hand. They clasped arms like old comrades.

"I thought I was going to be punished!" Tol said over the cheering.

"Just wait," Draymon said wryly. "You have been!"

Amaltar sat down and called for a commission in the city Horse Guards. A blank parchment was found. Tol's name was about to be filled in when Valdid stopped the scribe.

"Your Highness," he said. "Master Tol is of common birth."

"So? Every bull has the horns his father leaves him."

"Of course, mighty prince, but the law enacted by Ackal II Dermount states no person of common birth may enter the Horse Guards."

"Such laws do not apply to me!" Prince Amaltar declared. Valdid maintained his long face.

"They do, gracious Highness. Only the emperor is above the law."

Murmured commentary among the onlookers increased, much to the crown prince's annoyance. He stood. "Ridiculous!" he said. "Am I not my father's co-ruler? Still, if they want the emperor's hand on this act, they shall have it! Come, Master Tol!"

Above the crown prince's throne, hanging from gilded ropes, were a series of curtains and tapestries which walled off the rear half of the massive hall from view. Dragging Tol along, and with a frantic Valdid in close pursuit, Amaltar charged through the hanging curtains, swatting them aside.

"Wait, Your Highness! Please, wait!" Valdid called in vain.

Amaltar perused the nest of cords and poles over head, then commanded, "This way!"

Baffled but obedient, Tol stuck close behind him. He found himself in a maze of rising platforms, each no more than a pace deep and separated from its neighbor by a shifting, soft fabric wall. As they climbed layer after layer, the curtains became progressively lighter, more sheer, until finally they were as filmy as clouds.

Tol looked at the ceiling. Below, it had been a good twenty paces away. Now that they had climbed up innumerable platforms inside the maze of hanging curtains, the roof was only half as distant. The layers of curtains deadened the noise from the hall below, lending the high platform an eerie, isolated feeling.

Amaltar parted the last gauze curtain to reveal a large and ornate table, long and narrow, with at least fifty high-backed chairs along each of its two long sides. The air was warm and muggy, tinged with the acrid smell of incense.

"Father?" said the crown prince. "Father, it is I."

Seated in the tallest chair at the end of the table, his back to Amaltar and Tol, was Emperor Pakin III. Tol went to his knees.

"Father?" said Amaltar, gently nudging the figure nodding in the chair. Pakin III stirred.

Tol stole a look. He could hardly credit that the gray-faced old man he saw was the vigorous ruler who'd received the adulation of the crowd in the palace courtyard just days before. His beard was whiter than Tol remembered, his face dry and colorless. He was still a large man, but in the courtyard had seemed powerful and strong. Up close he looked bowed by years and the weight of command.

"What is it?" Pakin said. Amaltar said a few words in the emperor's ear. Pakin III nodded.

"Come here, boy."

Tol came round the side of the great table and knelt again.

"Amaltar tells me he wants to give you the Order of the Silver Saber." Tol held up the heavy medal for the emperor to see. "It is a rare honor. No one has been awarded it since the reign of Ergothas III."

"I'm really not worthy—" Tol tried to say. Pakin III cut him off.

"Tosh, boy. I've heard about you. Thanks to you, I was able to send the insufferable ambassador from Silvanost home with a flea in his ear. That alone was worth the Silver Saber." A laugh rumbled deep within the emperor's chest. "Better still, you settled Morthur for us. You've already done more for this throne than most of the noble warriors in Daltigoth.

"Amaltar needs a man like you. He's a thinker, but he's no warrior. Be his champion. Defend him from the wolves who circle the throne every day, seeking to snatch him from his seat. Will you do that?"

"I will do whatever Your Majesty commands," Tol said fervently.

"Don't give yourself too readily, boy. They are plenty of people in this land who will gladly take from you until nothing's left but skin and bones!"

Pakin III settled back in his chair and folded his hands across his belly. He sighed, a gusty sound of great tiredness.

"To placate Valdid and the snobs in court, I'll create you a lord of the realm. What is your full name?" the emperor asked.

"Just Tol, Your Majesty."

"A sound name, but not enough for the velvet-robed nitwits around here." The emperor closed his red-rimmed eyes briefly. "My ancestor, Ackal Ergot, was a savage who drank blood from the skulls of his enemies. Did you know that?"

Tol shook his head. The emperor laughed, saying, "Now they call him Ackal the Great. He *was* great, a great savage. It took a ferocious warrior to carve out an empire, and it takes new generations of cunning and bloodthirsty warriors to keep it going. If we don't defend the empire, someone else will tear it from our hands, a worse savage than I or my son."

"Father," Amaltar said, trying to keep the emperor's mind on his task.

"Yes, yes." Pakin III extended a hand scarred by many a battle. "There was a warrior, one of Ackal Ergot's boon companions. Your name starts out like his, so I'll give you the rest of it."

Clearing his throat, he said, "Arise, Tolandruth, Lord of the Realm, commander of the Horse Guards, champion of the House of Ackal."

Tol stood, slowed by his aching leg, and by the full burden of a new name and weighty titles.

"Father," Amaltar said, "didn't Ackal the Great cut off Tolandruth's head?"

"He cut off all his friends' heads, eventually," murmured Pakin III. In moments he was asleep again, snoring softly.

Amaltar and Tol departed. They found Valdid lurking outside the innermost ring of curtains. The crown prince relayed the news of Tol's elevation.

"His Majesty's will be done," replied the chamberlain, bowing his head. "But it may not go well for Master Tol—that is, for Lord Tolandruth. The nobles of the empire are proud, Highness. They may not accept a newly made peer born of peasant stock." Valdid nodded to Tol. "No offense, my lord."

Tol blinked at the title, but said automatically, "No offense taken."

The fact was, his head was swimming from his sudden change of fortune. He'd wakened this morning believing it might be his last day of life, and instead he'd been raised to nobility by the hand of the emperor himself, awarded an honor shared by the greatest warriors in the empire's history, and named to command a prestigious body of fighters. He could scarcely take it all in.

Crown Prince Amaltar presented him to the crowd in the audience hall as Lord Tolandruth, commander of the city

Horse Guards. The assembled courtiers and favor-seekers cheered, as was their wont, but Tol wasn't fooled by their enthusiasm.

There were a few who didn't bother applauding. Most of the silent ones clustered around Prince Nazramin, Amaltar's younger brother, loafing at the far end of the hall. Since seeing Prince Nazramin abuse Valdid in the back halls of the palace, Tol had heard many stories of the prince's monstrous pride and cruelty. The stony silence of Nazramin and his cronies seemed louder than the cheers of the crowd. Valdid's prediction of Tol's poor reception was already coming true.

❦ ❦ ❦ ❦ ❦

Lord Enkian was thunderstruck. Gone was the eighteen-year-old foot soldier he knew, and in his place stood the new commander of the city's mounted garrison, wearing the ancient Order of the Silver Saber, and Enkian's own equal, Lord Tolandruth.

"I am bewitched," Enkian said. "How can this be?"

"If it's witchcraft, my lord, then the emperor cast the spell," Tol replied. He was giddy with the ability to bandy words with his once forbidding liege.

The rest of Enkian's entourage from Juramona stood by, likewise dumbfounded. Relfas asked, "So, you'll not be coming back with us?"

Tol shook his head, grinning foolishly.

"Fantastic," said Enkian. "Egrin will not believe it."

Mention of Tol's old mentor deflated his elation. What about Egrin? Would he never see him again? He thought fast.

"I have two requests for you, my lord," he said to Enkian. "I'd like to send a letter to Egrin—will you see he gets it?" The marshal nodded, and Tol added, "I also want to keep some of the Juramona footmen here with me—as many as ten, if that's all right."

Enkian shrugged. "Keep them all, if you want," he said, and Tol ignored the slight against his men.

The Juramona delegation was due to depart in two days. Tol would not begin his duties as commander of the Horse Guards until the following day. In the short interim, he rounded up the foot soldiers from the canal quarter and told them his news. To his surprise, they already knew.

"The whole city rings with your name," Narren said. "They say you were ennobled by the emperor's own hand. Is it true?" Tol admitted it was.

He told them of his plan to keep ten men in Daltigoth as his personal retainers. To a man, they all volunteered. Tol chose Narren, then picked nine more based on special skills or talents they had. Tarthan, Allacath, Wellax, and Frez he chose as the four best spearmen in Juramona; Darpo and Lestan were the bravest and steadiest of the footmen; Fellen, son of a builder, was a skillful field engineer. Valvorn and Sanksa, formerly of the Karad-shu tribe, were gifted scouts and trackers. Only Frez and Tarthan were older than thirty, and all the men were fine warriors.

To the rest of the soldiers he was obliged to bid farewell. "Wherever service to the emperor takes me, I shall always be Tol of Juramona, a foot soldier of the Household Guard."

The cheers raised for this declaration echoed from the blackened rafters of The Bargeman's Rest.

After sending Narren off with money to find lodgings for his new retinue, Tol returned to the Inner City. He crossed the open courtyard, pausing before the Riders' Hall. On a whim, he turned away from the hall and entered the wizards' garden. It was growing dark among the elms and yew as he made his way to the Font of the Blue Phoenix.

She was there, curled up on the pool ledge. Tol moved silently up behind her, thinking a little scare would do Valaran good.

"Grown men shouldn't tiptoe. You look silly," she said, raising her head.

"I thought you were asleep."

"No. Reading." The light was so poor she had had her nose pressed to the parchment. *The Confessions of Milgas Kadwar.*

What nonsense! No one can reach Luin by ladder!" she scoffed.

He didn't know what she was talking about, and didn't care. He took her in his arms, lifting her bodily from the low marble wall. Valaran did not resist, nor did she return his ardor.

"You always have one thing on your mind," she said.

"You inspire me," he replied. He entwined his fingers in her thick brown hair and tried to kiss her, but she dodged him.

"We must be careful, Tol," she chided, pulling back. "I'm to wed the crown prince in seven days."

The words were cold water thrown in his face. "You don't have to remind me!"

"You must be a man about this." Valaran tucked her legs underneath and smoothed her robe.

He looked away at the fireflies glittering around them. "If I were a man, I wouldn't let anyone take you away from me, not even a prince!"

"You're a noble now, Lord Tolandruth, so start thinking like one. Poor people marry for love; nobles marry for advantage. Don't confuse the two."

Even as she said the harshly practical words, she laid her head on his shoulder, and his sullenness vanished. He stroked her smooth cheek.

"I will take a house in the city," he whispered. "My men will be quartered there. Will you come and see me now and then?"

"What of your wives, the forest women?"

"You know," he said earnestly, "they're not really my wives. I've never touched them. They're hostages to the good behavior of the Dom-shu tribe." Realizing his words made Kiya and Miya sound unimportant, he added, "They're like sisters to me, big, tough sisters. They take care of me in their own rough way, and they'll take care of you, too."

Hand in hand, they walked back toward the square, surrounded by dancing fireflies.

"Will you write a letter for me if I tell you what to say?" Tol asked.

The dimple appeared at the corner of her mouth. "Dismissing a girl back home?"

He told her about his old friend Egrin, warden of Juramona. "He'll want to know what happened here, and I don't trust Enkian to give him the straight tale. Egrin is the man who trained me in the art of war—and how to be honorable."

"Why not send for him?" she said. "Make him one of your retainers. Many lords with less rank than you have twenty or thirty followers. You can afford eleven."

"He would not come. He's loyal to his place in Juramona."

Val sighed. "Men's loyalties make me tired. I'll ask Amaltar to make it an order. Will that move your warden?"

"Yes!" he exclaimed, and slipped his arm around her waist. "You'd really ask the prince to assign Egrin to me?"

She stared up at him. "I'd do anything for you."

In the deep shadow of the west wing of the palace, they kissed and reluctantly parted. Tol waited at the door of the Riders' Hall, watching as Valaran's slight figure was slowly engulfed by the darkness of the lane alongside the palace.

He went inside with a smile on his face. He did not notice that two floors above, an unlighted window in the Riders' Hall silently closed.

Chapter 16

The Bargain

Happiness is sometimes best measured at a distance. Close up, small flaws show more clearly. The three years Tol spent in Daltigoth were like that. During this time, he knew many fears and frustrations. Only later did he realize they were some of the happiest years of his life. In one hand he held the reins of a powerful formation of seasoned fighters; in the other, the slim, warm hand of the girl he loved. The two halves of Tol's life balanced well, helping him avoid the temptations of power, and giving him the satisfaction of knowing that he was loved—even if his lover was married.

Tol took a large house in the bustling canal district. Two stories high, built of brick and stucco around an open courtyard, it housed his retainers, Kiya and Miya, and a scruffy band of locally hired cooks, washerwomen, valets, and grooms. The highlight of life in Juramona Hall—as the inhabitants dubbed it—was when Egrin arrived to take up residence there. Summoned by Prince Amaltar's order, Egrin reclaimed his role as Tol's second father. Officially in charge of training new members of the Horse Guards, the former warden easily commanded the respect of the young guardsmen.

Tol had a somewhat more difficult time with the guardsmen, at least at first. His youth and widely known peasant origins were held against him by the well-born riders. They saw him as a palace favorite thrust upon them for political reasons. Nobles in the guard opposed him in every way short of open defiance. They pretended his provincial accent was unintelligible. Orders and dispositions were conveniently forgotten, drills and exercises ignored or performed in such a half-hearted manner their value was lost.

At first he was tolerant. He respected the experience of his subordinates. A warrior of Ergoth began riding a horse not long after he learned to walk. Some of the men under Tol's command had fifteen or twenty years in the saddle, compared to his scant seven. They felt Tol had nothing to teach them. Fighting was the birthright of an Ergoth warrior, a trait born in their blood, not a trade to be learned like throwing pots, or weaving cloth.

When a few guardsmen "forgot" to stand and salute when Tol entered their hall, however, his tolerance came to an abrupt end. Fourteen of the offenders were demoted in rank and sentenced by Tol to ride around the city's outer wall, night and day, until they dropped. Failure to obey would have meant immediate execution. A further thirty of the most recalcitrant warriors were taken to the practice field outside Daltigoth for a lesson in unity and soldierly obedience.

It was a mild autumn day, dry and clear. Tol's ten-man retinue, drawn from the ranks of the old Juramona foot guard, marched into the open field. They carried poles the length and weight of their regulation spears but lacking lethal iron heads. Tol asked his truculent horsemen how many of them it would take to rout the foot soldiers, to break their formation. No one replied until he ordered them to do so.

"Five," said one sullen warrior, a distant cousin of the House of Ackal.

"Then take four with you and show me."

"Your men will be killed."

"My men know how to defend themselves. Do your worst. I want to see if your fighting skills are equal to your arrogance."

The imperial cousin chose four of his friends, and they galloped away to gain room to charge. At Tol's nod, Narren marched his men across the dusty field. Yelling like fiends, the horsemen drew sabers and spurred their mounts at the foot soldiers. At twenty paces, Narren's band of ten made a quick turn to the left and formed a circle, presenting a hedge of blunt poles to the onrushing riders.

Seeing their targets thus arrayed, the riders tried to veer off, but Narren wouldn't let them. The footmen on the safe side of the formation swung their poles over the shoulders of their comrades, and the foot soldiers charged the horsemen! Taken aback, confused, the riders let them close, and all five were knocked from their saddles.

"Now you understand what trained, determined men on foot can do," Tol said, moving among the unhorsed men. "We taught ourselves these tactics at Juramona, an outpost on the eastern plain. Imagine what Tarsan mercenaries can do, or the host of the Speaker of the Stars!"

The noble, twice Tol's age, looked up at his young commander for a moment, then saluted smartly. "Will you show us how to beat trained footmen, my lord?" he asked.

That was the beginning of Tol's acceptance. Using his own ideas, and the sound lessons he'd learned as Egrin's shilder, Tol set about creating a new kind of horde. The Horse Guards came first to respect him, then admire him, and finally felt something akin to worship. He transformed them from a dandified street patrol into a true fighting force, a warrior band of brothers.

Not everyone accepted Tol's leadership. More than twenty well-born warriors left the Horse Guards, openly condemning Tol as a dangerous radical and a military impostor. The disaffected warriors found a champion in Prince Nazramin, who despised the new lord. He rallied the defectors to his personal standard, adding them to his already large private retinue. Riding forth from the prince's villa in the Old City, the band became known as "Nazramin's Wolves," a feared new feature of city life. They beat up courtiers and officials who affronted them, started brawls in taverns, and harassed clerics and sorcerers loyal to Prince Amaltar. More than a few times Tol had to lead a contingent of Horse Guards to arrest a wolf accused of mayhem. The guards usually got their man, but few of Nazramin's followers were ever punished. The pattern was grimly similar in each case. When the accused malefactor was brought before an imperial magistrate, no one showed up to press the complaint against him. Without the offended party, the magistrate had to release the ruffian.

Such a state of affairs never would have been allowed under a strong emperor, but each passing season made Pakin III's failing health more apparent. The day-to-day rule of the empire fell heavily on the crown prince, but many in the empire preferred the harsh, warlike Nazramin to his cold, scheming brother. To warlords accustomed to settling matters with a sword, Nazramin was seen as strong, and Amaltar as effete.

Not long after Tol assumed command of the City Horse Guards, Valaran, fourth daughter and youngest child of Lord Valdid and Lady Pernina, became Princess Consort Valaran. The elaborate marriage ceremony marked the longest time she had spent with Amaltar to that point, she told Tol. Once wed, she dined with the prince every third day, played draughts by the fireside on rainy evenings, and occasionally read aloud to him. Such, she told Tol, was the life of a princess consort.

Tol knew he should let that be enough, but he couldn't. "Has he . . . known you?"

"The marriage is not legitimate until that happens." She would have left it there, but he asked her again and she said bluntly, "Amaltar is my husband, Tol."

That had been early in their relationship, and they had moved beyond such jealousies, beyond the need to pry into each other's secrets. When the weather was warm and fair, they went together to the Font of the Blue Phoenix, to be alone, to share love. It was the perfect place for them to meet. Outsiders could not breech the spell surrounding the garden, and the sorcerers within kept far away from the Irda nullstone Tol still carried. For three years, their idyll continued, but like all perfect things, it could not last. Forces of ambition and disorder, never defeated, marshaled anew.

Paul B. Thompson and Tonya C. Cook

❦ ❦ ❦ ❦ ❦

In the autumn of the tenth year of the reign of Pakin III, war finally broke out between the empire and the city-state of Tarsis. Long-smoldering disputes over tariffs and trading rights in Hylo finally ignited into open conflict when the Tarsan fleet stopped patrolling the southern waters and pirates began to run rampant along the Ergothian coast. Kharland buccaneers, usually restrained by the powerful Tarsan navy, raided the far west coast of Ergoth, seizing captives, burning crops, and plundering villages. Lacking a large fleet, the Ergothians demanded the navy return and suppress the pirates. Tarsis refused.

The western sea raids were a diversion. The merchant-princes of Tarsis hoped to shift Ergoth's attention westward while they landed a sizable mercenary army in Hylo. The city-state had long entertained designs on the kender kingdom, nominally independent but in fact dominated by Ergoth. A few discreet agents had attempted to foment discord and resentment among the kender, but the chaotic kender proved resistant to Tarsan influence. More direct action was required, so with Ergoth's attention focused on its ravaged western coast, Tarsis put troops ashore in Hylo Bay. Ignoring the principle towns—which they could capture at their leisure—the Tarsan army marched south to meet the expected Ergothian counterattack.

Twenty-six imperial hordes rode north under Lord Urakan, commander of all imperial armies, to drive the Tarsans from Hylo. Urakan was opposed by two forces. The first was the army of Tarsan mercenaries under an elf general named Tylocost; the other, a collection of plains tribes and other hired barbarians led by the nomad chieftain Krato. Lord Urakan easily drove the plainsmen back over the Thel Mountains, but the left wing of his army was sharply defeated by Tylocost in the river country of eastern Hylo. Lord Urakan struck back by sending nine hordes up the east side of the Thel Mountains, trying to cut off Tylocost from his seaborne supplies. Fighting continued for two years, neither nation gaining the upper hand.

In the spring of Pakin III's twelfth regnal year, Prince Nazramin and his wolves, reinforced by four additional hordes, joined Lord Urakan's host. They won a bloody victory over Krato's plainsmen, utterly destroying a band of nomads in the pay of Tarsis. In the spirit of Ergothian conquerors of old, Nazramin massacred the enemy and sold their families into captivity. The red-haired prince's reputation rose high as a consequence of his victory. He returned to Daltigoth in triumph, though his only lasting accomplishment was to fill the other plains tribes with hate, driving them into the arms of Tarsis.

Tol saw no fighting in the first part of the war. Still haunted by the death of his uncle Pakin II, Prince Amaltar was more and more consumed by fear of assassination. He would not allow his champion to leave the capital, and Tol chafed at his enforced inactivity. Returning one night after chasing bandits who'd been harassing travelers on the Ackal Path, he poured out his frustrations to Egrin.

"Patience," the elder warrior counseled. "We are doing honorable service here. How many brigands did we kill this day?"

"But I want to try my men in real battle, against the Tarsans," Tol said peevishly. "Tylocost is counted the best general in the world. I want to put him to the test!"

"You'll get your chance. Neither Prince Nazramin nor Lord Urakan is a match for the elf. When the empire needs you, you will be called."

For a time it seemed his mentor was wrong, and Tol would get no chance to fight. And then, while camped in the forest outside the kender port town of Far-to-go, Lord Urakan's army was stricken by the Red Wrack, a dreadful plague. Soldiers perfectly hale at sunrise developed a hacking cough and irregular red spots on their skin by midmorning, were crimson from hair to heels by afternoon, and spitting blood by next dawn. Death followed for most in only a day. Sufferers afflicted by the worse forms of the plague would bleed from their ears and eyes before dying, which was why easterners like Tol knew the disease as "the bloodtears."

Hoping to leave behind whatever miasma was causing the disease, and save the remainder of his army, Lord Urakan abandoned his coastal camp and retreated twenty leagues into Ergothian territory, the Northern Hundred.

The Tarsans fared little better. Taking advantage of Urakan's withdrawal, Tylocost's host crossed the bay to attack Hylo city, but were repulsed with heavy loss. Kender reports (never very reliable) told of death on a massive scale, bodies piled high on the beach and in the surf, the waters of Hylo Bay stained red with the blood of ten thousand mercenaries. Problem was, no one, not even the local kender, could say who had inflicted this signal defeat on Tylocost. It wasn't Urakan's doing, nor Prince Nazramin's—he was by this time once again comfortably ensconced in Daltigoth. A third force, as yet unknown, must have joined the fray.

Tol and Egrin were present at a council of war, held in the audience hall of the Imperial Palace, when a delegation of kender arrived in Daltigoth with their account of the Tarsan disaster. Warlords filled the hall to hear the kenders' tale, and Tol knew the ailing Pakin III listened from his aerie, concealed by the curtains above and behind Amaltar's throne.

"How large was Tylocost's army?" asked the prince, perusing the enormous map laid at his feet. Drawn on a single oxhide, the map lapped at the foot of the imperial throne on one side, ran down the dais steps, and ended at the waiting kender on the other.

"Twenty thousand men," said one kender, wearing a sort of turban made of shiny cloth. It was too large for his head and had obviously been "borrowed" from someone with a bigger skull.

"Thirty thousand, you mean," corrected the second kender. He was dressed like a plainsman, in buckskin and feathers.

"Where did they land?" the prince demanded.

The turbaned kender crawled onto the map and pointed to a long, wide beach east of Hylo city.

Egrin had been staring at the turbaned kender and now said, "I know you. You came to Juramona a few years back, seeking the help of Lord Odovar against the monster XimXim."

The kender pushed his drooping turban up, and declared, "Never been there."

"He's not *that* Forry Windseed," said his buckskin-clad companion. "And I'm *not* Rufus Wrinklecap."

Egrin's eyes narrowed. He was certain he knew better, but only asked, "Could it have been XimXim who attacked Tylocost?"

By navigating a typical fog of kender exaggerations, embroidery, and outright lies, they gradually pieced together the strange tale. When Tylocost had half his army ashore, a thick gray fog blew down the bay, covering the Tarsan ships. Before long, a terrible chorus of shrieks and screams arose from the cloud. The fog turned crimson from all the blood spilled, and disciplined mercenaries threw down their arms and fled. Many boats capsized as panicked soldiers tried to row to safety. Hundreds who had escaped the carnage on the beach ended up drowning.

"Coulda been XimXim, I guess. We found no tracks on the sand—just lots of dead soldiers," Windseed said, genuinely puzzled. "Never knew ol' Xim to take on so many at once, though."

"Something must be done."

Heavy silence followed this declaration from Crown Prince Amaltar, until Lord Tremond cleared his throat. Once renowned as the handsomest man in the empire, he had become red-nosed and bloated from the soft life of the capital.

"Perhaps Lord Urakan—," he began.

"Lord Urakan has five thousand men sick, and he's lost twice that many horses to the plague. I will not ask him to do more."

"Regobart has mustered eighteen hordes, Your Highness, ready to ride north," offered Valdid cautiously.

"Lord Regobart's army is needed to safeguard the eastern border," the prince replied. "His absence there could bring on an uprising by the forest tribes, or trouble with the Silvanesti."

More silence. A loud, sneering laugh came from the far end of the hall. The assembled lords slowly turned toward the sound, and Prince Nazramin sauntered out of the dimly lit recesses of the hall. Draped in a black pantherskin mantle, his armor clinked with each footfall. Having recently returned from the war in the north, his normally long hair was still cropped, his curled mustache clipped, to fit his closed helmet. The contrast between his flaming hair and black attire was striking. He gripped a large pewter flagon in one hand.

"Such brave men!" he said in a loud voice. "Heroes one and all! Won't anyone here visit the little kender and see what's amiss?"

Tol opened his mouth to speak, but Egrin restrained him. When Tol shot him an inquiring look, the warden shook his head briefly and mouthed one word: *Beware!*

"Will you go, brother?" asked Amaltar.

"If my liege sends me, I will go." There was no respect in the words, only sarcasm. "I have piled up two thousand heads for the empire, and filled the workhouses with five thousand slaves. Still, if the emperor my father needs me again, I shall go."

He lifted the heavy cup to his lips and drank, his hand trembling ever so slightly.

"Of course," he went on, "I'll need a new army. There are plenty of salon soldiers and polished peasants in Daltigoth to fill out the ranks of a new horde, aren't there?"

Gasps echoed in the audience hall, and several warlords muttered angrily at the slander spoken against them. Many eyes glanced Tol's way. He broke Egrin's hold on his arm and stepped forward.

"Don't," Egrin warned in an undertone. "He's baiting you."

"And I'm taking the bait." Tol faced the crown prince and saluted, bringing his heels together with a loud clank. In a voice meant to carry, he said, "Your Highness, I volunteer to go."

Amaltar shook his head. "No, Lord Tolandruth. I cannot spare you. Your place is here."

"Guarding the imperial bedchamber," Nazramin sneered. "My brother cannot sleep otherwise."

"Be silent!" the crown prince snapped. "Comport yourself like a prince, not a drunken oaf, or I'll have you removed!"

Nazramin's brown eyes glittered. "As you will."

"Your Highness," Tol said, "the Horse Guards can remain in Daltigoth. With the kender as guides, I can reconnoiter Hylo with foot soldiers."

Even Tol's allies among the warlords chuckled at that.

Tol folded his arms and declared, "Give me three hundred men and I will comb Hylo from end to end. If the monster XimXim is there, I will discover him and destroy him. If he's not there, I will find out what attacked Tylocost and determine if it is a threat to the empire." He smiled briefly. "Who knows, I may find an ally in Hylo, and not a monster."

From laughter, the hall now filled with contentious words. Amaltar called for quiet, and Valdid rapped the mosaic floor with his staff until the warlords reined in their tongues.

The crown prince sat back on his throne, rubbing a finger across his clean-shaven chin. "What do you say, Mistress Yoralyn?" he asked.

Seated far to the side, the head of the White Robes in Daltigoth could not address a council of war unless spoken to by the prince or emperor. Having been given leave, though, she now said firmly, "Put your trust in Lord Tolandruth, Your Highness. He will succeed." Nazramin snorted into his pewter mug.

"We'll go with Lord Tolandruth," offered the turbaned kender, who was not Forry Windseed.

The wrangling threatened to resume, but a tall, gaunt figure emerged from the curtains behind the throne, silencing all arguments.

Although no longer the vigorous warrior of earlier decades, Emperor Pakin III still commanded the deep respect of his subjects. Everyone knelt, even Nazramin. Pakin III looked them over calmly.

"My, how you all talk. Too much talk will be the death of us," he said. "The council is over. Amaltar, send Lord Tolandruth. Give him what he wants and let him go to Hylo."

Amaltar stood, clapping his heels together in salute to his liege. "It shall be done! Lord Tolandruth will be given his pick of three hundred soldiers, and all the supplies he needs. The kender will show him the way. He will take orders directly from the throne. Let it be so recorded."

The emperor shuffled back up the dais toward the curtains. The legion of scribes seated below the prince's dais made the proper notations. Egrin shook his head at his former shilder. Prince Nazramin looked triumphant.

❧ ❧ ❧ ❧ ❧

Once he was alone with Tol in the courtyard of the Inner City, Egrin gave vent to his misgivings. "Prince Nazramin maneuvered you into this," he said. "He wants you out of Daltigoth. He'll do anything to ensure your mission fails."

"Then I'd better not fail."

As the vexed Egrin headed off to return to Juramona House, Tol remained behind. He wanted to make an offering to Mishas in the garden temple, he said, to ask the goddess to watch over him on his journey.

Over his shoulder, Egrin said, "Give her my good wishes also." And Tol was left to wonder at the import of his words.

When he reached the grove surrounding the College of Sorcery, Tol paused. The last light of the setting sun illuminated the Tower of Sorcery. The structure had reached a height of twenty paces, a massive octagon of stone encased by a rising web of scaffolding, overtopping the trees. Above the line of dense stone, the phantom tower remained, shimmering and translucent. The magical double of the tower, formed of cherry blossoms from the natural life-forces present in the college and garden, glowed shell-pink in the sunset. At night it shone white and solid, like a brilliant lamp.

Progress on the tower had been slow, for work proceeded in daylight only. At night the sorcerers activated their wall of sleep to keep intruders out. They had enlarged their spell to encompass the entire garden, even the Font of the Blue Phoenix. Of course, the barrier had no effect on Tol, protected as he was by the Irda nullstone. He'd threaded a strong copper chain through a small gap between the smoky glass and the braided circlet, allowing him to wear the nullstone on his left wrist.

Valaran had felt the metal on Tol's wrist and knew he had a talisman there, but she asked about it only once. He told her knowing the secret could end her life, and so she did not ask again.

When the sun was fully set and he was certain he was unobserved, Tol called her name softly. She stepped out from a niche in the wall. Wrapped in a dark gray cloak, she seemed a part of the warm twilight. He held out his arm, and she rested her hand lightly on his wrist. Together they walked unfazed through the invisible barrier of sleep.

The fever of their early days together, stoked by their mutual fear of discovery, had mellowed with time. They now passed some nights in conversation, even in scholarship, as Valaran enlarged on the rudimentary reading and writing skills Tol had acquired in Juramona.

This evening, Tol wasn't thinking of books. He hadn't seen Valaran for three nights. As soon as they were safe, deep in the enchanted garden by the fountain, he pulled her into his arms.

"Poor lad," she said, teasing. "You've missed me, have you?"

"I always miss you. And I'll miss you more still. The emperor has ordered me to go to Hylo and find out who defeated a Tarsan army there."

Valaran kissed him ardently. "I can ask Amaltar to keep you here—"

"No! You don't understand—I asked to go."

"You want to fight?"

Tol sat on the low wall that encircled the fountain pool. He pulled Valaran down beside him.

"I'm tired of chasing footpads through back alleys and brawling with Nazramin's thugs!" he said. "A warrior must fight, else he's just an over-dressed fool in an iron hat."

Valaran trailed her hand in the cool water, causing the reflected stars to shatter and shimmer. She looked up from the moonlit basin and regarded him seriously. "You must obey the emperor's will, as I must. But it will be terrible, being apart from you."

She leaned toward him and pressed her fist against his chin, saying sternly, "If you get yourself maimed, I'll never forgive you. Killed, however, is acceptable. I'll grieve most ardently, then find another lover. But I can't bear the sight of cripples."

Feigning shock, Tol twined his fingers in her long, soft hair and gently drew her head back. "You are a heartless woman," he said.

"I am."

"You admit it?"

"Certainly. I gave my heart to a peasant boy long ago. He keeps it still."

They read no books that night.

❦ ❦ ❦ ❦ ❦

Valaran lifted the hem of her skirt to keep it out of the dust as she hurried across the plaza to the palace. She entered through the stifling hot kitchens, quiet now that no meal was expected until breakfast. In a small room beyond the kitchens, she found Kiya and Miya. They sat at a table, heads resting on their arms, asleep. Her arrival woke Kiya, the lighter sleeper.

"Ah, it's you, Princess," Kiya muttered. "Is your visit done?"

"Done. Thank you again for helping Tol and me."

The oft-repeated words were like a ritual among them. The

Dom-shu sisters were part of Valaran's deception. Anyone in the crown prince's suite who went looking for the princess would be told she was with Kiya and Miya, collecting information about their forest tribe for a book she planned to write.

Kiya re-tied the thong that held back her long blond hair. "Don't mention it. What's a wife for, but to help her husband meet his lover?"

Kicking her sister's ankle, Kiya said sharply, "Miya! The market's open! Go buy us some venison!"

"No more 'n three silver pieces apiece," murmured the sleeper.

Val laughed softly, but Kiya rolled her eyes. "She's always been like this. Our mother used to pinch her nose shut just to wake her."

"Why don't you do that now?"

"Same reason Mama stopped doing it: Miya punches hard!"

Kiya hauled Miya to her feet, and hoisted her over one shoulder. Valaran led her through the empty kitchens.

Outside in the fresh air, the princess said, "Tol is going away, to Hylo."

"We heard. News moves like the wind in this pile of stone."

"Will you be going with him?"

Kiya yawned. "I think so. Do us good to get out of the city for a while."

"I envy you. You get to go with him. I must stay here."

The towering Dom-shu woman patted Valaran on the shoulder, and the princess said, "Take care of him. Bring him back to me."

"He doesn't need much care. But we'll watch his back, Miya and me."

With the inert Miya over her shoulder, Kiya strode off. Some distance away, she stopped and dumped her sister unceremoniously on the ground. Miya awoke, flailing her fists. After an exchange of familial insults, the women walked away together. Valaran could hear them sniping at each other long after the night had wrapped them in darkness.

She re-entered the palace. She needed no candle to light her way through the echoing, darkened corridors. So familiar was every inch of the sprawling palace, she could have run to her room blindfolded and never touched a wall or piece of furniture.

In the crown prince's suite, she ascended the stairs. As she turned off the landing, headed for her own rooms, someone stepped out of an alcove and seized her by the arm. A cry of alarm formed in her throat, but a large gloved hand covered her mouth, stifling it.

"Quiet, lady, if you please. You're in no danger. It's your brother, Nazramin."

Heart hammering, Valaran nodded her head to show she understood. His hand came away from her mouth.

She jerked her arm free, and said icily, "Brother by marriage. What is the meaning of this rude imposition?"

"Nothing of import, lady. I wanted to inquire after your health. Cavorting outdoors at night can be hazardous. All sorts of nasty vapors lie in wait for the unwary."

Valaran had mastered her surprise at his sudden appearance. "Speak plainly, sir, or do not hinder me further!"

"Fine. Hear me, Princess Betrayer: You deceive my brother with a peasant upstart!"

Alarmed anew, she drew back a step. Nazramin advanced the same distance. He was taller than his half-brother Amaltar, and more strongly built.

"Mind what you say," she snapped, eyes narrowing. "I am not some serving wench you can bully into submission!"

Nazramin came closer. "You and that farm boy are lovers, and have been for years."

"Spare me your dirty insinuations. I know the penalty for infidelity." Under Ergothian law such petty treason was punishable by burial alive. Haughtily, Valaran added, "Would I risk disgrace and death for any man? Now stand aside and let me pass!" He advanced on her until she was pressed against him. She stared up at her tormenter not with fear but stubbornness and contempt. Nazramin rested his hand on the wall, just over her shoulder, and smiled.

"Princess, I have informants everywhere. I've known about you and the peasant from the first. Days, places, how long you were together—would you like to see the catalog of specific infidelities I've compiled?"

Valaran regarded him without any change of expression, yet inside she was quaking, her heart hammering against her ribs. She didn't doubt for a moment Nazramin had her and Tol dead to rights. He could have denounced them already, but he hadn't, which meant he wanted something other than their destruction.

After only a moment's pause, she spoke, and was proud that her voice still sounded cool and steady.

"What do you want?" she asked. "Gold? You're richer than my entire family. Power? You're second in line to the throne, with all the privileges and none of the responsibilities my husband has to bear. What more does a serpent like you crave?"

He smiled, a flash of teeth behind his red mustache. His breath smelled of stale beer. "I'm not here to avenge my dear brother's honor," he admitted. "I'm more interested in having an informant in his innermost circle."

Now she was confused. "Amaltar tells me nothing—"

"Not your husband's circle, lady, your swain's."

Fury rose up in Val's breast and she cried, "I'll not betray Tol!"

"Mishas bless you, lady, of course you won't!" he said, chuckling. "And if I wanted to hurt him, I would simply reveal what I know to the prince. So please do continue your dalliance with Lord Tol. All I want from you is a record of his plans and movements—plus any letters he writes to you. Share that with me, and I won't ruin you both."

"Lord Tol" was a deliberate insult, but Valaran hadn't heard it. She was busy turning over in her mind how to escape Nazramin's suffocating coils. In spite of her outward show of bravery, she knew her fate was in the prince's grasping hands. He would certainly be believed, especially if he had specific information about her activities. For what she'd done, there was no clemency. Amaltar could not spare her even if her wanted to. She'd be entombed alive in the palace wall, and Tol would lose his head. But if all Nazramin wanted was information about the Hylo campaign—?

He read her thoughts in the frown of concentration on her face. His look of triumph infuriated her all the more.

"There may not be any letters! He'll be much too busy to bother writing me," she snapped.

"Not write to his beloved? What country swain would fail in such a pleasant duty?"

Nazramin put his hand to her throat. Valaran immediately knocked it away and ducked under his outstretched arm. The prince's low voice carried to her as she hurried up the wide stairway.

"You cannot refuse me, Princess Betrayer. My eyes and ears are everywhere. I'll know when every letter arrives. Try to hide them from me, and I'll tell a pretty tale to my brother and father."

Valaran lifted her skirt high and ran the rest of the way to her rooms. Nazramin's deep chuckle followed on her heels, terrifying, inescapable.

Chapter 17
Helpful Stranger

Without fuss or fanfare, Tol's expedition departed Daltigoth at dawn. They passed through the Old City and out the main north gate, known as the Dermount Portal, for Emperor Ackal II Dermount was entombed there directly under the gate. As an old man, he'd prepared for one last campaign against his lifelong enemies, the Wak-shu tribe. Moments after declaring he would return victorious or be buried where he fell, he dropped dead from his horse as he rode out the north gate of his own capital. His loyal retainers honored his word and buried the doughty old warrior exactly where he died.

For the first time, Tol led his three hundred men from horseback, riding Cloud, a fine dappled-gray stallion and the son of his old mount Smoke. Egrin had brought the horse with him from Juramona.

The bulk of the men given to Tol were city guardsmen, hired commoners like the foot guards he'd once led in Juramona. They were tough and competent fighters, but few had seen any campaigning outside the city. Some had never been out of Daltigoth in their lives. To guide and instruct them in foot soldier tactics, Tol appointed each man of his personal retinue, as well as Egrin, to command a company of thirty men. Each commander was also mounted.

Unlike a typical Ergothian army, Tol's demi-horde boasted no cumbersome baggage train. Each man carried ten days' supplies, his arms, and a bedroll. If more was needed, they would have to forage. Once his band left the imperial road, Tol wanted the soldiers to be able to move fast, unencumbered by slow-moving wagons or gaggles of camp followers.

Kiya and Miya walked with the soldiers. Horses weren't used in their dense forest homeland, and both women disliked the animals. They trusted their own two feet to get them where they needed to go.

Flanked by Egrin and Narren, Tol surveyed his men as they marched past. Alongside him as well were the two kender mounted on their own ponies. Forry was still clad in fringed buckskin, but Rufus had exchanged his oversized turban for a pointed cap with a sweeping plume as long as Tol's arm. Both cap and feather were a startling shade of yellow-green.

Tol found his eyes drawn away from his passing troops to the walls of the Inner City, tinted rose by the rising sun. It was ridiculous to think he might spot Valaran on the palace battlements from this distance, but he cherished the hope.

Leaving Daltigoth behind, the demi-horde marched due north, along the unfinished Kanira Path. This broad paved road, begun by the Empress Kanira over one hundred years ago, was supposed to connect Daltigoth with Hylo by way of a new city, Kaniragoth. Neither road nor city was ever completed, however. Sixteen years after deposing her husband, Emperor Mordirin, Kanira was in turn overthrown and imprisoned by Ergothas II, a fine ruler much revered in the provinces. Kanira's extravagant building schemes were quietly forgotten, and the erstwhile empress finished out her life imprisoned on a rocky pinnacle overlooking Sancrist Bay.

The distance from Daltigoth to Hylo was ninety-three leagues. At a foot soldiers' pace, it would be an eighteen-day journey, and even without the paved road, this early part of their trip would have been an easy one. The land north of Daltigoth was all flat floodplain, watered by several tributaries of the Dalti. On both sides of the elevated Kanira Path enormous fields of green wheat and barley stretched to the horizon. Walnut and burltop trees lined the road as well. Planted by Kanira's builders, they were lofty, mature giants now.

Raised in hill country, Tol found the utterly flat, ordered vista and open bowl of sky a revelation. All day he gazed ahead as clouds built from small, white streaks on the afternoon's eastern horizon into vast towers of vapor by evening. The open terrain allowed them to view some spectacular sunsets, but offered little respite from the torrential downpours.

Leaving the river bottoms behind, they entered the wooded foothills of the mountain range that encircled Daltigoth on the south, west, and north. A dozen leagues from the capital, the paved road ended, and the Kanira Path shrank from four wagons wide to a scant two. Trees and thick undergrowth encroached on the edges of the old road. Decades of freezing and thawing had crisscrossed it with ruts and exposed tree roots. This was still the chief land route to Hylo, but these days most heavy trade goods went by sea. Only peddlers, pilgrims, and plunderers used the old track. For their part, the Dom-shu sisters were happy to be done with stone under their feet. They joyfully discarded their city sandals and resumed going barefoot.

In five days, they reached the mountains proper. Camping below the ridge that evening, Tol continued the letter to Valaran he'd begun his first night away from Daltigoth. As a result of her tutelage, writing was less difficult for him than it once had been, but he still found it a tedious chore. However, he was determined to include a letter to Val with the regular dispatches that he would send off before they crossed the mountains in the morning. When dawn arrived, he would give the courier two silver crowns to deliver the sealed and folded parchment to Draymon, captain of the Inner City Guard. And Draymon in turn would pass it to a trusted servant, who would leave it in a certain alcove in the palace from which Valaran would retrieve it. The precautions seemed clumsy to Tol, but the safety of his lover was worth any amount of trouble.

Once they crested the ridge, the great western plain of the Western Hundred lay before Tol and his men. Removed from the direct influence of Daltigoth, it was a patchwork of rugged frontier towns, vineyards, and vast herds of cattle. The natural abundance of the land made it easy for them to buy victuals along the way.

On the evening of the sixth day, they reached Ropunt, the forest of central Ergoth. Nowhere near as forbidding as the Great Green, Ropunt was riddled with logging trails and dotted with woodcutters' camps.

Even so, Tol halted his men at the edge of the wood. Though there was plenty of daylight left, the forest was silent. No axes thudded into tree trunks, no shouts rang out warning of falling trees. When the Dom-shu sisters scouted ahead and saw no one at work, Tol ordered his soldiers to take up a defensive position in a field of scattered boulders. They were a long way from the coast, but Kharland pirates were known to make land raids now and then.

Preparing to ride forth with Narren, Egrin, and the two kender, Tol left Darpo in command. A steady, imperturbable warrior, Darpo had served for a time on a merchant ship. The scar that bisected his left eyebrow and ran down to his left ear was the result of that service; a line had snapped, whipping across the deck and lashing his face.

Tol's small party proceeded down a crude logging road, listening hard and watching for signs of trouble. Their kender guides had not passed this way before; they explained that they had come through a little further north.

A quarter-league along the logging trail they found a clearing. At its center sat a blockhouse, a stout, two-story log structure surrounded by a shoulder-high stockade of sharpened timbers. The upper story overhung the lower and was pierced with narrow window slits. No door was visible in the lower level. A thin ribbon of smoke oozed from the center of the roof.

Around the blockhouse, cut logs were piled, ready for shipment south. Axes and adzes lay about, many with blades pointing dangerously skyward. Egrin examined several blades. Bare metal rusted in a day, sometimes even quicker if it rained. These tools were still shiny; they hadn't been idle long.

Tol rode straight to the stockade gate. When he was twenty paces away, someone inside the blockhouse lofted an arrow at him from a window slit in the upper story. The missile stuck, quivering, in the dirt ahead of his horse.

"Who goes there?" called a muffled voice.

"We're from Daltigoth, on imperial business."

"Daltigoth? Then what are them kender doing with you?"

"They're our guides."

After a short delay, a trapdoor opened in the upper story. Five women and four children emerged.

"Our men went to cut oak two days ago and never come back," explained a rawboned redhead who gave her name as Shancy. She held a stout bow with an arrow nocked. "All the game in the woods has been scared off, so we've had no meat for eight days. There's plague about, too, so we can't be too careful."

"What sort of plague?"

"The Red Wrack."

This was the same sickness that had eroded Lord Urakan's army, and its dreaded name caused the kender to shift uneasily on their mounts. Although usually fearless when it came to confronting danger, kender had a dread of disease.

"Anyone sick here?" Tol asked. The women and children shook their heads.

Shancy said their men had gone northwest, to log a shallow valley. The Oaken Bowl, as it was known, was filled with some of the oldest oak trees in the forest.

Tol had Egrin get the names of the missing men and sent Narren back to fetch the rest of the demi-horde. Before long, they came marching down the trail.

"We'll camp here tonight," Tol announced. He set sentries to walk a line fifty paces from the blockhouse, and another line to patrol twenty-five paces in from them.

A garden of woolen bedrolls blossomed around the squat blockhouse. Campfires were built, and the men ate their rations under a dazzling aerial river of stars. For soldiers accustomed to walls, roofs, and the lights of the capital, the open blackness of the clearing was unsettling. Wolves howled in the distance. Owls, foxes, crickets, and other creatures of the night made their own noises. The Juramona men moved among the restless city soldiers, calming them with jokes.

Narren returned to the fire where Tol and Egrin were seated with Kiya, Miya, and the former Karad-shu in Tol's retinue, Valvorn and Sanksa.

"The kender are gone," he announced, and held up two kender-sized bedrolls. "They stuffed these with leaves and straw." He wondered aloud why the kender would run away. Did they know something the Ergothians didn't?

"Rotten little peckerwoods!" said Miya. "I always said you can't trust short people." Tol had to smile. Almost everyone present was shorter than the Dom-shu women.

"What do we do without our guides?" Narren asked.

"Push on," Tol replied. To Kiya and Miya: "Will you scout ahead with Valvorn and Sanksa? We need to know what's in front of us as we go along."

"These woods smell bad," said Miya, "but I'll go if Sister does."

"I'd rather scout ahead than walk behind these filthy horses. I had to wash my feet four times today," Kiya said.

Sentinels were posted, and the camp settled into a watchful rest. Tol sat with his back against an elm stump, bare saber on his lap.

❦ ❦ ❦ ❦ ❦

His eyes snapped open. Tol listened, wondering what had interrupted his doze.

A pre-dawn mist filled the clearing. All seemed normal, save a fetid smell, like decaying leather, which hung in the air.

Sword in hand, he stood up. "Narren! Egrin! On your feet!"

The men did not respond. Tol shook them, and they rolled limply under his hand. Both men still breathed, but would not wake.

Cursing silently, Tol ran along the circle of sleeping soldiers, trying to rouse them. He had no luck. Realizing it must be magic, he cast about for Miya and Kiya, but the women were gone, as were Sanksa and Valvorn. He wondered if they'd departed on their scouting mission before this unnatural lethargy had claimed the rest of his command.

Horses, tied to a picket line, snorted and pawed the ground. Tol was relieved. At least they were awake, unlike the animals stricken by the power of Morthur's ring. He freed Cloud and mounted.

On the north side of the clearing, dark shapes were moving through the fog. There were eight or ten of them, strung out in a line. Whoever they were, they were armed. The clatter of metal and squeak of tanned leather was unmistakable.

On horseback, Tol could see over the low mist. He slid his shield onto his left arm and seated his helmet on his head. The clearing was a mess of tree stumps, limbs, and sawdust, all waiting to snag an unwary foot or hoof, so he rode with care.

Twenty paces beyond his insensible troops, Tol raised his saber and called out, "Halt! In the name of Pakin III, emperor of Ergoth!"

The prowling figures did halt—then dived down into the thick mist. The sound of twigs snapping revealed the figures were drawing closer, creeping toward him.

He sheathed his sword and drew one of the two spears from the quiver on his saddle. Cloud chivvied and pranced. Trained from birth as a war-horse, he was not usually skittish. Now he flared his nostrils, unhappy with the strange noises and odors assailing him. Tol tried to steady him, but the animal churned in small circles, stirring the thick mist.

All at once a figure leaped up out of the fog. In one hand wielding a broad, curved sword, he was completely covered in strange gray-green armor made of small, jointed plates. Hissing, he chopped at Tol.

Cloud sidestepped, and Tol thrust hard with his long spear. It struck his armored antagonist in the chest, and the iron tip went in. To his shock, Tol realized the green scales weren't painted armor, but the creature's own skin!

Yowling in pain, the nightmarish apparition jumped back and swiped at the spear. Answering its cry, more scaly foes erupted from the fog.

Tol rapped his heels against Cloud's sides, and the charger lunged forward. Bending low, Tol drove the bloodied spear into the injured creature's gut. Dark fluid welled from the fresh wound.

Grasping the spear with webbed claws, the creature tried to unseat Tol by yanking on the weapon. Tol let go in time. The impaled creature fell heavily to the ground and was swallowed by the fog. Tol whipped a second spear out and turned to face his other scaly opponents.

They were armed with a mix of weapons—falchions, battle-axes, and even a morning-star flail. Tol held them off with his longer-reaching spear, jabbing at their faces and chests. One of the creatures dodged a little too slowly, and the iron head of Tol's spear raked over its shoulder. The monster let out a tremendous hiss while simultaneously spreading a wide, leathery frill that had been furled around its neck. The frill of skin filled with blood, turning bright scarlet.

The sight was too much for Cloud. The terrified horse began to rear and buck.

Tol dropped his spear and clutched at the reins, but to no avail. With a clang, he landed on his back in the mist. Cloud cantered away, eyes rolling wildly.

Shaken by the fall, Tol could hear his enemies padding toward him through the fog. He rolled onto one knee and started to draw his saber, then thought better of it. They couldn't see him under the veil of vapor, but the scrape of iron would give him away. Quietly he took out his war dagger, kept in a suede sheath under his left arm. Two spans of cold iron would have to do.

Sweeping the mist in front of him with his flail, the nearest creature grunted and squawked to his comrades. Tol heard the studded flail swish over his head. He sprang forward, driving his dagger between the creature's ribs. He aim must have been true, because his hand and arm were promptly drenched with blood. Gravely wounded though it was, the creature cracked Tol on the jaw with the handle of his flail. Tol reeled to the ground and spit out two of his back teeth. His strength spent, the creature collapsed with no more than a grunt.

Up close, the monsters were even more fearsome. Two paces tall, they were built like well-muscled humans, but their faces and scales spoiled any human resemblance. Dish-like eyes with vertical pupils, slit nostrils and thin gashes of mouths, and small ear holes made the creatures resemble oversized lizards rather than men.

Another lizard-man came pounding out of the mist, sword upraised. Tol flung the dead creature's flail at him, then stood, reaching for the pommel of his saber. He got it out just in time to parry his foe's powerful overhand attack. Tol's hand stung from the force of the blow. When he forced the lizard-man back with a riposte, he saw his iron blade was deeply nicked.

The sun was up now, brightening the sky, but the encircling trees kept the clearing in shadow. The remaining creatures closed in. Tol traded cuts with two of them, then three. Parrying a chop, he thrust home, his saber biting hard flesh. Hissing, the monster spun away, clutching its armpit. Tol followed, impaling his wounded opponent through the back. It had enough life left to backslash at Tol, the heavy falchion scoring a line of hot blood from Tol's ear to his chin.

Tol gasped, feeling like a blazing brand had been pressed to his face. He drew back, wiping blood from his jaw. Shock quickly gave way to deep fury. They would pay for this!

He faced seven lizard-men now. The surviving foes surrounded him.

Parrying overhand, he twisted to his left and slashed sideways at one, burying his battered blade in the creature's ribs. Fighting with his dagger in his left hand, Tol fended off another pair of axe-wielding monsters. The shield on his arm slowed him, so he slung it off.

"Juramona!" he cried, in case there was anyone who could rally to his side. "Juramona!"

No one came to his aid. His only hope was to end the battle sooner rather than later, before the lizards wore him down.

The fourth lizard-man succumbed to a feint with the saber, followed by a close-in thrust of the dagger into its belly. Tol made sure of his kill, finishing his dagger thrust with a hard twist. Spine severed, the lizard-man went down and did not twitch.

A tremendous blow caught Tol on the side of the head. The iron helmet saved his skull, but he went sprawling in the mist, stunned. Fortunately, the sun had finally topped the tree line. As it shone down on the fog in the clearing, it reflected enough light to make the mist seem opaque. Flat on his belly below the surface, Tol was momentarily invisible.

He finally shook off the blow and hauled himself up to a crouch. He could see the legs of his enemies as they prowled the fog for him. With a bow he could have picked them off easily, but he had no bow. Instead, he located the spear he had dropped.

The ground around him was littered with stumps and tree limbs. With the butt end of the spear braced against a stump, he raised the point to waist height and supported it with a forked hardwood branch.

Rising suddenly out of the fog, he shouted, "Scaleface! Here I am!"

They came at him helter-skelter. Tol leaped sideways onto a stump. The blade of an axe snagged his tunic, and he whacked the passing lizard-man on the back of his blunt head. A second attacker spitted himself neatly on the spear, running full tilt into the iron tip hidden by the fog. He howled and fell, thrashing out his life as the mist at last began to thin.

Panting and aching from his accumulated hurts, Tol was still outnumbered five to one, though one of the lizards was staggering from Tol's blow to his head. Spying a gleam of metal at his feet, Tol took up a lizard-man's axe. He used it to block the sword of one of his charging foes, then brought his saber down in full swing on his opponent's bare shoulder. Split from neck nearly to breastbone, the lizard-man fell back screeching, tripping his oncoming comrades. Tol backed away, whirling the axe in wide circles to clear fighting room.

Shaken by the skill of the lone warrior, the remaining lizard-men turned tail. Grateful to see the last of them, Tol let them go.

The mist was almost clear when he staggered to his camp. All around the blockhouse his men were stirring, blinking in the sunshine, coughing from their long sleep on the damp ground. Tol found Egrin standing on shaky legs, clinging to the iron tripod over the cold campfire.

"My lord!" Egrin said. "How do you come to be hurt?"

Tol related the story of his morning battle as Narren and the rest pulled themselves together. Egrin professed shame at having slept through his commander's struggle.

"It's no fault of yours," Tol answered. "You all were laid low by a spell of some kind, a magical mist that made you sleep like the dead."

Darpo and Narren cleaned their commander's wounds, applying pungent salve to the long cut on his face. When they were done, Tol led them to where the fallen lizard-men lay. Egrin's strained face paled further.

"Bakali!" he said. "Draco Paladin preserve us! There haven't been bakali in the empire since Pakin Zan conquered their last stronghold in the Western Hundred a century ago!"

Tol stood over one of the slain creatures. He'd heard tales of the bakali. It was said that during the Great Dragon War, fought a century before Ackal Ergot founded the empire, a swarm of bakali had appeared in the east, doing the bidding of an alliance of evil dragons. They invaded the Silvanesti realm, inflicting many casualties. The elves used magic to defeat them, but the spells went out of control. In the resulting chaos, thousands died in earthquakes and lightning storms that lasted days at a stretch. Later, isolated colonies of bakali were discovered in the west, where they'd fled to escape the power that had overcome their dragon masters. The early emperors crusaded long and hard against the bakali, finally wiping them out, as Egrin said, during the reign of the vigorous usurper, Pakin Zan.

Narren asked Tol why he hadn't been affected by the unnatural sleep. Unwilling to reveal the existence of his Irda artifact, Tol shrugged off the question, saying that since he'd slept sitting up, the soporific vapors must not have reached him.

As he told the others of the disappearance of Kiya, Miya, and the Karad-shu men, Tol realized Egrin was still coughing, as were fully half his men. The magical sleep had dissipated with the fog, but the coughing persisted. Oddly, the older warrior's face was no longer pale, and small red blotches had begun to appear all over his skin. Narren and the others were showing the same strange coloration on face and hands.

Shancy emerged from the blockhouse to fetch a pail of water. When she saw the stricken Ergothians, she gasped, covering her mouth with the hem of her apron.

"The Red Wrack!" she cried, retreating.

Tol felt the pit of his stomach fall away. His men had the plague! Since they'd not encountered any contagion directly, he realized it must be spread by the fog. Neither he nor Egrin could believe the bakali clever enough in sorcery to manufacture the mist themselves, which meant a wizard must be involved.

Five bakali lay lifeless in the clearing, the final wisps of fog clinging to their bodies. The city guardsmen looked over the slain lizard-men and regarded their commander with new respect. Tol brushed aside their admiration.

Shancy and the other woodcutter women were terrified by the sight of the dead lizard-men. They wondered if their men had met the same fate the bakali had obviously intended for

Tol's troop. Tol promised them he would look out for their missing loggers as his troop made its way north.

The soldiers' coughing was growing worse, and many complained of severe headaches. Although they were obviously suffering, Tol ordered them to prepare to move on. They had to find the missing scouts.

🦉 🦉 🦉 🦉 🦉

They headed deeper into the wood. Although they called periodically to their missing comrades, their cries attracted no answers. Stealth was out of the question anyway, what with half the men or more coughing ceaselessly. The tiny red splotches were growing, covering the men's faces with a crimson stain. The Red Wrack was upon them, and Tol didn't know what to do. Lord Urakan's army was served by an entire train of healers, yet they were said to have barely held out against the disease.

He contrived to touch both Narren and Egrin with the Irda nullstone, thinking its power might transfer, but their symptoms did not abate.

Tarthan and the thirty men under his command had been farther from the clearing than the rest and seemed less affected by the plague mist. Tol sent them ahead as a vanguard. Before midday Tarthan sent back word they'd found a recent trail.

When the main body caught up with Tarthan, Tol found the warrior standing in a dry creekbed that wound through the woods. A grim expression on his dark face, Tarthan pointed to several bare footprints, surrounded by three-toed bakali prints.

Tol knew those long, narrow footprints. One of the Domshu sisters had been abducted by the lizard-men.

Taking the lead himself, he drove his men relentlessly onward. The tracks continued, following the old stream bed.

Near dusk, they found Sanksa and Kiya hiding in a tree. With happy shouts, the two swung down, and for the first time in their "marriage," Kiya threw her arms around Tol and embraced him with real ardor.

"I knew you would come!" she said. "Hurry! They have Miya!"

As they moved out, Kiya explained that she, her sister, and the two men had risen well before dawn and gone out to reconnoiter as planned. When the mist first formed, they climbed trees to see over the fog. Then the bakali appeared. Communicating by hand signals, the scouts decided Valvorn and Miya would warn Tol, while Kiya and Sanksa stayed aloft to keep an eye on the lizard-men. Once Miya and Valvorn were in the fog, they lost consciousness, however, and the bakali fell on them. Valvorn was slain immediately and Miya taken captive. Sanksa and Kiya had been following the lizard-men all day. Tol had caught up with them as they rested briefly in the treetops.

"Miya is in their camp, two hills away," explained Sanksa. The plainsman's copper-colored face was grim. "I counted twenty-eight lizard-men."

Tol drew his saber. "Let's rush them!"

"Wait," Egrin said, struggling to draw breath. "Why not work around the camp and take them one by one?"

"There's no time. Besides, the way everyone's coughing, the bakali will surely hear us coming."

Tol sent Tarthan's healthy men straight on, while four companies under Narren, Wellax, Allacath, and Lestan followed as closely as they could. Egrin's band would swing wide on the right, while Frez's men took the left. The remainder, under steady Darpo, would wait in reserve, moving up where and when the situation warranted.

Tol followed Tarthan's men through the widely spaced trees. Light was failing fast, and he didn't want the bakali to elude them in the coming darkness.

From the top of the hill, they plunged down the slope, slipping and falling in the loose leaves. Deaf oldsters could have heard them coming, and as they advanced up the facing slope arrows flickered through the trees. A few men were hit, and the first wave of Ergothians faltered.

Rallying his men, Tol hacked through a wall of briars and kept going. Arrows thudded into trees and turf around him. Gasping and coughing, but still slogging forward, Narren's company topped the hill and started down behind Tarthan's. Tol heard crashing in the underbrush, punctuated by hacking and wheezing, and knew Egrin's men were on their way as well. He saw the dark silhouettes of several bakali as they stepped out from behind trees to loose their missiles. More of his men toppled, arrows in their chests.

"Long live the emperor!" shouted Tarthan, raising his sword high.

The soldiers answered in ragged fashion and charged uphill the last twenty paces. Confidently, the small group of bakali waited, thinking the line of sharpened stakes around their camp would halt the humans, who could then be punished by a rain of arrows. Tol reached the stakes first, and wormed between them without much trouble. The lizard-men had bungled. They had spaced their stakes to stop enemies as bulky as themselves, not such slender humans.

The bakali were poorly equipped with plundered weapons. Although they fought tenaciously, by the time Egrin's men closed in from the opposite side, the lizard-men were all dead. Tol searched the camp for Miya, finding her under a flimsy lean-to of willow leaves and moss. She was staked out on the ground, hands and feet bound with thick rawhide straps. Tol was shocked to see her at first because she'd been stripped of her clothing and her skin was covered with bloody red streaks.

"Husband!" she shouted. "Glad to see you. Get me loose, will you?"

Egrin and Narren arrived at the lean-to, and Miya managed a surprising yelp of modesty. Startled, the two men withdrew.

Tol sawed at her bonds with his dagger. "What happened? Did they hurt you?"

"Nay, I'm not harmed." She stared in the direction where Narren and Egrin had come and gone, making sure they did not return.

"What are all these marks?" He rubbed a finger down her arm. The red streaks smeared at his touch.

She explained the bakali had been in the process of marking her for butchering when Tol and his men arrived.

"These lizards eat humans!" she said. "Lucky for me, they like certain cuts better than others. They took too long, arguing over who would get what part of me."

The image she conjured up was horrible, but Tol found himself grinning with her.

"What part did they consider the choicest?" he asked, thinking thigh or calf, but Miya pinched the ball of her left thumb.

"Two of the lizards were going to fight to the death over who got this part of my hands," she said with a shrug.

Miya recovered her discarded clothing, using a scrap of hide to scrub away the bakali's butcher marks.

Tol said, "I'm glad you're well. Kiya would never forgive me if anything happened to you."

"Huh! She stayed safe in a tree. Next time, she gets to run from lizards."

Shouts from the bakali camp sent Tol dashing out of the lean-to. Tarthan was waving to him.

"We found another prisoner, my lord," Tarthan called.

Tol followed him into a crude bark hut, expecting to find one of the woodcutters. It was dark inside, but he could see a man sitting in the dirt, legs crossed.

"Someone bring me a light," Tol said.

"No need," said the stranger. "I have one."

A glowing yellow ball formed, hovering over the stranger's outstretched hand. By its light, Tol saw that the man was somewhere past thirty years of age, with thinning brown hair and a high forehead. He wore a belted gray robe, striped on the sleeve and hem in blue satin. The linen was much-mended, yet the garment was still far too fine for the forest. His fleshy face was drawn and haggard, the countenance of one accustomed to easy living, but who hadn't experienced much lately.

He uncrossed his legs, standing awkwardly. "I am Mandes," he said, pronouncing his name as though it were recognizable and important. "At your service, sir. And to whom do I owe my deliverance?"

"I am Tolandruth of Juramona."

"Ergothian, aren't you?" Tol nodded. Mandes gave a slight bow, saying, "Thank you for rescuing me, my lord. I thought my days were truly numbered!"

In response to Tol's original call for light, Allacath arrived, bearing a blazing brand. Kiya and Narren were close on his heels. Mandes drew his outstretched fingers together, and the globe of light he had created flared and died.

"How long have you been a prisoner of the lizard-men?" Tol asked.

"Many days. I've not eaten in so long. Can you spare a crust or two?" Narren gave Mandes what rations he had on him. The former captive devoured the stale bread and smoked beef strips.

They left the tiny hut, Mandes wincing with every step. He had large, soft feet, and was obviously unused to being barefoot. He looked around the camp, counting the dead bakali.

"Five are missing," he said.

Tol waved a hand. "Don't worry. They're all dead. I killed the others this morning."

Mandes's thin brows arched. "You? Alone?"

"Yes. My warriors were paralyzed by a sorcerous mist."

"And you weren't affected?"

Tol let the question fade, as the answer was obvious. He was watching the reunion of the Dom-shu sisters. Kiya and Miya did little more than grunt and nod at each other, but he could tell they were delighted to be together again.

The bakali camp yielded little else of value—a handful of coins, a woman's silver torque, and a hodgepodge of weapons, most in poor condition. Tol set a party of his healthiest soldiers to work building a pyre for the lizard-men's bodies. There was enough disease abroad in the land without adding rotting corpses to the mix. Six men in Tol's band had died in the fight, and they would be buried more traditionally, as befitted Ergothian warriors.

Tol sat on a log while this activity whirled around him. He had a quiet word with Narren and Egrin and they herded Mandes over to him.

"Tell us your tale, wizard," Tol said, poking a small fire on the ground in front of him. "Who are you, and how did you get here?"

Mandes drew a deep breath, throwing out his chest and striking a pose. "I am from Tarsis, as my manner of speech no doubt told you," he began. "I was once a respected exponent of the theurgical arts in the city of my birth. That changed, however, as the guilds took over, forcing independent practitioners like myself to conform or face summary punishment."

"Guilds? You mean the White and Red Robes?" said Tol.

"Yes! May they stew forever in the belly of Chaos! I, Mandes the skillful, Mandes the learned, was hounded to join the Order of the Red Robes. I refused."

"So they ran you out of town?"

Mandes's proud posture deflated, the firelight playing over his dejected expression. "Alas, yes. I fled one step ahead of their ghostly enforcers, vile wraiths raised to steal my wits as punishment for defying their orders!" He stamped his foot, grimacing when his heel struck a sharp stone. "The guilds would reduce the noble art of magic to a trade, with apprentices, journeymen, and masters who decide who can practice and where. Mandes the proud, Mandes the free, will not submit to such coercion!"

"Hmm." Tol flexed his fingers, nicked and scarred from the day's battles. "What happened after you left Tarsis?"

"My self-imposed exile was precipitous," Mandes said, face flushing. "I departed without food or proper clothing. I wandered the countryside for many, many days, coming at last to the shores of the sea. There I chanced upon a Kharland trader stranded on a bar. In exchange for my help freeing their vessel, they conveyed me to their destination."

"Ergoth?"

The sorcerer shook his head. "The Gulf of Hylo. Specifically, a kender town on the eastern shore called Free Point. There I remained for half a year, selling my services to those magically deprived folk. It was a miserable place, I must say. No culture, no real stimulation for a man of intellect like myself." He grimaced. "That, and the kender stole back almost every fee I collected. I resolved to leave, but the bakali descended on the port before I could do so."

Mandes described how a fleet of six ships, disguised as merchant vessels, landed bakali warriors on the Free Point waterfront. Before the day was out, the town was theirs. All non-kender were rounded up. Some were killed immediately and eaten by the lizard-men. Others were made to work as slaves. Mandes would have suffered one or the other fate had he not demonstrated his magical talents to the bakali commander.

"What happened to the kender of the town?" asked Tol.

"Oh, a few were caught and killed," said Manes. "But most got away. Kender have a way of making themselves scarce."

"Why didn't you use your spells to escape?" Egrin said.

"I was preparing a conjuration that would have transformed the entire scaly mob into pillars of sawdust, but one of them hit me on the head before I could finish the third incantation—"

"Why did you create the stupefying mist for them?" Tol asked, rising to his feet.

Mandes blinked once, slowly. "If I had not, they would've killed me."

"And the plague that goes with it?"

"The illness is not my doing. I know nothing about it!" the wizard proclaimed, throwing out his chest.

"Can you cure the sickness?"

"I shall do my best for your gallant men," Mandes said. "After all, you saved me from those awful lizards, and for that I am deeply grateful."

Tol did not readily trust the mage. He might be nothing more than an innocent prisoner, or he might have been in league with the bakali. Regardless, if he could cure the plague, Tol would use him, trustworthy or not. He appointed four men to watch over Mandes while he prepared a cure for the Red Wrack. Once his men were well, Tol would take the wizard to Lord Urakan, so he could work his cure on the imperial army. After that, Mandes's fate would lie in Urakan's hands.

Using an old brass cauldron salvaged from the bakali camp, Mandes made a decoction of roots, bark, and herbs, gathered skillfully despite the dark night. Two sips of the hot potion, and the sick men could immediately breathe freely. In short order their red splotches faded, and their coughs ceased.

The wizard's swift success only made Tol more suspicious. How would Mandes know exactly how to cure the illness unless he'd created it in the first place? It was enough to make Tol extremely wary of the wayward sorcerer.

Tol had doses of the cure sent back to the blockhouse for the woodcutters and their families. The same two riders were charged with carrying to Daltigoth Tol's report on the bakali and the plague, as well as another missive to Valaran.

When they were ready to move, Tol had Mandes placed on a horse and led the animal himself, so he could keep an eye on the strange fellow. Lord Urakan was camped above the head-waters of the West Caer River, twenty-two leagues away. Tol tried not think of how many Ergothian soldiers might die of the Red Wrack in the five days it would take for them to reach the camp.

Ally or Monster

The sprawling imperial army camp looked more like a shanty town than a military encampment. The pall of smoke which hung over the site was visible five leagues away. Twenty thousand men, plus at least as many traders, sutlers, and camp followers, had carved out a blight on the once-pristine grassland. Intermittent bouts of heavy rain had drenched the great army of Ergoth, which was now sinking ignobly into a lake of mud. The camp was too large to protect with the usual stockade, so the hodge-podge of tents and shacks were surrounded by a deep, muddy trench. An appalling odor permeated the scene—the combined stench of disease, death, and the manure of horses, cattle, and chickens.

Afraid to expose his men to Urakan's tainted hordes, Tol left them outside the vast, ill-favored camp and rode in with only Egrin, Narren, and Mandes. Kegs of the sorcerer's curative potion were slung on the backs of four sturdy horses.

On the journey from Ropunt, Mandes had proved an entertaining, garrulous fellow. There was no doubt he was clever, and when he wasn't being blindingly arrogant, he was fascinating company. He knew all the gossip of Tarsis (at least up to the time he fled), and he entertained Tol and his comrades with colorful accounts of life in the wealthy port city.

The sentries they encountered were listless and gray-faced. More than the Red Wrack was plaguing Urakan's army, the men reported. Ague and flux were rampant. The sentries themselves were so weak they could barely stand.

Outside Lord Urakan's tent, Tol and Egrin dismounted, leaving Narren to watch Mandes and the kegs. They entered and found Urakan at his table, alone, with his head in his hands.

"My lord?"

Urakan looked up. The arrogant, iron-limbed general Tol had known in Daltigoth was gone. In his place sat a tired, dispirited man, his beard starting to go white.

"Lord Tolandruth! And Egrin, Raemel's son, isn't it?" he said hoarsely. He stood, propped up by his hands on the table. "By the gods, I never thought to see you here!"

They clasped arms all around. "I had word from Prince Amaltar you were on your way north, but he didn't say you were coming to see me," Urakan added, somewhat plaintively.

"This wasn't part of my original mission," Tol replied. He described their encounter with the bakali and the subsequent capture of Mandes. Tol expected the old warrior to demand the sorcerer's head for aiding the lizard-men, but the instant Urakan heard the word "cure," that's all he cared to know.

"I'm burying fifty men a day," he said, eyes dark with pain. "Is there enough potion for the entire army?"

"If there isn't, Mandes will make more," Tol vowed.

Lord Urakan received the first dose, then the kegs were sent to the great tent serving as the temple of healing, with instructions to the priests and priestesses of Mishas as to how to administer the potion. Word of the cure quickly spread, and hundreds of warriors and camp followers dragged themselves painfully to the healers' tent. Once the distribution was well underway, Tol had Mandes brought before Lord Urakan.

"What do you have to say for yourself?" asked Urakan gravely.

Not the least intimidated, the wizard launched into his tale. When he reached his enslavement by the bakali, the general interrupted him.

"Did you make this plague people call the Red Wrack?" Urakan demanded.

"No, my lord. It has always existed. I did give the bakali chief, Mithzok, certain magical perfumes and unguents, compounded into large balls of resin. When burned, the resulting fumes created a soporific veil of fog, which only sunlight could disperse."

"The plague, wizard. How did it get into the mist?" Tol interjected sharply.

Mandes lifted his hands in a gesture of ignorance. "Forgive me, lords, but is it proven the Red Wrack was a component of the mist? It did strike Lord Tolandruth's men right after the fog arose, but the sickness has long lurked in this land." The sorcerer folded his hands across his belly and furrowed his high brow. "It could be a conjuration made by the bakali, my lords. They have knowledge of poisons and sickness spells. Mayhap one of their shamans joined a coughing spell to my fog-making incense."

They cross-examined the wizard for a long time, trying to trick him into admitting he had created the plague for the bakali. But Mandes deftly avoided every trap laid for him and steadfastly maintained his innocence.

"Very well," Lord Urakan said finally. "I accept your story. Under duress, you helped the lizards. You are forgiven that weakness. Today you've done a greater service to us by curing the Red Wrack. So you are free to go."

"My lord!" Tol protested.

"What would you have me do, Tolandruth?" Urakan asked, a hint of the old arrogance coloring his voice. "I have a war to pursue. Thirty days we've lingered in this stinking morass, while Tylocost and the Tarsan army have overrun eastern Hylo. When my men are fit to fight again, I intend to retake the province. I don't want to worry about this wizard."

"What of Tylocost's defeat? Whoever destroyed half his army may still be at large in the western part of the country," Egrin observed.

"Could it have been the bakali?"

"Possibly, but I doubt it, my lord. Tylocost's defeat took

place well before the bakali are known to have arrived," said Tol.

"Solving that enigma is your task. Mine's defeating Tylocost." Urakan's strength was returning, and he plainly burned to come to grips with the elusive elf general.

Mandes cleared his throat. "May I speak, gracious lords?" At Urakan's nod he said, "If there is some unknown force at work in Hylo, Lord Tolandruth may need help dealing with it—sorcerous help. I am willing to offer my services."

Tol folded his arms and said, "That might be wise."

Even Mandes was surprised at the easy acceptance. "I'm honored by your trust, my lord," he murmured.

"Don't be. We don't know what we'll be facing up there. It may be the monster XimXim or more bakali. Who knows? Maybe there's a dragon loose in Hylo. Feel up to tangling with a dragon, Master Mandes?"

The wizard crossed his arms, insolently imitating Tol's pose. "My lord, what you can face, I can face."

For several heartbeats they gazed at each other, faces masks of measured stoicism. Suddenly Tol smiled, giving way in the end to a full-fledged grin.

"You have grit, wizard."

"I seek only to serve a worthy master," Mandes replied modestly.

✦ ✦ ✦ ✦ ✦

The change in the imperial camp was profound. Healing tents emptied, and men who'd been without appetite for days crowded around the cookfires, stuffing themselves on beef and bread. The camp took on a new air of confidence and action. As Kiya observed, Tylocost and the Tarsans had better take care. Urakan's hordes were looking to end their bored inaction, and the enemy would feel the force of their frustration.

From this scene of grim energy, Tol's column moved quickly and quietly away. An army the size of Lord Urakan's always attracted spies, especially when it remained in place a long time. Tol wanted no one to learn of his mission.

They made good progress up to the border between the Northern Hundred and Hylo proper. Beyond the stone markers bearing the arms of Emperor Ergothas II lay the kender kingdom, forested and sparsely settled. Four-fifths of the population of Hylo lived in six towns: Last Land, Windee, Hylo City, Far-to-go, Old Port, and Free Point. The rest wandered the countryside, doing incomprehensible kender things. One of Tol's captains, the former seaman Darpo, had served on a merchant ship that traded in the Hylo ports. As they camped at the edge of the forest surrounding Hylo City, Darpo spoke of his experience with the kender.

"Everyone knows their light-fingered ways," he began. The shifting light and shadow played eerily over his scarred face. When his audience snorted at his words, Darpo grinned, saying, "But kender don't steal the way human thieves do, to enrich themselves. They do it out of mischief more than anything else."

"Are there female kender?" Miya asked. They snickered at her, and she added hotly, "I've never seen one, that's all!"

"One of the ones with us before Ropunt was female," Darpo said, and took a long swig of beer, a parting gift from the grateful Lord Urakan.

"Eh? Which one?" Tol asked.

"The smaller one—the one we called Rufus."

"I don't believe it!" said Kiya. "He had a face like a spoiled apple, and no shape whatsoever!"

Darpo smiled, pushing dark blond hair back from his face. "Well, she was pretty old. Kender cultivate a vague appearance. They also change their names whenever it suits them."

"Darpo's quite right," Mandes remarked. "I lived among the kender for half a year, and I seldom could tell male from female, or get one to answer to any name I thought I knew."

As the Dom-shu sisters continued to dispute with Darpo over the gender of their erstwhile guides, Tol said to Mandes, "Once the kender know we're from Ergoth, they'll not resist us, will they?"

Paul B. Thompson and Tonya C. Cook

Mandes shrugged. "No one can predict a kender's mood, not even another kender."

"In that case, we'll keep clear of them as much as we can." He ordered a standard bearer to ride at the head of the column, displaying the colors of the empire.

They moved out at dawn, fording a shallow stream and entering the ancient forest. Trees here were twice the size of the oldest specimens in the smaller Ropunt woodland, giving the forest more the look of the primeval Great Green. Kiya and Miya were quite taken with their surroundings. It reminded them of home.

According to a map Tol had borrowed from Valaran, the stream they crossed was called Fingle's Creek. It flowed directly into Hylo Bay, by the town of Old Port. Several well-worn paths followed the creek to the sea. Tol's column glimpsed a number of kender in the woods, but they melted into the trees at the sight of so many armed men. Ever after, though they saw no one, the Ergothians knew many sharp eyes were watching them with great interest.

The creek broadened into a sizable river about the same time the first whiffs of sea air reached the marching soldiers. Tol reined in Cloud and surveyed the water from bank to bank. A few rickety piers poked out from under the trees, and nothing larger than a canoe was in sight. The kender were indifferent sailors but fanatical traders, and the lack of activity on the river told Tol that either word of the Ergothians' coming had quieted traffic, or the force responsible for Tylocost's defeat had cleared the area of commerce.

He asked Mandes, "Can you sense anything untoward?"

"I'm not a seer, my lord. My specialties are potions and perfumes, and I've begun studying ways to command the clouds—"

"I didn't ask for your life's history, just if you sensed danger!"

Mandes sniffed. "No better than you, my lord." His tone implied he did not consider it a useful trait.

Tol halted his men. He sent Sanksa and thirty skirmishers ahead to look for trouble. Another company of thirty, under the command of the seasoned Frez, he sent back as a rear guard. The high ground west of the river looked harmless, but Tol sent his engineer, Fellen, with thirty more men to look around there. The balance of the demi-horde resumed its march.

The land remained hilly right down to the sea. Before leaving the cover of the trees, Sanksa's men returned with word they'd overlooked Old Port and all appeared ordinary.

"What?" Egrin exclaimed. "Is there no garrison of Tarsan troops for us to contend with?"

"We watched all afternoon and saw naught but kender," Sanksa replied.

Old Port was on the other side of the estuary. Curious to see for himself, Tol told his men to keep to the trees and continue up the shore to the next town, Far-to-go.

"Darpo, Mandes, Miya, and Kiya will accompany me to Old Port for a closer look around," he said.

Egrin protested, saying a commander should not enter an unknown town without proper escort. Tol assured him no one would know his rank.

He proceeded to take off his helmet and red mantle. He tied a strip of homespun around his forehead as a sweatband. Dressed plainly to start with, without his cloak and helmet Tol looked like an ordinary man-at-arms. He shifted his dagger from his belt to his boot, a style affected by wandering mercenaries. Darpo likewise dressed down, commenting that Mandes already looked like a vagabond. The sorcerer pointedly ignored the slur.

Tol gave Egrin command in his absence, telling him to keep the men out of sight but moving. He wanted the demi-horde in Far-to-go by nightfall.

"How will you catch up with us?" Egrin asked.

"If there's no danger in Old Port, we'll hustle up the coast in time to rejoin you before the next town."

"And if there is danger . . .?"

Tol let the question hang. He turned Cloud over to Narren, and with his four companions set out for the kender town.

As they walked, they spoke in loud, unguarded voices of ordinary things—food, work, the weather. At the water's edge they found a kender lying in a flat-bottomed boat, face covered by a woven-grass hat. Snores rose from under the hat.

"Wake up," Tol said, rapping on the gunwale. "We want passage to town."

The kender said, "So what's stoppin' ya? Ya think I row folks across the river?"

"You mean we have to row ourselves?" said Kiya.

"Yep. One silver piece each, please."

They all looked to Miya, the renowned haggler. Eyes brightening in anticipation, she rose to the challenge.

"For a silver piece, we could hire a Tarsan galley!" she declared. "A copper per head is plenty."

"Four coppers per head," said the kender.

"One!" Miya insisted. "Plus one when we get to the other side."

"One more each?"

Miya would have continued disputing, but Tol caught her arm and nodded. "Done," she said to the kender. "One per head now, one per head on arrival."

"Done." The kender stretched out one hand. Miya gave him the first half of the payment. They piled in, sat down, and searched in vain for oars or poles.

"Where's the oars?" demanded Tol.

"Oars would be one silver piece each—"

"You try me, little man!" Miya fumed. "Nothing more! Two coppers each was the price!"

"One was just to get in, and the other pays for getting out. Nobody said anything about oars."

Tol was somewhat amused, but the Dom-shu most assuredly were not. Kiya seized the kender by his vest and dragged him up. Oddly, the grass hat clung to his face, even when she had him upright.

"Oars!" she bellowed.

The boat owner merely hung limp in her grip. Furious, she flung him into the water. Darpo and Tol rushed to the side to help the unlucky kender, but he bobbed to the surface out of reach. He had a swarthy, sunburned face, despite his clinging hat. Floating serenely on his back, the kender boatman kicked lazily away.

"Now that's negotiation," Mandes said dryly.

Tol and Darpo went ashore and cut a pair of saplings. They trimmed off the branches and used them to pole the boat out from shore. The current was strong, but they managed slow progress across the river.

From the water, Old Port lived up to its name—weather-beaten, innocent of paint. The houses were tall and narrow, worn brown by years of sun and rain, but every building bore a brightly colored pennant or metal totem, swinging in the wind. Eight merchant ships of modest size were tied up at the docks. They looked deserted and neglected. Streaks of black mold stained the canvas sails, and many lines were broken or untied. A few smaller craft crawled around the harbor.

Tol guided the boat to an empty berth on a long, ramshackle pier. A single kender, pot-bellied and possessing enormous ears, sat in a small kiosk at the end of the pier. Kiya leaped out and secured a line. They climbed out, and Tol nodded politely to the kender in the kiosk.

"Are you the harbormaster?" Tol asked.

"I am. That's Gusgrave's boat. Where's Gus?"

"He went for a swim. We borrowed his boat," Darpo said.

"Oh." The harbormaster closed his eyes and held out a hand. "Docking fee, two silver pieces."

Miya gave him two coppers. "We docked ourselves." The kender shrugged and put the coins in his shirt pocket.

"Quiet, isn't it?" said Tol. "No ships coming or going, no one loading or unloading."

"Blockade. Tarsis," the harbormaster said, yawning.

No blockading warships were in sight, but the long, narrow bay could be sealed easily at its mouth, over thirty leagues away.

"How long has the blockade been going on?" asked Darpo.

The harbormaster scratched his brown cheek. "Since the dark of the moons," he said. The night when no moons rose was forty days past.

Tol asked, "Any Tarsans here?"

"A few traders, some sailors. Flack the feather merchant, he lives in the high street." The kender looked slantwise at his interrogators and asked, "Will Ergoth attack our town?"

"How should we know?" Tol replied casually.

"You talk like Ergos. Word is, an army's coming overland from Ropunt. Are you them?"

Tol denied it, but he was perplexed. Despite their precautions, the kender seemed well informed of their presence. And if the kender knew, the Tarsans likely knew too. What of the unknown menace that had repelled Tylocost—did it (or they) also know the Ergothians' movements?

"We're mercenaries," Tol announced. "We heard there might be work here for good fighters."

"Try the Tarsans, 'cross the bay." The kender pointed vaguely northeast. "Big camp over there. General Ty-something. Maybe he'll hire you. Or maybe he'll hang you as Ergo spies."

The harbormaster leaned forward and closed the shutters of his kiosk, indicating their conversation was over.

It was late afternoon by the time they finished their explorations and regained the western shore. They tied Gusgrave's boat where they'd found it, and Miya tossed five coppers in it, the second half of the price she'd agreed to pay for use of the craft.

Tol led them quickly through the lengthening shadows. Mandes hampered their progress. He puffed and wheezed like an old man, and complained constantly of the too-brisk pace.

The setting sun colored the bay crimson, like an Ackal banner. On a bluff overlooking the calm sea, they paused to let the magician catch his breath.

"Look there!" cried Darpo, pointing out to sea.

Crawling across the flat water came a large vessel, a quinquireme of the Tarsan Navy. It ploughed ahead steadily against the offshore wind, oars flashing in the fading sunlight. Foamy green water curled back beneath the bronze ram on its prow.

Tol and his comrades took cover in the trees. Lying on their bellies, they watched the Tarsan galley approach. Three flags whipped from a pole mast stepped amidships.

"Wizard, whose pennants are those?" Tol asked.

"Topmost is the flag of Tarsis," answered Mandes. "The second is a naval flag of some sort. I'm not a warrior, but I'd guess it shows what flotilla the ship belongs to. The bottom banner"—he squinted at the colored fabric, tiny with distance—"looks like the flag of the Syndic House of Lux, the guild of goldsmiths and gem merchants."

"Merchants on a warship?" scoffed Miya.

"Wealthy merchants rule Tarsis," Mandes explained. "The House of Lux is a rich and powerful guild. Many city officials, ambassadors, and diplomats come from their ranks."

"Like Ambassador Hanira?" asked Tol, remembering the woman he'd seen in Daltigoth.

Mandes betrayed surprise. "Why, yes. Lady Hanira is mistress of the largest gemstone house in the city. How do you know her?"

"I don't know her, but I've seen her. She leaves a lasting impression."

The galley slowed as it came abreast of their position. From their high perch, the Ergothians had a clear view of the ship's main deck. Some kind of violent activity had broken out there. White-clad figures swarmed fore and aft, wrestling with mysterious gear mounted on the forecastle and poop.

Suddenly, a shadow, larger and darker than the surrounding trees, fell over the cliff top. Tol looked up as something huge and airborne rushed in, snapping off treetops above them. Silent till then, it began emitting a loud buzzing sound, louder than anything Tol had ever heard. He could feel it in his bones.

Zimm-zimm-zimm—

He knew at once what it was: XimXim was here!

The droning buzz slowed and stopped. All around the hidden Ergothians, tree limbs cracked and popped, showering them with leaves and twigs. Through the thick canopy, all Tol could see was a large, dark green mass smashing its way through the trees. He saw long, articulated limbs moving in the treetops. He counted five and stopped. Whatever XimXim was, it wasn't a dragon. Dragons were not common these days, and this monster had too many legs to be one anyway.

Loud, hollow thumps echoed across the water. Catapults on the deck of the Tarsan galley hurled giant darts at the monster. One missile hit an elm tree near Darpo, shattering the trunk.

"Tol, what should we do?" said Kiya, feeling trapped.

"Do nothing! Be still! No one knows we're here!"

A trio of ancient alders crashed down. The monster was moving straight ahead, to the edge of the bluff. Catapult darts sailed in at a steady rate, but none hit their intended target.

Miya lay by Tol's left hand, and she took hold of his arm in a grip made painfully strong by her astonishment. She didn't have to say a word. They could all see it now, emerging from the woods.

The sun was behind them, nearly set. Its bold, ruddy glow darkened the monster's green color almost to black. Rearing up nearly twenty paces, XimXim had an enormous three-sided head, with two faceted green eyes at the upper corners and a mouth equipped with many scissor-like palps. Two antennae, thick as a man's wrist, sprouted from the creature's forehead. Its head was perched on a thin stalk of a neck, which joined a relatively slender torso sheathed in green armor. Three pairs of legs supported the monster: four at the rear of the torso, and two enlarged arms hinged where the neck joined the body. Its forearms were shaped like a pair of downward-hanging scythes, their inside edges lined with sharp, saw-toothed spurs as long as a man's hand.

One mystery was solved: XimXim was a monstrous insect, a mantis of truly gigantic size.

The monster gazed coldly at the Tarsan galley. In the

center of its gigantic eyes, tiny black pupils tracked to and fro, following the movements of the terrified sailors. As more catapult darts whizzed by, XimXim unfolded stiff, bone-colored wings from its back. The wings didn't flap or flex like a bird's. They vibrated. The sound they made filled the air with the deafening, distinctive noise that gave the creature its name.

Tol wanted to shout a warning, but the men on the galley couldn't possibly hear him. He and his companions watched open-mouthed as XimXim rose lightly from the bluff and flew slowly over the bay to hover over the ship. It was completely safe from catapults there; the machines could not elevate high enough to hit it. After watching the Tarsans' futile efforts for a moment, XimXim dropped on them.

Slashing back and forth, the creature shredded the galley with its scythe-like forearms. Rigging and masts went down, entangling the hapless crew on deck. XimXim's arms tore through the stout hull planking like a farmer's blade mowing hay. After four horrible passes, the great ship was reduced to several large pieces, all sinking. By twilight's glow, the Ergothians could see black dots bobbing in the water—the heads of the crew as they swam frantically for shore.

Not satisfied with sinking the warship, XimXim swept over the water, slashing the helpless survivors to pieces. When no one was left, XimXim climbed steeply into the evening sky and flew off to the northwest.

The teeth-rattling vibration of his flight eventually faded with distance. Soon, only the lap of waves and the steady sigh of the sea breeze remained. None of them spoke for several long minutes but simply stared in numb horror at the scene below.

"By all my ancestors," said Kiya, breaking the shocked silence. "How can such a thing exist?"

"The gods' ways are unknowable," said Darpo flatly. His scarred face was ashen.

"Wizard, did you know about this?" Tol managed to say.

Mandes shook his head, whispering, "I've never seen or read anything about a monster like this in my life." It was obvious he spoke the truth; he was as shaken and gray-faced as the rest of them.

"The kender have lived under XimXim's threat for decades," Darpo said. "They have a kind of understanding with it. It eats a few of them every year, takes their cattle, sheep, or pigs, but leaves them enough to live on."

Tol remembered the day long ago when the kender delegation had come to Juramona to ask for Lord Odovar's help against the monster. Odovar had chosen to send his hordes to fight in the Great Green, a choice that cost him his life—but probably spared the men of Juramona from wholesale slaughter such as they'd just witnessed.

It was clear now what had happened to Tylocost's army, and to the eleven expeditions sent by the emperors of Ergoth to find the monster. XimXim had destroyed them all.

After years of equilibrium with the kender, the monster must have felt threatened by Tylocost's army. Perhaps it thought the mercenaries were coming to attack it, so it struck first. Sorcerers in Tylocost's pay raised a mist to hide their landing from Hylo's Royal Loyal Militia, but the mist also hid XimXim. He had torn the invading Tarsans to bits, sunk their ships, and slaughtered ten thousand armed warriors in half a morning's work.

"What now, husband?" Kiya asked.

"What can three hundred do against a beast that mighty?" Miya said. "We should go back."

Tol's response was immediate. "No," he said. "The emperor himself chose me to deal with the monster, and I will not fail! First, we must catch Egrin before he goes too far. I don't want XimXim doing to our people what he did to Tylocost's!"

The Dom-shu regarded him with respect for his staunch words. Darpo was still shaken by what they'd witnessed, but didn't question his commander. However, the reaction of Mandes, the city-bred sorcerer, surprised Tol.

For a man who had complained steadily about the pace of the march, his sore feet, and the bad food, Mandes seemed remarkably undisturbed by the prospect of facing XimXim. Once his initial shock had passed, his mood seemed more curious than afraid. "A fantastic creature, and a most unnatural one," he observed. "The world is not generally populated with monsters so great. Someone, somewhere, may have created XimXim by magical means. Perhaps on purpose."

His pale blue eyes were thoughtful as he added, "Sorcery that powerful should be studied. I would like to get a closer look at this monster, perhaps examine its lair. There may be much to learn from it."

Tol was pleased to have the sorcerer's support and felt obliged to say so. "I'm glad to have you along, Master Mandes. You may indulge your curiosity, so long as it doesn't delay our mission. But take care! My first lord, Odovar, marshal of the Eastern Hundred, sent a priest, Lanza, to investigate XimXim five years ago. Lanza ended up dismembered like a feast-day chicken. What he might have discovered, no one will ever know."

"Knowledge sometimes comes with a high price, my lord," Mandes said primly, adjusting his worn, dirty gown. "How else would you know its worth?"

Chapter 19
Toe to Toe to Toe

ol and his scouting party rejoined the rest of his command by the mouth of the Lapstone River, which began in the Sentinel Mountains to the west and flowed down to Hylo Bay through the capital city. Hiding from Tarsan patrols, Egrin and the soldiers had not caught sight of XimXim, though they too had heard the drone of his wings.

From a hilltop five hundred paces away, Hylo City was the picture of happy chaos. The town was a warren of narrow streets, market squares, and half-timbered houses cheek-by-jowl with inns, taverns, and courtyards. A riot of colors—if they were painted at all—Hylo's buildings ranged from sky blue to beet red. Fowl flapped and squawked, pigs ran squealing (pursued by squealing kender), and all sorts of commerce filled the streets. But as Tol's men drew near, the Hyloites fled inside, bolting every door and shuttering every window behind them. By the time the Ergothians halted in the main square, not a single kender could be seen.

"I thought kender were curious," said Miya.

"Such gratitude!" Egrin said. "Here we've come to save them, and they don't even greet us!"

"They don't view us as saviors," Tol said slowly, as he surveyed the houses around the central square. "We didn't help them years ago, when they first asked for it. On their own they had to learn to live with XimXim, and now I suppose our war with Tarsis has ruined their peace." His pointed to the tallest rooftops. "Look there!"

All around the town, the tops of the highest buildings had been ripped open. Long parallel slashes showed where XimXim had raked his sharp claws over them. Every house above a certain height bore severe damage.

It had been impossible to convey the horror of the monstrous creature to the city guardsmen. They had snorted dismissively at the notion of a giant bug terrorizing the countryside. But the visible destruction throughout Hylo, along with the clear reluctance of the kender to greet them, put an end to their cynicism.

Egrin asked if they should pay their respects to Lucklyn the First, king of Hylo, whose residence, just across the square, was shuttered and silent like all the rest. Tol, after thinking it over, decided against forcing their welcome.

In the midst of the empty square, Tol held a council of war. All his captains, plus the Dom-shu sisters and Mandes, crowded around as Tol spread a large goatskin map of Hylo on the cobblestones. He pointed out the bay, the river they'd followed, and then tapped the tip of his sheathed dagger on the little triangle representing Hylo City. A short hop west of the kender capital were the brown, jagged lines of the Sentinel Mountains.

"Our best information is that XimXim lives in a cave, somewhere in the lower reaches of the mountains," Tol explained. "The monster is said to be able to see the city from his lair, so we can assume his cave is somewhere here." He traced a short arc in the hills west and south of Hylo. "Anyone know anything about this region?"

No one did, not even Mandes or Darpo, the former seaman.

Tol continued, "Then we'll have to reconnoiter as we go. Given the nature of the enemy, I propose to disperse the band into small, individual companies—the better to stay mobile and hidden from XimXim. Each company will explore the region directly in front of it, and stay in contact at all times with their comrades on either flank."

He arrayed the ten companies across the map from south to north. Egrin was given thirty men in the center, with Narren on his left flank and Tol on his right. Tol took personal command of Valvorn's men, the Karad-shu having been slain by bakali. Mandes would accompany Tol, as would Kiya and Miya. Any group encountering the monster was to signal its comrades immediately, by bonfire at night or with rams' horns by day.

"Defend yourselves, but don't try to fight this thing by yourselves," Tol warned sternly. "XimXim is too powerful to be fought with sword and spear. Our purpose is to locate the creature's lair. If you do, don't signal. Hold your place and send a runner to me. If we can discover the monster before it knows we're hunting for it, we may be able to find a way to trap it in its own den. Believe me, we don't want to confront it in the open. This beast walks, flies, and kills with the speed of a whirlwind."

"My lord?" said Darpo. "What about the Tarsans? What do we do if we come upon any?"

"Kill 'em quick," said Narren, and the men laughed.

Tol said, "As far as I can tell, no Tarsans have made it across the bay. Small parties of scouts or spies may be abroad. Deal with them as you see fit, but remember Lord Urakan might appreciate a few prisoners to question."

The company leaders studied the map a while longer, each noting his line of march. The countryside between Hylo City and the mountains was hilly and wooded, though not so densely as Ropunt Forest. The Lapstone River divided southwest of town, and the fordability of it and its two tributaries was unknown.

One by one, Tol said good-bye to his retainers. All Juramona men, they had known each other for a large part of their young lives. Last to go were Narren and Egrin. The younger soldier Tol embraced.

"We're a long way from mucking out the stables for the Household Guard," Narren said almost wistfully. "You, me, and Crake were quite a trio, weren't we?"

Tol forced a smile at the mention of Crake. He'd never told

anyone the masked assassin in Daltigoth was their old comrade—only that he had fairly fought and slain the fellow who attacked him.

After Narren gathered his men and departed. Egrin stepped forward.

"My lord," he said, and saluted in the old-fashioned way, with his bared dagger.

Tol colored. "I'm not your lord. I'm still the stupid boy you trained to be a soldier," he said.

"You are my lord and commander. And you were never stupid."

Tol blinked, surprised at the warmth in the old warrior's words. Clearing his throat in embarrassment, he took a sheaf of parchment from under his tunic and gave it to Egrin.

"Keep this for me," he said quietly. "If I'm unlucky, will you see those letters get to the person named on them?"

Egrin tucked them away without glancing at them. They clasped arms. A hint of the old taskmaster came through in Egrin's voice as he urged, "No heroics. The gods favor you, Tol, but this creature does not abide by the gods."

"Never fear. My life is dear to me, but I shall do my duty."

Egrin led his men out. All that remained in the square were Valvorn's company of twenty-two, with Mandes, Miya, and Kiya. Tol told the sisters they were risking their lives by going, and should stay behind.

"I don't want to go," Miya said frankly. "I hate crawling things! Especially *big* crawling things! But I won't stay if Kiya goes."

Kiya's face was implacable. "Our father, the chief of the Dom-shu, owes much to you, husband," she said quietly. "Where you tread, we shall tread. Where you sleep, we shall sleep. And where you perish, so shall we die."

She drew her knife and grasped her long blond horsetail of hair. It reached the middle of her back. She cut it off just below the thong she used to tie it back at her neck. Miya gasped. The only time Dom-shu warriors cut their hair was before a battle to the death. Hair was sacred to the god Bran, lord of the forest. By cutting it, Kiya was making a serious sacrifice to her patron deity.

Tol said nothing, but clasped Kiya's arm as he would a fellow warrior's. She took her place with the soldiers. Miya, still looking a bit shocked, followed her sister.

Tol ordered his company to move out. They shouldered their gear and marched away. He swung onto Cloud's back and looked down at Mandes. The sorcerer had picked up the heavy hank of Kiya's hair.

"Leave it," said Tol. He explained the Dom-shu custom of sacrificing their hair to Bran.

"Strange ways," murmured the wizard, fondling the sheaf of golden hair. "The other one, her hair isn't very long."

"Miya isn't a fighter. Her sister was pledged to the warrior society of the Dom-shu while still in her mother's womb. Boy or girl, she was chosen to be a warrior. Miya was not."

Mandes let the hank of hair fall to the ground. Picking up the bindle containing his rations and magical paraphernalia, he departed the square, following Tol's troop.

🦅 🦅 🦅 🦅 🦅

The wind freshened, shaking the trees. Dust scoured the faces of Tol's party as they worked their way through a notch in the low hills west of the kender capital. They continued to find copious evidence of XimXim's wrath—an earthen dam torn asunder, orchards uprooted, isolated homesteads smashed to kindling. Everything bore the tell-tale slash marks of the monster's claws. They came upon a herd of cattle— some torn in half, others pierced by wounds strangely neat and precise. Equally precise and more horrible was the fate of the four herders accompanying the cattle.

The four were human, probably from the northern reaches of the empire. Nomadic herders often drove their cattle into Hylo to take advantage of the mild sea climate and abundant fodder. Usually the only risk they faced was from pilfering kender. These men had met a far worse fate. XimXim had struck off their heads and placed them neatly in a row beside their bodies.

Although he hated to leave the poor herders unburied, Tol could not delay long enough to do what was proper. He and his company had to stay in contact with the others in case there was trouble. They moved grimly onward.

The brown slopes of the Sentinel Mountains grew more distinct in the distance. Not a mighty range like the Khalkist, the Sentinels were called the Not Much Mountains by the kender. They were not much high, not much rich in minerals, not much inhabited, and not much of a barrier to trade and travel. However, at seventy leagues from end to end, they made a big pile of stone to shelter a monster.

Near dusk, Tol's group paused in the shadow of a vine-covered ridge. Wind was still gusting over the mountains, gaining force as it rushed down the slopes to the sea. While they rested, Mandes opened his bindle and spread the square of brown cloth on the ground. He sorted through various knots of dry herbs and shriveled roots, putting a chosen few in a small agate pestle. With a small mortar, he ground the ingredients to a fine powder, adding pinches of other powders he carried in small wooden tubes. Sniffing the resulting mixture carefully, he nodded with satisfaction.

"What are you making?" asked Tol.

"Balm of Sirrion. It creates the impenetrable mist."

"Like the one you gave the bakali?" The sorcerer nodded. "Doesn't it work only in darkness?"

Mandes smiled smugly. "I put that limitation on the balm I made for the lizard-men. Properly compounded, the mist will work in sunlight or darkness."

He warmed a plug of beeswax in the hollow of his hand. When it was soft, he pressed his thumb into the center, making a hole. This he filled with the balm powder. Pinching the wax closed, he rolled it between his palms to make a round pill the size of a hen's egg. He likewise filled three more wax balls, using up all the magical mixture. He presented the four to Tol.

Tol picked up one of the yellow wax balls, handling it carefully with the tips of his fingers.

"Tylocost and the Tarsans tried to land under the cover of a magical mist," he said. "XimXim flew right through it and tore the mercenaries to bits. How do you know he won't be able to see through your fog?"

"I don't. But some things require experiment."

"Experiment! You're talking about our lives!"

The wizard put the wax balls away, repacked his paraphernalia, and tied the four corners of the cloth into a bindle again. "My lord, you're gambling with all our lives," he remarked. "My magic improves the odds in our favor. Why else did you bring me along, if not to try my means?"

A runner came crashing through the underbrush. Tol and Mandes stood, and everyone idling under the trees got to their feet, spears in hand.

The runner proved to be a soldier from Narren's company.

"My lord," he panted. "Narren bids me tell you, we think we've found the cave of the monster!"

"Are you sure?" demanded Tol.

"Dirt mounded outside the cave mouth is marked with huge claw prints. Narren explored a score of steps inside. He found many bones of cattle, pigs, humans, and kender. And this—"

The messenger reached inside his overshirt and brought out a dull yellow spike as long as Tol's hand. It was hollow and light, and made of a hard, hornlike material.

"Narren thinks the monster sheds these spikes, my lord," he explained. "The floor was littered with them."

The cave was in the first valley beneath the Sentinel peaks, three-quarters of a league away. Tol sent a fresh runner to spread the news to Egrin's company. Commanding all to be stealthy, he set his men on the trail blazed by Narren's runner, who led them back through the woods.

Night had fallen when they found Narren. Crouching in a rocky defile a hundred paces from the black, gaping entrance to the cave, Narren greeted his commander in a fierce whisper. He held his helmet in one hand, letting the wind dry his sweaty hair.

"Any sign of the creature?" Tol asked, keeping his voice low as well.

"None." Narren wrinkled his sunburned nose. "Stinks like a slaughterhouse in there."

Tol grimaced at the too-apt description. "I notified Egrin. He'll join us when he can, but I want to have a look myself now. Mandes, come with me."

Kiya also followed him, as did a reluctant Miya. Tol told them to remain in camp, as this was only a scouting expedition.

"No, I am with you," Kiya said stubbornly.

"And I am with Sister," added Miya. "Though I wish she'd stay here!"

He ordered them to go back, but Kiya said flatly, "I'm not one of your warriors. I'm your wife, and I don't take orders."

Mandes chuckled. Tol glared at him, then hissed at Kiya, "All right! But please keep quiet!"

It was a foolish injunction, and he knew it. Having grown up in the Great Green, the Dom-shu were far stealthier than Tol or the city-bred sorcerer. They moved along silently as wraiths in the gathering night, while Mandes dislodged loose stones with every step.

At last they were crouching at the entrance to the cave. Sixteen paces wide and half as high, it was amply sized to admit the monster, and Narren had been right about the stench. Warm air emanating from the cave smelled worse than a charnel house. Mandes audibly gagged. Tol had to swallow repeatedly to keep from doing likewise.

Digging through his supplies, Mandes brought out a wooden tube of ointment. He put a drop of the oily stuff on their forefingers and bade them smear it under their noses. The sickening reek faded, replaced by a faint aroma of roses. Mandes explained the effect was only temporary.

The ledge at the mouth of the cave was a single slab of brown granite. Overhead, Luin had risen high enough to cast its reddish light into the opening. Tol could tell the cave had been gouged out of the living rock by force, most likely by XimXim himself.

At Tol's request, Mandes cupped his left hand, and an orange-white orb materialized, throwing off a soft glow. Tol and Kiya started in, he drawing his sword and she nocking an arrow in her bow. Mandes walked between them, lighting the way. Bringing up the rear and glancing constantly over her shoulder, Miya also carried her sword.

The tunnel plunged straight into the mountain, slanting downward at a fairly steep angle. Heaps of stinking refuse lined the walls—bones of various victims with scraps of flesh drying on them, along with dozens of XimXim's cast-off spikes, which had a musty reek all their own. Normal subterranean life was absent. No bugs scuttled away from their light; no bats clung in furry clusters from the cave roof.

Two dozen steps inside the cave, the muggy air gave way to a much warmer current, rising slowly from the depths of the tunnel. The passage continued straight as an arrow, with no end in sight.

"Let's go back!" Miya said. Her whisper sounded booming in the stone-walled cave.

"Yes," Kiya agreed. "There's nothing to see."

Tol wasn't satisfied, and asked Mandes if he could throw the light farther down the tunnel.

"I can send it as far as I can see it," replied the wizard.

He mumbled a brief incantation, and the little orb flew out of his hand. It sailed down the center of the passage, on and on, growing ever smaller with each passing heartbeat. Tol was astonished by the length of the tunnel.

Miya, still rearmost, suddenly cocked her head. "Do you hear that?"

"What? The monster?"

"No! More like . . . horns."

That jolted Tol. Narren wouldn't sound horns unless there was a grave emergency.

"Go back!" he shouted, shoving Mandes and Kiya around. "XimXim must be coming!"

It was hard going back up the slope. Mandes's soft slippers lost purchase, and he fell repeatedly. The Dom-shu sisters finally grabbed him by the arms and dragged him along.

The journey seemed to take forever, but finally Tol was close enough to the cave mouth to see the stars beyond. Unfortunately, he also heard the dreaded sound—*zimm-zimm-zimm*. The creature flew past, blotting out the sky for an instant, and Tol's heart spasmed in terror. If XimXim entered the cave now, they'd be trapped, with no hope of escape or place to hide.

Below the cave entrance, Tol's men realized the same thing. Egrin had arrived with his company, and it was as he listened to Narren's explanation of their commander's personal reconnaissance that the dreaded hum filled the night air. Egrin immediately ordered all signal horns blown, though there was no way to know whether Tol could hear them.

Hoping to draw XimXim's attention away from the cave, Egrin called forward the soldiers in each company who carried clay urns of live embers. In camp each night, the embers were revived for cookfires. Egrin ordered them thrown on a bed of dry leaves. The brisk wind fanned the glowing coals, and a lively fire erupted as XimXim's hum grew louder.

Overhead, the monstrous creature spied the leaping flames so close to his lair. His large but primitive eyes made out warm-blooded figures moving in the darkness around the fire. He landed in a dry streambed upwind of the fire, and then, rearing up, front legs cocked and ready to strike, he advanced toward the flames.

A shower of spears arced out of the darkness. Reflexively, XimXim halted as they whizzed by. His slender legs were difficult to hit, but several iron-tipped missiles struck his thorax. They bounced harmlessly off his armored hide.

Palps clacking, XimXim strode rapidly into the shadows beyond the bonfire. He could see the dull white faces of his enemies. Powerful forearms lashed out, scattering the humans. Raking backward with his right leg, he caught one man and hoisted him high. He tried to cut his captive in two, but the man's iron breastplate resisted. The man screamed and struck at him with a sword. More men rushed out of the darkness, shouting.

XimXim watched, curious, as they swarmed around him. Humans did not usually rush toward him; they ran away. One of the odd humans thrust a spear into the tender joint of his left middle leg, bringing forth a stream of green ichor.

Furious with sudden pain, XimXim snipped the head off his captive human and dropped the limp body. He gathered his legs together and leaped six paces. Humans scattered as he landed hard among them, his narrow feet driving into the stony soil. Since their torsos were protected by iron, he proceeded to cut the humans down at the legs, which were not armored.

Crouching by a boulder, Narren wiped blood from his eyes. "That thing must be made of metal!" he cried. "Swords and spears don't hurt it!"

"I hurt it," Egrin replied, showing the younger man XimXim's green blood on his spear. "It doesn't have many soft spots, but it has some!"

The fire, ignored by the battling Ergothians, spread quickly from the masses of fallen leaves and licked at the abundant dry tinder. It filled the ravine with crimson light and grotesquely wavering shadows. Men screamed as the monster found them. Others roared defiance and tried to muster their comrades. Eight men of Egrin's company climbed a tall outcropping that put them level with XimXim's massive, angular head. They tried to spear the beast's huge eyes, but it deftly parried their weapons with its massive forearms.

Bringing both arms together like interlocking scythes, XimXim mowed down every soldier on the outcropping. It seized the last one alive and bit off his head. Flinging the torso at the men below, it climbed the rock to gain a height advantage.

Egrin, noting the creature's movements, shouted, "The beast shows his back! At him now!"

He, Narren, and eleven men rushed from cover. Two grabbed XimXim's right rear leg, just as he was about to lift it off the ground. Weighed down, the monster swiveled its head to see what held him. While he was so engaged, Egrin ducked under the tree-sized limb and drove a spear into his lower joint.

XimXim shivered from one end to the other. His injured leg kicked out with enormous force, hurling free the men hanging on it. Reversing his stance, he butted four of the creatures who'd caused him such pain. They went down, and XimXim tried to bite the man closest to him. The fellow's iron cuirass saved him for the moment, but XimXim kept biting at the hard metal plate.

"Egrin! Egrin!" Narren cried, seeing the older warrior pinned down by the monster. He scrambled to his feet. "Juramona!" he shouted, and attacked with his saber.

With one terrific slash, Narren chopped off the end of XimXim's drooping right antenna. The monster gave a high-pitched shriek of pain and fury. Back came the terrible forearm, snapping like a spring. The blow caught Narren on his breastplate and slammed him against a sharp-edged boulder. His helmet flew off, and he slid to the ground. Blood welled from a terrible head wound, drenching his fair hair. He did not get up again.

Egrin rolled away from the angry monster. He heard death whisper by, as XimXim's left forearm drove into the dirt, just missing him. With his antenna damaged, the creature's aim seemed to be off.

"Get back! Fall back!" Egrin bellowed.

The Ergothians were only too happy to oblige. In the brief melee XimXim had killed twenty and wounded twice that many more. As the soldiers took cover in the scrub forest, several flung dirt over the burning brush, extinguishing the fire they had started.

Showing a distinct distaste for continuing the fight, XimXim clambered up a short pinnacle. His wounded leg stuck out behind him, trembling. Green blood stained the boulders, mixing with the red shed by the Ergothians. He opened his wings and took off, flying directly to his lair. When he had rested and was sound again, he would sally forth and destroy these reckless little pests, not only in his immediate domain, but everywhere he encountered them.

❦ ❦ ❦ ❦ ❦

As sentries stood watch, graves were dug and wounds tended.

Egrin knelt by Narren and closed the young warrior's life-less eyes. Lifting his own gaze, Egrin ran a hand down his cuirass. The hammer-forged plate was dented and chewed as he'd never seen iron damaged before. Juramona iron had saved his life.

No, the armor had only protected him. Brave Narren had saved his life. How Tol would grieve when he learned his old comrade had died—and how proud he would be to know how courageously Narren had sold his life!

Drawn by the signal horns and the blazing bonfire, the scattered companies of Tol's demi-horde gathered in the ravine below XimXim's cave. Egrin dispersed them, so the monster wouldn't find them too easily come daybreak.

He watched as Narren was consigned to the ground. So much death he had seen in his long life, so many young lives lost. Egrin stared up at the black hole in the mountain. Did his commander—his friend—still live?

❦ ❦ ❦ ❦ ❦

From the blaring horns and flickering firelight, Tol correctly divined his men were trying not only to warn him, but to distract the returning monster. He couldn't fault their gallantry, but he fumed at their disobedience. Hadn't he told them not to fight XimXim?

He, Mandes, and the Dom-shu women were only a dozen steps from the cave entrance. The women released the magician to dash out the opening, and Mandes promptly slipped again. Tol grabbed for the collar of his robe, but missed.

Mandes, squeaking in alarm, rolled down the sloping tunnel.

Miya ran after him. She caught hold of his robe, planted her feet—and was yanked head over heels by his considerable weight. Hopelessly tangled, they slid on.

"Sister!" Kiya shouted and sprinted after Miya.

Tol yelled at her, knowing she wouldn't abandon her kin any more than he would abandon the pair of them. The cave entrance was so close he could feel the night breeze, but without hesitation he too turned back.

Down and down Mandes and Miya tumbled, him grunting and her cursing eloquently. In the course of her whirling progress, Miya spotted a dull red glow in the distance, felt the rise in temperature, and finally realized what lay ahead. Drawing her arms in, she pushed away from Mandes with all her strength, and they shot apart. Mandes's robe snagged on rough rocks in the curving wall of the tunnel. He jerked to a halt. Miya, no longer tumbling, slid on her rear briefly, then suddenly ran out of floor altogether.

Her legs dropped into open air. She scrabbled for a handhold, but there was none. For a terrifying instant, she teetered on the edge of a precipice, then plunged into the abyss—

—and landed hard on her back a few paces down. Dust flew up around her.

Mandes's white face appeared above her. "Lady, are you all right?"

"Just wonderful!" she yelled at him, coughing. She tried to sit up, but her sides stung as though thorns had been hammered in. "I think I broke some ribs!"

"Don't move!" said the wizard. "Don't even turn your head!"

As soon as he said it, of course she had to do exactly that. There was rock under her head, but when she turned to the right, her cheek met only sweltering, stinking air.

She'd landed on a ledge just wide enough to catch her. Beneath her was an enormously deep pit. Intense heat, a red glow, and nauseating vapors rose from the depths below.

As Mandes tried unsuccessfully to reach her, Tol and Kiya

arrived, feet skidding as Mandes shouted at them to beware the pit.

Tol had a length of rawhide wrapped around his waist, a spare bridle for his horse. He dropped one end to Miya. She lifted her hands and grasped it, but couldn't pull herself up— not with her broken ribs.

Tol made ready to go after her, but Kiya stopped him, announcing she would go.

Tol planted his fists on his hips. "For once in your life, will you do as I say?"

"Someday, husband, but not now."

Kiya laid aside her bow and quiver, then tied the hide rope under her arms. With Tol and Mandes anchoring her, she backed over the rim of the pit, feeling for footholds with her bare toes. The two men grunted under the strain.

"Sulfur," Mandes muttered, gasping with effort. "That smell. Must be molten rock down there."

Tol played out the rope a little at a time. "How can rock be molten?" he asked, eyes streaming moisture from the stinging vapors.

"Same way metal can. Deep underground . . . is heat enough to melt solid stone."

"Where does the heat come from?"

"Some say Reorx's divine forge. Others—" The rope slipped. Mandes drew in breath with a sharp hiss, as the hard hide cut the palms of his hands, then continued, as though speaking to a student. "Others believe the heat . . . is a natural state of the deep places."

The line went slack, and Kiya shouted she had arrived.

"Where do you stand on the matter?" asked Tol, looking over his shoulder at the wizard as they both relaxed momentarily.

Mandes carefully patted his sweating, blistered hands with a corner of his robe. "I await further evidence before ascribing to either theory," he said.

On the ledge beneath them, Kiya pulled her sister briskly to a sitting position, ignoring Miya's squawks of pain. She set to work tying the rope under Miya's arms. Both women were coughing, their eyes streaming tears. Fumes rising from the depths enveloped them in a noxious fog.

Tol's face suddenly appeared above them, eerily highlighted by the glow from the chasm.

"Quiet!" he hissed. "Something's coming!"

"Something? *Something*? It's that monster!" Miya exclaimed.

"Haul me up! Let me die fighting!" Kiya cried, but Tol's face disappeared.

Tol and the wizard heard, far down the passage, a series of rapid clicks—the sound of hard-shelled feet on stone—and an occasional loud whirr. Tol had seen wasps vibrate their wings when they were angry. XimXim must know intruders were in his lair, and was probably furious.

Tol stood, slowly removing his crimson mantle. Stripping to his iron breastplate and leather trews, he kicked his clothing out of the way, then drew his sword and war dagger. He tossed the empty scabbard away.

"You don't think you can fight that thing single-handed?" said Mandes. He was sitting on the tunnel floor rifling through his clothing.

"What else can we do? We have no escape, and I doubt it knows mercy."

Mandes produced the four wax balls containing the Balm of Sirrion and half a dozen other objects: two dried clay pills the size of acorns, a speckled bird's egg, two stoppered wooden tubes, and a small glass cruet sealed with red wax.

"The sum of my life's work," the wizard said drily.

Tol gripped his weapons hard, pondering the sum of his own life. What did he have? A chest of gold coins, an old house, and the patronage of the future emperor of Ergoth—a man married to the woman Tol loved. Was that all he'd accomplished in his short life?

"Tol!" Kiya shouted. "Don't leave us down here! I want to fight too!"

"Aren't you going to answer her?" asked Mandes.

"Not this time," he said.

That was something else he had, the Dom-shu sisters. Wives in name only perhaps, but faithful and honorable companions. He would do his best to die honorably for them.

The clatter of many limbs grew louder. Several times Tol thought he saw movement in the shadows, but could discern nothing tangible. The sulfur vapors were making his head and chest hurt. If XimXim simply waited, the fumes would do his work for him. Yet Tol doubted there was much danger of that. The monster enjoyed killing too much to miss an opportunity to cleanse his home of invaders.

The drifting streams of smoke suddenly parted, revealing an enormous triangular head, half as wide as the tunnel. In the dull ruddy glow and tight confines of the cave, XimXim looked even more monstrous. The black pupils in his huge eyes swung round until they fixed on the two men. Two pairs of sharp palps clacked, as though eager to taste blood.

Tol felt a sharp stab of fear in the pit of his stomach. He could face any number of human foes with equanimity, but this creature was an abomination, an unnatural and terrifying evil.

Mandes shakily fell to his knees. At first Tol thought he was praying, but the sorcerer was simply adopting a more convenient posture for throwing his tiny arsenal of balms and vapors.

XimXim made a high-pitched noise and drew his lethal forearms slowly forward.

"May I?" said Mandes politely.

"By all means!"

The wizard chose one of the wooden tubes. Pulling the plug with his teeth, he flung it toward the monster. As soon as it left his hand, he intoned, "*Ama, Ama, Kozom-dosh!*"

The tube hit the floor in front of the oncoming creature. At once a bright blue, viscous tendril popped out. It spread rapidly across the floor, sprouting new tendrils as it went. Surprised, XimXim halted his advance.

The azure creeper climbed the walls and formed a web of glittering filaments, filling the lower half of the tunnel. XimXim threw up an arm, intending to slash the web apart.

"That's right," Mandes muttered. "Touch it! Go ahead!"

XimXim did not slice through the tendrils. Instead, the filaments stuck fast to him and continued to grow, moving up his leg. He backed away. Although the blue web stretched with distance, it did not break. In no time, his front leg was covered.

"Wonderful!" shouted Tol, relief washing over him.

XimXim retreated a bit, but the weird substance clung to him. Instead of using his other arm to try to cut himself loose, he brought his entangled limb to his mouth and began to chew the blue tendrils.

Tol hoped the monster's mouth would become glued shut, but that was not the case. The palps worked and worked. Saliva dripped from the fast-moving fangs. The blue tendrils were shortly reduced to bits which fell inertly to the floor.

While the monster was thus occupied, Tol decided to attack. Knowing he couldn't break through XimXim's natural armor, he adopted a new tactic.

"Keep it busy!" he shouted to Mandes.

He dodged between XimXim's many legs, dropping low beneath the creature's underbelly. Here the dark green armor faded almost to white. With both hands on the hilt, Tol thrust his sword hard at the monster's abdomen. There was resistance for a moment, then the thin shell gave. Green blood, black as ink in the dim cave, gushed over Tol's hands. XimXim snapped violently from side to side, tearing the saber from Tol's hands.

Mandes picked up one of his Balm of Sirrion pills and pressed it lightly between his palms. Uttering an incantation, he rolled the soft wax pellet across the stone floor. It stopped just short of the blue web and dissolved into a patch of white mist.

Flexing his six legs, XimXim brought his ponderous abdomen down hard, seeking to crush his tormentor. Tol rolled aside, grabbing his sword hilt and yanking it free. The creature tried twice more to quash him, but Tol evaded him.

By now Mandes's mist was filling the tunnel. In response to Kiya's shouted demands, the magician retreated to the edge of the precipice and gave the Dom-shu a terse account of the battle.

"Get me up there and let me have a crack at him!" Kiya roared.

"Sorry, lady, there's no time. Ah! He's bitten through the Phoenix Web!"

Mandes threw the second wooden tube, but this time XimXim saw it coming and batted it away. It sailed back over Mandes's head into the pit. The wizard watched its fall with wide-eyed alarm.

"Uh-oh . . ."

Tol crawled on his belly until he emerged behind the monster. He could see XimXim's bulbous abdomen waving in the fog as the beast attempted again and again to crush him. When the body dropped once more, Tol ran and sprang. He landed on the monster's back.

XimXim, free at last of the clinging blue tendrils, whirled in a complete circle when he felt Tol's weight on him. Tol slid over the hard armor, only halting his fall by driving his dagger into a hairline gap between the plates covering XimXim's wings. More ichor oozed from the new wound, but Tol had found a secure handhold.

XimXim went berserk with pain and outrage. He ran up the tunnel's side, his clawed feet easily keeping their grip. Tol tried to hang on, but when the monster turned him upside down, he lost his hold and fell to the floor. XimXim promptly let go and with astonishing agility twisted in mid-air to drop on top of his human antagonist. Quick reflexes saved Tol's life. XimXim's armored feet struck sparks off the hard floor, but just missed the young warrior as he scrambled clear.

The monster's frantic movement had brought it closer to Mandes and the rim of the pit. Snatching up two clay pills, the panicked sorcerer hurled them at XimXim. One after the other they detonated in a silent flash. Mandes was blinded, and on the ledge below, the Dom-shu were dazzled. The flash instantly dispersed the magical mist and the remnants of the blue webbing, leaving the tunnel clear and open.

Fortunately, XimXim's bulk protected Tol from the eye-searing blast of light. The young warrior's vision went red in the glare, but he didn't lose his sight. XimXim, though, was stricken sightless. The terrified monster charged back and forth, butting his head against the granite walls. Shards of rock and dust fell, and Tol feared the crazed creature might bring the whole mountain down on them.

Tol retrieved his sword, dropped when he fell from XimXim's back. Gripping it in both hands, he stalked toward the monster. Blood ran down his face from cuts in his scalp. His arms were raw from scraping against the cave walls and floor.

On the other side of XimXim, Mandes groped for the last weapon at his disposal. His fingers found the glass cruet, but there hardly seemed any point to this last throw. If Balm of Sirrion, the Phoenix Web, and thunderflash powder had failed, what good would Oil of Luin do? It was all he had left.

The wax seal was hard, and Mandes couldn't pry the glass stopper out. He could hear XimXim raging, feet pounding and palps grating, the sound reverberating through the tunnel. He had no idea what had become of Tol.

XimXim inadvertently kicked the prostrate wizard, a stunning blow. The cruet flew from Mandes's fingers. Tol saw it sail through the air and shatter on impact. The contents spattered on the floor, shiny as quicksilver. He tensed for some big effect, but the liquid merely lay there. Mandes must not have had time to speak the proper words of power.

XimXim's vision was returning. Having accidentally located the wizard, he turned to snip him into pieces. He hoisted the unconscious wizard high, holding his arm fast in the crook of one claw—

"Juramona! Juramona!"

Shouting to distract the beast, Tol ran under an arch of green legs, turned, and thrust his saber hard into XimXim's gut. The creature convulsed in agony, his front legs twitching spasmodically. Mandes's left arm was severed at the shoulder.

XimXim dropped the sorcerer and lurched away from his attacker, tearing the sword from Tol's hand. Tol's dagger was still buried in XimXim's back. The young warrior was weaponless now.

Fluids green and black gushed from the monster's belly wounds. XimXim opened his wings part way, but there was no room in the tunnel for flight. He staggered closer to the edge of the chasm. His middle legs trod on the Oil of Luin and promptly slid out from under him. He fell heavily on the thin pool of oil and slid toward the rim of the pit. Unable to stop himself, legs flailing, the monster skidded over the edge.

Kiya and Miya cried out when they saw the huge monster plunge by their narrow perch. It tried to spread its wings, but failed, and, helpless, clacking his palps in terror, XimXim plummeted into the pit. The awful noise he made was cut off abruptly when he splashed into the pool of molten rock far below.

A thick column of white smoke rose from the pit, filling the tunnel. The Dom-shu choked and gasped. Kiya had been hammering the rock wall with the pommel of Miya's sword to make shallow toeholds. She began to climb.

When Kiya gained the tunnel floor above, she spied Tol kneeling by Mandes, working feverishly. Both men were covered, as was she herself, with a layer of white ash from XimXim's immolation. She crawled to Tol, and he didn't even flinch when she appeared suddenly at his elbow.

"What happened?" she asked.

"The monster cut off his arm. I've made a tourniquet, but I fear it's too late!"

"Let me," she said. "Help Miya." Her hands were scored bloody from her climb, but she took over with the tourniquet. Beneath its coating of ash, Mandes's face was pale as wax. His lips were purple in the red light of the tunnel.

"Miya!" Tol called, crawling on his hands and knees to the edge of the pit.

Miya still had the rawhide rope tied around her, so she tossed the free end to him. It took four tries, but he finally caught it and hauled her up. By the time she reached the top, her face was stiff with pain.

"Mind that silver stuff," he said, indicating the magical oil. "That's what did in the monster."

"Poison?" she asked.

"Bad luck."

Tol left her lying on the floor, nursing her cracked ribs, and went back to Kiya. She was threading a needle with a length of sinew, supplies from the kit she used to mend tears in her buckskins.

"What are you doing?" he asked.

"Sewing up his wound. Have you never seen it done? In the woodland, we often do it to gaping injuries."

He watched, fascinated, as she used deer sinew to close Mandes's terrible wound. It took time, but when she eased off the tourniquet, no blood flowed from the stump of the wizard's arm.

"Now, let me see you," she said.

He waved away her concern. "I'm fine."

Kiya took Tol's head in her strong hands and glared at him, looking like a stern ghost in her coating of ash. "I'll tell you when you're fine!" she said. "After all, what's a wife for but to bind her husband's wounds?"

C h a p t e r   2 0

A Place by the Sea

The moons had set and sunrise was still a few hours off as the victors picked their way carefully down the mountain from XimXim's cave. Tol and Kiya carried the badly wounded Mandes. Miya followed, slowly and painfully, clutching her sides. They saw no one in the gully at the foot of the mountain. Bloodstained rocks and charred earth gave evidence of the battle that had raged in their absence, yet all was quiet now.

Lowering Mandes's limp body to the ground, Tol cupped a hand to his mouth and shouted, "Juramona! Juramona!"

The bushes stirred, and soldiers emerged. Some had their heads bandaged, or wore an arm in a sling. Seeing their commander, they raised a glad shout.

"The monster is dead!" Tol yelled.

The jubilant noise became a deafening tumult. Waving swords and spears, the soldiers engulfed them. A few ran down the ravine to inform the rest of their comrades. Tol ordered saplings cut to make litters for Mandes and Miya, then slumped to the stony earth. He sat with arms propped on his knees, head hanging tiredly. Something firm pressed against his back. Kiya had adopted the same posture, her back to his. He relaxed slightly against the welcome support.

The defile soon was full of happy, shouting men. The Ergothians cheered Tol so incessantly he gruffly ordered them to cease.

His officers soon got the troops in order. Torches were lit. Tarthan, Wellax, Allacath, and Frez sorted the men into companies and had them lined up in proper formation by the time Egrin arrived with the balance of the demi-horde.

Egrin, Darpo, Sanksa, and Fellen came forward and saluted. Tol lifted a hand and Darpo, his scarred face wreathed in smiles, hoisted him to his feet. Kiya rose as well, on the arm of Sanksa.

"My lord, I rejoice to see you!" said Egrin.

"I rejoice to be seen," was Tol's sincere reply.

"XimXim is destroyed?" Tol nodded. "Then this is a great day!" Egrin proclaimed.

In truth, Tol did not find it so. He was very glad to be alive, and happy the Dom-shu sisters and Mandes lived, but he wasn't exactly proud of his victory.

"It wasn't a battle, it was a bloody farce," he growled. "We went up there just to have a look around! We had no plan. We just fought for our lives and managed to win—barely!"

Egrin nodded. "There's no antidote for victory. It often leaves a bitter taste." He told Tol of their losses in XimXim's attack.

Narren's death hit the young commander hard. He stood with eyes closed until the burning in them subsided.

When the litters were ready, Miya and Mandes rested a bit more comfortably. Frez, who as a boy had apprenticed to a sawbones in Caergoth, wrapped a tight linen bandage around Miya's ribs. It was the only treatment he knew for her condition. After a few drafts of strong wine, though, the Dom-shu woman fell asleep.

In addition to his arm, Mandes had lost a great deal of blood, but he was still breathing, thanks to Kiya's timely attention. Frez had a strengthening broth of bone marrow, herbs, and red wine prepared, and a soldier was appointed to spoon small amounts between the sorcerer's slack lips.

Kiya washed the ash from her hands and face, and ate cold rations from a leather pouch. By this time the rising sun was beginning to color the eastern sky and Tol realized he was ravenous. He cleaned up and broke his fast.

A young soldier brought Cloud. Muscles aching, Tol swung into the saddle. Seeing Kiya limping along, he held out his hand. "Will you ride, lady?"

"A Dom-shu walks," she replied proudly.

"Get on and spare your feet."

To everyone's surprise, she did just that. She cut a curious figure, seated behind Tol. Her arms and legs were covered in cuts and scratches, and she was a head taller than her ostensible husband. At first, she looked uncomfortable on Cloud, but soon leaned her head on Tol's shoulder and fell asleep.

"What now, my lord?" asked Egrin.

Tol said, "Back to Hylo town. We'll rest there a day, then march to the coast. By now Lord Urakan should have reached Old Port. The Tarsans will not sit and wait for him to find them. I mean to join our companies to his army."

"Very good, my lord."

Egrin gave the orders, and the foot soldiers assembled in marching formation. They should reach Hylo City by late afternoon.

※ ※ ※ ※ ※

Word of XimXim's demise spread ahead of the Ergothians. The journey out from Hylo's capital had been desolate and lonely; the return was like a festival. Kender turned out in droves, lining the road to cheer the Ergothians. Lacking flowers so late in the season, they stripped off the most colorful leaves from nearby trees and spread them before Tol's horse.

Riding alongside his commander, Egrin said drily, "Victors are always popular."

Kiya, still mounted behind Tol, eyed the cheering crowd with distrust. "Just keep an eye on your valuables. Kender are even more dangerous when friendly!"

The soldiers did lose equipment to kender "curiosity"— haversacks, gauntlets, a few mantles—but nothing vital. By the time the Ergothians entered Hylo town, the crowds were tremendous. None of the soldiers, not even the oldest and most experienced, had any idea there were so many kender in all of Hylo. Little people cheered from every window, some waving bits of scarlet cloth tied to sticks, like miniature imperial banners. Kender children ran alongside the marching column.

"XimXim is de-ad! XimXim is de-ad!" they chanted, drawing the last word into two syllables.

Their procession bore left into the main square, packed from side to side by the shouting throng. The mob had left a clear lane across the square. It led straight to the door of the royal residence, where Tol halted the column.

"Looks like we're expected!" Egrin shouted over the din.

Tol nodded. "We represent the empire—let's pay our respects to the king." He looked back over his shoulder at the unmoving line of men. "Find Darpo! Tell him to join us up front."

Soon, the former sailor rode through the double line of soldiers to Tol's side. Tol raised his hand to signal the soldiers forward. The kender took this as a greeting and let out a high-pitched roar of delight. Tol managed a smile, then waved his men to follow between the two walls of cheering kender.

Hylo's royal residence was no bigger than any other house on the square. Three stories high, built of cut stone, and half-timbered, the residence was guarded by a detachment of the Royal Loyal Militia. These seventeen kender were dressed in a hodge-podge of military finery—Ergothian iron helmets, Tarsan octagonal shields, mantles in the Silvanesti style. Their weapons were the usual swords and spears, though reduced in size for kender. According to Lord Urakan, the kender imported weapons from the dwarves of Thorin, so the implements were likely made of very good iron and bronze.

Standing at the top of the steps was a fellow slight even by kender standards, almost lost in a long pinkish-brown cape.

"Is that the king?" Tol asked Darpo, but Darpo could only shrug. He had visited various Hylo ports, but had never caught sight of the kender king.

Tol halted Cloud at the foot of the steps. Kiya dismounted and stretched, her limbs unused to riding. Tol tried to mask the exhausted tremor in his own muscles. At his order, Egrin, Darpo, and Kiya joined him in climbing the steps of the royal residence. The tiny kender in the cape resembled a wooden doll, his face seamed with a thousand fine cracks and his long white hair pulled back in a tight bun.

The crowd quieted somewhat. With a respectful nod, Tol said, "Do I have the honor of addressing Lucklyn, king of Hylo?"

"You have more honor than that," said the wizened kender. "I'm Casberry, the queen. Lucklyn's gone on a wander and left me in charge."

Tol and his party knelt. "Forgive me, Your Majesty!"

The queen cackled. "Never mind. At my age, I don't mind being mistaken for a king. It's better than being taken for a corpse!"

"Very true," said Tol. The Ergothians rose.

The queen took out a long-stemmed clay pipe and stuffed a brown weed into it. She stamped her foot and one of the militia left his post to fetch a burning twig from within the house.

While he waited for the queen to get her pipe lit and drawing, Tol noticed she had extremely bright green eyes, like the color of new spring leaves. They reminded him, with an unexpected pang, of Valaran's.

At last the queen said amiably, between pulls on her pipe, "So, you finally killed XimXim?"

"I did, Your Majesty, though not alone." Tol introduced Kiya, and gave credit to Miya and Mandes as well.

Queen Casberry choked on smoke. "Not Mandes the Mistmaker?"

"It may be, Majesty. He is skilled at making fogs."

"He owes us money," said the queen. "For practicing magic in our realm without a license."

Tol promised to settle the debt, and the queen moved on to another subject. She tottered over to the Dom-shu woman, gazing up at her considerable height.

"Did someone hex you?" she demanded. "You're tall as a vallenwood!"

"We of the Dom-shu tribe are all of goodly height," said Kiya.

The queen tapped the pipe stem against her yellow teeth thoughtfully, then asked, "How'd you like to work for me?"

"Doing what?"

"Bodyguard." The ancient little queen stepped closer and continued in a loud whisper, "This bunch of empty pockets aren't much good, you know. When XimXim attacked the city, all of them hid in the cellar!"

"Probably a wise decision," said Kiya, remembering the terrible toll XimXim had taken on the trained warriors of Ergoth.

The queen snorted. "So? Want to be my royal guard?"

Kiya's open face revealed the blunt rejection she was prepared to make, but a warning glance from Tol prompted her to say, "Sounds tempting, Your Majesty, but I'm not a free woman. Lord Tolandruth here is my husband."

The map of fine lines on the queen's face drooped in unison. "Oh. Well, if you ever get tired of him, come see me. I pay good. Ask anybody." With a sparkle in her green eyes, she returned to the center of the landing.

"Thanks very much for killing XimXim," she said to Tol. "He's been bothering us for a long time. Ate a cousin of mine, Rufus Wrinklecap. Not *the* Rufus Wrinklecap, mind you. *That* one once borrowed—"

"You're welcome, Your Majesty," Tol said hastily, forestalling what he supposed would be a long tale. "By your leave, we would like to camp for the night just outside the town. We'll be marching off to Old Port in the morning."

"Fine, fine. There's the matter of the fee, though."

Tol again promised to meet any fine levied against Mandes for his unlicensed practice in Free Point. He was grateful to Mandes—and not a little worried about his recovery from the battle with XimXim.

"There's another fee," Casberry said, stroking her pointed chin. "For killing XimXim."

Tol's comrades exploded with outraged exclamations. The queen was unmoved by their protests.

"Our law requires all hunters pay a fee, since all game in the kingdom belongs to the crown. That's me," she explained. She rapped the bowl of her pipe against the heel of her hand. Burnt weed spilled out, soiling the front of her belted robe. "You being foreigners, I don't hold it against you that you didn't pay first. But I must have the hunting fee before you leave my domain."

Kiya muttered something about thievery. Egrin looked grim, and Darpo scratched his scarred brow, trying to think of a reasonable argument to offer for why they shouldn't be required to pay.

Tol simply said, "How much, Your Majesty?"

"It's based on the weight of the game killed. Rabbits are half a copper each, wolves three, deer five, pigs seven, elk and wild oxen go for one silver piece per carcass," Casberry said, regarding Tol slyly. "XimXim was a rather big fellow, was he not?"

"Yes, Majesty. Yet his carcass weighs surprisingly little."

"Eh? What?"

"He fell deep into the mountain and burned up in a pool of molten rock. All that's left of him is smoke and ash, probably weighing no more than a grown boar." Tol put two fingers in his belt pouch. "Seven coppers, you said, for pig-sized game?"

Plainly unhappy, Queen Casberry ignored the snickers of her militia and grabbed the coins. "How do I know XimXim burned up?" she asked, once the money was in her hand.

"You have my word as a Rider of the Horde and a lord of the Ergothian Empire," Tol replied loftily. "Of course, Your Majesty could visit the cave and see for herself that the monster is dead. I myself will mark a map for you."

"Yes, yes, thank you very much!" she said, waving away Tol's offer. "You may camp outside our city for as long as you like." The crafty look returned to her wizened face. "Your Lord Urakan is already defeated, though."

Tol advanced two steps until he was standing over her. The Royal Loyal Militia tried to interpose their spears, but he would not be deflected.

"You have news of Lord Urakan?"

"I do," answered the queen, not in the least intimidated.

When she offered nothing further, Tol said, "Perhaps my men and I should remain in Hylo City, to defend it from the Tarsans. We could camp here in this square—"

"They aren't coming here!" Casberry snapped, then began fussing with her pipe, trying to stuff more brown weed into the bowl.

"How do you know?"

When she ignored him, stubbornly persisting in loading her pipe, Tol delved into his pouch and produced five gold coins— part of the original treasure paid to him by Prince Amaltar after the battle in the Great Green. The coins were imperial crowns, rated at twice the value of a typical gold piece. The haughty profile of Ackal Ergot marked each thick, heavy disk.

Seeing the coins, the queen of Hylo forgot her pipe completely. Tol put the imperial crowns in her hand and gently closed her tiny fingers around them. She could hardly hold them, they were so large.

"I may have been wrong about XimXim's weight," he said in a low voice.

Casberry bit one coin. Satisfied, she tucked all five up one voluminous sleeve. "I'm told on good authority that Lord Urakan's army tried to cross Three Rose Creek two days ago," she said, naming a shallow stream northeast of Old Port. "When half his army was across, the Tarsans attacked. Many Ergothians were slain, and Lord Urakan withdrew into the town."

Tol chewed his lower lip. Timing like that was no accident. Tylocost was living up to his reputation. He'd probably had Urakan's hordes under observation the whole time, and struck when he could do the most damage.

"How do you know the Tarsans won't come here?" he repeated.

"Don't have to," was her acute reply. "If they destroy Lord Urakan, Hylo is theirs, isn't it?"

When Tol turned to order his men to march away, he was stunned to see the square, formerly packed with deliriously cheering kender, was now empty, save for his ten companies. He heard a rustle of cloth and the clink of armor and spun around in time to see the last of the Royal Loyal Militia closing the door of the royal residence behind him. The Ergothians were alone in the square.

❦ ❦ ❦ ❦ ❦

It was raining by the time they pitched camp, halfway between Hylo City and Far-to-go. A pile of thunderheads had risen out of the bay and rolled ashore, loosing a deluge that drenched everyone.

Tol made sure Mandes had a warm, dry place to sleep. The wizard was still in his litter, face wet with sweat. Tol lightly pressed two fingers to the vein in Mandes's throat. His pulse was rapid, his breathing shallow.

Surprisingly, the sorcerer's eyes opened. "My lord?" he said weakly. "The monster . . . defeated?"

Tol smiled. "We're alive, aren't we?"

"Filthy creature . . . mangled my arm, didn't he?"

Tol didn't know how much to tell the weak man, so he said, "You made the difference, Mandes. If it hadn't been for your magic, none of us would be alive now."

"Thank you, my lord." His gaze flickered around the tent. "Where . . . ?"

"Outside Hylo town. We saw the queen today. She claims you owe her money."

For the first time Tol heard Mandes use a foul word. "Some thieves get hanged," he murmured. "Others get crowns."

"Never mind. Take your ease while you can. We'll be on the march tomorrow. Lord Urakan has been bested by Tylocost again, and we're marching to his aid."

Tol was leaving when Mandes rasped, "My lord, a thought!"

Tol returned, and the sorcerer said, "It's no betrayal of the empire to help yourself, instead of Lord Urakan. To win the war, you must overcome Tylocost, even if that means letting others taste defeat."

Mandes's strength was exhausted. He closed his eyes and slept.

Outside, rain poured down Tol's face. What did Mandes mean? The words of a feverish man were often like divination—a glimpse of truth through a veil of mystery. Was there a way Tol could defeat Tylocost with fewer than three hundred men?

Tol walked around the camp, weighing what he knew about the situation in eastern Hylo. He turned the facts over in his mind, considered, pondered, mulled. Although several of his soldiers called greetings, he never heard them.

There was a way, he decided at last. A very dangerous way, calling for extreme coolness and the utmost courage from his men. He was prepared to try it, but what of the others?

He stalked through the rainy night, calling for Egrin and his captains. It was time for a council of war.

✦ ✦ ✦ ✦ ✦

"With all respect, my lord, the notion is insane."

The flat statement came from Egrin. As a life-long warrior, his opinion carried considerable weight, but for once Tol was unmoved by his mentor's caution.

"Very well," Tol replied. "Other opinions?"

Darpo, as stalwart a man as ever lived, looked at the movements marked in charcoal on Tol's map.

"If it works, it would be glorious," he said, chewing his lip.

Egrin was adamant. "Our men will be slaughtered."

"I don't think so," Tol countered. "Tylocost is a clever, accomplished general, but who has he faced all these years? Lord Urakan?—a stout fighter and steady leader, but a dull tactician. Lord Regobart?—a brilliant general, but impetuous and unstable. Prince Nazramin—" Tol paused, unwilling to

343

speak his mind even in front of his loyal officers. "Prince Nazramin thinks war is like a boar hunt: Whoever sheds the most blood wins."

A few tired chuckles greeted this comment. The council of war had gone on a long time, first with Tol explaining his idea, then with his subordinates discussing it. Midnight had come and gone.

"I believe in this plan," Tol said. "Tylocost knows nothing about us. If he's heard we went after XimXim, he might even believe us destroyed. Should word of the monster's demise reach him, he'll not credit it. After all, his army of trained mercenaries was decimated by XimXim. What chance would three hundred Ergothians stand?"

"It took only four," said Sanksa, with a rare smile.

Tol remained serious. "We must attack," he said, "but I want each of my commanders to believe in my plan. Anyone who doesn't should remain behind in Old Port."

The men from Juramona didn't hesitate.

"We'll follow you anywhere," Darpo vowed, and others echoed the sentiment.

Only Egrin remained silent. He stared down at the map with a frown on his bearded face. All eyes turned to him.

At last he looked up. "I go where you lead, my lord," he said.

"That's not what I want," Tol said. "Do you believe the plan can succeed?"

When the elder warrior pursed his lips and said nothing, Tol nodded. "Very well. I have a special task that needs doing. You will undertake it."

Although Egrin looked chastened, Tol clapped him on the shoulder warmly. He was ordered to head south with Miya, Mandes, and the seventeen men who had been badly wounded in the fight with XimXim. Mounted on all their remaining horses, Egrin and his party would seek out Lord Urakan and inform him of Tol's intentions against the Tarsans.

Egrin saluted. "That mission I shall fulfill."

The soldiers caught a few hours of rest, then, before dawn, with the rain still falling, they broke camp. The demi-horde was reorganized into eight companies—some two hundred and sixty fighting men, plus Kiya. They parted company with Egrin at Fingle's Creek. The line of wounded, some in litters, others hobbling on crutches fashioned from spears, moved slowly away in the rain. A two-wheeled kender cart, acquired in Hylo City, carried Mandes and Miya. Miya was still asleep, which was just as well; conscious, she would never have agreed to be parted from her sister.

Egrin raised his hand in farewell, then rode away. He and his limping command were quickly veiled by the gray morning.

"I wish he was with us," murmured Frez, at Tol's side.

Tol, equally sorry for Egrin's absence and still grieving the loss of Narren, stiffened. Frez's downcast words penetrated his gloom, reminding him how important their fighting spirit was to his plan.

"Regret nothing!" Tol said staunchly. "Egrin has nothing to prove, to us or anyone." Assuming a light-hearted tone, he gave Frez a slap on the back and added, "Would we not gladly die for the empire?"

"Why not?" replied Tarthan, a wry look on his dark face. "I've done most things, but I haven't been killed yet."

Muddy to their waists, the foot soldiers turned south. When Fingle's Creek shrank to a narrow stream, they forded it and mounted the eastern bank. The woods were thin here, crisscrossed by footpaths and cart trails. The Ergothians hugged the creekbank, and by midmorning had reached the slapdash defenses of Old Port.

Kender weren't known for keeping buildings in repair, and the Old Port wall was no exception. The stones were cracked open by vines, and the wooden gates were rotten. None of the wall seemed to be guarded, but Tol and his men avoided the south gate just in case. They slipped silently into the sleepy town.

In the high street they came upon a pair of armed humans, each carrying a bucket. Wellax's company swiftly captured them. They proved to be mercenaries—men from the eastern lands beyond the Khalkist Mountains. Astonished to find

Ergothians in Old Port, they finally answered Tol's questions after a little encouragement.

They had been looking for fresh water to take back to the Wave Chaser Inn, three streets away. A few score Tarsan soldiers were quartered there, and a late night revel had used up every potable in the place. The main Tarsan army was south of Three Rose Creek, outside Old Port. Tylocost was preparing to strike south and destroy Lord Urakan's army once and for all.

The number of men in the Tarsan army was somewhere between ten and twelve thousand. All the rest of Tylocost's fifty thousand strong had been lost in the past two years—in battle, to sickness, and to XimXim. More troops were on the way from Tarsis, the prisoners said. A reinforcement of twenty thousand was expected before autumn.

This news added urgency to the Ergothians' plan. Tol had the two men bound, gagged, and heaved into a convenient cellar. He sent half his men up the high street. He and the rest of the demi-horde surrounded the Wave Chaser Inn, a stout stone structure built by a Tarsan sea captain as a haven for his fellow countrymen in the kender town.

Slipping on a helmet and yellow cloak taken from one of the mercenaries, Tol walked boldly in the front door.

The great room was full of soldiers sleeping off the effects of too much drink. Tol took a deep breath and shattered the silence.

"On your feet!" he bellowed. "Lord Tylocost comes! Get on your feet, you stinking swine!"

His training-ground voice stood him in good stead. Blearily, the mercenaries got to their feet, shaking their more sodden comrades awake.

"Turn out! Turn out!" Tol shouted. "The army's moving out! Any man not on his feet and in the street will be considered a deserter. We all know what Lord Tylocost does to deserters!"

In threes and fours, the soldiers staggered into the rain-swept street. Tol's own men were drawn up in two double lines, and the befuddled Tarsan troops obligingly formed up between them.

Meanwhile, an officer, from the look of the gold leaves on his helmet, approached Tol. "What's happened?" he asked in a hoarse voice. "I thought we were staying in Old Port for at least a fortnight—"

"General's orders. He's routed the Ergothians and needs every available man to join the pursuit."

The officer nodded. Looking down to buckle his sword belt, he noticed Tol's Ergothian-style riding boots.

The Tarsan's head came up. "You're—!"

Tol whipped out his saber and laid its edge against the man's neck. "Be wise!"

The Tarsan officer glared at Tol with bloodshot eyes. His hesitation lasted only a moment; he had no choice, and knew it. He surrendered.

Tol prodded him outside, where the bewildered Tarsans were facing four lines of Ergothian spears. At their officer's command, the Tarsans grounded their arms.

The wine cellar of the inn proved a perfect dungeon, albeit filled with casks of north plains wine and Tarsan-style beer. Tol had the disarmed enemy soldiers herded into the cellar and the door bolted. Laughing at their easy coup, the Ergothians demolished the wooden stairs leading up from the cellar and used the heavy timbers to brace the door shut. Full casks, long feasting tables, and heavy bags of flour were piled against the braces. It would take the Tarsans a full day to break out.

"Let's go," Tol said. "Time is short! Egrin should have reached Lord Urakan's camp by now."

The rain had ended at last, and the sun was breaking through the tattered clouds. Tol's men sorted through the cloaks and weaponry given up by the mercenaries. One entire company—Darpo's—was outfitted with saffron-colored cloaks and peaked Tarsan helmets. They also tied red cloths around their right arms to identify themselves as imperial soldiers.

They left Old Port by the east gate, heading toward the alluvial plain between Fingle's and Three Rose Creek. A low ridge dominated the north side of the stream. Tol could not imagine crossing the creek and climbing that ridge in the face of an entrenched enemy, but stubborn Lord Urakan had tried. Tol was counting on that same stubbornness now. Stung by defeat, Urakan would fall back, but slowly and reluctantly. Tylocost would swoop down upon him to complete his victory.

That's what Tol would do, and what he expected the skilled elf general to do.

The south shore of Three Rose Creek was covered with rafts, scows, and barges used to ferry the Tarsan army across. No guards remained behind. Tylocost had cut loose from his base and was going all out to catch Urakan's retreating hordes.

As most of Tol's force hurried on, Fellen's company stayed behind. They proceeded to sink or set adrift all the watercraft the Tarsans had left behind. There would be no escape for Tylocost.

The enemy's trail was easy to follow. Thousands of men and horses had trampled through the waist-high cattails as they climbed up from the creek into the sparse pine woods. Just inside the woods, Tol paused, waiting for Fellen's company to rejoin them. A distant rumble came to his ears—Tylocost's army, on the move.

"Twelve thousand men," Allacath muttered.

"Equal parts foot and cavalry," Tol added. "The Tarsans hire plains nomads for their riding skills."

"They can't stand up to our horsemen," said Darpo staunchly.

"They've been doing a pretty good job so far," was Allacath's gloomy reply.

When Fellen's men had caught up with them, Tol ordered his men into battle formation. Five companies would lead: Tarthan's on the far left, then Wellax, Allacath, Frez, and Darpo on the right. About fifty paces behind them would come the second line, the companies of Fellen, Sanksa, and Egrin, the latter now commanded by Kiya. In ordinary times, it would have been impossible to convince Ergothian warriors to follow a tribal woman into battle, but her part in defeating XimXim had won Kiya much respect from the hard-nosed soldiers.

Darpo's company, disguised by yellow cloaks and peaked helms, advanced slightly ahead of the rest of the line. Several times they came within sight of the rearmost echelons of the Tarsan army, but Tol held them back, allowing Tylocost to keep ahead. The time was not yet right to strike.

Midday came. The sky was bright blue, flecked with clouds only at the far eastern and western horizons. It was summer, and the warm wind off the sea combined with the sun to make the day sultry.

Tol and his men ate and drank on the march, passing waterskins back and forth in the ranks. Off to their right, the west, a distant shout went up, closely followed by the telltale clatter of arms. Tol tossed his waterskin to the man behind him and drew his sword.

"Close up the line. Shields up," he said quietly.

Two hundred round shields swung into line; two hundred long spears protruded beside them. Darpo's company scattered into a thin skirmish line. They trotted through the slender pines toward the din of battle, but hadn't gone far when an officer on horseback cantered back to them.

"What are you men doing here?" the Tarsan demanded. "Get to the front! We've caught the Ergos. They won't escape this time!"

Darpo hurled a spear, killing the officer. The riderless horse galloped away. While the Ergothians were searching the dead man, a troop of enemy cavalry came riding by. They were lightly armed nomads, wearing Tarsan colors, but rode past without stopping. Darpo let them go.

In the dead officer's cuirass, Darpo found a dispatch. As he was skimming its contents, Tol and the main body of soldiers came jogging through the trees. Darpo handed him the letter.

"'Proceed at once to the enemy's left, and charge home,'" Tol read aloud. "'Their unhorsed cavalry won't fight on foot.'" He looked up swiftly. "It's signed 'Tylo.'"

"What are we going to do?" Wellax said.

Tol crumpled the strip of parchment. "We go straight in," he replied.

He knew his plan would work better if the Tarsans routed the battered, horseless Ergothian riders. It was a harsh decision, but there was no time to waste explaining to his men. Mounting Cloud, he urged his soldiers forward.

The sounds of combat increased. Atop a sandy knoll Tol took in the panorama of battle. On his right, the Tarsan cavalry was swarming around a large body of Ergothians on foot—the horseless riders mentioned in the dispatch. Had Tol commanded them, the Ergothians might have formed a tight circle and held off the enemy light horse, but the imperial riders had no proper training in fighting afoot. They sallied forth in groups of ten and twenty to attack the nomads, who easily evaded them. Then the Tarsan cavalry charged and tore the isolated knots of Ergothians to pieces, trampling them underfoot or impaling them with their long, light lances.

In the center of the battlefield, a strong force of Ergothian horsemen was holding out against combined forays of Tylocost's cavalry and heavily armed foot soldiers. Encased in armor, using shields so large and heavy it took two men to shift each one, the Tarsan infantry could push the Ergothian cavalry back. But the Tarsans' great weakness was their lack of maneuverability.

On the left, another mixed force of enemy foot and cavalry was driving steadily through a small force of riders. Judging by the stout resistance in the center, Tol deduced Lord Urakan was there, his granite-hard resolve steadying his men. Tylocost would gravitate to the center as well, looking to overwhelm the imperial hordes and complete their destruction.

"Darpo, off with those rags!" Tol said.

"Yes, my lord!" Darpo's company shed their Tarsan cloaks and helmets.

"Juramona!" cried Tol.

"Juramona!" answered his chosen retainers. The city

guardsmen under their command raised spears high and added, "Daltigoth! Daltigoth!"

Tol's men fell on the rear of the Tarsan force. His hardy footmen drove through the nomad cavalry but slammed to a halt when they reached the armored infantry. The nomads reformed and swarmed around the rear of Tol's formation, expecting to scatter the few Ergothians. To their immense surprise, Kiya's company formed a tight block bristling with spears and ran at them, trapping the Tarsan force against Sanksa's company in the rear. At least a hundred nomads fell, and the balance fled in consternation. A few of Sanksa's men picked up stones and contemptuously flung them at the fleeing barbarians.

Deep in the fight, Tol saw none of this. He was in formation with Darpo and Frez, and they hit the enemy foot soldiers hard from behind. The rear ranks died where they stood, unable to face about in the press, but the middle ranks managed to turn and meet Tol's onslaught. The Tarsan troops were armed with short, heavy swords, shields, and halberds. Tol's spearmen kept the short swords away, battling the halberdiers to a standstill. The fight degenerated into the kind of slashing match Tol could not afford with his slender line of men, so he called for Fellen's company to hit the enemy's flank. The engineer arrived like a whirlwind, bowling over the mercenaries in their weighty suits of iron mail and bronze plate. In the center, five thousand Tarsans were pinched between Tol's two hundred sixty and Urakan's three thousand. Lighter troops might have fought their way out, but the heavily armored foot soldiers were trapped by their inability to maneuver.

Lord Urakan felt the tide turning, even before he understood why. The pressure lessened on his beleaguered riders. By his side, Egrin declared, "My lord, Lord Tolandruth has hobbled them! It's up to you to knock the enemy down!"

Brandishing the standard of his own horde, the Golden Riders of Caer, Lord Urakan charged straight into the center of the melee. His Ergothians broke the first line of infantry, then the second; by the time they reached the third, however, they had no momentum left. Mercenaries closed around Lord Urakan. Halberds whirled and struck the standard from his hand. He replaced it with his saber, but the foot soldiers used the hook ends of their pole arms to drag him from the saddle. Fighting furiously, brave, arrogant Lord Urakan was pulled into the mob of Tarsan soldiers, and brutally slain.

Seeing this, an angry Egrin took command and re-formed the center of the imperial line. The center held, but the Ergothians were now in difficulty on both flanks. The unhorsed warriors on the left had been beaten and were streaming away from the fight with howling nomads in pursuit. On the right, the Tarsans and Ergothians battled back and forth, neither side gaining an advantage. Everything depended on the center, on which side would outlast the other.

Tol left the front line long enough to climb a small pine tree and survey the battlefield. The enemy center was pinched in the middle, leaving two large blocks of troops joined by a thin line. Egrin was sending waves of mounted attacks against this narrow line. Men and horses were piling up in heaps.

Sunlight flashed off a brilliant object in the midst of the Tarsan center. Tol shaded his eyes and saw an officer on foot wearing a tall, silver helmet with a brightly polished comb. Such workmanship had to be elven. Could this be Tylocost himself?

Shinnying down the tree, Tol shouted for Darpo. Covered in blood not his own, the intrepid warrior raced to his commander's side. Tol pointed out the shining helmet.

"Tylocost?" Darpo exclaimed, his scarred face brightening. "I'll bring you his head!"

"Only if it's still attached to the rest of him!"

Darpo grinned, nodding. He knew his commander did not approve of butchery. He called together a dozen men and prepared to thrust deep into the enemy formation. Tol joined them, moving shoulder to shoulder with his brave foot soldiers.

They rushed through a gap in the line and used their spears to lever apart the armored Tarsans. Because they didn't stop to fight, Tol and Darpo were able to force their way through enemy lines quickly. They found a gap, where wounded Tarsans were sheltering from the battle. Idle archers, their bowstrings made slack by the recent rain, grabbed maces and tried to drive the Ergothians out, but were no match for the spears and shields of Tol's men. Half the archers perished. The rest broke and ran.

From the open ground, Tol could see Lord Urakan's army as it pressed forward, and the mercenary infantry bending back under the strain. He spotted the bright helmet again. Its owner was up a birch tree, watching the attack of Urakan's hordes.

Tol, Darpo, and their small group ran through the wounded and dying men, leaping over them as they lay on the blood-stained soil. They reached the birch tree with Tol in the lead.

"Tylocost! Come down!" he shouted, striking the slim trunk with the flat of his sword. "Come down, or I'll cut the tree down with you in it!"

The warrior in the shiny helmet showed no sign of hearing, much less complying. A handful of nearby Tarsans rushed to their leader's rescue. Darpo's men fought them off while Tol, Darpo, and two guardsmen chopped at the tree with discarded Tarsan swords. Chips flew. With a loud crack, the slender birch sagged and began to fall.

Hardly had the tree come to rest when Tol and his men swarmed over it. The Tarsan in the bright helmet stepped nimbly from the branches and whipped out a fine sword with a long, slender blade. Tol rushed in, dagger in his left hand, saber in his right.

The Tarsan's blade flickered in and out, close to Tol's throat and face. He knew his opponent was trying to unnerve him, but he refused to be cowed, and bored in with his saber while blocking his opponent's attacks with his dagger. At last Tol pinned his foe's blade with the dagger and brought his own weapon down on the Tarsan's grip. The cup hilt saved the fellow's hand, but the blow broke three of the Tarsan's fingers. The slender sword fell to the ground.

Tol brought the edge of the dagger to his opponent's neck. "Surrender!" he panted.

"Will you spare my men if I do?"

"Yes!"

The Tarsan pulled off his helmet. He was an elf all right, but not at all what Tol had expected. Instead of the handsome gallant of bardic song, Tylocost was downright homely. His hair was long, but more gray than yellow, and his pale blue eyes were closely set over a long, thin nose. His fair skin was blotched with large brown freckles, and he was thin to the point of emaciation. He asked Tol's name, then confirmed his own identity.

"I am Janissiron Tylocostathan, called Tylocost by the Tarsans."

The men of the storming party surrounded the enemy general. Tol guided his prisoner at sword point to the center of the Tarsan line, where Tylocost called for a cornet. A youth answered, standing just outside the ring of Ergothian spears, but hesitated when ordered to sound "ground arms."

"Do it, boy," Tylocost told him. "We've lost today. There'll be another time, another day to fight."

Blushing with shame, the cornetist put the brass horn to his lips and blew a four-note signal. He kept repeating it until the Tarsan foot soldiers threw down their weapons. The Tarsans' nomad cavalry, not inclined to submit to Ergothian mercy, galloped away. Weary imperial horsemen let them go. The Battle of Three Rose Creek was over.

Moments before, twenty-five thousand men had been fighting to the death. Now a hush fell over the battlefield. The survivors of Tol's small band pushed through the Tarsan army, most of whom were sitting dejectedly on the ground. Tol saw Tarthan and Frez, Fellen and Sanksa, leading their men toward him. He strained his eyes and stretched his neck until, with great relief, he saw Kiya among the survivors. She had an ugly cut on her sword arm, but walked her with head held high.

Tarthan, the eldest of Tol's retainers, saluted with his dagger. "My lord," he said. "I present the demi-horde of Daltigoth and Juramona, one hundred forty-eight blades fit for duty."

Before Tol could reply, Kiya walked past the gathering Ergothians and threw an arm around his shoulders.

"You are well?" he asked, smiling up at her.

"Sore." She eyed him up and down. "And you haven't got the slightest scratch, have you?"

"No holes. No missing parts."

With a rumble of hoofbeats, the imperial hordes arrived. Tol was surprised but pleased to see Egrin leading the riders.

"Greetings, my lord," the elder warrior said. "The day is yours!"

"Well, we won, at any rate. Where is Lord Urakan?"

Egrin shook his head once, and Tol understood. "Are you in command of the army then?" he asked.

A smile ghosted through Egrin's gray-flecked beard. "No." In answer to Tol's puzzlement he added, "You are the victor, my lord. The army is yours."

Tol was about to protest when Kiya raised a cheer: "Tolandruth! Tolandruth! Tolandruth!"

Tol's retainers added their hoarse voices, then the multitude of Ergothians took up the cry. Tol felt his face burn.

Turning away, he found himself face to face with the homely but clever General Tylocost.

"To the victor goes all praise," the elf said calmly. "Savor it—for now. Soon enough it will be only a memory, given the fortunes of war." When Tol grimaced and kept his flushed face averted, Tylocost frowned and asked, "Forgive me asking, but just how old are you, my lord?"

"Twenty and one years."

The elf looked pained. "Merciful Astarin! I've been beaten by a child. What will they say in Silvanost?"

Tylocost's chagrin cheered Tol considerably. He raised his head, and his grin incited fresh cheers. Tol stared in bemusement at the sea of dirty, bloodstained men, all happily bellowing his name.

Paul B. Thompson and Tonya C. Cook

"Don't just stand there grinning like a lout," Tylocost said.

Nettled, yet unsure, Tol said, "What should I do?"

The elf sighed. "A child, a veritable babe! Raise your sword or spear, my lord. Such devotion should be graciously acknowledged."

Tol took out his nicked and battered saber one more time. When he lifted it high above his head, the chant of his name became a great single roar. It was heard as far away as Old Port.

It would soon be felt in both Tarsis and Daltigoth.

The Reward of Trust; The Silence of Virtue

The days that followed the battle were frantic and noisy. Imperial soldiers, elated by their hard-won victory, celebrated long and heartily.

Tol retired to the tent that had been Lord Urakan's. Amid the carpets and tapestries, gilded braziers and leather camp chairs, he felt very out of place and very much alone. His first night there, for reasons he did not understand, he was seized by violent fits of trembling. He downed a cup of Lord Urakan's best vintage, and the shivering faded.

Scattered across the dead general's trestle table were sheets of the finest foolscap. Tol sat down, took up an ink-stained pen and wrote a lengthy missive to Valaran.

The battle is won, he wrote in a neat but slow hand. *But I would give up all the cheers I hear now and the honors I will receive, if I could be with you tonight...*

He was still at the table when Egrin found him, slumped forward, sleeping with his head resting on his folded arms. The conqueror of XimXim, liberator of Hylo, and victor over Tylocost had ink on his fingers and a black smudge on his nose, the result of a careless scratch while he was writing his long missive.

Egrin did not try to wake him. Tenderly, the elder warrior draped one of Urakan's heavy capes around Tol's shoulders, then went out to begin the reorganization of the scattered imperial army.

❦ ❦ ❦ ❦ ❦

Within ten days of Tylocost's defeat, all opposition to
Ergoth was overcome. Tol marched through eastern Hylo,
driving out the Tarsan garrisons posted in Free Point and
other towns. Tarsan mercenaries not captured at Three Rose
Creek fled the country, taking ship or escaping over the
mountains. Although they expected vengeful Ergothian
hordes to pursue them, the imperial army had little strength
left to chase anyone.

Tol halted his tired hordes at Old Port and requisitioned
all available ships. Then he turned all the captured Tarsan
soldiers loose. Stripped of arms and armor, with only
enough food to get them home by the most direct sailing
route, nine and a half thousand men were sent on their way.
They were all that was left of the force of fifty thousand
who'd come to Hylo to wrest the kender kingdom from the
empire's sway.

Veteran warlords under Tol's command, including Egrin,
argued against such clemency, saying the freed men would
only take up arms against Ergoth in the future.

"They're defeated," Tol said. "Let them go back and show
their masters in Tarsis their humiliation. Let the wealthy syndics of the city feed and house them, not us."

Tol defied accepted custom in another way: He did not
send Tylocost's head to the emperor. The elf remained his
prisoner. To disguise him from vengeance-minded Ergothians,
Tylocost's hair was cut to chin length, and he was dressed
in nondescript yeoman's clothes. He was hidden in plain
sight among the enlarged retinue of warriors and servants
now attached to Lord Tolandruth. Tylocost took captivity in
good stead, but proved to have a melancholy nature to match
his eccentric looks. His life depended on Tol's good will, so he
readily played the biddable captive.

One evening, during supper in the vast tent Tol had inherited from Lord Urakan, Miya blurted, "I thought all Silvanesti
were finely made. What happened to you?"

Tol nearly choked on his roast, but Tylocost took the rude query calmly.

"It's said my mother, while burdened with child, beheld a human woman in the forest, and the image of the wretched creature was impressed on my features before birth." After a brief pause, he added, "It was a Dom-shu woman she saw."

Miya flushed, and Tol smothered a laugh.

"No Dom-shu is as ugly as you!" Miya said hotly.

And so the evening's wrangles would begin. It seemed more than passing strange to Tol to have the former terror of the empire at his side, shabbily dressed, matching jibes with his boisterous wives. Even so, Tol held no illusions about Tylocost. The acute mind that had defeated Lord Urakan and three other Ergothian generals in the past twenty years had not been thrown out with his gaudy helmet. Tylocost was biding his time.

Knowing he needed a sharp pair of eyes on the elf, Tol designated Kiya to act as the elf's guardian. He had no specific suspicions but realized Tylocost might try to escape or foment a plot from within Tol's camp.

Hylo was firmly in imperial hands, but the war continued. Tarsan fleets raided the west coast of Ergoth. Far to the south, Tarsan gold raised the pirate fleets of Kharland into open war against the empire. Elaborate and flattering treaties were proposed to convince the Silvanesti to enter the war as Tarsis's ally. Thus far, the elves had resisted Tarsan blandishments, but the pirates quickly choked off all trade in the Gulf of Ergoth. Something would have to be done about them.

Victory had not ended the war, only changed its venue.

❦ ❦ ❦ ❦ ❦

Before the winds of autumn set in, Tol organized the return of the sick and wounded to their homes. More than one thousand Ergothians were seriously injured, and another two thousand were needed on their farms to finish the harvest. Tol gave Egrin the task of leading the sizable column south, calling first at Caergoth, then Daltigoth. He prepared lengthy documents describing the death of XimXim and his subsequent victory over Tylocost. With Egrin busy rounding up wagons and carts to transport the sick, Tol decided to entrust his dispatches to another— Mandes the wizard.

Mandes had weathered his personal catastrophe well. The loss of his left arm was a hard blow—a wizard needed two hands to perform most incantations—but Mandes proved surprisingly adaptable. By the time the imperial hordes returned from clearing out the last Tarsan garrisons, Mandes was up and walking. He spent most of his time in Old Port, drinking in noisy kender taverns or prowling the seedy shops lining the waterfront. Such shops were treasure troves of odd merchandise, brought in by wandering sailors or "found" by kender on their wide-ranging travels.

One afternoon, with the chill of early autumn in the air, Tol found the wizard in the Wave Chaser Inn, the same place they'd captured the Tarsan soldiers. The wizard was seated in a snug corner by the hearth, at a table heaped with moldering manuscripts. A wooden tankard of mulled wine steamed by his right hand.

Tol greeted him. Unlike nearly every other soul in Hylo, Mandes did not rise and salute the now famous warlord, but he did bid Tol join him in a pot of warmed wine.

Tol dragged up a three-legged stool and accepted the offer of a drink. When the wine arrived, it proved to be heavily spiced. Though not to Tol's taste, he sipped it politely.

"You've heard I'm sending men home to be discharged for wounds or work?" he said. Mandes grunted assent. "Would you like to go along?"

That brought the wizard upright on his bench. The wool blanket draped around his shoulder fell away, exposing the empty sleeve of his velvet robe. The cuff was pinned to his chest.

"I, go to Daltigoth?" he said, and Tol nodded. "That is a handsome offer!"

Tol smiled. "There's a price to be paid. Some letters and dispatches I've written must be delivered. Will you see to it?"

Mandes leaned forward, knocking old scrolls from the table top. "Gladly, my lord! To whom will I give them?"

"Crown Prince Amaltar gets the reports bearing Lord Urakan's seal." Tol had inherited the old warlord's signet with command of his army. "The remainder—only one—goes to his wife, Princess Consort Valaran."

He expected some comment, but Mandes showed no sign of recognizing the unusual nature of the second recipient.

"I've long dreamed of going to Daltigoth," the sorcerer said, sinking back in his bench. "Tarsis was too tight-fisted, too mercantile for me. In Daltigoth, a man can be recognized for his talent and rewarded for his deeds. When do I leave, my lord?"

"Tomorrow morning, first light. I've secured a conveyance for you. Not a wagon or a kender's cart, but a real coach-and-four. You'll have company on the ride, but it's still better than a ox-drawn wagon, eh?"

Tol called to a pair of soldiers waiting by the inn door. They brought a strong box, strapped with iron, and set it on the floor at Mandes's feet. Tol opened it. Nestled inside were eight short, thickly wound scrolls. Seven bore the seal of the warlord, pressed into the red wax enclosing the parchment. The eighth scroll was tied with white ribbon and sealed with ordinary white wax.

Tol looked over the brief legends inked on the outside of the rolls. Finding the one he wanted, he tapped it with a finger.

"I haven't forgotten you," he said. "This dispatch mentions the bakali, your role in helping to stop the Red Wrack, and our battle with XimXim. I would be very surprised if His Highness Prince Amaltar didn't reward you for your deeds."

He closed the box and clamped a soft lead seal around the hasp. Rising, he said, "I thank you, Mandes—for everything. And I know you'll see my words safely into the proper hands."

After Tol departed, Mandes rose from his chair, swaying slightly from too much wine. He summoned two kender from the kitchen to carry the box to his room on the second floor. Gathering up his old manuscripts, he followed them upstairs.

Alone in his room, he sagged heavily on the straw-stuffed mattress. His features lost their carefully neutral expression and twisted with omnipresent pain. Agony lanced through his shoulder, throbbed down his left arm, and ended as it always did, in the tips of the fingers of his left hand—arm, hand, and fingers he no longer possessed.

Mandes held up his right hand, palm down, and felt his crippled shoulder flex as though lifting his left as well. He could see his left arm and hand alongside the right; the phantom limb glowed faintly in the gloom. His searches through the scrap shops of Old Port were not merely a cure for idleness. Mandes was looking for magical tomes that might contain secret recipes to restore his arm, or at least give flesh to the phantom limb he was certain he possessed. He'd found nothing so far and had begun to despair. But now—

Now he was to go to Daltigoth!

The empire's capital contained perhaps the greatest concentration of wizards and sorcerous literature in the world. Only the libraries of Silvanost could rival it, and they were beyond the reach of a mere human.

Mandes shivered, more in anticipation than from the autumnal chill. Lord Tolandruth's offer was a gift from the gods. Yet it was a gift he felt he had more than earned with his suffering.

Pain was replaced by the equally familiar rage. Mandes stood and flung the useless manuscripts across the room.

Tolandruth! It was that fool's fault he'd lost his arm! True, he had consented to help in the fight against XimXim, but he'd never imagined he'd have to battle the monster himself in that hellish cavern!

Now, Gilean's book of fate had turned a new page. He was getting that which he most desired: access to the great and powerful. In Daltigoth he would place his magical skills at the disposal of whomever offered him the highest rewards. It was only right and proper. Wealth and power belonged to those who could *do*, whether they were warriors, woodcutters, or sorcerers. One day, he vowed, he would be the most powerful wizard in Ergoth. When that happened, his persecutors in Tarsis would have cause to regret their past injustices to him.

Giving the bakali the Balm of Sirrion had been a mistake, he now realized. Embedding the Red Wrack in the mist had been an even greater folly. The lizard-men hadn't asked for a plague. That had been his own idea. Since the Tarsans and kender were not sufficiently admiring of his talents, he'd decided to repay them with pestilence. But the dead bakali had taken the blame, and no one living knew the truth but him. Even so, he wondered if Tolandruth still suspected.

The sealed box sat by the door, black and bulky. Within were Tolandruth's thoughts on the events of the past sixty days. His decisions, his opinions, his praise, his condemnation— all were locked inside that box. Mandes needed to know what had been written. It would be to his advantage to embellish adulation of himself and expunge any criticism.

The lead seal was weighty in his hand. He knew no spells to remove seals intact, but he did know how to re-forge broken ones.

Mandes was awake till dawn. He read and wrote all night, scraping off Tol's carefully penned letters and inking in his own. The former farm boy had little skill as a writer; his simple handwriting was easy to alter.

The last scroll, addressed to Princess Valaran Mandes found most interesting, but it mentioned him not at all. He did not bother changing any of it. Instead he made a copy.

❦ ❦ ❦ ❦ ❦

The caravan rolled out at sunrise. Tol saw it off. Egrin led the homeward-bound column on horseback. He saluted his former shield-bearer proudly, and Tol returned the gesture with enthusiasm. Egrin bared his dagger and raised it high, holding it there long after he'd passed Tol.

Behind Egrin came those riders going home to their families and farms. Most were from the Caergoth region. They raised four cheers for their valiant commander as they rode.

In their wake came the walking wounded. Weakened, they did not shout so lustily, but there was pride in their stride and gratitude in their eyes.

Lastly, a long, irregular parade of carts and wagons rolled by, filled with warriors too hurt to walk. Leading the line of wagons was a black coach drawn by four matched bay horses, once the property of a rich Tarsan merchant who spent some months each year in Old Port. Tol's men had found the coach hidden away in a barn and liberated it for their commander's use.

Mandes sat in the coach's rear seat. The other places were taken by riders who'd lost limbs or sustained other grave injuries. The wizard did not wave as he passed, but did incline his head to the author of his new opportunity.

Tol called out, "Farewell, Mandes! When I return to Daltigoth, we'll feast at Juramona House!"

He remained until the last cart in the long caravan was gone, then turned Cloud about and rode back to camp.

It was the middle day of autumn. Tol expected that once his letters were received, he would be recalled to the capital to confer with the crown prince and the highest warlords of the empire. Fresh hordes would be needed if Tarsan territory was to be invaded. Tol had fewer than seven thousand men, enough to defend Hylo but not enough to conquer the powerful city-state.

He knew no attack could be mounted until spring. Winter's snow would close the roads and make troop movements laborious and expensive. Tarsis might launch coastal raids in the meantime, but the loss of a huge army and their best general had to give them pause. Time would tell how much.

Riding back into camp over ground crunchy with frost, Tol was stricken anew with longing for Valaran. She'd been much on his mind during the journey north, but once they encountered real danger, his mind had been fixed on the peril in front of him. His pent-up desire surfaced with a vengeance now. How long would it be until he saw her again? The letter he'd entrusted to Mandes begged her to write to him. Before, when he'd been on the move, there was no way for her letters to find him, but he would be in camp for some time now and regular correspondence was possible. He was lord of the northern hordes. The thought made him smile with pride.

A few flakes of snow drifted down, melting on Cloud's gray hide and Tol's bare hands.

It will not be long, Val, Tol vowed. Not long.

† † † † †

Snow was falling in Daltigoth. The sun shone warmly over the Inner City, as it always did thanks to the college of sorcerers, but the outer city lay muffled under a fresh mantle of white.

Treading carefully through the drifts came a man swathed in furs from head to heels. He made directly for the gate of a darkened villa sited in a cramped corner of the Old City. Stucco was peeling off the villa's wall in wide patches, exposing red bricks underneath. Snow padded the spikes atop the wall.

Few people dared approach the crumbling mansion. It was inhabited by a gang of disreputable nobles, former members of the city Horse Guards, drunkards, wastrels, and thugs. They were called—though not to their faces—Nazramin's Wolves, in honor of the prince who was their patron.

The gate was shut, so the fur-clad man tugged on the chain hanging nearby. A bronze bell tolled dully. The wicket opened.

"Who is it?" demanded a deep voice from within.

"A visitor to see your master."

"Go away before I set the dogs on you." The deep baying of hounds within proved the threat was not an idle one.

The wicket started to close. Quickly, the stranger held up his hand, palm out, and muttered a short cantrip. A brightly glowing ball of fire, no bigger than a hen's egg, shot from his hand through the wicket.

Exclamations and curses from the other side told the visitor his credentials had been noted. The wicket widened, and a fiercely scowling face appeared.

"Why didn't you just say who you were?"

The man's clean-shaven face, lined by recent suffering, twitched into the faintest of smiles. "I just did."

The old gate swung inward, scraping back a wedge of newly fallen snow. Seven hard-looking men, cloaked and hooded, stood on the other side. One jerked his head to indicate the visitor should proceed straight ahead to a columned porch and a great brass door much dulled with tarnish. The visitor strode on, only to be stopped by the point of a sword against his breastbone.

"Open your furs. I have to search you for arms."

Wordlessly, the stranger allowed the guards to probe him for weapons. One of them noticed his left sleeve was pinned to the breast of his robe.

"What's this?" he said, snatching the cylinder of cloth free. It swung limply by the man's side.

"As you can see, I have no arms to hide," said the stranger. The guards grunted, and sent him on his way.

The villa's interior was almost as cold as the evening outside. Only every third wall sconce held a burning torch, giving the hall a dim and forbidding air. Suits of armor hung on stands along the walls, and racks of spears and swords were everywhere. The villa had more the air of a barracks than a fine old house.

A stooping servant, bearing a tray with a tall beaker on it, scurried down the stairs and entered the door at the far end of the hall. When the door opened, a blaze of heat and light washed out. The visitor followed the servant and stood, unannounced, in the open doorway.

The room beyond proved his host was not averse to comfort

after all. It was well illuminated and heated by crackling fires in two large fireplaces. Between them was an enormous chair padded with leather. A table to one side was laden with food and drink, heavy plates and goblets wrought in bright gold. On the chair's right was an identical table, covered with partially unrolled scrolls. Two wolfhounds lolled by the fire. They growled at the visitor.

"Come forward, Master Mandes," beckoned Prince Nazramin. He set aside the document he was reading and leaned back in the leather chair.

Mandes pulled off his cape and let his robe hang open. Although he'd been cold before, the heat here was stifling.

The prince waved to the pile of parchment. "You bring amusing gifts. The peasant boy has been busy, hasn't he?"

"Indeed he has, sire."

Nazramin's brown eyes narrowed. "I am not my brother," he said slowly. "Do not call me 'sire.'"

"Forgive me, Lord Prince. I am but lately come to Ergoth. My sojourn in the uncivilized wilds—"

"You altered these dispatches, wizard. What parts did you change?"

Sweat beaded on Mandes's high forehead. "Only those portions that mentioned me, Lord Prince. Some I embellished to make more flattering; others I repaired because they were, ah, critical of my deeds in Hylo."

"I see." After a moment's thoughtful pause, Nazramin added, "You left Lord Mudfield's description of his own successes. Those will have to go. In fact, I intend to change them all. I know several expert forgers—though for this lout's handwriting, a pig with a pen would suffice. When I'm done, no one will care a whit about farmer Lord Tolandruth!"

He drained a golden goblet in one toss. He did not offer his perspiring guest any refreshment.

"Lord Prince, many soldiers were present at the battle of Three Rose Creek," Mandes said carefully. "Lord Egrin himself is now in the city, and knows the truth. How can you take Lord Tolandruth's acclaim away without arousing suspicion?"

"First, Lord Urakan won the battle," the prince said, refilling his goblet. "I'll put those words in the upstart's own mouth. That Urakan died is both poignant and useful. He was a military blockhead, but also a noble of the first blood. Let Urakan have the glory. He'll bear it better than a peasant boy, no matter how high my brother elevates him!

"Second, the situation in Hylo is delicate. Very delicate. Lord Mudfield will request permission to remain there, to keep an eye on the machinations of Tarsis. He will be granted permission. And stay there he will—until he rots!"

Without warning, the prince flung his goblet on the stone floor. It rang loudly, and showered yellow nectar on Mandes's feet. The wolfhounds, each one hundred fifty pounds of muscle, teeth, and fur, rose and stalked to the nervous wizard, sniffing the spilled wine. They began to lick the sticky droplets from the floor and Mandes's boots.

Mandes bowed his head. He would have bowed more deeply, but didn't dare shift his feet. The hounds were still busily licking them.

"An excellent stratagem, Lord Prince," he said. "The frontier is a dangerous place. Lord Tolandruth may perish amidst its dangers."

Nazramin gave a disgusted snort and scrubbed strands of red hair from his face. "I doubt it. Peasants are like cockroaches: Try to stamp on them, and they survive." Slightly drunk, he mimed his own words, lifting one foot unsteadily off the floor. Letting it fall heavily, he added, "I prefer he survives anyway. I'll savor it more if he wastes his life away on a distant frontier."

"Alive, Lord Tolandruth is a threat," Mandes offered.

"Perhaps to you, wizard. Not to me."

Gauging his words carefully, Mandes said, "May I ask, gracious prince, why you loathe Lord Tolandruth so?"

Nazramin seized the front of Mandes's robe, dragging him close. Nose to nose he whispered, "He offends me, wizard. Because he's not in his proper place. Because he does the deeds of a hero, even though he was born to grow turnips. A proper order must be maintained if the world is to turn as it should. Don't you agree?" A dangerous glint came to the prince's eyes. "Most of all, he gives me a convenient way to torment my brother."

He shoved Mandes away, swept a hand through the scattered scrolls, and came up with the one Tol had addressed to Valaran. He smiled at it—and Mandes suppressed a shudder at the singularly unpleasant expression.

"And this," Nazramin murmured, caressing the scroll. "This gives me a chain I can bind around Valaran's slender throat. I pull, she comes. I let the chain go slack, she flees— but never very far. She is privy to my brother's doings, which I otherwise would not hear of. By making certain alterations to this"—he tapped the scroll against his palm—"I can twist the chain, convincing the princess to give voice to the words I want said."

"Your vision far exceeds mine, Lord Prince," said the sorcerer. "I confess it is beyond me."

The prince gave a dismissive wave. "Get out. Do not approach me again unless I send for you."

The dogs had gone to sleep, forsaking Mandes's boots, so he stepped back and bowed deeply.

"As you command, Lord Prince." Necessity required Mandes to add, "A reward was mentioned for what I placed in your hands . . ."

Nazramin took a weighty purse from the folds of his dressing gown and tossed it to Mandes. The sorcerer was not yet adept at catching with one hand, and the bag of coins thumped into his belly and fell to the floor. The clatter of heavy coins woke the dogs. In a flash the wolfhounds were on their feet, barking and snarling. Mandes paled and drew back.

The prince rocked with laughter. "Take your reward, wizard! Buy yourself a new arm!"

Mandes scooped up the purse and backed out of the sweltering room. As he was about to close the door, Nazramin said a word to the dogs, and they leaped for him.

Mandes shut the door just in time. The savage beasts hurled themselves against the oak panels time and again, howling like the cursed hounds of H'rar. Sweating and shaking, he beat a quick retreat. Out in the snowy streets, he clenched his fingers tightly around the prince's gold.

Buy yourself a new arm. Nazramin had meant it as a cruel joke, but that's exactly what Mandes planned to do. With a new arm, his campaign would start. Not for him the petty plans of Prince Nazramin.

His goal was nothing less than the magical conquest of Daltigoth.

¥ ¥ ¥ ¥ ¥

Valaran let Tol's letter fall from her hands.

On the sunny battlements of the Imperial Palace, she looked over the silent, gray city. Snow always stole the color from everything. All the poets said so, and for once, she saw the truth in their fanciful words.

"Duty demands that I remain here, to guard the borders of the empire," Tol had written. "I cannot say when I will see you again. Our lives mean little compared to the glory of our nation . . . here I can serve the empire best, instead of rotting away as the crown prince's lackey."

She could hardly believe it. He had promised to come back—and now seemed in little hurry. The realization stung like a slap in the face. If he'd been ordered to stay, she might have accepted it—they both had their duties—but he didn't want to come back! At first she couldn't fathom it, then her eyes found the letter's final sentence, and all was made dreadfully clear. That cheery postscript had stolen the breath from Valaran's lungs and driven her, pale as a wraith, to this great height.

"The Dom-shu sisters have been of great worth to me. Kiya is an excellent warrior, though she still cannot cook. Miya has proven herself in other ways. Our child will be born in the spring."

Valaran looked down in despair. It was a long way to the plaza. Unblemished by winter's snow, the heroic mosaics sparkling in the sunlight seemed to mock her, ridiculing her pain. She could see every one of the thousands of stones in them. In a moment she would see them closer still.

Two women crossed the plaza slowly. From this height Valaran couldn't recognize their faces, but their elaborate gowns and deliberate, stately tread marked them as imperial wives. How they and the rest of the Consorts' Circle would coo and jabber over her fate! Poor Valaran the Wisp, the skinny, unfeminine scholar who had somehow caught the eye of the hero Tolandruth, and killed herself when he was unfaithful. Silly girl! Didn't she know *all* men are unfaithful at some point in their lives?

Anger flooded her, sending hot blood to her face. No! Not for any man would she throw away her life—certainly not for an upstart, arrogant peasant who imagined himself a noble!

Upstart, arrogant, *lying* peasant! What a fool she had been to believe him!

The wind dried her tears. Valaran turned away from the parapet and made her way with firm steps down the winding stone stair into the palace. She went directly to the imperial library and filled her arms with books. Ignoring courtiers and servants, she moved purposefully through the halls, back to the corridor between the kitchens and the Consort Circle's salon. She wanted nothing now but to seclude herself in her old hiding place, where she'd first met Tol.

She shook her head savagely, excising that event from her memory. It hadn't happened. *He* hadn't happened. How stupid she had been to order her life around such a ignorant, unfeeling farm boy!

Valaran closed the curtain and sat down to read.

❦ ❦ ❦ ❦ ❦

Through the cold and achingly dull winter, rumors began to circulate among Daltigoth's elite. People having problems with health, love, or business dealings could seek help from a man who could solve any problem, a wise and discreet man, said to be unknown to the college of sorcerers. Skilled in many magical arts, he was new to the city. For gold, or the right sort of favor, this clever wizard would unravel even the most difficult problems, no questions asked. Fortunes changed hands. Enemies disappeared, or succumbed to the worst "luck" imaginable.

When word of this dangerous freelancer reached Yoralyn's ears, she attempted to find out more about him, but she had foresworn spies, and could find out little with her own resources. By the time the name of Mandes became better-known to the college, the rogue wizard was too entrenched, too popular, too protected by powerful patrons, for the White Robes or Red Robes to move against him. It was said that even Prince Amaltar consulted Mandes— most discreetly.

Emperor Pakin III took ill that winter and never left his bed again. Tough and stubborn still, Pakin III clung to life but gave up his power. No longer simply co-ruler, Prince Amaltar was proclaimed Imperial Regent by a conclave of warlords. Formerly a penniless outcast, Mandes now moved closer to the most powerful man in the empire.

The sorcerer settled into a sumptuous house only a short distance from the entrance to the Inner City, living there alone. The day Prince Amaltar was made Imperial Regent, Mandes stood in the center of his beautifully appointed, scroll-filled study and rubbed his hands thoughtfully. One hand was pale and soft, like the rest of Mandes's flesh. The other was muscular and brown. Unable to grow a new arm, he'd found a suitable replacement. Its former owner had not given his limb willingly, but he was past protesting. His lifeless body had been consigned to the Dalti River before it froze over for the winter.

Too easy, too easy, some part of Mandes's mind told him. His goals may have been too modest, for everything he wanted had seemed to fall into his hands within six months of his arrival in Daltigoth. Only two things still vexed him, in minor ways. Prince Nazramin, whose power behind the scenes had grown enormously, remained indifferent to Mandes and rarely sought his counsel. The other niggling problem was Lord Tolandruth. Consigned to the distant reaches of Hylo, the young warlord still lived. Even with half the nobles of Daltigoth on his side, the other half under his thumb (for he knew too much about their indiscretions), even with the patronage of the regent himself, Mandes could not contemplate Tolandruth without foreboding.

❦ ❦ ❦ ❦ ❦

Days passed into months. New hordes arrived to bolster Tol's army, but no word came with them—not from Prince Amaltar, Egrin, or Valaran. The silence was so troubling that Tol wrote new letters to Valaran and Egrin.

When the sun broke through on the first day of spring, sixteen new hordes arrived under the command of Lord Regobart. Many years Tol's senior, Regobart bore orders from Regent Amaltar which named him commander of the northern army. Regobart had been charged to convey the prince's appreciation to Tolandruth for keeping station through the winter, and his continued affection for his champion. That was all. No words of praise or gratitude for last autumn's victories. No personal missive came from Valaran.

When a private message finally did arrive, it came in the form of Sanksa, one of Tol's chosen retainers. The Karad-shu man had gone to Daltigoth with Egrin. He returned looking haggard and grave, and Tol's heart fell. He feared the worst.

Muddy and trailworn, Sanksa gratefully accepted a flagon of warm grog.

"Egrin's at the Bay of Ergoth. Been there since before the first snowfall," he told Tol. Upon their arrival in Caergoth, Sanksa went on to say, they had been ordered to the south coast to train six hordes to fight the Kharland pirates, who plundered the empire's coasts at the behest of Tarsis. The rest of the caravan, including Mandes, went on to Daltigoth.

Tol had heard about the depredations of the pirates from other new arrivals and wondered why Egrin hadn't written him before this. Sanksa's response caused fresh worry.

"From then until now he couldn't write because our raising of seaborne hordes was counted a secret," the Karad-shu said. He lowered his voice. "To bring you this word, I left our camp on the bay and stole my way to you!"

"Desertion? What could possibly make you, a loyal warrior, do such a thing?" Tol asked.

"I will not water the wine, my lord, but pour it straight: That faithless villain Mandes has set himself up in the capital as a free sorcerer, taking on clients for gold and defying the edicts of the colleges. The Red and White Robes would have moved against him, but he has made powerful allies, chiefly Prince Amaltar. The colleges dare not provoke the prince, as he now rules the empire in his father's stead. Worse to tell, Mandes must have altered or destroyed your reports, offering instead to the prince his own lies. He claims to have bested XimXim alone, and gave sole credit for the defeat of Tylocost to Lord Urakan, who he said died of his wounds on the very doorstep of victory!"

Sanksa clawed dirty blonde hair from his face and drained the flagon. "The final clod of dirt on your grave was a letter claiming, in your name, that all you wanted from life was to remain in Hylo with the army until Tarsis was defeated. With Mandes performing wonders for him, Prince Amaltar's fears for his own safety have been greatly eased, and he does not feel so strongly the need of a champion. So, my lord, you, Egrin, and the good men of Juramona are condemned by lies and villainy to exile at opposite ends of the empire!"

Stunned and silent, Tol wandered to the tent flap. Outside, the imperial camp was alive with activity as Lord Regobart's new arrivals sought their billets.

"And Regobart?" Tol said, casting an ugly look over his shoulder at Sanksa. "Is he also a part of this web of deceit?"

"Egrin says Lord Regobart is not to blame for your predicament, being an honorable soldier and a loyal vassal of the emperor. 'Serve him well, as you did Lord Urakan,' Egrin told me to tell you," the lanky warrior said.

Tol turned away, his shoulders hunching slightly in defeat. Rising to his feet Sanksa exclaimed, "Do not despair, my lord! The gods know virtue and will punish evil. You will best your enemies as you did XimXim and Tylocost, two mighty foes!"

Tol thanked the earnest warrior for his efforts and bade him stay in Tol's own tent to rest and eat. He promised to make right Sanksa's desertion.

Stepping outside the modest tent (he had ceded the larger one to Lord Regobart), Tol inhaled the cold air of early spring. It had been a morning like this, many years ago, when he'd gone to the onion field to work, and instead ended up saving the life of Lord Odovar. What would he be doing now if he had run away and left Odovar to the Pakin rebels? Still hoeing onions on a frosty morn? He banished such thoughts. There was no going back. Whatever destiny the gods intended for him, it was not on a hardscrabble farm in the wilds of the Eastern Hundred.

He looked south at the greening sward of forest between the camp and the plains of Ergoth. Juramona lay that way, and beyond, Daltigoth. Valaran was there. Had Mandes altered his letter to her, too? Loneliness like a fist gripped his heart. Had she been told he was staying away by his own choice? Would she believe that of him?

"My lord!"

The call did not penetrate Tol's troubled thoughts. Fellen approached, saying, "The new infantry spears are ready for your inspection. Will you see them now?"

Tol's gaze was still fixed southward.

After a moment, Fellen asked, "My lord?"

"Take it back!" Confused, Fellen asked him what he meant.

Paul B. Thompson and Tonya C. Cook

Tol looked at the engineer and proclaimed, "I will crush my enemies, and when they are dust, I shall take back what is mine!"

Fellen took him to mean the Tarsans. Later he would remember Tol's words, and know the truth.

The Minotaur Wars

From *New York Times* best-selling author Richard A. Knaak comes a powerful new chapter in the DRAGONLANCE® saga.

The continent of Ansalon, reeling from the destruction of the War of Souls, slowly crawls from beneath the rubble to rebuild – but the fires of war, once stirred, are difficult to quench. Another war comes to Ansalon, one that will change the balance of power throughout Krynn.

NIGHT OF BLOOD
Volume I

Change comes violently to the land of the minotaurs. Usurpers overthrow the emperor, murder all rivals, and dishonor minotaur tradition. The new emperor's wife presides over a cult of the dead, while the new government makes a secret pact with a deadly enemy. But betrayal is never easy, and rebellion lurks in the shadows.

The Minotaur Wars begin June 2003.

Collections of the best of the DRAGONLANCE® saga

From *New York Times* best-selling authors Margaret Weis & Tracy Hickman.

THE ANNOTATED LEGENDS

A striking new three-in-one hardcover collection that complements *The Annotated Chronicles*. Includes *Time of the Twins*, *War of the Twins*, and *Test of the Twins*.

For the first time, DRAGONLANCE saga co-creators Weis & Hickman share their insights, inspirations, and memories of the writing of this epic trilogy. Follow their thoughts as they craft a story of ambition, pride, and sacrifice, told through the annals of time and beyond the edge of the world.

September 2003

THE WAR OF SOULS Boxed Set

Copies of the *New York Times* best-selling War of Souls trilogy paperbacks in a beautiful slipcover case. Includes *Dragons of a Fallen Sun*, *Dragons of a Lost Star*, and *Dragons of a Vanished Moon*.

The gods have abandoned Krynn. An army of the dead marches under the leadership of a strange and mystical warrior. A kender holds the key to the vanishing of time. Through it all, an epic struggle for the past and future unfolds.

September 2003